KING OF HEARTS

RAKE FORGE UNIVERSITY BOOK 2

ASHLEY MUNOZ

King of Hearts
Copyright © 2021 by Ashley Munoz & ZetaLife LLC
ISBN: 9798372324206
ALL RIGHTS RESERVED

No part of this book whether in electronic form or physical book form, may be reproduced, copied, or sold or distributed in any way. That includes electronic, mechanical, photocopying, recording, or any other form of information sharing, storage or retrieval system without the clear, lawful permission of the author. Except for limited, sharable quotes on social media, or for the sake of a review. There is absolutely no lawful permission permitted to upload a purchased electronic copy of this book to any free book sites. Screen shots of book text or kindle passages are not allowed to be shared on any public social media site without written permission from the author.

This book is a work of total and complete fiction. The story was thought up from the authors curious and thoughtful brain. Any names, places, characters, businesses, events, brands, media, situations or incidents are all made up. Anything resemblances to a real, similar, or duplicated persons or situations is purely coincidental.

The author acknowledges the trademarked status and trademark owners of various products referenced in this work of fiction, which have been used without permission. The publication or use of these trademarks is not authorized, associated with, or sponsored by the trademark owners.

Cover Design: Amanda Simpson from Pixel Mischief Designs
Editing: C.Marie
Proofing: Tiffany Hernandez

❋ Created with Vellum

To Kaitlin:
You're hard as nails, baby girl...marching to the beat of your own war drum.
But you're mine, and I've never not been completely proud of that.
I love you more than you could ever know.

PROLOGUE

Taylor

I was seven years old the first time I saw someone die.

The man had fallen to the floor after my father pointed a gun at his chest, a dark red circle appearing immediately over his heart and making my own beat against my ribs. I remembered the fear that had gripped me, like a rope tied with the tightest knots, keeping me in that room even after I had left it. My small feet felt as though they had suddenly been stuck inside cement blocks for how fast they carried me.

It wasn't nearly fast enough to avoid my father's grip. My ponytail was strangled in his meaty fist as the man I knew as Father tugged me downstairs, returning me to the place where he'd just committed a heinous crime. My body shook as he crouched next to my ear and spoke of duty, penance, and lessons. I was so young I didn't see that I was just a blob of clay in my father's palm, his to mold, to shape, and to utilize as he saw fit. He forced his lessons on me, not so that I would be desensitized to murder or bloodshed...but so that I would learn to fear him.

It was when I was thirteen that I realized no matter how many lessons I was forced into, my father's appetite for executing them would never be staunched.

"So this is what you choose, értékes?" my father asked, narrowing his icy glare on me.

My breath hitched at the use of the name my father had called me since I was little. I used to think it meant something endearing, yet I couldn't remember one time ever feeling precious to the man who shared my DNA.

He stood tall, his hair like a flash of lightning against his pale skin. It made his eyes stand out, pale blue...the eyes of the devil. Some said I was blessed that mine were like my mother's, starker, like specks of glittering water pulled up from the ocean.

"Yes." My voice was a shutter, like a feeble piece of wood protecting a pane of glass in a hurricane.

My mother's light touch on the small of my back forced my spine straight, reminding me to stand tall regardless of how badly my gut wanted to cave.

"You know you have already been promised to the Mariano family... little Markos." My father casually grabbed the clear glass that usually contained vodka and brought it to his lips. How could I forget about the boy who had made my life a living hell? Markos was an angry boy, perfectly paired to his evil, menacing father.

My mother's touch disappeared; I knew she did it so I would stand on my own. She'd never been overly maternal, but I craved her touch. Especially while staring down Ivan, the wolf of the east.

"I am prepared to fulfill that promise." I watched as Jakob, my father's second-in-command, shifted on his feet. It was barely noticeable, but from the man who'd been more like a father to me than my own, I recognized the movement. He was prepared to defend me if necessary. I could count on both hands the number of words Jakob had spoken to me in the past thirteen years, but his acts of kindness were unmeasurable.

My father's glare cut to the woman at my back. My mother made no sound, inhaled no breath, did nothing as my father challenged her with his angry glare.

"I will allow this, but only because I have business back in Hungary." The air in the room seemed to thin as we waited for him to finish his sentence. He set his glass down carefully, as if he was setting down a loaded pistol and hadn't yet chosen his target.

"I will let you go free, with no more visits...but I hope your mother doesn't allow you to soften over time, Ari, for the man you marry will also deal in blood as I do. It is in your future, whether you deny it now or embrace it later. You cannot escape it."

I gave him a firm nod, as stable as my feeble head could give. Thirteen years old, staring down the most dangerous man on this side of the country. My mother told me it was brave, but I only felt foolish. Within seconds he could change his mind, decide to kill my mother, and sell me off. I only knew a small portion of the plans Ivan had for me, but none of them were decent or noble.

They were blood-soaked oaths that cost more than a soul could bear.

I turned away, resigned to my fate. At the age of twenty-one I would become a bride. No amount of shouting or screaming would change it, but at least for the next few years I'd get a reprieve, a break from the lessons my father forced on me...relief from the red that stained my father's garden every summer, from seeing the bodies lie in wait for burial. It would be well worth it.

I'd make sure to make every second count, for once I returned to this life, it would be without a soul or a single hope.

CHAPTER ONE

SENIOR YEAR OF COLLEGE

Taylor

March

"Are you going to say anything?"

The stark question bled into my thoughts, spreading like spilled ink over all my possible justifications. I'd just kissed someone, and they had no idea why I had done it.

The problem was, the truth...the real reason I had kissed him might as well have been written on a rock in Braille and dropped into the deepest part of the ocean. There was no way I'd be telling him why I'd randomly pulled on his shirt, slamming my lips to his, letting his tongue sweep into my mouth and consume every inch of me. I'd take it to my grave.

Instead, I stared into his whiskey eyes, committed them to memory, and pulled on the façade I perpetually wore.

"What do you want me to say?" I moved away, straining my fingers against the air as if the invisible force could take away how good it had felt to have his body pressed against mine.

He made a sound, a scoff or something else that came from his sculpted chest. I wanted to spin on my heel and see if those lips had curved in that same sensual way they did when he tried to coax me into movie nights with his friends.

"So, you text me, tell me to come over, then make out with me the second I walk in...and you have nothing to say?"

He sounded like he was trying to clarify the situation, but I didn't understand why. We had both been there. We both knew what had happened...he was just pissed that I wouldn't explain the reason behind my actions. The fact that he wanted a reason made my heart swell.

I busied myself with digging through my purse, finding lip gloss then my phone. I had to push away the sensation that had flared, taking on a life of its own. I'd been obsessively daydreaming and regular nighttime dreaming about my sister's best friend for four years, and since we would be going our separate ways after graduation, I felt like I had to make a move.

I had to because I'd written it down in my goal book.

Dream goal for the year: kiss Juan Hernandez before graduation.

That was literally the extent of my aspirations. Mallory, my stepsister, would have been horrified if she learned I had only dreamed of kissing a boy and not starting or running a business, or literally anything else beyond being wrapped in his arms for the rest of my life.

I was a terrible feminist.

My chance had finally arrived to make my move, by way of getting Juan's number from my sister's cell phone. I wasn't proud of it, but I had stolen it while she was in the shower. Knowing Mallory was busy and Juan wasn't, I had texted him, asking if he could come over and help me with something for Mal.

I'd lied.

Wasn't the first time, but it was my first lie to the man I'd been crushing on for four years.

The plan was he'd come in, we'd talk and laugh, and I'd make him want me—like all the other guys seemed to without issue. Juan never seemed to be interested, though.

No matter how I dressed or how I acted, nothing would get him to look at me in any other way except as Mallory's little sister. This would be my only chance. He knocked, I opened, and before either of us could say a word, I slammed my lips to his.

Thankfully, he didn't push me away. I would have died if he had.

He froze for a second, those warm, silky lips firm against mine. A moment later, he groaned and moved into it, finding a rhythm with me. His tongue and lips moved against my mouth, his hands going to my hair, gripping and tugging with perfect pressure. It was everything I had dreamed it would be. The second he walked us back and pushed me against a wall, I knew I had gone too far.

I had to stop because all I had ever allowed myself to hope for from him was a kiss. There could never be more. That was why my random hookups worked so well for me. I enjoyed sex, and there were never any strings attached.

Juan was the only man I had ever allowed myself to dream about, and he wasn't even aware of it.

The way he rubbed his lips now while looking at the ground, shaking his head like he couldn't believe what he'd just done...it made something in my chest fold in on itself like a piece of junk mail, discarded and forgotten.

He was already moving toward the door, and my chest ached with the need to pull on his arm so he'd stay with me. No one ever stayed with me. I was always forgotten, and after a while I had gotten used to it, finding my own form of entertainment...but none of that was the same as having Juan's body pressed against mine or the way his scent wrapped around me.

I felt as though a blood pressure cuff had been wrapped around my heart as I watched him open the door. A sound escaped my mouth, forcing Juan to pause with his hand on the knob.

I had one chance to say something to make him stop. He'd kissed me back, so there had to be a part of him that wanted me...right? Still, as I watched his tall frame slouch against the entrance, the only sound that came out of me was the rehearsed string of words that would act as a wall of protection for anyone I ever dared to care about.

"It was a mistake…I was waiting for Holden, thought you were him. Got a little carried away."

I ducked my head. Tears burned the backs of my eyes as I bit back all the words I wanted to confess. I never would. Juan was the type of guy who would do the right thing and would actually want to date me—assuming he even cared about me in that way…but if he did, my father would find a way to kill him. My twenty-first birthday was at the end of the year, and no man in my life was safe.

Juan's eyes flashed with hurt before his head canted in obvious frustration. His hand came up to rub at his smooth jaw, and I tried to commit it to memory, how good he looked standing in my house, there for me and not my stepsister.

"You know, I thought…" His eyes flicked to the carpet for a second before he collected himself. "I guess it doesn't matter what I thought. You just proved me wrong."

The door slammed shut as I blinked away a tear. I'd tuck it away like a carefully folded note, into the darkest places of my heart. One day, after I'd married Markos, I'd pull it out and look at how I could have loved Juan, how it could have been everything.

CHAPTER TWO

Juan

May

A RUSH OF ADRENALINE HIT ME IN THE CHEST AS I PUSHED THE silver key in and turned the lock. This wasn't my house, not my door, and yet going inside always felt like home. Smirking at the teal color Mal had never wanted and the ridiculous wreath that hung on the front of the door, I pushed my way inside.

The sun warmed the floors and walls, revealing two open windows, their lacy curtains billowing in the light breeze, and it shouldn't have bothered me…but it did. Having windows open meant they weren't closed and locked. Mentally I chided myself for caring whether or not she was safe; it really shouldn't have fucking mattered. She was just a job, a favor texted in by my best friend on my way to practice. Like watering a plant.

"You're here again." A soft voice spoke up from behind me, and that jolt of energy pummeled through me once more.

Turning on my heel, I mentally readied myself for seeing her, for feeling her indifference.

"You're sleeping in again." I clicked my tongue in reproach.

That pouty mouth of hers turned into a frown while those blue eyes rolled. Sunshine, silk, and sadness—that was what this girl was made of, and for some fucked reason, it called to me. Sang like a song, thrumming in my blood, pounding in my ears and inside my chest to get closer to her, hold on to her...keep her. Except I never would. She was a door that occasionally needed to be opened but required being slammed shut within seconds. Open too long and she'd sink her hooks in, likely aiming for my heart this time. Last time it had just been a case of blue balls she caused... I'd never let her any closer than that.

"Why are you an asshole every time you come to my house?" She picked up the coffee I had brought myself and sipped it. Of course she'd think it was for her. She was selfish enough to assume me coming here was for her sake.

It was only for my best friend who worried about her little sister so fucking much that I agreed to come over once in a while. My best friend cared too damn much, enough to give herself an ulcer, or worse, a heart attack. Meanwhile, Taylor didn't give a single fuck if Mal was okay or taking over a job she didn't want. I resented her for it; Mal didn't know that I did, but I was angry that my best friend had given up so much and her sister couldn't seem to lift a goddamn finger.

I walked toward the kitchen, too angry to notice that she was wearing mere scraps of clothing. The way her tank top pressed against her bare breasts clearly showed her pert nipples and the fact that she wasn't wearing a bra. Then there were the shorts that rode up so high her ass cheeks were on display. I'd never deny that Taylor Beck had a body made for sin; I'd just follow that up with the fact that I'd rather become a Catholic priest and take a vow of abstinence before ever indulging again. One kiss was enough.

"Am I the only asshole you've encountered in your precious, sheltered life?" I peered over my shoulder while tackling the dishes in the sink. Don't ask me why I was suddenly washing dishes, except that it bugged the hell out of me that there were dirty ones in the sink. That paired with a myriad of takeout boxes on the counter...the place was a mess. Taylor was supposed to have moved out since she was done with school, but every few days I'd check and, sure enough, she was still here.

"You don't know anything about my life," she stated, her voice wavering just the smallest bit.

I knew enough of her life to know she wasn't worth the time I spent checking on her. I knew she was selfish and self-centered. I knew she was stuck in my head, and I didn't understand why. Whether I was skating, fighting, or fucking, there she was: blonde hair the color of sunshine on a cloudless day, her blue eyes glittering with unshed tears—the ones she thought no one ever saw—and that skin.

I turned my head, ignoring her tan, smooth skin. I'd touched it, and it was stuck in my head too. Occasionally that image would guide my hand while I fisted my cock in an attempt to get her out of my system.

"I know your gold-digging mother found herself a winning lottery ticket in the form of her magical cunt, married Charles Shaw, and became a millionaire's wife overnight. I know you've been spoiled for the past six years, making your stepsister's life a living hell. I know you're selfish, conceited, and an easy lay."

Her blue eyes sparkled with tears, but none fell. Her chin rose, her lips thinned, and I noticed her fists clench at her sides. *Yes. Get angry, baby girl. Fight me. Fuck me. Put me out of my misery.*

Suddenly she laughed, letting out a huff of air before pushing her silky blonde hair out of her face. It fell past her shoulders, and it had been a fantasy of mine to one day wrap it around my hand while I pounded into her from behind. A fantasy and a nightmare.

"You're a waste of my energy. Completely forgettable." Taylor sauntered past me, grabbed my cup of coffee, and then moved down the hall to her room.

I knew my words stung her. I wanted them to, but fuck, I didn't want to admit how badly hers hit and landed like a missile into all my insecurities.

"You want to know why I'm an asshole to you every time I see you?" I suddenly said to her retreating form.

She paused in the middle of the hallway and spun on her heel. "Because we kissed, and I thought you were someone else?"

Fire. Ice. She made me feel too fucking much.

I took a step toward her, narrowing my eyes. "I'm an asshole because you're selfish. You don't deserve Mallory as your stepsister. She does everything for you, and you fucking throw it in her face. Everything you do makes her life harder, and because *she* has *me* in her life, someone who actually cares about her, I'm not going to sugarcoat how badly I wish you'd just fucking disappear. Trust me, the fact that you kissed me has nothing to do with it. I just can't stand you, but neither can anyone else, so at least I'm not alone in that."

I had finally done it. I'd made her cry. Thick tears fell from her black lashes in little drops while her neck turned an angry red color, crawling up into her cheeks. I ignored what it did to my chest to see her react to what was likely the harshest thing I'd ever said to anyone in my life. She stood there crying while I just walked past her and out the door. I thought maybe I should just tell Mal I couldn't come over anymore…maybe after this, she'd be out of my system for good.

♥

June

JUAN: Are you going to the wedding?

Taylor: Who is this?

Juan: Don't play stupid.

Taylor: Juan?

Juan: Gold star.

Taylor: (Insert rolling eyes emoji) What do you want?

Juan: A fucking answer would be nice

Taylor: You don't have to be a jerk

Juan: And you don't have to be a tease, yet here we are…

Taylor: Fuck off

♥

JUAN: I heard you're going to be the maid of honor...kind of a strange role for you, isn't it?

Taylor: Why do you keep texting me?

Juan: I haven't texted you for an entire week...

Taylor: You counted the days?

Juan: Do you have a date for the wedding?

Taylor: ....

Juan: Hello?

Juan: So you're just going to ignore me?

Taylor: You're an asshole...did you forget what you said to me the last time you saw me?

Juan: Was it any different than calling me to come over and putting your tongue down my throat only to realize you were kissing the wrong person?

Taylor: Didn't think you cared.

Juan: ....

Taylor: Guess I'll see you at the wedding...

Juan: Guess so...

CHAPTER THREE

Taylor

September

My pink fingernail ran along the magenta flyer, tracking each word.

"One roommate needed- must be clean and tidy. Eight hundred dollars...what the hell?" I voiced out loud, narrowing my eyes. Was this for real? Nearly a grand a month for just a bedroom?

My hand fell away from the message board while my lungs let out a sound similar to a balloon deflating. The sun was a blanket of humid heat, boxing me in on all sides as I wiped at my damp brow. It seemed more and more difficult to regulate how hot I was every day with this damn weather. I'd managed to make it through the worst parts of summer, but now carrying this massive book bag and my Hydro Flask...it was all a little too much.

For the first time since I had the heart-to-heart with my stepdad, I was starting to worry. We'd had brunch weeks ago, when I was entertaining the idea of living all alone and had plenty of time to make up my mind. He'd offered to buy me an apartment, but since I had witnessed my older stepsister stepping up and refusing handouts from Charlie, her biological father, I decided I could do that too. I didn't need his millions or free apartments; I could tuck away with a few roommates and finish the last few credits needed to obtain my bachelor's degree.

I couldn't, however, currently afford eight hundred dollars a month. Not only that, but now, as I had begun the hunt for a place to live, I realized how stupid I'd been. There was nothing left, and thanks to the massive surge in new residents, there was a significant housing bubble that was forcing people to pay astronomical prices on anything that *was* available. Since turning down my stepfather's money, there was just no way I could afford it. I obviously didn't qualify for any kind of financial aid, but I had a small trust fund my mother had created for me. It felt vastly different taking a handout from the woman who birthed me than it did doing so from Charlie. Besides, it was something she'd started back when we were dirt poor. There was only about ten thousand dollars in it, which would be enough to float me for a while, but otherwise, I was completely on my own and in need of a job.

My phone rang inside my pocket, which temporarily diverted my anxious thoughts.

"Hey," I said, pulling it to my ear.

"Did you find a spot yet?" my stepsister asked, sounding like she'd just heaved something across the room.

"What was that?"

"I lifted a box of paper. Can you believe I don't have an assistant to do that shit for me?" She let loose a strained chuckle while something else slapped against the floor on her end.

I laughed in response. "What about your baseball player husband?"

"He's ironically at the gym, and he may have told me to wait on picking up these boxes, but I'm feeling a little defiant today," she explained proudly. My older stepsister, whom I referred to as just my sister, had just recently taken over Charlie's New York office with her brand-new husband, Decker.

"I don't want to know about your defiance with Decker. Save it." I laughed, swinging my water bottle while I walked down the path. College students bustled around campus, darting around to get set up, find classes, and move into dorms. I looked longingly at a freshman who had a box in her arms. She wasn't homeless.

"You're out of breath," Mallory said with a hint of concern in her voice.

I moved my wrist to swipe at my brow, returning the phone to my ear. "Yeah...it's a bit hotter than I realized it would be. I feel weird."

"Tay, be careful. Those heatwaves can be really dangerous."

I rolled my eyes. "I know. I've lived here just as long as you have, sis."

"Yeah, but—"

"You know I love you, Mal, but you called for a reason."

She let out a super dramatic sound as another slap echoed through my phone.

"I just wanted to know if you found a place."

I let out a sigh and sank down on a bench by the administration building. "I definitely have options." My feet hurt, my shoulders too, and I hadn't even started my first day yet.

"That means you have nothing." Mal laughed, and I could feel my chest loosen as I joined her. I already missed her, and I'd just driven back to Rake Forge from her penthouse the week before. I had spent almost the entire summer with her, and I was still struggling with how badly I missed her.

"I don't know what I'm going to do, Mal." I shook my head, unsure why it suddenly felt so heavy. More sweat gathered at my brow, soaking my neck and back. I knew I needed to take a quick drink of water, so I pulled the heavy flask up and began opening the lid.

"You know all I have to do is make one phone call," she said hesitantly.

My brows crinkled as I considered what she was talking about.

"Hillary?" One of my sister's best friends had moved to Chicago last I heard.

She clicked her tongue. "You know that's not who I'm talking about."

I played dumb. "Hmm, not sure then."

Right as I said it, the person in question who I knew she was referring to was headed in my direction with his head down, looking at his phone.

My heart did a little flip while my neck suddenly stretched, straining to see every inch of him, maybe to ensure he wasn't a mirage or just simply because it was an odd sensation to see him after so many months. Mostly it was because he wasn't supposed to be here. He'd graduated and was now employed as a professional athlete; there were zero reasons he should be on campus.

"Juan asked about you," Mal hedged, likely worried how I might respond. We hadn't talked about Juan, except for one time on my bedroom floor when I had admitted that I would be returning to school this year. She had no idea of my past with him, or my crush...she just thought we didn't get along because I was arguably difficult for most to get along with. I supposed after her wedding, I'd been a little immature regarding her friendship with him. In my defense, there wasn't a soul on this planet who had hurt me the way he had, and that included my psychopath father.

"Please refrain from telling him anything about me," I droned while I watched Juan walk casually toward the door that was almost directly across from me. I took a second to catalogue how handsome he was, only so I could tuck it away for later use. He wore dark denim that fit him so perfectly he might as well have been a jeans model. Brand new white Nikes were on his feet, not a single speck of dirt on them.

"He's a good guy, Tay. He'd help you in a heartbeat."

She didn't know about Juan's little visits last year; no one did. No one understood what sort of hell it had been to see him at her wedding, or what lengths I had gone to to ensure he stayed away from me.

"Mal, I have to go," I said in a rush, realizing too late that as I was ogling Juan, he was bound to lift his head and see me any second.

"Okay, but call me back."

I hung up on her and began gathering my things. I stood and, keeping my eyes on the enemy, began walking to the left. I was almost clear of him entirely, thanks to the random group of students that had congregated. I slipped past a tall jock and in between two girls, still moving, peering over my shoulder one more time. The heat was sweltering, and I hadn't actually sipped any water while I talked to Mal. Now my heart seemed to be thundering at a sickening pace. I tried to take a deep breath while looking once more, but I lost sight of Juan. Just as I felt my brows crinkle in confusion, I ran into something hard and went down.

"Aw hell," I muttered, lying flat on my back, breathing hard. Sweat dotted my hairline while a few black dots danced along the edges of my vision. Faces came in and out of focus as a few people stood over me. Where was that damn Hydro Flask? Had it rolled away?

"Help her up, omagosh, is she okay?" a female asked briskly between bubble gum chews.

"I didn't see her...she just ran into me," a guy murmured as hands came to my elbows to help me up.

"It's really fine, it's not a big de..." I faltered as dizziness danced inside my head.

One of the guy's hands shifted from my elbow, easing me back down.

"Be careful. You don't want to..."

A familiar, deliciously tempting smell wrapped around me as the guy helping me tipped his head back.

"Remove your hands from her body." Crisp and cold, Juan's voice echoed around the circle like a war drum.

I closed my eyes and let out a sigh. Two seconds and I was already annoyed with him.

"I didn't see her," the guy repeated, letting go of me like he'd just been caught robbing a bank.

"How can you *not* see her?" Juan snapped, helping me to my feet.

I didn't want to stick around to see if he gestured to my stomach or not, or if he said anything else. I tried to walk forward, but Juan held me in place.

Looking down, I saw my bookbag and the Hydro flask rolling around, water spilling out because I had never secured the lid. I bent to get it but was again stopped by Juan's hands.

"Stop trying to fucking hurt yourself," he snapped, bending down to grab my things. People dispersed, moving on from the random person who'd just fallen like a pancake in front of them. I could hear a few people murmuring things under their breath about me, about my condition, and my eyes narrowed as anger swept through my chest.

"Come here." Juan tugged me into the shade, finding a tree with lush grass beneath it.

I peered down at it but wasn't sure what he wanted me to do. I wasn't one to sit on the ground; I hated the outdoors and nature.

"Sit." He eyed the grass, the bark of the large tree, and then my stomach.

Feeling a fresh wave of heat hit my face, I did as he said, and he helped me lower myself to the grass, gripping my hands in the process. Once my back was against the tree, I could feel a cool breeze blow across campus, and the sensation immediately helped to calm me down.

Juan settled in across from me, watching me with a calculated look. In his hands, he gripped my water bottle with the lid open.

"Can I have my water?"

His whiskey eyes narrowed. "How about a please, or a fucking thank you?"

"I was fine." My voice was shuddery as I tried to push down my anger. It was difficult to stay irritated with him as the sun peeked in and out of the tree branches above us, casting Juan in a glow so beautiful I wanted to grab my phone and snap a picture.

He turned his head to the side, giving me his profile, and that jaw of his...fuck, he had a really great jawline. I was no stranger to being around good-looking men, but there was something about Juan that was devastating, in a teenage-crush sort of way. A man who was unattainable but impossible not to watch, to crave.

"So, what...you fainted on purpose? You that desperate for everyone to see your little bump?" Juan asked, ripping out a patch of grass near his knee. The way his eyes flicked to my stomach and to the lush lawn we sat on made me think he was hiding emotions. I still wondered how he'd responded to the news of my pregnancy...actually, it was likely a good thing I hadn't been there for that conversation. He had likely said I was a slut or something; maybe he'd bet on me getting knocked up. Either way, he'd made it more than clear the previous spring how he felt about me.

A little flame licked at my spine, tingling, whispering of things I wanted from this man but would die before ever asking for. I would admit I grew up deranged and with monsters, but there was a villain inside of Juan Hernandez that called to me. It always felt like we were in this dark room, playing hide and seek with one another, him always beckoning me to come and play.

"I didn't faint. I was trying to get through the crowd and ran into someone. Besides, it's not such a little bump anymore." I rubbed a hand down my stomach, feeling protective as this was the first time Juan had ever acknowledged it. A few people walked past our tree, smiling and nodding at Juan in a manner I had seen men do with my father while growing up.

Everyone knew Juan was on the local hockey team and was powerful in his own right, but even beyond that, he just wasn't the kind of guy one would mess with. Danger radiated from him, anger a palpable taste when you got too close to the man—which reminded me that he shouldn't have been on campus. He should have been on the ice, prepping for his first season with the Hornets.

Juan's eyes raked over my body as if he was collecting what little details about me that he could. I wondered if he would ever pull out those tiny pieces to inspect later, like I did. His perusal was always a challenge, but this time, he seemed more worried than prickish. I hated it. Maybe once upon a time I would have preferred his kindness, but not now. Now I was only interested in his indifference.

I had successfully avoided him and everyone else for the past several months, but with me failing out of school the year before and leaving with my sister…it had been more like four or five months since I'd seen him. During those first few weeks, I had no issues hiding it, and after that, I utilized massive sweatshirts, but it was September now, and I was too hot for that sort of coverup.

Juan had briefly seen me at my sister's wedding in June, but the way the cut of my dress had fallen across my body, there was no way anyone would notice that I was knocked up. He had been there with a date, so it wasn't like he'd paid attention to me anyway.

"When you wear shirts like that, you're right, it's not so little. Haven't you heard of maternity clothes?"

I bit back a sharp response. He wanted to fight with me, and I had once entertained the cutting and sometimes devastating blows he'd deliver, but today I was exhausted and didn't have the energy for it.

I sipped my water in silence, watching the campus buzz with excitement. Freshmen were getting tours while upperclassmen held their phones and walked without looking up. A few people were moving into the dorms, so they carried boxes and large duffle bags. Parents were tagging along with a few here and there, and it made something in my heart drop. My mother hadn't come with me on my first day of college all those years ago. Charlie had come with both Mallory and me, but I'd always known it was more for her than me. I was just the obligatory stepsister, starting in the same year and grade as her.

I remembered so distinctly that Mal wanted to live on campus, in a dorm with Hillary. I hadn't had a friend, had never made them very easily. I also hadn't wanted to share a room with a stranger when I knew my coping mechanisms weren't healthy. I had sex. A lot of it. Not because I was a slut, or I guess I didn't consider myself one...but growing up, I was always feeling something. Terror. Fear. Anger. When Mom married Charlie, I had no idea how to deal with the lack of emotions that came with my new life, so I found out that first time, when I lost my virginity, that I could summon new ones.

Sex became an outlet, a form of control. So, I asked Charlie to force Mallory to live with me in a large townhouse where I would have my own space to have my hookups while also not having to be alone. Back then I didn't even feel guilty for it. He had to bribe her because there was no way she'd ever want to live with me of her own volition, and now, that seed of shame that had been planted all those years ago had grown and blossomed into something horrible. I had always hated myself. There was always something to hate, especially after the lessons my father would deliver...and then knowing Mom had to do unspeakable things to secure housing for us, food...it was always on her shoulders. Even her marriage to Charlie was my fault.

It was hard to shed that kind of self-hate and even harder to convince everyone you had gotten past it. I was a good liar—I had no other choice but to become one—so it wasn't difficult to conceal my emotions and true feelings from others. I'd been practicing it my entire life.

"Haven't seen you since the wedding." Juan finally spoke up, his voice more curious than angry.

I withheld the urge to roll my eyes. He'd likely had a hard time seeing anything past the brunette he couldn't stop kissing and groping at my sister's wedding. The only time they hadn't been attached at the face was during the vows, and even then, his hand was up her skirt.

"Yeah, I've been busy getting ready for classes," I muttered in between sips of water.

Juan seemed to consider that for a moment before his eyes narrowed on my leather bag. My gaze darted there too, but a second later, he dragged it closer and began digging inside. His large hands roving through all my things had my stomach knotting up.

"What are you looking for?"

"Well, I was looking for snacks, to feed you something…I'm assuming you aren't used to being pregnant, especially in this sort of heat. You need to keep your water up and eat like a baby elephant. Instead, you look like you're barely eating enough to keep a bird alive."

I dipped my head, staring at my belly as shame washed over me. How did he know more about what I should be doing than me? I had a doctor's appointment set up for the following month. The first few had been…uncomfortable but basic. They said I needed an extra number of calories a day, but I was usually getting that from my meals. I didn't think I could add that in with extra snacks, regardless of how hungry I became. I wasn't eager to put on any extra weight with this pregnancy other than what was specifically required.

Juan scoffed, shaking his head as his eyes stayed on the inside of my book bag.

He wanted me to react. I wouldn't, but I really wanted to. I hated how he always made me feel—as if I was an idiot, or just simply failing at everything. I was already insecure about being a mother, especially knowing what my father had in store for me. Even my own mother told me I was being stupid and selfish for keeping the baby.

"What kind of mother would you be, Taylor? You are too selfish to care for anyone but yourself."

Her words were stuck on repeat in my head, playing over and over again every time I entertained the idea of indulging in motherhood, of talking to my belly or planning for our future. Her words would play, and I would stop.

Juan was still looking through my bag, and after a few seconds I looked over in confusion when I realized he held my cell phone in his hand.

"What are you doing?"

His eyes narrowed, his large hands cradling my white device. "Unblocking my number."

Panic forced me to move, half rolling to the side to get to him, my fingers outstretched.

"You don't have the right to touch my things." I seethed, crawling on my hands and knees to get to him.

He leaned back, lying down on the grass, my phone was still clutched in his hand. I had blocked his number at the wedding, after Juan had made eye contact with me then kissed his date. I had wondered if she knew he'd been texting me before he decided to bring her. I had realized in that moment I didn't want anything more to do with him, so I'd cut him out of my life.

"Sure I do." He laughed, typing away.

I crawled until I was hovering over him, my hair hanging down like a curtain over us, my hands on his chest. The muscles under my palms were solid, so fucking delicious I had to resist the urge to dig my fingers into each groove and indent. I'd been with jocks, felt their bodies, but Juan's chest was so different, the muscles more defined and trained in an entirely different fashion.

"Give me my phone," I demanded, reaching for it, but he lifted it behind his head where I couldn't reach. My grasp brought my face closer to his, our noses nearly colliding. My breath caught as I realized my error, but it was too late.

Within seconds, my phone was abandoned, and Juan's hands were cupping my face, pulling me down. His lips pressed against mine in a firm, scorching kiss. He wasted no time prying my lips open, demanding entry with his tongue. One sweep inside my mouth and I was moaning. I realized just seconds into it what we were doing and tried to pull away, but he held me there.

Branding me.

I'd have been lying if I said I didn't want to pretend it was real for a few seconds, pretend he felt for me the way I had once for him, pretend he had suddenly grown feelings too big to conceal for me. That thought was what made me give in and begin kissing him back, tangling my fingers in his hair.

The second I engaged, he pulled away. With wide eyes and a thin smile, he warned, "Try to cut me out of your life again and it won't just be a kiss that I steal."

He moved, sitting up and getting to his feet at a speed that shouldn't have been possible, and before I could even muster a single thought in my head, he was walking away.

CHAPTER FOUR

Juan

I knew I had company the moment I parked my car. The Range Rover with wide, chrome rims and blacked-out windows sat in a parking space reserved for the owner of the building. I knew it was for the owner, everyone knew it was...but when El Peligro parked in front of your establishment, you didn't say a goddamn word. Richie, the owner of my apartment complex, only had to learn that lesson once.

I grabbed my bag from the back of my car and trudged upstairs, wishing I could sulk over my encounter with Taylor alone. Seeing her again, after months of nothing...it was definitely a mind fuck. She'd cut me out of her life cold turkey, moving and giving me no indication of where she went, and then she'd blocked my number. We weren't friends...or friendly in any real way, but she had to know I would be there for her if she needed me to be. I had been when she needed to get in touch with Mal and couldn't seem to on her own. I had helped then...I'd always help her if she really needed it, so her being alone on campus without anyone didn't sit right with me.

Even without our failed kiss, I was somehow coming to protect her... scaling one wall at a time. It was partly why I was so harsh with her, because she was always one second away from falling apart, and the only thing that seemed to drive her was fire.

So, I had determined to be her own personal dragon, breathing fire down her neck as often as I could…until her fire came back strong enough to force me out. I hadn't anticipated she'd turn into a mouse and sneak away without a word. Mallory had told me that Taylor was pregnant and had even asked if there was any way I'd ever accept Taylor as a roommate, but I had merely laughed as the idea rolled through and left me. There was no way I'd ever be stable enough to room with Taylor Beck, especially not while she was pregnant with another man's child, a man she had mistaken me for when we kissed.

My apartment door sat ajar as plumes of vaping smoke billowed from inside.

I hated when he smoked in my space, even if it was just vaping…I hated that he thought he could come in and do whatever the hell he wanted to.

"Primo." My cousin reclined on my couch, wearing a pair of navy blue Dickie shorts, a blue and white checkered flannel buttoned to his throat, and a pair of stark white Nike Cortezes. I had the same shoes in my closet, and once upon a time I had sported the blue colors of El Peligro, but that was a long time ago.

I shoved the door closed with my foot, giving him a slight nod.

Hector was bald with varying tattoos inked into his skull, face, and neck, most of which he'd acquired while in prison.

"Don't fucking vape in my house." I set my things down and walked to the fridge. My cousin laughed, shaking his head, but he put away his vaping pen.

When he laughed like that or even smiled in any way, it reminded me how close in age he was to me. I was on the brink of twenty-two, and he was only twenty-five. I tried to remember a time when we were just kids, playing on our abuela's floor with a few cars and army figurines. Those were good times, back when we were unaware of our family being mixed up with the messy business ethics they'd adopted. My mother and biological father were born in America, but their parents weren't, and incidentally several of my aunts and cousins were immigrants. Most of them were working toward getting their citizenship, regardless of how fucking difficult the government made it. The others didn't give a flying fuck about papers or any of that shit.

They saw an opportunity and took it.

"Speaking of houses...why the fuck you still in this tiny-ass apartment?" Hector lifted his eyes to the ceiling, his nose scrunching in distaste.

I glowered at him while fixing myself a sandwich. I would have loved to move out of the shitty apartment, but one visit from my uncle at hockey practice and that was all it took. Everyone in Rake Forge knew of El Peligro and knew the further you were from them, the safer. I was let go from the Hornets immediately afterward, told it was a conflict of interest with the team. I had no idea what the fuck that meant, but it essentially meant they didn't want to risk being involved with a notorious gang.

"Why are you here?"

Hector rubbed a hand over his head, letting out a sigh. Things between us had been a little tense over the past two years. My uncle had found out about my best friend, Mallory Shaw, and decided maybe it was a good idea to try to scam her or her dad for a couple million. When I told him to go fuck himself and said I'd kill anyone who touched her, they backed off. They weren't the only ones who had a reputation in the family.

"Pops feels bad about your hockey gig...he wants to make it up to you." My cousin shrugged his shoulders, his massive shirt nearly swallowing him whole.

I eyed him, slapping turkey on my bread. "I don't want anything from Tío."

I'd handle my own shit. Just because I had lost my position on the Hornets because of my family didn't mean I'd resent them for it. Family was family at the end of the day.

"Too bad, primo. He bought something for you, no strings attached...

we all know how you feel about those." He dangled a pair of keys in front of me.

I turned my back on him. "I don't fucking want anything from El Peligro either. I'm not taking whatever is attached to those keys. I'm not in…I'll never be in." Not again at least.

"Such dramatics. Relax, homes." He laughed, walking forward to shake my shoulders. "It's just a gift, no cords…and you won't exactly have a choice. Poppy bought this shit hole, and everyone is getting evicted."

He said it like it was no big thing, like all my neighbors losing their place to live would be perfectly fine. This was why I'd never consider being a part of El Peligro again…that and the murder and theft they committed.

I let out a sigh and rubbed my eyes. I wouldn't be able to afford a down payment anywhere new, and the market had just flexed and popped like a goddamn rubber band. Getting into a new spot would be nearly impossible.

Reluctantly I tugged the keys free of my cousin's fingers. "What am I going to find at the end of this?"

His brown eyes lit with excitement. "A sick-ass place." He rubbed his hands together. "It has a pool."

♥

"HIJO MÍO." My mother's whiney voice echoed from the back of the kitchen, and I rolled my eyes at how dramatic she always was. I usually tried to stop by and help them in one of their restaurants whenever I had a free moment, but since signing with the Hornets, I hadn't been in months.

"Mom," I replied, walking toward her then kissing her cheek.

"¿Dónde has estado?"

Where had I been? Hilarious. It may have seemed like a harmless question, but coming from my mother and delivered in that tone of hers, it was like being slapped across the face. I may have been blessed with her eyes, but hers were always twinkling with judgment. Which was really fucking rich, coming from her—or my father, for that matter. Their restaurant was a front for running drugs, and while she made the best street tacos in Rake Forge and I loved her dearly, she helped dirty the streets of this city. I loved my family, and while our past was complicated and most of it I just accepted with a devotion that would never waver, I never accepted guilt from my parents. I wanted a life free of this shit, free of hiding and doing backdoor deals, running drugs, all of it. I wanted the Hornets, or some other team where I could play, but it was likely word would spread about my family and anywhere on the east coast wouldn't touch me.

"I've been working, and now I'm going back to school." I turned to stir a pan of chicken. "You added way too much pepper to this," I said to one of the cooks.

"Talk to him." Rodrigo pointed at the man who'd raised me, Leo, who was viciously flipping a dish of sauteed veggies and shrimp.

"Papá, you can't add so much pepper."

"Don't speak to me about this. I was cooking before you were even a thought," he rumbled in that grumpy tone that only made me laugh.

I considered Leo my father, even if we didn't share DNA. He hated the life that came attached to my mother's as much as I did, but like me, he made the best of it. Originally, he started the restaurant as a way to distance himself from El Peligro and my biological father, but my uncle just roped him in, giving him little to no choice in the matter.

"Juan, when are you going to bring a wife for me to meet?" asked my Aunt Maria.

She was flattening a few tortillas, something that made our restaurant so successful. Her tortillas were an obsession for most of Rake Forge, especially the university students.

"Not sure. Guess when I find someone who can put up with me."

"What about that girl who keeps coming by here asking about you?" my father asked, and I had a feeling I knew exactly who he was talking about. Angela, the girl I had taken to the wedding, had gotten the idea in her head that I wanted a relationship instead of just a distraction.

She'd hopefully learn soon enough that her tagging me in pictures on Instagram and sending me vague texts wouldn't be doing her any favors.

"Hector was here earlier—he wants to talk to you about something," Maria said, rolling more dough into a ball.

"I know, I saw him."

"So what did he want?" my mother asked, dicing a tomato.

I felt weird not helping with something, especially while discussing that I had accepted something from my uncle.

"Victor bought a house and is letting me stay in it while he purchases the building I'm in." I shrugged, grabbing a piece of chicken from one of the serving plates. Way too much pepper. I coughed.

"A ese diablo no le recibas nada," my mother rattled off in a quick rush. It was her brother, so I didn't know why she was even trying...or if maybe she didn't know that I was aware of what she was currently accepting from him for allowing the restaurant to act as a cover for his drug running. Her calling him the devil and telling me not to accept anything from him was just one more thing I had to bite my tongue about.

"It's done."

"Undo it," she begged, and I shrugged. She also knew her brother had effectively ruined my place on the Hornets.

I had nowhere to go, and I knew even if I tried to find a place, it would just be a headache I didn't need at the moment. This way I could take my time and be comfortable for a few months while I figured out my next step.

My mother's firm grip tightened around my wrist as she pulled me away.

"My son, I love you very much...but I beg you not to do this."

I hated when she whined like that, as if me not following in her footsteps would somehow save my soul. "Madre, stop. It's just a house."

She blanched and looked down at her feet. I was about to walk away when she said, "It's never just anything with El Peligro. They'll take your whole life, my son, one I don't think you even know you're ready to part with."

CHAPTER FIVE

Taylor

"Why don't you just live here?" My mother kept her gaze down on her cell phone while she spoke. I was used to it, but now that I was pregnant, it felt more annoying than usual.

"I've already told you why I don't want to live here. It's too far, and my first class is at seven thirty in the morning." I gripped the duffle bag by the handles and moved it toward the door. Gareth, our driver and house manager, jogged across the foyer to grab it from me.

"It only takes half an hour to get to your school from here." She shook her head, tapping away on her phone. My mother's blonde hair was styled to perfection as well as her makeup, and somehow, she was already wearing Chanel.

I tried to remember back to when I was younger, back when she wore Walmart brands and we ate at fast food joints, but only if we had a coupon. It was what had endeared my stepfather, Charlie, to her. He had been poor once too, but right around the time we made a break for it to get away from my father, Charlie became a self-made millionaire. She met him on accident while trying to con another man out of money, and she said their story was one for the ages. As quick as it happened, it was something I had no doubt would last forever.

Here she was, almost seven years later, and they were madly in love. He was a widow, and I had instantly wanted to become just like his daughter Mallory because of how untainted she was. You could tell she'd never had to use a gun in order to learn lessons as a child, had never stumbled upon dead bodies. She wasn't being stalked and watched methodically by a sociopath that shared her DNA.

She was bright and all things good, and I was a moth drawn to her.

"It's forty-five minutes without traffic. I go to school on weekdays, Mom… that means I would have to hustle out of the mansion by seven in the morning and sit in traffic. I don't want to do that every day, especially pregnant."

Her eyes finally flicked away from her screen and darted toward my protruding stomach.

Today I wore a halter maxi dress with sandals. It essentially swallowed my whole body, except my bump. My mother never really spoke about the baby…she wasn't naturally maternal, even on a regular basis. She was protective, but not maternal. I struggled with her most of the time, especially with the way she treated Mallory. She was always comparing the two of us, and I knew it was because she saw in Mallory what I did…that she was good, and I was not. A tiny lamb tossed in with a wolf pup, and everyone trying to convince us that we were the same. My mother spent too much time trying to play it off to everyone that I had wool instead of fangs…I didn't understand why she bothered.

"Don't you think you should hide that a bit more?"

My throat grew tight as her tone chafed along my soul. My hand went to my stomach on instinct, as though I could protect my baby from its grandmother's brash words.

"No…why would I need to hide it?" I played dumb, though I remembered her words the day I told her I was pregnant.

I'd explained to her and Charlie at the same time, and while my stepfather rushed to hug me and tell me how happy he was, my mother stayed still as stone, her lips thinned, her eyes narrowed into angry slits.

Later that night, she pulled me aside and slapped me across the face.

"You know he's coming for you. It was the only requirement when we

made the deal to be let out of summer visits. Twenty-one and you're his... what do you think he'll do with your baby? Why would you bring a child into that world, Taylor? You know better than this..."

I sobbed silent tears and even went to a clinic that next day...but I was already in love with my baby, and I didn't know how to reconcile that with what she'd said. Somehow, I thought I could figure out a way to get free of the monster I knew as Father.

"So, what then...you said you've looked everywhere. What are you going to do?" She finally lowered her cell entirely and watched me with reserved frustration.

I understood it. I had put off living on my own for so long that now it wasn't even an option. The housing market had imploded, and nearly every available house, apartment, and condo was gone. There was nothing left. Charlie had sold the townhouse complex Mallory and I had shared the year before, as well as the units on either side that had been occupied by his security teams. He had offered to keep a unit available for me, just in case, but I had told him to sell it. I couldn't live in that big of a space on my own.

Now I felt senseless saying that, or even suggesting that I had options. I was naïve and too inexperienced to know that something trivial like the housing market would end up screwing me over.

"I'll figure something out, Mom." Maybe I could look into living in a tent. I could tuck away on the football field while the weather stayed warm, which in North Carolina would be a decent while.

The drive back to school was filled with traffic. It was as though a few thousand extra people had moved to Rake Forge over the summer, and now our roads were entirely overwhelmed. I was probably being dramatic as I had never had to make the drive from my parents' house so frequently, and usually not on weekdays.

I listened to a podcast about being pregnant, missing my history stations, but now that I was getting so close and I literally knew nothing about bringing a child into the world, I decided to sacrifice my pleasures and beef up my knowledge on becoming a mother.

It was right when the commenter began talking about ligament pain that I saw a familiar-looking sports car.

Juan's two-seater, red Mustang was parked where my Beamer had sat the previous day. I gripped my steering wheel aggressively as I searched for a different spot. I had been parking in that spot for days now, and it seemed oddly timed that the idiot now had it.

With a huff of frustration, I finally snagged a space in the overflow lot. I pulled my book bag free, along with my water bottle and cell phone. Right as I shut and locked my doors, my phone rang.

Smiling, I pulled the phone to my ear. "Hey sis."

"Are you ready for your first class?" Mallory asked happily—too happily for not even eight in the morning. Why was she even up so early?

"Do you ever sleep in?" I shuffled my bag to the side and grabbed the handrail, trekking up the concrete steps.

"I'm married to a horny twenty-two-year-old who wakes me up in filthy ways every morning." She laughed, sounding like she'd taken a bite of something and was now chewing.

"And there's that little bit about you being a CEO now..." I laughed along with her.

"Oh yeah, and that bit." She acted like it was nothing, but I knew it had been difficult for my stepsister to take over the New York branch for Charlie. I was silly enough to think it could have been me who did it, like if I somehow had a purpose and something to do then my murderous father wouldn't come knocking on my door. That or he'd see me as more valuable than just a piece of property to marry off.

My swift walk carried me past the nose of Juan's sports car, forcing an inferno of frustration to bubble up to the point that I couldn't hold back.

"So, your best friend is a dick," I stated evenly, fighting the urge to key the gorgeous cherry coloring of the car.

My sister choked on whatever it was she was chewing. "Uh...what?"

"Seriously, he's here on campus. He stole my parking spot, and he's being..." I bit my tongue, realizing I had never shared with her the cruel words Juan had spoken to me, or our kiss. I couldn't see what she saw in the prick. They'd been best friends for years, and I still didn't get it. Why put up with such dickery?

"He's on campus?" Mal seemed to overlook my drop in the sentence, likely to avoid having to hear gossip about her best friend.

"Yes." I held my hand out in front of me like she could see me.

"That's strange...last I heard, he'd landed a spot on the Hornets. Maybe he's there giving an encouraging speech about how to chase your dreams or something," Mal guessed, already dismissing the whole thing.

"Maybe he's dating a teacher and is trying to get in an early orgasm or something," I offered, biting my lip. The idea of Juan fucking someone caused a strange twinge in my chest.

"No, Juan hasn't been dating anyone...for like a long time, as far as I know," my sister said firmly, sounding like she was opening and shutting a door.

"He was hot and heavy with someone at your wedding."

I hated on way too many levels that I'd noticed him with that girl, and I hated that it had bothered me for months. I hated that the image of his hands on her hips, his fingers on the back of her head, his lips on hers had made me jealous.

"Oh yeah...but that was nothing. Just a fling, like you always have. Juan dumped her right after the wedding, like he didn't even take her home. It was rude. But he hasn't dated anyone in like a year, or longer. Now that I think of it, it's really weird that he hasn't. I know of at least two girls who were texting and calling him, but I guess he's not in the right headspace to date."

I thought back to the kiss we'd shared when I had lied to him right after. I still had no idea why he'd kissed me back or seemed so upset when I pulled away.

"Anyway, I have to go...but tell me you found somewhere to live."

I cringed, knowing she'd likely freak out if she knew I hadn't.

"Yeah, I did...I'm still working out all the details, but I'm good."

Her silence told me she didn't believe me.

"Okay, well send me the address as soon as you have it." That was her way of saying she didn't buy my bullshit. I was drawing close to my first class, so I smiled and said goodbye.

I shrugged my shoulders, trying to dislodge the feeling of defeat. I was currently, technically homeless, and while I knew I could go to a hotel without issue or even go live at home, I didn't want to. I desired to be more like my sister and stand on my own two feet, especially now that I would be responsible for a baby.

I grabbed for the door as butterflies erupted in my stomach. It had been happening a lot lately, along with tiny little kicks along my abdomen. Two doors in and I was already seeing people I had partied with the year before. Most of my friends were seniors, but a vast number were underclassmen...including the father of my child. It had taken some time to narrow it down, but now I was absolutely positive.

I saw his broad shoulders first and his tousled dark hair second, and even though he hadn't responded to the text I'd sent to him, I owed it to my child to see if he would agree to a paternity test.

"Holden..." I gently placed my hand on his arm, hoping to turn him. He was engrossed in a conversation with two players from his team and a few girls. They all eyed me warily.

"Taylor..." He turned, his eyes dropping to my stomach immediately. His face turned ruddy, his eyes wild as fear crept in.

"Hey, I was wondering if we could talk?"

"Uh...I have class." He gripped his neck while frantically searching the hall.

Was he looking for help? I almost laughed at how ridiculous he was being.

"Maybe after class, or later today or something?" Because I didn't want him to freak out, I added softly, so the others couldn't hear, "You know, I don't want anything from you...I just want to know."

He visibly softened, and his hand came up to cup my hip as he bent down to whisper in my ear. "Okay, yeah...I'll call you later."

Then he pressed a kiss to my cheek before walking away. Holden Winters was a pretty decent guy, and honestly, as far as relationships went, he'd probably be the only guy I'd ever had one with. I was almost positive he was the dad. I had thought back to how often we'd been together and realized it couldn't be anyone else.

We'd hooked up in his dorm room, then later that day in the locker room...and then the next day in the back of his truck and again at my house. We weren't exactly thinking clearly; we weren't drunk, just horny, and if I were truly being honest, I was struggling with the fact that Charlie's birthday had come up and Mallory had gotten him the perfect gift. The way he looked at her, the photo album she'd gifted him...it was all so sweet. We all passed the images around to view, my mother glancing my way a time or two, as if she'd shield me from seeing what a happy childhood looked like.

It was no secret to me that Mallory had a good childhood. Even with losing her mother at the age of ten, she had two parents who loved her unfathomably. I had purchased Charlie a watch, and it garnered a fake smile and a half-hug from him. He saved all his big hugs for Mallory, and how could I begrudge him that? Still, it brought out some unhealthy behavior in me, and that weekend, I just needed to feel. So, when the tip of Holden's cock slipped past my thong, I let him thrust into me over and over. I was on birth control, so I figured it would be fine if he didn't pull out; besides, the orgasm was so much better when they didn't have to. My cheeks heated as I considered how reckless I'd been. After our weekend together, we went our separate ways, and I ended up getting really sick and needing antibiotics, which likely was the reason my birth control was ineffective.

Shaking away the memory of my reckless decisions, I moved down the hall and into my class. It wasn't until I slumped into my chair that I realized someone's stare was burning a hole through the back of my head.

CHAPTER SIX

Juan

Hockey was off the table until I had time to decide on where to go. Inevitably I would move to play within the same division or a different one—hell, I'd even take on a coaching position at a school—but until then, I was figuring out what else I could do to fill the time. I already had my bachelor's degree, and until I decided what I wanted to do next, I was aiding professors with their extra work, just wasting time until I figured out my next step. I could lie low and just work at my parents' restaurant, but the closer I was to them, the likelier it was that I got tangled up with the gang that had claimed my biological father's life. I knew with a little bit of time, I could probably get picked up by another division team along the east coast or leave this area entirely and try somewhere else. That would likely be my best choice, to just leave the east coast, head west, and start a new life, away from my fucked-up family... and away from having to see Taylor get kissed by other guys.

Holden Winters had held her possessively in the hall earlier and kissed her on the cheek, and I knew he'd fucked her close to the time she would have gotten pregnant. I was way too aware of her life, of her absence, and knew he was probably the dad. For whatever fucking reason, that just dug at me. Maybe because it was him she had said she'd been expecting when we had our kiss, or because she'd acted like it was all just an accident. Either way, I hated the guy, and by extension, I resented Taylor for having his baby.

Walking down the street from my parents' restaurant, I quickly stopped in at my favorite frozen yogurt shop. There were a few students milling about while I eyed the flavors. I didn't pay any attention to them until I heard my name being called. As I turned, a muted flash of blonde hair caught my attention, those honey strands I knew so well tied up on a head that was bent over a book. It wasn't Taylor who'd called my name, but her eyes were on me as Angela came into view.

"Juan, oh my god! Where have you been?" Angela exclaimed, tugging on my arm while her two friends staggered beside her. They'd already grabbed their frozen treats and were likely on their way out of the restaurant, which was good for me. They wouldn't stay long.

My eyes kept going to the girl two tables behind her who happened to be watching me with an odd expression. It was the same one she'd had at the wedding when she saw me with Angela. Taylor had been watching us, and for whatever reason I'd wanted to know if it would piss her off if I pulled Angela close and kissed her. I wanted to know if that pink flush that had crawled up her neck would increase if I shoved my hand up Angela's skirt. Taylor, in the end, had given up nothing except a flash of hurt and a few other odd expressions. No words, and certainly no groveling of any kind, asking if I would forgive her for what she had done to me back in the apartment. Maybe I wouldn't have cared so much if her lips weren't the ones I had been stuck fantasizing about, or if it weren't her eyes that I'd subconsciously sought out at every party and rager I had attended last year.

Letting out a sigh, I ran a hand through my hair and thought of how to answer her.

"Busy...with work and school stuff." Was there no one else who frequented this fucking shop? I looked around, seeing my earlier observation had been all wrong: only three employees in the back on their phones, and just Taylor sitting amongst the tables. It must have been close to ten, so why the hell was Taylor still there?

"I've been texting you." Angela pawed at my shirt, grasping the black material and tugging. She should have gotten the hint or had enough self-respect not to call me again after I ditched her ass in June. I hadn't even had sex with her that night, yet here she was...begging for more affection.

"Yeah, I saw that." My eyes flicked back, seeing that Taylor continued watching us. The last time I tried to use Angela against her, it ended with my number being blocked. Call me crazy, but I wasn't eager to have her kick me out of her life again. Not that I was in her life, but if I wanted to text her right now, I technically could, and that was a good feeling. Only because it meant I could keep an eye on her for Mallory's sake.

"But you didn't text me back." Her brown eyes went wide as she considered what I had implied.

I gave her a half-smile. "I've been busy with family stuff."

She seemed to understand what that meant with a small bob of her head and a downcast look. Thank fuck.

"Okay...well I guess we better get going. Just call me if you want." She braided her fingers together, looking down while her friends leaned in to whisper to one another.

I rubbed the back of my neck. "Okay...yeah."

I wasn't sure what else to say; it felt awkward. I didn't want to cause a scene, but I also didn't want to encourage her, especially in front of Taylor.

Once Angela was walking out the glass doors, I headed toward the flavors. Once I had grabbed my cup, I paid and walked toward the blonde in the middle of the café.

Dragging back the metal chair, I flipped it around and straddled it.

"Why are you here?" I took a bite of my dessert, my eyes flicking to hers.

She wasn't wearing any makeup, and honestly it was how I preferred her. Little strands of hair falling in her face, her blue eyes alert and aware, the small number of freckles she had proudly splattered across her nose on display.

She grabbed the spoon from my carton, pulling up a decent amount before gently pressing the bite of cake-batter-flavored yogurt into her mouth. My dick twitched, watching her pink lips work around the spoon, those blue eyes not giving a single fuck that it was my dessert or that my mouth had already been on it.

"I'm studying," she finally said, flipping another page of her book.

Sure enough, she had a large history book in front of her, but it didn't look like a textbook.

"It's ten at night." I grabbed my spoon back, taking another bite.

Her eyes scanned the page while her elbows rested on either side of the open book. I took another bite then left the spoon, hoping she'd steal it again.

"Why do you care?"

I tilted my head, watching her intently. Why was she always so fucking difficult?

"Who says I care?" I waited to see if she'd take another bite. For whatever reason, her using my spoon was the equivalent of her agreeing to hold my hand—which I didn't want, not really. I just wanted to see if she'd do it.

Finally, her hand darted out, grabbing my spoon. She scooped a huge bite before bringing it to her lips then slowly licked the spoon clean. If this was the only foreplay I'd ever get with this woman, I'd fucking take it, but I'd never talk about it with anyone.

Once she cleared the spoon, she set it back in my cup before scooting her chair back. The metal grated along the floor.

"Where are you going?" I stood with her, watching as she slid her book into her bag and grabbed her cell.

She canted her head toward the door. "To bed...it's late."

Right—it is late, so why is she out here? She's never done this before.

I walked over to the garbage can, tossed my cup inside, and opened the door for her.

I had no idea where she'd ended up living, but I'd have been lying if I said I didn't want to know.

She walked ahead of me while pushing her bag up her shoulder.

"You don't do this often, right?" Just as I asked it, a gunmetal grey car rolled by us, going slow. The windows were heavily tinted. I lifted my hand to wave, hoping they'd see the tattoos on the upper side of my arm and keep driving. Their red brake lights lit up for only a second before tires screeched and they gunned it down the street.

Taylor shrugged, completely oblivious to what had just happened. She could have been abducted, raped...fucking list was endless, and she had no idea.

"Can you do me a favor and not come out here, this late at night alone, please?" I walked next to her, seeing her car parked up ahead.

The streetlight accentuated her bare shoulder, the leather strap of her bag, and the small wisps of hair that kept falling out of her bun. "Sure. I'll make sure I bring someone next time."

This girl pissed me off a thousand fucking different ways. I gritted my teeth while she unlocked her car.

"Whatever, just don't be out here alone."

She signed off with two fingers to her forehead, then she ducked inside her car and started it up.

As she pulled away from the curb, I watched her taillights for longer than I probably should have. Taylor was a dead end. We were too volatile, and she was pure venom. If I ever surrendered to her, she'd dice me up, and any hope at having her at all would be ruined.

So instead of spending another second thinking of her, I turned toward my car and headed home.

♥

"THIS HOUSE IS INSANE, MAN."

Hector walked through, keeping his eyes up along the ceiling. There was an entire mural painted on it, like the house was a cathedral or some shit.

"It's a little over the top," I said, dicing up an avocado and throwing it in the salad I'd prepped.

"Like your cooking—have you heard of Hungry Man meals?" My cousin held his hand toward my salad, shaking his head. He was right, but I loved cooking. It came naturally to me and actually helped me to work out any extra stress I was carrying. I could get lost in a recipe and not think about the fact that I hadn't seen Taylor for a week or heard from her in any capacity. I could have texted her, but I hated being the one to reach out to her. It made me seem desperate. It wasn't like I needed to insert myself into her life again...we'd gone months without talking, and we didn't need to start back up.

I moved on to a yellow bell pepper, mulling over why she hadn't been around and where she had ended up living.

"So...there's this chick who keeps coming around the restaurant, looking for you." Hector grabbed a piece of avocado and tossed it in his mouth.

"I heard. Your mom actually told me Angela keeps coming by." I chopped, then moved on to a tomato. Had Taylor ended up shacking up with Holden? I had thought I heard he was living in a fraternity house and had maybe even signed on with the new baseball team. After my best friend Mallory's story hit the world, outing the strange-as-fuck secret society Devils team, they'd been investigated by police and shut down.

The school board was rearranged, and several faculty members were fired and replaced. There was now a new team operating, but they hadn't disclosed if they'd continue on as the Devils or get a new team name.

"If she keeps it up, there are going to be some assumptions made," my cousin hedged, walking over to the massive fridge and sticking his head inside.

I paused working on my salad and looked up. "I'm not in."

"I know...but you're still Manny's son. You're still you. They will always look to you."

I laughed, shaking my head. This was fucking nuts. "So, what? They're assuming she's mine?"

"The guys are nervous to touch someone who belongs to you." Hector pulled the tab on his soda with a loud click.

I let out a laugh, licking my finger. "I'm sure they're not worried about backlash."

Hector's head tipped back as he drank.

"Well, she's hot, so if you're not going to make a move..."

I diced a few more pieces of tomato before looking up at him and smiling.

"Trust me. If I wanted to mark her, everyone in the fucking city would know, and not a single soul would fucking touch her."

My cousin laughed, shaking his head along with me. We both knew how this worked. If there was a girl I didn't want anyone to touch, I'd get a heart inked in black, positioned over my heart. It was the El Peligro way, but that wasn't even what I was talking about. On her she'd get my name or an identical heart tattooed on her chest. That ink held other meanings as well. Sometimes it was just a bribe to get men into the gang. Something my grandfather had started as a symbol of honor had been twisted into bribery by my father.

If you didn't get your girl marked, other men in the gang could have her. Rape wasn't an issue in El Peligro because any female inside knew the score, but once that ink was on your skin, your body belonged to El Peligro.

If I had a girl I didn't want anyone to touch, I'd be there to make sure no one touched her. Simple as that. I didn't need to ink shit into my skin for it, but if that were to happen one day, then fine...I just wasn't counting on it, and I wasn't getting involved with the gang my father ran. There was no place for me in it, and I would never accept it even if there was.

CHAPTER SEVEN

Taylor

September was already almost over, and I'd been successfully sleeping in my car for two weeks. I had an entire routine down. At night, I'd park over by the stadium, close to the girls locker room door. It worked because first thing in the morning, I could sneak in, shower, and get completely ready without anyone knowing I was there.

Even if anyone did see me, they'd just assume I was there for a sport... though on second thought, with my baby bump, they might have a few questions. Still, didn't matter. I had a groove going. On the weekends, I'd go home and stay at my mom's, do all my laundry, and then repeat the whole process. I'd spend as much time as I could working in the library or at random food spots. I'd use coffee shops mostly, but every now and then I craved dessert, or something different.

I had been tempted to stay in a hotel a few times, and there were definitely a few conversations I had with myself about why I was being so stubborn, but the only credit card I had belonged to my stepdad, and while I hadn't previously minded putting it to use, I did now. I had to learn how to care for not only myself, but my baby too. I was still looking for a place to stay, but for now, the car worked. At least until the temperature changed.

I had just shut the shower off in the private stall I'd snagged when I heard someone laughing. Freezing in place, wrapping a white towel around my body, and wringing my hair out, I waited to see if they'd moved on or stayed put. I had never had company a single time I had showered or gotten ready in the locker room, so maybe it was just someone passing through or grabbing their things.

A second later, I felt the stall shake as someone probably pushed into it a little ways down. The water came on a second later with a girl giggling and laughing. My clothes were on the bench outside of the stall, so they didn't get wet, but that meant whoever was out there would see me. I decided to stay put until I knew they were in the shower.

I cradled my arms to my chest, waiting, and then I heard a familiar laugh.

"Why did you pull me in here?"

"Because I know what you want," the girl responded.

My gut sank as I processed what was about to happen.

"So you saw me lifting weights and thought it would be a good idea to have me come in here with you...to do what exactly?" asked the smooth-as-velvet voice, and I could picture his lips slinging to the side in a mischievous smirk.

"I thought maybe I could help you work out. You seem stressed..." The girl sounded like the one I had seen at the yogurt shop...the same one at the wedding with him over the summer.

"How do you suggest we do that?" Juan asked.

God, I was two seconds from putting my finger down my throat. Were they really going to fuck right here in the locker room? What sort of bad luck did I have that this would happen to me?

"I don't think this is going to go the way you think it is. I didn't sleep with you after the wedding, and I don't want you to get the wrong impression," Juan said gently.

My heart leapt a little. He was shutting her down. I walked closer to the door, trying to get a peek at the couple, but I couldn't make anything out.

"I'm not asking for anything, just like I didn't back then. Just let me make you feel good."

That didn't sound good. Fuck, was this bitch about to...

"Fuck, Angela...shit." Juan made a startled sound through the shower corridor. He sounded like she had just taken his cock into her mouth. It didn't exactly sound like pleasure, but I'd been known to make sounds that seemed like I was being murdered when I came, so I couldn't really tell.

Either way, her mouth was on him, and I wanted to scream.

He made a strangled sound again, the echo of the water hitting tile stopped, and all that was audible was the sound of her gagging every few seconds.

Anger flared to life inside my veins like an angry virus. Juan wasn't mine; he could never be mine, but he sure as fuck wasn't about to be hers. Maybe one day I'd look back on what I was about to do and think better of it, but right then the only thing on my mind was making this pain in my chest stop.

I pushed my palm against the stall door, and it slammed open with an angry echo. I stalked out to where my clothes waited, not giving a single fuck that Juan's back was up against the stall door, his gym shorts pulled down enough to allow his thick cock to be swallowed by the brunette kneeling in front of him. She had on a low-cut tank, revealing her minimal cleavage, and exercise shorts.

Juan's eyes flew up, seeing me standing there. His hands immediately went to the girl's head and pushed her away. Her lips let him go with a smacking sound, her pinched expression revealed she had no idea why he'd stopped.

"Oh, don't mind me. Please continue," I said happily while dropping my towel and grabbing for my lacy underwear. Juan's face flushed red while he tucked himself back in, his raven hair askew. Those whiskey eyes stayed fixated on me...on my body, moving from my chest to my bump and down further.

I dressed briskly while the girl in front of Juan stood, whispering something to him, but he only shook his head, giving me one last look before he walked away.

She turned, giving me a death glare before exiting through the back doors.

Good riddance to them both. I had no idea why either of them cared. Any other guy would have pulled the girl who was sucking him off closer, not pushed her away, but Juan had done the opposite. If I were blowing Juan, there's no way some random chick walking out of the bathroom would stop me.

Once I dressed, I walked out through the weightlifting doors and found Juan working on the squat rack with a reserved expression. I paused, taking him in, letting him see me take in his appearance, how his jaw clenched. A few other guys milled about, including the father of my baby. Smiling, I walked past Holden, waving, acting as though Juan was no one of consequence to me. In the end, he wasn't.

I'd never tell him what it did to me to see him get taken in by someone who wasn't me. It was a stupid crush, and he'd crushed me...so why wasn't I over it yet? I walked through the weight room, feeling the heat of his stare, giving small smiles to the men pumping iron, save for one. I acted as though he didn't exist.

My feet carried me straight through the space until I was in the hallway, heading toward the science building.

"Taylor," Juan called at my back.

I smiled, thrilled that I had moved him, like a chess piece.

I didn't stop though, because if I did then he'd say something that would hurt me, and I didn't want to feel that sort of burn this early in the morning.

"Hey!" The sound of his shoes squeaking on the floor hit my ears, indicating that he was likely jogging over to me. His grip landed on my elbow, spinning me around. "Just wait a second..." He stared down at me with those worried eyes and smooth lips.

I ducked my head so I wouldn't have to see those parts of him I still thought about on a regular basis.

"Why were you in the locker room this morning?"

My eyes jumped up to his.

"What?"

His jaw tensed, his hand on my elbow loosening. He wore a black tank top with black basketball shorts and black Nikes. Against his tan skin and dark hair, he looked like a fucking weightlifting model, if those existed.

"Why were you in there?"

I tilted my head, twisting my lips to the side. "You upset that I interrupted your little suck-off session?"

His eyes narrowed, his lips thinning into a firm line. "Not even a little bit. You did me a favor..." His head tilted to the side, mirroring mine. "I don't appreciate my dick being sucked by someone who can't even properly gag without nearly passing out. She ended up just lapping at it, like a puppy."

I couldn't help it. I snorted, ducking my head while a laugh rolled through me.

"Tell me why you were there."

How easy would it be for me to lean into him, to have him touch me... maybe mention that I had nowhere to go? He was an asshole, but my sister wasn't wrong—deep down, he was a good guy, and he'd take care of me. I had no doubt of that. I also knew he could never actually help me, not without me putting him in danger. So, I bit my lip, holding back the words I wanted to say, and pulled on that same façade.

"Same as you." I gave him a sly smile, rubbing my hand down his chest while I walked away.

"What the fuck does that mean?"

I stopped and turned. "Holden met me before you two came in... what can I say? He's a little more talented with his tongue than your girl is." I winked and stalked off.

He didn't follow. My eyes burned with tears that needed to be shed, but I wouldn't allow a single one to fall. If I did then it would be admitting that I cared, and I couldn't afford to. My soul was damned, and no matter how badly I wanted to stay above ground with Juan Hernandez, the devil was coming for me.

CHAPTER EIGHT

Juan

It was late. I'd had two morning classes assisting professors with grading and making copies, then I had rushed over to my parents' restaurant and worked a shift there all afternoon, and then I had come back for an evening class. Now I was finally headed home, just as soon as I picked up my car. Parking at RFU was a bitch and a half. There weren't enough spaces to accommodate how many students were there. They offered busses and a few commuter options, but for the most part, students spent up to twenty minutes finding a space.

I was driving out of the lot, about to turn left, when I saw Taylor's white Beamer illuminated under the white parking lights. No other cars were out there, and at first, I wondered if Holden had picked her up. The two of them would likely have a cute little romp in the sheets when finally connecting over the shared pregnancy.

Fucker.

Seeing her in the locker room a few days ago had been a punch to the gut. I didn't even know why I cared that she saw me...and not that it even mattered, but I didn't want Angela to drag me in there; I also didn't make it a habit to be an asshole to every girl I saw. Usually that was just reserved for Taylor. I had planned on thwarting any attempts Angela made toward me, but I hadn't realized she was going to go down on me the first chance she got. She was all teeth and sloppy tongue, so it made things a thousand times worse in turning her down. When I saw Taylor slam that door open, there was no mistaking the flash of anger that bled into her face. She didn't like that I was with Angela. It was the same look I'd seen her use at the wedding, then at the yogurt shop. With everything in me, I didn't want to care that hurt flashed in those ocean eyes, or that she bit her lip in a similar fashion to when I had eviscerated her in the apartment last spring. I didn't want to admit that seeing it hurt her made my chest ache in a way that was unwelcome.

Seeing her car in the lot only took those flashes of hurt and ideas of jealousy and tossed them into the fire she'd set by going with her baby's father. Why act as though she felt something for me but go and play house with him? She couldn't have it both ways, and with me, she'd never have it at all. Like it did back when she'd told me it was Holden she meant to kiss, the walls around my heart fortified, reminding me that I felt nothing for Taylor, nothing but common decency to keep her safe as my best friend's little sister.

Ready to leave her car and the feelings associated with Holden and her reuniting behind me, I continued forward, only to catch sight of the indoor light in her car popping on through the partially uncovered part of her front window. The tinting job made it nearly impossible to see anything, but I knew someone was in her car. Fuck, if she was in there with Holden, I was going to punch him in the goddamn face.

Swinging back toward her spot, I quickly parked and jumped out. I could hear music playing as I drew closer, and now that I was feet from her, I could see the glow of a screen inside.

Knocking on the tinted window, I waited to see what in the hell was going on.

After a few seconds, the passenger door opened, and a head of blonde hair poked out.

"What do you want?"

I looked down, confused about what exactly I was seeing. Takeout bags sat on the floor of the seat she was currently perched on, wearing sweats and an off-the-shoulder sweater. A duffle bag sat in the driver's seat, and the back seat was currently set up for someone to sleep there.

"What are you doing out here?"

"Nothing, just hanging out," she explained—poorly. Her dainty fingers toyed with the handle of her car door as she awkwardly held it open, looking up at me.

"Right." I moved, opening the back door, realizing she had to have unlocked the doors to open hers.

"Hey," she protested from the front seat.

I was right—there were blankets, two pillows, and a sleeve of Ritz crackers resting next to the makeshift bed.

"Are you sleeping in here?" I moved so I could catch her expression.

Even though it was dark, I caught her reddening face and the way her stature faltered.

"I...it's just temporary, until I can find a place. I only plan on staying in here two, three nights a week. The rest I'll drive back to my parents' house."

I shook my head, because this girl was unreal. Only Taylor, darling stepdaughter to the millionaire Charles Shaw, would consider sleeping in her car over a hotel, a damn house, or with the fucking father of her child.

"Why aren't you in a hotel, or with Holden?" Fuck if I wanted to suggest the prick, but he'd be better than this.

She wet her lips, still half kneeling on the passenger seat, her arm holding the door open.

"I'm not staying with Holden...and regarding the hotel, I considered it, but it's such a waste of money, and it's so hard to get a parking spot here. I figured why not just park here and kill two birds with one stone?" She shrugged.

I rubbed my forehead, the dots finally connecting. That was why she had been in the locker room, not because she was getting fucked by Holden...but because she had nowhere else to shower, which might mean she wasn't with her baby daddy at all. Some kind of warm sensation moved through my chest as if a piece of ice was thawing, but anger quickly came through like a fire and burned the sensation up.

"Do you have any idea how dangerous this is?"

That bare shoulder rose toward her ear again in a shrug. "I'll lock the doors."

"You don't know what sort of monsters roam these streets at night, parking lots like this, looking for some stupid college kid who was dumb enough to leave his fancy car. Locks don't keep them out, baby."

"How would you know?" Blue, daring eyes tried to search mine, but I looked away.

"I just do...now get in the driver's seat and get ready to follow me."

I turned away from her, already annoyed with the imaginary images of her getting robbed in the middle of the night.

"No, I don't need you to—"

"Don't argue with me on this," I warned.

We were already sitting ducks in a war waged on these streets when the civilians of Rake Forge went to sleep. She was naïve and ignorant to how dangerous it was to be outside during their business hours.

"Juan, I don't want..." She tried again, but I gave her a look so severe it shut her up. The next thing I knew she was letting out a huff, attempting to climb over the console.

"What are you—stop, you can't fit."

She gave another huff while her shoulder moved toward the steering wheel. "Yes I can."

So goddamn stubborn. I shook my head, bringing my fingers to the bridge of my nose.

"See...just had to wiggle a little." She beamed up at me, pushing the tip of her finger to the start button.

I turned and headed back to my car, preparing to drive and watching to ensure she followed. Once I saw her lights flick on, I put the car into gear and started out of the parking lot. Just as we passed the gate to the first parking lot, I saw a familiar set of wheels drive past. El Peligro was already out and hunting tonight and likely had set their sights on her car. A shudder ran through me at the idea of what they would have done once they broke in and saw her inside.

I drove just ten minutes away from the school and then continued up the hill toward the nicer homes until I turned onto the tiny slice of driveway that led to my new house. Fury fueled me forward, faster than I probably should have been driving. How long had she been sleeping in her car? Why would she rather risk her safety—her baby's safety like that over asking me for help? I had seen her out at ten at the yogurt shop —what was that, two weeks ago? Fuck. How long had she been doing this?

I keyed in the code and waited for the gates to open and for the white Beamer behind me to follow me in. Tall trees lined the path, providing ample privacy. Small lights were woven into the branches, allowing us enough light to see the property ahead of us.

We slowly maneuvered forward until we were both parking in the circle driveway. It was a massive, white, stucco-style house with clay shingles and arched windows, and gaping openings stood to my left, like a small mansion. It was nicer than I'd initially assumed, but as soon as I had driven through the gates and saw how many small touches my uncle had requested for me, it was beyond anything I could have imagined.

Taylor's door slammed; her thin frame came up close to mine.

"This is your place?"

"Yeah…it's new." I walked forward, not in the mood to explain it all to her right then. I was still too angry that she'd consider sleeping in her car over asking to stay with me.

I opened her passenger door and dug for her duffle then slammed her door.

"Get the shit you need for tonight."

She scuttled toward her car and dove inside, grabbing a cord and her phone and a pair of sandals. Then she was at my back, her arms full and her eyes wide as we walked in through the oak door together. It felt just like it had when I'd opened her door, knowing she'd be on the other side —like coming home. Strangely this place hadn't felt that way until now.

I heard her let out a tiny gasp as we entered the foyer with its marble floors and the mural on the ceiling.

"My uncle designed the place," I explained, moving into the house. The living room was my favorite place with its lush sofas and lounge chairs. There was a massive fireplace, big enough to stand inside, and I couldn't wait for rainy weather to try it out.

Taylor followed on my heels, not saying a word. The house was already lit up with small lights here and there giving accents and enough light to see the small pieces of furniture that littered each space in a complementary way.

"The kitchen is open, get whatever you want." I walked past it, not going inside. She could make out the ten-foot island, the chrome hood over the gas oven, and the butcher block counters. The whole house had more of a bohemian theme with potted plants and cozy touches.

We crested the stairs; she was still on my heels as we walked past a bathroom.

"You can use whatever you want in the house...it's still new to me, so there might be something I'm not sure about. I don't have staff or whatever the fuck you're used to at your parents' house, so hopefully you know how to make yourself food."

"You don't have to be rude," she meekly said from behind me.

She was wrong. If I wasn't mean, I'd be nice, and if I were nice, I'd do something I'd regret, like I had when she had dragged me by the collar and kissed me. I had kissed her back with as much passion because I had wanted her. She had been a constant beat in my chest that wouldn't stop, a rhythm that wouldn't change chords. She was constant. Then she had finally pressed her lips to mine, gently tugging my heart from my chest, only to trip over it on her way out the door.

"Here's your room." I ignored her and walked along the padded carpeting. There was already a queen-sized bed with fresh, white linens. "There's an attached bathroom suite, so make yourself at home."

Taylor moved around me, setting her things down on the white dresser. I set her duffle down, realizing the initials MS were inked into the handle of the red fabric.

"This is Mal's duffle bag."

Taylor shrugged from her spot near the bed. "I didn't exactly want to lug around my Coach luggage while apartment hunting. I was hoping to find a spot by now, but I wanted to keep a low profile."

"Using Mal's stuff is perfect since it's so peasant-like, right?"

Her face turned red, her fingers turning into fists.

"Look, I didn't ask to stay here. I didn't ask you for a handout."

She stormed past me to the bathroom.

"You're just not used to people treating you the way you deserve to be treated. Thought you were fucking Holden—how come you aren't in his dorm right now?"

I watched as she turned the handles, starting the bath in the massive sunken tub.

She didn't answer, just started stripping.

I turned away, hating how quickly she was able to thwart my asshole attempts. She knew I wouldn't stay in her bathroom, being a dick to her when she was getting naked. She was my best friend's little sister. There was no way I was crossing that line...not again.

"I'll be gone by tomorrow," she said to my back, her voice sounding muffled as if she was pulling material up over her head. I blinked to get the image out of my head.

"You're staying here until you have an actual address to send your mail to."

"You don't get to tell me what to do," she yelled at my back, and because I was sick of having a screaming match without seeing her, I turned around.

The sight of her naked rendered me speechless. She had perfect, round breasts with pink, peaked nipples. Mallory had once mentioned that Taylor had had them worked on, but fuck if I cared about that right now. They were perfect.

Her stomach was still trim, except for the roundness near her belly button forming a bump. The way her hips flared in perfect proportions, cradling her naked cunt...fuck me.

She walked closer, seemingly aware of the effect she was having on me. It wasn't until she was directly in front of me that she tipped her head back and arched her back, making her tits press against my chest.

"You know what I think?" she whispered, wetting her pink lips. Her blue eyes darted up and down my face.

I didn't respond.

"I think you want to touch me, and I think you don't want to stop, and that really bothers you."

She wasn't wrong, but like hell would I cave and let her win. I tilted my head to the side.

"How exactly do you think I want to touch you?"

She stepped closer, bringing her hands to her breasts. "I think you want to touch me here."

I eyed her, not moving an inch. "Where else?"

Her chest heaved, but her eyes stayed locked on mine while her left hand drifted down her body until she was cupping herself. "Here."

"You know what I think, Taylor?" I tucked my hands into my pockets, keeping a blank expression. "I think you want *me* to tell *you* to touch yourself."

Her small intake of breath told me I was right. I took a step closer until her forehead nearly pressed into my chin. Our bodies were almost touching, all her soft curves fitting perfectly against my hard edges.

"I think you want to stand there, touching yourself while I watch. I think you want to get yourself off with an audience. Do you like the way you feel, Taylor? Are you wet?"

Her eyes briefly closed while her fingers worked in and out of her folds. I could hear that she was wet, and if she looked directly at my cock, she'd see that it was indeed hard.

"I'm soaked." She leaned her head to the side, letting out a small sigh.

I waited, unsure if I should go there. It would bypass where we'd just started taking things, but fuck...I couldn't help myself.

"Taste yourself."

I'd just confirmed what she'd suggested about me wanting to tell her what to do.

I expected a smirk, or for her to break away from me saying she told me so, but there was no smirk. She kept her eyes locked on mine while she slowly brought her fingers to her mouth and sucked on them. Her eyes closed briefly as a low moan left her chest.

I ached to unzip my jeans, fist my dick, and play along with her, whatever this game was where we told each other to touch ourselves, but this was something we shouldn't have been doing.

"Do you want a taste?" she whispered, returning her hand down to her wet entrance.

My chest inflated with desire as I watched her eyes close once more, waiting for me to decide. One problem with this scenario—and there were many—was whether or not Taylor was hoping to call my bluff. She could easily seduce me to the point of obsession, only to walk away, leaving me with blue balls and a healthy dose of embarrassment.

Instead, I decided to take the choice from her entirely.

"Taylor." I breathed against her neck, her eyes dilated while her fingers worked in and out of her center. "Get in the bath." I took a step back, sneering down at her. "You're filthy."

Then I turned on my heel, ignoring the pull in my chest and the ache in my dick.

♥

I WOKE up the next morning feeling hungover. It was ridiculous, really; I hadn't had a sip of alcohol, but the fact that I'd jerked off in the shower to images of Taylor standing there, lowering to her knees, and going down on me had burned so hot inside me that I was hard again the second I crawled into bed.

I dreamed of Taylor sneaking into my bedroom and waking me up with her lips, her blue eyes watching me in the dark while her fingers roamed over my body. I had a wet dream like I was in middle school again, and just like then, I wanted to burn my sheets so no one would ever know.

"Good morning," Taylor said cheerily, walking into the kitchen dressed and ready for the day—a small mercy, as was the fact that she wasn't acting mopey about the previous night's interaction. She had every reason to be pissed at me. What I'd done was fucking shitty, but like always...she bounced right back.

"Morning," I muttered in response.

She seemed much more chipper than I did. Had she slipped that hand back in between her thighs once she crawled into the tub? Had she thought of me or imagined someone else? Fuck this wasn't good. I didn't want her to think of me, and we needed to stop seeing each other naked and standing in close proximity to each other while aroused.

"I wanted to thank you for allowing me to crash here last night. It meant a lot...but I have some other plans on where I can stay for the time being."

I sipped my coffee, watching as the sun invaded the kitchen from the skylights. The living room was bathed in it too.

"You have a new address already?" I thought I had made myself pretty clear.

She faltered, tucking silky-white hair behind her ear. "Well, not exactly...but I have some ideas."

"Then you're staying here." I moved past her.

"Juan, seriously...drop the act. What the fuck is your issue with me? I didn't ask for you to be all big brother with me, or to take care of me since Mallory isn't here. No offense, but I'd rather be homeless than deal with your surly remarks every day."

Shit.

I watched the floor, waiting for some kind of idea to pop into my head. If I was nice to her, I'd be truly fucked because I wouldn't be able to resist her, and I knew my heart would never survive her again.

"Okay..." I gripped the counter. "Fine."

Her posture shifted, like this announcement surprised her.

"Why do you care where I go?"

Because for whatever fucked-up reason, my blood boils at the idea of you being hurt or not having somewhere safe to stay.

I shrugged. "You're my best friend's little sister...I care."

Her lips twisted to the side as if she was considering what I'd said.

I sipped my coffee and toyed with my phone, swiping my thumb across the screen. Angela had tagged me in a post on Instagram again. It was the third time since the wedding, and the pictures she kept using were old, back from our very short time together two years prior. Inviting her as my plus-one had been a mistake, but at the time I was being reckless, and I didn't want to face Taylor without a buffer.

"Okay, then I'll stay. But you have to promise to tell me if I begin to cramp your style, and if you have an expectation of when you want me to be gone by."

I nodded. "Done."

"Do you have any rules for me?" She tied her hair up into a bun on her head. I swallowed thickly as I realized how difficult and likely stupid this whole idea was.

"No guys. Here's the key code to get into the house—you don't have to have a key with the way the lock is set up, just a code, and a thumbprint if you want to get that set up." I tipped my cup back, keeping my eyes trained on hers. Her thin eyebrows rose, but she didn't fight me.

"Okay, thank you." She cradled the paper in her hand before looking up at me again. She wore a pair of jean shorts paired with a tight tank top again, showing her little baby bump.

I hated that she somehow looked even hotter with that bump. That saying about glowing wasn't a lie...she was radiant, and all I could think about was how she had looked standing in front of me cupping herself.

"And you don't have to worry about guys—I don't plan on dating while I'm pregnant."

I scoffed. "Just last night you had your fingers in your cunt, and then you offered to put them in *my* mouth...so forgive me if I don't exactly believe you. Besides, what if Holden comes around and suddenly wants to play daddy?" Fuck, why did I sound so petulant?

"First of all, what happened to you being nice?" She quirked a brow, her hands going to her hips, making her look cute as fuck.

I suddenly had the urge to walk up, cup her face, and taste her lips again. I hadn't allowed myself to really think about the kiss I had stolen from her the other day. How it felt to taste her, have her pressed against me...it was something I'd done just to shock her, piss her off, anger her, like she'd done to me. If I really wanted to be an asshole, all I had to do was tell her I was rebounding from Angela or something...but once I'd had her there, words hadn't come, save for the warning I'd given and would keep if she kept trying to keep me out of her life.

"Fine." I blinked, running my hand through my hair. "But I should still be allowed to be honest with you."

"You can...and you're right. The purpose of last night was to see how far I could push you. I didn't expect..." She trailed off, her face and neck turning red.

"You didn't expect what?" I moved around the kitchen so I wouldn't think of the night before or how close we'd gotten to crossing a line. Part of me wondered if she'd only pushed me like that so she could turn around and turn me down.

"Well...uhh, this pregnancy has done some really weird things to my body. Anyway, once I started toying with you, it felt so good, and the hormones kind of kicked in then suddenly I wanted to do a lot of dirty things with you, regardless of how angry I was." Well fuck, maybe she wouldn't have stopped us. Maybe she would have gone all the way, or at least far enough, so I wouldn't have had to deal with blue balls all night.

She shouldn't have told me that. It was going to stick in my head like a guidebook on all things Taylor now. Every single thing would lead back to her being pregnant and horny and wanting dirty things done to her.

"Okay..." I tried to clear the need and lust out of my throat.

"So, no guys, and no more seeing each other naked." She laughed, spinning on her heel.

I watched her head toward the front door, an objection on my tongue that I'd never once said we shouldn't see each other naked...but she was right. We couldn't and shouldn't do anything more like that, because next time I wouldn't be able to stop.

Taylor gave me a cute half-wave before turning, walking out the door, and starting her car. I realized she had never addressed my question regarding Holden coming around and playing daddy.

CHAPTER NINE

Taylor

Dr. Phoss was so long-winded. How long did it take to explain the basic behaviors of humans in the first few centuries of time? I was going to pee my pants if he didn't wrap this little discussion up soon. My legs jiggled under the desk as I watched the clock count down to two. It was my last class of the day, and I was so ready to be done. I was beyond exhausted. After my little routine the previous night, I had been so embarrassed and aroused that I didn't end up getting to sleep until well after three in the morning. I had tried to fix the issue myself, but it was like nothing could take the edge off after seeing Juan Hernandez respond to seeing me naked and offering him a taste of myself.

God, how embarrassing. Regardless of what he'd said, there had been no hiding the bulge in his jeans, or the way his eyes turned to fire when they trailed down my body. I knew he wanted me. I could feel it, like a crackle of electricity in the air, or like the way the sky darkened before a storm.

Even still, the image of him watching me had been on replay in my head for hours, and nothing could relieve me. I had eyed the pool outside my window at least three times, curious if a lap or two would help...but I had chickened out because everything had happened so fast with moving in that I didn't feel comfortable wandering.

It didn't help that Juan was so insanely hot and cold with me. One second he was devouring me with his eyes, smoldering and clenching his molars to the point where that muscle in his jaw ticked, and the next he was saying such horrible things to me. I honestly had no delusions that this living situation would last long. I wasn't kidding when I said I would rather be homeless than deal with his rude remarks.

"Okay, that's it for today. Be sure to follow up with the notes I posted online and the assignment posted for next week." Dr. Phoss finally ended the class, and since my books and laptop were already packed, I dashed up the steps and out the hall, heading straight for the bathroom.

"Excuse me," I muttered, pushing past a few students. I was doing the pee-pee dance at this point, and if people didn't move, I was going to make a scene.

"Tay..." Someone grabbed my elbow. I could see the bathroom sign; I was so close. Groaning, I turned toward the person who'd snagged me and sagged in place.

"I am literally going to pee my pants," I practically cried, wishing I could take it back. Some things didn't need to be said out loud.

"Sorry..." Holden let me go, wincing while he hefted his backpack higher on his shoulder. His dark hair was covered by a dark snapback, making him look broody and hot.

Looking around, I grabbed his hand and pulled him after me into the bathroom. There were a few girls milling around, but all of them exited quickly enough for us to lock the door and for me to snag an empty stall.

"What's up, Holden?" My voice echoed, and maybe in a different life I would have cared that this was awkward, but not today.

He cleared his throat on the other side of the closed stall door. "Uh... you never called or came over yesterday."

No, I hadn't, and that was still on replay in my head too.

Finishing up, I flushed, opened the door, and washed my hands while watching him in the mirror. He stared at my protruding stomach as though it was something he had to fix. *A problem.*

"I was busy."

"Well, what did you want to talk to me about?" His brows dipped in concentration.

I turned, crossing my arms over my chest. It pushed my cleavage up, but I didn't care. I was running out of space for where I could put them.

"Did you not get my text a few months ago after we fucked like six times back to back without protection?"

The idiot blanched, glancing at my stomach again before dropping his gaze to the floor. He *had* gotten it; I knew it.

"My phone said you read it."

"What do you want me to say?" He turned away from me, and my dumb heart deflated. What had I expected? For him to say he'd been out of the country and would do anything to be a part of the baby's life?

"I just wanted you to know...I don't want you to say or do anything."

"It's not like you need me—your dad is a millionaire, Tay." He shrugged again, and I was getting really fucking tired of seeing those lousy excuses for shoulders rising toward his ears. Juan had taken me in without a second thought, not dating me or related to me...not even obligated because he'd knocked me up, and yet this guy couldn't even reply to a text.

"I already said I don't need anything from you, but some guys want to be involved with their kids' lives...just wanted to give you that opportunity."

He stared at the floor, unmoving.

Letting out a small sound of disbelief, I went to leave, but his hand darted out to stop me.

"Can I think about it, have time to wrap my brain around it?"

Why did he need time? I had texted him months ago...still, because I was weak and some small place existed inside me that wanted my baby to have their father in the picture, I nodded like an idiot. I let the man who'd knocked me up lean in and kiss the corner of my mouth.

"I miss you," he whispered in my ear. "You know that I miss you...I tried calling you after, but you wouldn't return my calls or texts. I know we aren't together and I'm still figuring this out, but if you need me...in other ways, I'm here for you."

He turned to leave before I could respond. My eyes watered as shallow breaths assaulted my pathetic lungs. He needed time to consider being a dad, but for a quick fuck, he'd come right over? It hurt, burned in ways I hadn't felt before, but I figured this must be how it goes, right? You fuck it up and then try to mash all the painful pieces together to make it work. That's how my mom and dad had worked, until she couldn't take it anymore and got out.

Swiping at my face, I headed for the parking lot, ready to hide in my new safe haven.

♥

I REALIZED once I started my car that I had no idea where I was headed. So, I had to text Juan to get the address.

Me: I kind of forgot to ask you for the address today

Juan: 4589 S Terrace Court—key code for the gate should be on the paper, but if it's not, it's 901.

Me: Thank you

He didn't respond, and I didn't expect him to. He could stay on his side of whatever it was he did, and I would stay on mine.

Punching in the address, I began driving toward the nicer part of Rake Forge. Ten minutes later, I was in front of the same wrought iron gate I had seen the previous night. Pulling up close to the keypad, I entered the code Juan had given me and tried not to feel too giddy when it slowly slid open. Questions about how he'd gotten this house swirled in my head. The one and only time I had ever tagged along with Mallory to one of his movie nights, his apartment had been on the other side of town, and it was old, run down, and tiny. The only redeemable thing inside had been his couch.

The sun peeked in and out of the trees that acted like a canopy for the long driveway. Now that it was daylight, I could see how much land stretched along the white fence that bordered Juan's house. A grove of trees was scattered along a large portion of his property, making me itch to walk under the branches to see what grew there.

I didn't even fight the smile that broke out on my face. An accompanying flutter erupted in my stomach, and I knew it wasn't a bout of nerves or butterflies. That was my baby.

"You as excited as me, little bean?"

I rolled down the windows and laughed as I felt a tiny kick prance along my abdomen.

"I wouldn't mind living here either. There's even a pool," I muttered, loving the feeling of peace that began to unfurl inside my chest. This was the first time I'd felt at peace since finding out about being pregnant. I tried to fight the feeling trying to take root. I had to remind myself this was only temporary. A plant in a pot. I'd be leaving soon.

Cresting the top of the path, I pulled into the circular driveway and put my car in park. I was used to opulence from my time growing up with my father and then moving in with Charlie, but this house still made me feel small. Maybe because there was also a part of me accustomed to poverty, thanks to the fact that my mother had accepted her freedom from my father, but only on the condition that she ask for nothing.

That extended to me as well for all the time I spent with her. It felt like a punishment more often than not, living in tiny one-bedroom hovels where the carpet smelled so strongly of mold and cigarettes that learning to hold my breath for as long as I could became a form of survival. I had folded my small body into tiny corners to sleep more times than I could remember. I was a mess, my head and heart a tangled mess of trigger wires.

Blinking, I reached in, grabbed my phone and purse, and then slammed the door shut. As I wandered to the front, a tiny little pulse point jumped in my chest as I entered the pin code into the keypad at the door. Once it clicked open, I let out a sigh of relief.

For however long, this was where I belonged.

I had grown accustomed to settling and adjusting...but something told me this would be an entirely different situation. As I looked around the living room and took in the cozy comforts, it looked as though the entire house was staged. Nothing personal was added. No photos of Juan's big family, none of his mother, whom I had seen but never met, none of his younger sister.

I moved into the kitchen and began digging through the options for food: Greek yogurt, oat milk, gouda cheese, fresh lettuce and tomatoes. None of it was mine, and regardless of how much I craved a snack in the form of a juicy apple and a few slices of cheese, I would wait until I bought my own groceries.

I didn't feel right about eating his food, so I shut the fridge and decided to stick to the snacks I had brought with me. They would have to do until I had a chance to go shopping for something fresh.

Back up the stairs and in my room, I let out a relieved groan. I liked the room. I loved the brilliance of light that was welcomed in and the attached suite, loved the plush bed and how simply the white and grey contrasts were arranged. I mentally put together a color scheme that would look amazing with some added textures and lamps, along with fresh flowers. If I did stay and this worked out, there was even ample space for a crib.

Sobering to the reality of my life and where it was headed, I sat on the bed and rubbed my belly. There was no way Juan would want a single mother and her baby living here. He had a life, he had girlfriends... and the memory of the night before rumbled into my chest like a runaway semi-truck.

He'd stood there, consuming me with his eyes...told me to taste myself. Then he told me I was filthy.

That couldn't happen again. Maybe Juan was just a player, used to fucking and flirting, and this would be no different. He was the male version of me, so I wouldn't judge...but still, we had to set some boundaries. Maybe with them in place, he wouldn't mind if I stayed for a while, even after I had the baby.

That was assuming my father or Markos didn't find me first.

Heaving a sigh, I stood and stretched. There were so many things out of my control and too many questions I had. There was no way to address them all, and for now, I just needed to let it go. I knew from listening to my podcasts that stress wouldn't be good for the baby. So, I walked to where my duffle sat and pulled out my bathing suit, ready to test out the massive pool in the backyard.

Right as I was about to slip into the restroom, my phone pinged, reminding me I had a doctor's appointment. I sighed as I looked out the window, realizing the pool would have to wait.

CHAPTER TEN

Taylor

I loved that Dr. Kline always managed to fit me in before he closed up. I didn't get out of school until after two and he stopped seeing patients at three, so by the time I actually got over to the side of the city I needed to be on, he was usually the only one in the small office when I arrived.

Opening the glass door, I found him in his blue scrubs, glasses perched on his nose while he filled out paperwork on the counter. The receptionists were gone, leaving just the two of us, like usual...unless there were other people milling around somewhere. I assumed there were, likely, janitorial staff or something.

"Taylor, good to see you," Dr. Kline said, smiling at me.

He was insanely hot, and each time I saw him, my face never failed to betray how his looks affected me. He was maybe thirty-something, no wedding ring, but I knew he had kids from the photos in his office. He was nice to me, super helpful and always encouraging me regarding my pregnancy.

"Let's get to it, shall we." He held his hand out, indicating I lead the way to the exam room. We always went to the same one all the way in the back with a small alcove outside so there was a little more privacy. It was closest to his office, so I assumed that was why he preferred to use it.

"How are you feeling?"

I led the way into the room, setting my purse down and toeing off my sandals. "Good. Really hot all the time and exhausted."

"Hop up." He patted the table. "Are you drinking plenty of fluids?"

I nodded, feeling a little flutter hit my chest. This part was always odd to me. Growing up, I'd never been to a public health practitioner. My father had always made sure I saw a private doctor, same with Charlie. They paid to have people see us, and we didn't have to go into offices. So, I wasn't sure how things were normally done, but I felt mostly at ease with Dr. Kline. It was just overcoming the nerves of having my body inspected like I was a lab rat. It didn't help that occasionally it felt like my doctor looked at me in a nonprofessional way, but that was probably just in my head because I wasn't used to it.

"Well let's take a look. Go ahead and strip down." He turned toward his computer, grabbed a gown from under the sink, and held it toward me.

I took it then began to do as he said. As often as I had stripped in front of men, I always felt so exposed when I did it in front of Dr. Kline. The first time, he'd just assured me it was policy and I'd get used to it. Still felt strange to me.

I lifted my shirt, unclasped my bra, and shed my shorts and panties, folding them all in a small pile. Once naked, I pushed my arms through the front of the gown and returned to my spot on the table.

"All set?" He smiled at me, rolling on his little stool toward me.

I nodded, feeling my heart beat a little faster. I loved getting to hear my baby's heartbeat. It was my favorite part of these appointments.

"Let's check your blood pressure first." He rolled over to me with a blood pressure cuff, placing it over my arm then tilting my wrist until his finger rested over my pulse. His face was so close to mine since I was still sitting up with my feet dangling off the table. "You're definitely getting sun. I can see you have new freckles." He smirked, tracing a small patch of skin along my nose.

I laughed, ducking my head while he began to pump the blood pressure cuff. It squeezed tight for a second before releasing.

The sound of Velcro being ripped apart filled the room while he jotted down my vitals. "Looks good, still healthy and strong, no worries there."

"Good." I let out a sigh and leaned back against the pillow.

"Let's check these next." He opened my gown by pulling on the little string that kept it closed in the front and palmed my breast. "Any pain here?"

I shook my head as his thumb rubbed over my nipple. Thanks to the frigid air, it had pebbled. I hissed as he repeated the process. When he inspected my chest, it was that same odd feeling I used to have as a little girl when my father's doctor would examine me. I had to remind myself I was grown and was probably just nervous about being inspected by a good-looking doctor. Every pregnant woman went through this.

"Sorry, guess they're sensitive, huh?" He grabbed the other breast and did the same thing until both his hands were full and his thumbs were running over my peaked nipples.

I hated that when he rubbed them, I felt my core clench, my thighs nearly squeezing together to hold off on feeling aroused. "Yeah, really sensitive."

He did the same thing with the other breast until he was finally skimming his cold palm down the expanse of my stomach, pulling the gown up, and scrunching it under my breasts, leaving my entire bottom half open and available for him to see. I always noticed how his eyes caught on the triangle of bare skin between my thighs. Maybe it was in my head, but it seemed like his gaze heated every time.

"Ready to listen?" He moved back toward his counter then returned with the plastic bottle and little machine used to hear my baby's heart. He squirted an ample amount of gel onto my stomach, some of it dripping down into my lap.

I nodded, holding the fabric of the gown over my breasts while the whooshing, beating sound filled the room. He kept the small wand there for a second, looking at his watch, then smiled again.

"Sounds great." It was always over far too soon, my little light snuffing into nothing within seconds. I once asked if he could let me listen for a little longer, but he'd chided me, saying he had to keep things moving. I understood, but that little wallop sound was the most beautiful sound I'd ever heard in my entire life, and all I wanted was to hold on to it forever.

Walking back to the counter, he grabbed a small towel and began to clean up my stomach, moving it down into the place the lube had fallen.

"Oops, looks like we got some down here." He swiped at my pubic bone with his fingers, covered by the rag, but the fact that he was so close to my center made my thighs clench together. This plus the nipple situation, and my hormones were officially out of control. "Okay, let's check you. Feet up, and you can lower the gown."

I did as he said, putting my feet up in the stirrups and lowering the gown so it covered my belly and lap. Even though his view now was of my entire ass, at least I felt covered.

"You're going to feel pressure here for a second," he warned while his gloved hand pressed at my entrance and then began to push in further. "So, how are the hormones? I know you're single…has that been difficult to manage?"

I watched the ceiling tiles while he navigated my cervix, or whatever it was he was after inside my vagina. "It's been horrible. I can't seem to get relief from anything that I try."

"Hmmm, interesting."

I didn't know what to say to that, but since being near Juan, things were exponentially worse.

"Well, there's a little stimulation trick I can show you, if you want?"

I looked down at him; his face was down, watching what he was doing. He must have found what he was looking for because he withdrew his hand, saying everything was in the right spot.

"What kind of trick?" I felt that same feeling, like nails on a chalkboard, like I was doing something wrong. Doctors talked about sexual things in front of couples all the time; this probably felt weird because I was all alone.

"Well...I don't want to make you feel uncomfortable, but I can show you if you want."

I considered it for a second, and then I thought of how hot and bothered Juan had left me the other night. I wouldn't survive if that kept happening, but at the same time...the doctor showing me something like that seemed odd. I considered all the weird shit they'd done to me since my first appointment...maybe him showing me a technique wouldn't be that far off.

With my voice shaky and my insides feeling like I was filling them with lead, I said, "Okay."

♥

THE SUN WAS a healing elixir I couldn't get enough of. I rested on the inflatable pool floatie with my face tipped back and sunglasses perched on my face. I had connected my phone to an outdoor speaker, and "Montana" by Daya danced along the water, forcing my wayward anxiety to settle and calm.

That is until a shadow fell over me, blocking the sun.

"Did you forget you're pregnant?" Juan's velvet voice boomed from somewhere near the edge of the pool.

I shoved my shades up, resting them on my hairline. "Excuse me?"

Juan crouched, his powerful legs straining against his denim-clad thighs. The crisp white t-shirt on his firm chest, a stark contrast to his mocha skin, made my mouth go dry. It was worse when I noticed how good he looked with his raven hair swept back and pieces falling into his face while a pair of dark frames covered his whiskey eyes. I loved Juan's eyes.

One night, while drunk on the stars and the beauty of New York's skyline, I had wondered what those eyes would look like on a baby girl and what kind of dad he'd be. I'd allowed myself thirty minutes to think rogue thoughts that would never do me any good, but still I thought them. I imagined what it would be like to be his wife and what kind of life it would be to have a husband who coached hockey for our kids or who built forts—or did anything my own father had not. The closest I'd ever come to having that was when Jakob had thrown a blanket over two chairs pulled together. It was during a thunderstorm, and I couldn't stop crying.

He seemed to know exactly what to do to calm me down after tears stained my clothes and my throat had gone raw from calling for my father. I learned later that we'd experienced a hurricane, and I'd had no idea. I had just known it was the scariest thing I'd ever experienced in my life.

Juan flicked his fingers toward me. "You're spilling out of that scrap of fabric—it's barely covering your cunt, and your tits are one harsh wind away from showing." Standing, he shoved his hands into his pockets but kept his eyes angled down at me. "So I'm wondering if you forgot that you gain weight with pregnancy...or are you just trying to show off?"

Since meeting Juan, I'd learned that my chest was an active volcano, the blood in my veins a fault line.

White-hot heat hit my chest as I processed his words, his arrogance, the fact that he'd never speak to my sister this way. He made me feel like I was worthless while making me feel like the only person to have ever captured his attention. For some reason, he brought out the worst in me. He brought out the girl who had hardened over time, the one who occasionally walked into the woods with a loaded gun.

He prodded me, knowing under this faux wool, a snout and maw of teeth ached for the taste of blood.

Instead of answering him, I sat up, exiting my raft with a dip into cool water, submerging myself completely in my effort to calm the fire in my lungs. Once my feet hit the bottom of the pool and I stood, my arms went back, my fingers tugging at the bow I'd tied at my spine.

As I crested each step and pulled myself free of the water, I let the sopping top fall to the cement, knowing my breasts were on full display to the asshole across the pool. I didn't care. He wanted to make me feel dirty, like I should be ashamed. I wouldn't give him the chance.

Once I cleared the steps, my fingers pushed down the material of my bottoms until I was stepping out of each leg.

"What in the fuck are you doing?" Juan's flat tone floated to me as I picked up a fuzzy towel. My body shook with the need to cover myself, but I wouldn't. Not yet.

I walked, drying my hair, leaving my nude body on display.

"You broke a rule...so I broke one."

"We agreed that I could be honest," he snapped, his hands out of his pockets, one of them blazing a trail through his hair, the other clenching at his side.

"You said you wouldn't be mean. If you're going to belittle me and make me feel like a whore, I'll save you the time and be one."

He smirked, his lips curving up in a delicious way. "Does that mean you'll get on your knees for me?"

His eyes were still covered, but I could feel the heat from him as thick and intense as a furnace. I was just a toy to him, though, a fascinating hamster now stuck in his cage, a pet he could poke and prod as much as he pleased.

"Is that what you want?" I stepped closer, dragging a finger down my chest, feeling my skin pebble against the cooling air. "For me to pull your thick cock into my mouth and suck?"

Juan's throat bobbed as he stared down at me.

I stepped closer. "You want to fist my hair while you slam your hips forward and shove your dick so far down my throat that I choke?"

Heat emanated from him, his jaw ticking, and I knew if I looked down, there'd be a bulge in his jeans.

Whispering, I said, "Because I'd never get on my knees for you...and I'd never allow you to touch me that way. You wouldn't even know what to do with a girl like me, Juan. I'd ruin you."

I walked off, finally tugging the towel around my torso, tucking in the sides. My fingers shook as I headed toward the sliding doors and took the stairs one at a time. My eyes burned with unshed tears, with fury at the one man who seemed to both light me on fire and burn me to ash.

Once inside my room, I showered and dressed, taking the time to blow-dry my hair and apply my makeup. I had realized long ago that my veins were black, my heart an inky stain, and my very blood a knot of ebony. Hatred seeped out of every pore as I tugged my cell up and entered the text that would seal my fate. The strength I'd found just one day prior had left, gone with the pin prick to my pride that Juan had delivered.

Me: I want to see you. I don't want to talk…just need a release.

I set the phone back on the counter for untold minutes, hating the burn in my chest. When I looked in the mirror, I saw a doll, a tool to be tugged free from a cage whenever needed…a hollow instrument with no dreams or aspirations. I was empty, and while I had grown used to the numbness I usually felt during hookups, now as I rubbed the palm of my hand over my swelling bump, there was only heartache.

I stared at my reflection, my golden locks glossy and straight, my lips a soft pink, and my eyes guarded with fake lashes and dressed up with dark tones that made my blue eyes pop. A single tear traveled down my cheek as I stared at my ample cleavage and tan legs. The dress I'd chosen was short, even without a bump; now, it was miniscule, but I didn't want Holden to have to work hard for what I needed from him.

A text came in as I grabbed my purse.

Holden: Come over…I'm alone tonight.

For some strange reason, I wanted him to deny me, wanted him to tell me we had to establish boundaries for our co-parenting to work in the future…but with that same desire, I also knew he never would and I would be doing this all alone. *Until my father finds me.*

Swiping at my face, I turned on my heel and exited my room.

CHAPTER ELEVEN

Taylor

The air was thick with something spicy, making my stomach grumble with hunger pangs. I pushed past the urge to ask what Juan had cooked. I didn't even know he could cook, but it didn't matter. I couldn't stay there while he treated me the way I saw myself. It felt like I was paper thin and somehow had found the one person in life who could see through my translucent skin and knew my deepest sins. I hated who I had become, but then again, my entire life was made up of death and denial... there was no way I'd confront the monumental mind fuck that Juan Hernandez was.

With one hand on the door, I was suddenly stopped with a warm hand on my wrist.

"Where are you going?" Juan's question was soft, almost pleading.

I knew if I turned to catch his expression, it would melt part of the ice I'd let expand in my chest.

Facing away from him, I answered, "Out."

"That's not going to work for us. I need to know that you're safe." He tugged so I'd face him. Although I resisted, it did nothing to keep him away. "Where are you going?" he tried again, and this time his tone was so gentle that my eyes rose to his.

Whiskey on a sunny day, daring me to answer him...challenging me to lie.

"Holden," I whispered, wetting my lips. My mouth was too dry, my heart too pathetic.

I expected Juan to scoff, let me go, and make me feel the way he had so many times. But he surprised me by tugging me forward until I was following him, his hand covering mine.

"Juan, did you hear me? What are you—"

"I heard you, I'm just not letting you go." He stopped at the stove, where he started stirring what looked like chicken. It smelled so good that my mouth watered and my stomach clenched. I hadn't eaten anything since lunch, and that was...what time was it? I looked around, noticing the clock on the microwave indicated it was past six.

"Why do you care? I—"

"When did you last eat?" Juan cut in, his gaze on the sizzling chicken.

"I..." I pulled at my hand, but he didn't let me go. "Lunch time." I finally gave in.

"So that was around noon...have you had a snack?" He let me go, but his warm arms came around me, caging me against the counter with my back to his chest. There was a wooden cutting board in front of me along with a sharp knife and three limes.

He lifted my right hand and forced a small green fruit into it.

"Roll this."

I wrapped my fingers around it, feeling its weight while trying to look up to catch his gaze. What did he mean by 'roll it'? I had never rolled a lime before; was that a normal thing? Perplexed and slightly intrigued, I did as he said and laid the lime on the wooden slab, making my palm flat over it and then rolling the round citrus.

"More pressure, like this." His hand swallowed mine, adding pressure as the limes rolled into the wood. I allowed his fingers to stay on top of mine while we worked all three. Soft music played in the living room, something with a heavy beat, making the feel of Juan's arms around me and the heat of his breath on my neck an intoxicating mixture.

"Where did you learn to do this?"

Juan shifted behind me, slightly moving to the right, letting me out of his cocoon. I stood there, unsure why I suddenly felt so cold and confused. Wasn't I headed over to Holden's house?

"My parents, aunts, my grandparents—everyone cooks. I've been around it my entire life." He flipped the chrome burner to the left, killing the flame. The pan was lifted above our heads while he shifted toward two empty plates. I hadn't even noticed them.

He carefully poured a small portion of cubed chicken onto each plate, which already had three round tortillas laid out.

"Can you quarter those limes for me?" He set the pan back on the burner and headed toward a small bowl of diced onion and another with something green inside.

"Uh…" I looked down at the cutting board and eyed the knife next to it. Heat flared and infused my cheeks as I realized I had no idea what he meant. I assumed he meant to cut them into four pieces, but was there a specific way to do that…or…?

Grabbing the knife in my right hand and the lime in my left, I wet my lips and aligned the blade to cut down the middle. I knew Juan watched me, which only made things a thousand times worse. I was almost twenty-one and had no idea how to quarter a lime. My face warmed as I paused, staring down at the two halves in front of me. I had baked things and even dabbled in cooking a million times, but I had never really made anything authentic.

"Now cut each piece in half again," Juan quietly murmured from the counter across the kitchen. His eyes weren't even on me, which made breathing a bit easier. How embarrassing. He'd been cooking his whole life, likely dated women who knew how to cook…then there was me, a spoiled entitled princess.

I cut the following two limes, hating myself with each swipe of the knife.

"Here," I whispered, cradling the pieces in my hands and walking toward the plates. I didn't even know what we were doing with them.

Juan turned and gave me a dazzling smile, one that stilled my erratic heart rate.

"Perfect. Now come sit down and eat with me." He steered me by the elbow, helping me sit on the stool.

"I was headed out. I'm happy to help cook anytime you need it...even though I'm not much of one, as you can tell...but I'm actually leaving for the night."

Juan's gaze fixated on the plate in front of him.

"Have you had tacos before?" he asked, ignoring me.

I watched as he spread onion and the green-looking leaf around the chicken then grabbed the lime and squeezed it all over.

My stomach grumbled as the smell of the spices and chicken assaulted me.

"I have...but they never looked like this."

"Eat, then if you still want to go see the dick face, be my guest." He folded the prepared taco and took a large bite of it.

I wanted to protest, get up, and walk out the front door...but I was only using Holden as a crutch, and it made me fucking weak to admit it, but I knew I should never have opened that door with him in the first place.

Copying what Juan had done, I lifted the taco and took a generous bite. Flavor burst along my tongue as a satisfied moan erupted from inside my throat.

Juan laughed beside me as I took another bite, and then another.

"Slow down, preciosa." He handed me a glass of water then sipped from his own.

"What did you say just now?" I smiled, trying to breathe between bites. The food was so good, and I hadn't tasted flavor like that in all my life.

"I called you a cow."

I rolled my eyes, knowing he was probably telling me the truth.

"Cow or not, this food is the best thing I've ever tasted. Does your whole family cook like this?"

He smiled down at me again, his bright eyes catching the dimming light of the sun. It was getting later, and I still hadn't texted Holden.

"My family owns a chain of restaurants. I should act offended that you've never been, but the most expensive thing on the menu is steak, which only costs just above twenty bucks. It's a place for the everyday person, not the one percent."

The jab landed and unfurled in my heart. He knew nothing of my life or my past...but that didn't matter. He didn't need to.

I nodded, sipping more water. "Well, I'd love to go sometime. What's the name of the restaurant?"

"Especias y Fuego." He stood and walked to the sink while I sat trying to tame the foreign word with my tongue.

Something niggled at the back of my brain. The sounds together were familiar...

"It means spice and fire," he added before turning again.

I let the thought go and finished my tacos, walking the plate over to the sink behind him.

"Well, I'll go sometime and pay my compliments. You could work there—you're that good of a cook." I smiled, but the way his face turned solemn told me I'd messed up again.

Not wanting to hear his insults, I spun away from him and started toward the front door.

"You're still going?" His clipped voice sounded at my back.

"You're the one who said I should eat and then I could go..." I shrugged, confused about why this bothered him.

"You like the pool?" He changed the subject, and my brows crinkled at the sudden shift.

"Uh..."

He grabbed his keys. "Let's get you a new suit."

"I don't fucking need one. What you did earlier was rude and uncalled for."

He smirked, which enraged me.

"You *do* need one. In fact, I'll get you several if you want."

I laughed, letting my petulant side flare. "You know who my dad is, right?"

"*Stepdad*...yeah, I do," Juan bit out, glaring at me.

"What is your problem with me? I didn't do anything to you." I crossed my arms defensively.

"I don't have a problem with you. In fact, I'm trying to help you." He let out a laugh that skittered down my spine and made a home in my soul.

"I don't *need* your help."

"You do, preciosa. That's why you're here...in my house, because I found you sleeping in a car."

"Oh my god, I'm not a COW! And I was fine in my car," I screamed at him, about to pick up a damn photo or vase, fucking something to throw at him. I hated him. "I'm leaving. I'll be back for my things when I can get Mallory to come with me." I spun on my heel and opened the door, slamming it shut.

I wasn't going back that night.

I wouldn't, not with his infuriating and frustrating mood swings.

Nearly to my car, I heard the door open behind me, which both thrilled me and exasperated me.

I quickened my steps, worried Juan would do something like block my ability to get to my car. I glanced up, seeing him jog down the stairs, bypassing me altogether and heading toward his sports car.

I stopped for a second as I realized he was leaving before I had a chance to.

"Oh no you don't." I tugged my door open, hopped inside, and started my engine.

Seeing his taillights flick on, I slammed my foot down on the gas pedal, but he was faster. There was enough room in the circle for two cars to drive side by side, but it narrowed once it straightened into the long drive down to the gate.

His red car moved in front of me and rushed down the road at a hazardous speed. I rolled my eyes, realizing he didn't care about my rage or my petulant defiance. My chest deflated as I progressed down the road and under the canopy of trees. This was so stupid, this idea that Juan and I could co-exist in the same house.

I tried not to care that he was likely headed to someone's house, maybe that brunette from the wedding. I hated that I cared, and that he was the only guy who'd ever seemed to make me care about where he went and who he saw or spent his time with.

Right as I rounded the corner on the path, veering for the gate, I saw a flash of red and slammed on my brakes.

Juan's car was parked parallel in front of the gate, blocking any entrance or exit.

"No." I breathed out, leaning over my steering wheel.

I was too busy watching the red sports car to realize my passenger door was opening.

"Let's go, princess."

Bereft of words, I stared at him. The way his form folded into my car, the way his scent filled up the space, erasing the smell of anyone else...

"Excuse me?" I scoffed, shocked by the fact that he'd just blocked my way out. Internally I smiled at his creativity and that he wasn't leaving.

"You can turn around right there. If you do it right, you'll only need a three-point turn. If you don't, it'll be more like a fifteen-point turn."

I stared at him.

"Need me to drive?"

Breathing through my nose and not in the mood to deal with him any longer, I cranked my wheel and began the drive back up to the house.

"So, you're not going to talk to me for the rest of the night?" Juan asked as I parked and slammed the car door shut.

"Why would you want me to?" I opened the door and tried to slam it shut, but he was right on my heels.

"You don't know anything about what I want," he muttered, following me up the stairs.

"Well, I guess not." I veered toward my room, and right as I was about to shut my door, he braced his hands on either side of the frame.

"I was two seconds away from fucking you today," he said with a sharp bite.

"What?" I whirled, my hair flying like a sheet in the wind.

He stepped inside my room, forcing me to back up a step.

"The way you looked in that bathing suit...the way your tits strained against the material, the way it rode up, right here." He carefully leaned forward until his finger traced over the outside of my mound, flaring to my hip.

I breathed through my nose at how close he'd gotten.

"That with your hair..." He tugged on a piece. "You can't wear shit like that around me, Taylor. You might think I don't care or I'm not attracted to you...but I promise you, it's quite the opposite." He watched me with those whiskey eyes. I wanted him to step closer, press his lips to mine, claim something that he already seemed to possess. "Eres peligroso para mi corazón," he whispered in a cadence that washed over me in a way that tugged at the strings of my heart.

I closed my eyes, committing the beautiful words to my heart, even if they meant I was a fat cow again. Something told me they were sweet words, ones he wouldn't be ready to say in English, which only made me crave the translation.

"Get into your pajamas and then come downstairs. Let's watch a movie."

He turned before I could say a single word or ask him why. I did as he said, hesitating only briefly over a pair of small sleep shorts and a tank that would show off my stomach and cleavage. He'd pushed me today when I made him feel out of control. While that wasn't my issue, I didn't have the energy to push him any further today.

Tugging on a pair of baggy sweats and an oversized shirt, I left my phone behind as I headed downstairs.

CHAPTER TWELVE

Juan

"Where have you been?" yelled my best friend Mallory as she lifted two iced coffees into the air. Her bright smile widened, and I knew her green eyes were animated as she looked over the house at my back.

"Me? I'm not the one who moved to New York, got married, and took over a company all within the last six months," I joked, pulling her into a hug as she made her way up the last few steps.

"I have called, texted, and even tried to FaceTime you the last time I was in Rake Forge. I come pretty often, actually," she argued, following me into the house.

I laughed, feeling my chest loosen at being in her presence again. Mallory Shaw and I met our sophomore year of college in a class neither of us took seriously or wanted to be in. We ended up playing tic-tac-toe, table football, and even hangman during each class, until I convinced her to let me have coffee with her every Saturday. It wasn't that she wasn't stunning, because she was. She was in a league of her own with her snarky comebacks, russet curls, and those curves that should have driven me crazy, along with every other guy, but it was never anything but platonic between us. She felt like a sister to me, a long-lost, adopted sister who was always meant to be in my life.

"How's Decker?" I asked, opening the patio doors and smiling at her gaping mouth. I'd missed her reaction to the house because I was in front of her, but seeing her freak out over this place was as fun as seeing our friend Hillary freak out over it. Our trio was split up for now, but I had high hopes of getting our little band back together.

"He's good. He's actually spending time with my dad today...fixing cars or something like that." She set the coffees down and settled her hands on her hips as she glanced across the kidney-shaped pool. Green grass stretched past the moon white patio until it dipped down a large hill where an orchard of citrus trees swallowed it.

"Juan, explain this to me..." She jutted her hands out.

I shrugged, chafing at the fact that I hadn't ever shared this part of my past with her.

"Signing bonus from the Hornets."

"Taylor said you weren't on the team anymore." She flicked her dark shades up until they rested on her head.

I shrugged again, grabbing for the coffee she'd brought for me. I pushed down the urge to reflect on the fact that Taylor had talked about me. I knew she would since she lived here, but I wanted to know what she'd said. Was there anything else she'd asked? How frequently did she bring me up?

"What happened?"

"Just a misunderstanding. Nothing I can't fix. I got to keep the bonus though..." This was true, but it wasn't nearly as big as I was making it sound—not big enough to secure or keep a place like this.

"What will you do now?" Mallory gently inquired, stretching into one of the lounge chairs.

"I'm keeping busy...going back to RFU actually as a TA, just for now." I rubbed my neck, feeling oddly embarrassed.

Mallory tilted her head to the side. "For now?"

I sipped the coffee, hating that she'd gotten mine like hers. She knew

I hated all the sugary shit she liked. I took mine black with a splash of milk, that was it.

"Yeah...I mean, I have to make a decision soon regarding hockey. I can sign on with other teams, out of the area."

"What's wrong with this area?" she asked in her reporter tone, and fuck, if my best friend caught wind of my family, I would be screwed. She worked for an international paper that worked tirelessly to seek out social justice. She'd rip my entire family to pieces if she knew what I was tied to.

"Nothing, just...might be time for a change..." I trailed off.

"Right," she murmured, like she didn't believe me, and I wasn't sure why she wouldn't.

"So, what's going on with you and my sister?" She sipped from her pink straw.

I had nearly forgotten about the little sisterly come-to-Jesus meeting where they overcame the term 'step' when referring to each other as siblings.

"She's a temporary roommate."

"Paying rent?" Mallory's dark eyebrow rose in question.

I almost laughed, just thinking of Taylor trying to offer it. I knew she probably would, but our tentative truce would likely implode if she did. I thought over the last week that she'd been here, starting with our explosive beginning where we couldn't seem to not want to hate-fuck each other every five seconds, and sadly how it had cooled and waned into a tentative lukewarm existence. She came and went to school without making a fuss. If she'd stepped foot in the pool again, it had been while I wasn't home. She had made a few meals on her own, leaving leftovers in the fridge, cleaning every single scrap of proof that she was ever there. The only reprieve from her silent, mouselike existence was when she'd come downstairs in her pajamas with a leatherbound book in her hand. I'd turn off the hockey highlights and turn on something for us to watch. She loved anything that had to do with history, whether historically accurate or not.

"She might be...we haven't discussed it yet."

"Cut the crap." Mal spun on her ass, sitting up to face me. "What is going on with you two? Why is she here?"

"Nothing is going on." I peeked over her shoulder at the pool, wondering if Taylor had mentioned what had happened. "She's here because I caught her sleeping in her car on campus."

"What?" my best friend yelled, confirming that Taylor hadn't told anyone about her little homeless situation.

"I guess she couldn't find a place or something." I shrugged, not really caring why Taylor didn't have a place to go, only that now she slept here every night and woke up here every morning. Not that I necessarily wanted her to...the knowledge just sort of sat inside my chest uselessly, right next to my black heart.

Mallory's face softened, the fire in her eyes simmering a fraction. "Well, thank you...I have no idea what in the world caused her to sleep in her car of all places. She could easily go to a hotel."

"I don't know either...something about parking at the school."

"Has she told you about the father yet?" Mal asked in that same reporter voice.

I hated this question. I didn't know why I hated it so much, or why the idea of Holden's hands on Taylor's body made an ice storm form in my chest cavity, but it did. Seeing them together in the hall the other week, knowing she wanted to go see him wearing that scrap of fabric she called a dress, especially right after I had seen her saunter toward me completely naked from the pool...

Fuck.

Pregnant or not, her body was pure temptation. I wanted to claim her, grab her by the hips, and let her know what seeing her in that tiny black bikini did to me. Never in my life had I been that hard in such a short amount of time. I saw her lying on that pool lounger, her tits pushed together, tan and glistening with sweat, and those bottoms...just a fucking string. Smooth skin greeted me, a tiny tantalizing fantasy just waiting for me to succumb.

I cleared my throat, remembering Mallory's question. "Holden, right?"

A huff of air left Mal's chest. "Yeah...such a loser. I'm so frustrated on her behalf. She just needs some place to lie low and build the confidence to be a mom. I know she'll move back to be near Dad's once she gets close to delivering, but her having a safe place to be right now means so much to me. Thank you, Juan." She stood and leaned over, kissing me on the head. "But if you try to sleep with her or break her heart, I'll totally force Decker to kick your ass."

I laughed, because Decker was a good guy, and even if he wanted to kick my ass, I knew he wouldn't. I also knew he couldn't. Mallory, however, probably could...the girl was scary as hell.

"Got it, M." I hugged her, forcing images of Taylor in my house, holding a new baby out of my head.

"Let's go FaceTime Hillary and meet her new girlfriend." She wiggled her eyebrows.

Shaking my head, I laughed. "No, I don't want to—they're always so mean."

Mal slung her arm over my shoulder and tossed her coffee cup. "Show me the rest of your house first."

♥

IT WAS NEARLY dark when I padded up the stairs to check on Taylor. I kept thinking she'd come down for our nightly routine, but she never did. I contemplated just staying put, keeping the sports highlights on, letting her do her own thing, and, more importantly, not giving in to how comfortable it had become to have her with me every night. I would have been lying if I said I didn't look forward to spending each evening with her, learning new little things about this woman who'd been stuck in my mind for too long. I realized she loved history books, the ones mostly about America. She had a huge heart and a lot of opinions about the early days of our country, and I loved hearing them. Sometimes she'd talk, not realizing I was there listening to every word, absorbing her and all the tiny pieces of what made her unique. She didn't like scary movies, nothing with a sad ending, unless it was historical. She loved food and eagerly helped me if I was cooking. Even if she wasn't sure what to do or how to do it, she would get up and offer to chop or dice. So, with her absence, it just felt empty...and then there was that part of my chest that began to fill with worry.

That part ached in a way I wasn't ready to fully examine.

Her bedroom door was unlocked and open, her slight form in the middle of her bed as she held her phone to her ear. I carefully stepped closer and heard a soft walloping sound come from the speaker. Taylor was staring off to one side of the room, on her side, her hand tucked under her face while tears ran down her cheeks.

"Hey, you okay?" I gently took a seat on the edge of her bed, and my hand went to her shoulder on its own.

She closed her eyes, which pushed out a few more tears.

Concerned, I tugged her phone free to hear what she was listening to. On the screen it said something about a sound clip of a fetal heartbeat.

"I'm pretending it's hers."

I set her phone back down, eyeing her stomach. "You found out the gender?"

She shook her head, swiping at her nose with her sleeve. She wore a large flannel over her pajamas; it looked like a men's shirt, which caused a strange pitch to my stomach.

"I'm guessing." She sniffed, unaware that I was reeling over whose shirt she was in.

"Why aren't you listening to her actual heartbeat?" I asked, moving past that feeling. It wasn't my business whose shirt it was or if she was with someone or had been seeing someone. I focused on her problem. I knew from my cousin's pregnancy that there were machines that would allow you to listen to the heartbeat with headphones.

She sat up, swiping at her face, and the devastation nearly broke me open. I'd never seen her so vulnerable. My thumb moved under her eye, swiping away her tears, and I cradled her face in my palm. Words danced along the edge of my tongue to comfort her. I clenched my molars together to hold off the odd sensation.

"The doctor said I wasn't allowed to record it."

What a prick, but I knew that was likely true for legal reasons. "Why do you need to hear it tonight?"

The small light from across the room allowed me to see her freckles and tear-stained skin. She was the most beautiful thing I'd ever seen. I hated that my mind had made the connection, because now it wouldn't be so easy to push it away. Taylor wasn't just hot or sexy; she was truly beautiful, with a soul that matched and a light that had somehow been smothered so many times that she just acted like it was a part of her when I knew it wasn't. She was hiding from something.

"It was just a hard day..." She shrugged, swiping at her face once more. "When I hear it in the appointments, it's like all of a sudden everything is better, and I don't have to worry anymore...it makes me feel like everything will be okay."

"What are you worried about not being okay?" My brows dipped, curious what concerned her so much. Something in my chest flared with a rogue emotion I hadn't ever felt before. It was fear, protection...things I didn't want to attach to her but couldn't seem to stop.

Her shoulder rose while she sat up straighter. "Nothing, just pregnancy stuff."

Something told me there was more to it than that, and the idea that her tears might be from not having Holden in the picture left me feeling empty and like I'd failed her somehow. I didn't know why or the cause of it, but it was like my rib cage was opening under taut skin, just painful and without a doubt would leave me ruined.

"Want to watch something in here?" I had to try to cheer her up, get her mind off of whatever it was that had bothered her so much.

She gave me a small laugh and moved over to make room for me. "I don't have a television in here."

I settled in next to her. "That's okay, I have my phone."

"I'm kind of a mess. I still need to brush and braid my hair."

I realized now, beyond just the pajamas, her hair was indeed wet. "Grab the brush, I'll help you." Why had I just offered that? I didn't want to touch her hair or sit with her between my legs. I didn't. I couldn't.

"Juan, it's fine. I'll just—"

"Taylor, let me help." *Fuck.* What was wrong with me?

She let out a sigh and moved. Bringing back her laptop and a brush, she eyed the bed and the open space between my legs. It was dim enough in the room that I couldn't catch whether her eyes flared or not, but the flush working into her neck told me she would be just as affected by this setup as me.

She set up a television show on her computer and then gingerly crawled onto the bed and in between my legs.

"This okay?" Her narrow chin appeared over her shoulder, her eyes questioning.

There was enough space to fit an entire extra person between us, so I gently gripped her hips and moved her until her back was flush with my chest...and her ass was nestled up against my dick.

"This is better." I grabbed the brush she'd brought and watched as she relaxed into me when I began brushing through her wet strands. The movie she'd selected was some historical show about a time traveler who had two husbands in two different times. Seemed odd to me, but Taylor loved watching it whenever she had the television to herself.

I'd finished brushing her hair entirely and was ready to start gathering her hair into a braid when she carefully asked, "Where did you learn to braid?"

I smiled at the memory. "When I was little, my biological dad was pretty rough with women, and since I had been spending a lot of time around him, my mom worried that I'd turn out like that—mean, brash, violent. So, she had me braid my little sister's hair every night. She was younger than me by about five years, but it worked. I learned to be patient and calm, especially when she would say I pulled too tight or tried to make the task difficult for me."

I felt Taylor's shoulders shake in laughter.

"What?"

She lifted a shoulder. "Nothing. I just can't picture you braiding hair...especially on a little girl."

"I'm braiding yours, aren't I?" I tied off the end of her hair and suddenly had no place for my hands except on my thighs. I could feel the heat from her own legs burning next to mine.

"True."

It was quiet for a while, the show played on the laptop, and then Taylor tried to move away.

"Where are you going?" I gently placed my hand on the top of her thigh.

"You're finished with my hair, so I can move if you want."

"Is that what you want?" I said low and close to her ear.

Fuck, what was I doing? This wasn't a good idea, and yet...her body was so warm, and she smelled so fucking good, and I couldn't quite remember why I hated her to begin with.

She let out a breath that seemed to be trapped in her lungs for too long then gave the slightest shake of her head.

"Lean back," I whispered, reclining into the pillows. She followed suit, bringing her elbows back to my hips until she was adjusted to our new position. From this vantage point, I could see the swell of her breasts move up and down as she took each breath.

"Your father was a violent man?" she asked carefully.

I watched the show playing out, trying to weigh how much I wanted to tell her, and how much I wanted to keep quiet. "Yeah...not so great. He died about five years ago."

"I'm sorry," she whispered.

"Don't be...I'm not."

She shifted again, her breathing becoming shallower. "What happened with hockey? You're an amazing player...I don't understand why they'd drop you."

I blinked, realizing my initial response had been to just open up to her, and while I didn't want Mal to know anything about this, something told me Taylor wouldn't tell her.

"I don't talk about this part of my life...but my uncle came to one of my practices..." I hesitated. "He's a part of a gang...it's pretty dangerous, and the team didn't want to have any connection to it."

"That's really shitty. I'm sorry that happened to you." Taylor moved her back like she was uncomfortable. She didn't seem scared that my uncle might be tied to me, or that I'd used the term gang... which was telling in itself. If she'd grown up alongside me or on the streets, I might have accepted her brushing it off, but Taylor had been raised with a silver spoon in her perfect mouth. Me saying my uncle was in a gang should have shaken her a bit, or at least made her tense up. I already knew how Mallory would respond, which was why I'd never tell her.

"It's fine...just means I'll likely have to relocate to sign on with a different team." I decided to move on, unsure how to even broach the subject of her lack of reaction. Maybe she didn't believe me.

"I hope you can. I couldn't imagine you giving up that dream," she said softly, and because I was so fucked in the head, I actually took offense to her encouraging me to move. That she hoped I would...*fucking hell*. I wanted her to turn in my arms and tell me not to go, then wrap her pink lips around my cock and let me show her how badly I wanted to stay.

I closed my eyes, releasing a shuddering breath...this was merely a physical reaction, just a response to her tits being so close. The tank she wore was practically translucent, and it was so low cut that it barely concealed her fullness.

There was that, and the fact that she kept squirming, brushing against my dick.

My hands went to her stomach, bracing her just above the line of her shorts. It was instinctual...I just needed to touch her. She froze for a few seconds, until she let out a tiny gasp.

"Taylor, are you wet?" I asked on a rough, needy rasp. I didn't know what we were doing or why we were doing it, but fuck if I could stop it.

"When am I not wet?" she admitted breathily. "This pregnancy is the worst. I'm horny all the time, and it's so painful because it's not like I can take care of it the way I usually do."

"You mean with sex?" I skimmed the edge of her shorts, moving my fingers to trace the top of her mound and in between her legs.

Her back arched. "Sex...my vibrator...nothing seems to be working.

My reach and the size of this growing belly might have something to do with it."

"You can't just rub one out?" I joked, but it was strained because the image that had just popped into my head was causing a problem in my sweats. I was so hard against her that it was painful.

"I can...it's just not the same. It's like my appetite is so much more intense than I've ever felt before."

Using my other hand, I teased down the elastic of her shorts and planned to tease her through her panties, but as soon as I moved inside, I realized she wasn't wearing any. I nearly cursed as her bare cunt was already wet and ready for my touch. Her little moan let me know she approved, so I indulged. Up and down my finger swiped while my other hand squeezed her breast. She put her hands on my thighs and pushed up so she was sitting taller and I had easier access.

Taking her breast out through the top of her tank, I roughly rolled the hardened nipple between my greedy fingers. Then I carefully used my finger to spread her pussy lips and gently push my middle finger inside her center.

"So fucking wet for me already. Do you have any idea what I would do with this if I were to fuck you?" I whispered in her ear, catching the lobe with my teeth.

"What would you do?" she asked breathlessly, her head rolling to my shoulder.

I did the same progression of swiping my finger along the seam of her pussy lips a few times, loving how wet she was and needing her to melt for me. Once she hissed, pushing into my chest, I began to rub her clit in circles.

"I'd wrap that silky hair of yours around my fist." I pushed two fingers into her. "And I'd mount you, up on all fours..." She bucked into my hand like she couldn't contain herself.

"So you'd..." she started, but her breathing turned ragged.

I added more pressure, gently biting her shoulder. "I'd make sure you were nice and wet for me, then I'd slide into you hard...but slow. I wouldn't want to hurt the baby."

I was still rubbing circles into her pussy when her body went rigid.

I paused, curious about her reaction.

"What?"

She paused again then sat forward. "Nothing...it's just..." She moved so my hand left her shorts and chest.

"Did I hurt you?"

"No."

She was moving now, trying to get off the bed. Her knee knocked into the laptop, causing it to fall off the bed and her to go sideways.

"Taylor—shit." I sat up, trying to help her. "You're going to hurt yourself, let me help you."

"I'm fine," she said coldly.

What the fuck had I done wrong?

She was still moving, righting herself, and smoothing her hair when the lights suddenly went out.

"Fuck."

"Did you not pay the bill?" she asked in the dark somewhere off to my left. The laptop was still going, but it was on the floor and dark, so it offered little light. What would she even know about bills not being paid or lights getting shut off because of it?

"I think it's storm related." Just as I said it, a gust of wind slammed into the house, making the shutters shake outside.

Taylor's voice trembled. "Oh shit."

Worried that she'd fall, I shuffled forward until I was grabbing her wrist and guiding her back to bed.

"Juan, no...I'll just—"

"I don't want you to hurt yourself or the baby."

She stayed quiet while I brought her back, helping her ease back in.

Settling in beside me, she finally whispered, "Why do you care about the baby?"

"Don't you?" I shifted to my side.

"Obviously...but I've gotten used to being the only one."

That made my chest ache, and I wasn't sure why. She wasn't my business, wasn't my problem, yet not having anyone care...that would be shitty as hell. Why didn't she have anyone who cared? Surely, Mallory did...and...fuck, who else did she have?

I folded my hands across my chest so I wouldn't be tempted to touch her. "Well, you're not the only one."

We waited in the dark while the storm raged outside, and while she didn't ask me to stay, for some reason I knew I needed to. So, I did, waiting until her breathing evened out and I knew she was asleep. Then I covered her and got up, all the while knowing I needed this not to go any further. She could stay...the baby too, for as long as they needed, but I needed to find somewhere else to be. Tonight, we'd come too close to crossing a line, and I'd obviously upset her. It was a mistake I wouldn't make again.

CHAPTER THIRTEEN

Taylor

Reds and creams all swirled in a chaotic mix around me as nervous energy thrummed under my skin. This was the third time I'd somehow wandered to this side of town and into this store. Each time I'd get as far as the greying carpet signaling the start of the baby section, then I'd stop and look around as though I was an imposter. I had no idea what I was doing, but I couldn't help but wander here, curious about what my little bean would need when he or she came. Rubbing my belly, I stepped over the invisible barrier and began thumbing through little outfits and rompers that were so cute my heart nearly burst. My eyes kept drifting to the girl clothes, the pinks and teals, even the little flamingo rocker...my heart thumped wildly in my chest as I took in all the possibilities.

"Can I help you find anything?" A woman in a red shirt smiled at me while wrangling a rack of clothes.

"Um...I don't know," I said in response, unsure of what I was looking for or why I was there, again. I greedily took in the highchair displays and cribs...there was so much, so many things I would need, and where would I store it all?

"Well...let's see, you're what, in your third trimester now?" She eyed my stomach.

KING OF HEARTS   99

I turned toward her, my brows hitting my hairline. "Yeah, how did you know that?"

"I just had a baby last year." She waved me off.

My eyes lit up, my heart soaring. "This one is my first. I honestly have no idea where to even begin, or what I need."

"Oh girl." She smiled and urged me forward. I followed after her while we headed away from the clothes and displays of cribs and rounded the corner. The first aisle had blankets and other cuddly things, along with bathtubs and a few lotions, and another had diapers...so many diapers.

"Holy smokes...why are there so many options?" I ran my fingers along one of the boxes.

The woman gave me a sympathetic look. "Anyone in your family who can help you?"

I snorted. "Not anyone who'd know anything."

"Well..." She hesitated, looking over her shoulder. "Here." She pointed toward the letter N in the bottom corner of the diaper box. "This stands for newborn. It's the first size for babies when they're born...then you go up to one, then two, and so on. You'll know as they get older when they're ready for the next stage."

Feeling empowered, I grabbed a red and white box with the N in the bottom corner.

"You'll need wipes—lots of them, and a ton of other things." She pulled out her phone and typed away. "This website will help you, and go on Pinterest, type in what to get as a new mom—there are a lot of really good blogs."

I eyed the screen of her phone, feeling a little stupid. Why hadn't I thought of that?

"Thank you, you've already been really helpful."

She smiled again, her flawless ebony skin radiant against her white teeth. "You're welcome. Listen, that N goes for the sizing on clothes too. First ones they wear have the N on it, then it goes zero to three months, and so on."

I nodded to communicate my understanding, feeling a little less like an imposter and a bit more like a soon-to-be mother. The feeling swooshed into my chest like a cold liquid.

"By the way...do you know what you're having?" she asked, nearly out of the baby section.

My eyes watered because I hadn't wanted to find out, afraid to get too attached. So, I just shook my head no. It was partly why it had been such a bad day the day prior. I'd had an O.B. appointment, and Dr. Kline was in a bad mood. He wanted to show me the stimulation technique again, and this time I told him no. It felt strange to have his hands on me, and wrong...and I wasn't sure if I had been rude by telling him no, but I felt like I should have the right to turn down medical services, even if they were as twisted and strange as him offering to get me off.

When he'd moved to check the baby's heartbeat, and I asked if I could record it, he shut me down so fast with a sharp denial and a scoff... almost making fun of me. He educated me on how that was illegal, then proceeded to talk down to me about the weight I wasn't gaining and how I needed to start taking this pregnancy more seriously. It was a downward spiral from there as I considered again that I was a terrible choice for a mother for this baby. I wouldn't be able to protect her from my father, or from Markos.

The reminder that my life didn't belong to me came in as swift as a turbulent thunderstorm. I could get as excited as I wanted, but it would never matter because I was owed to a monster, and it was only a matter of time before he came to collect.

"Well, that's okay...and one last thing." She eyed my belly and the way the material scrunched up, showing my skin. "You might want to start wearing maternity clothes, not that I'm judging...but you mentioned not knowing where to start, so I thought maybe you weren't sure about that part either."

I blinked, a little overwhelmed that she'd had to point out that I needed to wear maternity clothes. She was right, and no, I didn't know where to start.

"Right over there, they have pants that you don't have to button or zip, shirts that cover your belly, and all sorts of things." She smiled once more, and then she was gone.

I spun on my heel and smiled, despite the cloud hanging over my head. I had learned to enjoy the breaks in the clouds, however few and far between the gaps were.

♥

I ENDED up going back to the store every day for a week, each day picking up something else on my list. I had read so many new mommy blogs and posts and links, so many pins and TikToks that I truly felt empowered. I knew what a nursing bra was and that I would need one, and a pump...I knew about storing breast milk, and nipple sensitivity.

I had purchased a ton of maternity clothes too and found out from some of the blogs that there were things called belly bands and tanks that helped and went with outfits. There was so much, and my head was still swirling with all the things I'd learned.

Walking with my hoard of purchases, I didn't expect to run into Juan on my way up to my room.

"Hey," he said, grabbing my elbows to stabilize me.

"Hey," I replied, my arms full.

He let me go, and I ambled past him. He'd been scarce the past week...more than scarce, he hadn't even been home as far as I could tell. Our movie nights were effectively ruined, because I'd ruined them. So, at night, I went down by myself and watched the massive television with all the lights on in the room, because I was afraid of being alone.

I hated it.

I read books to my baby and made homemade face masks and hair masks, but in the end I was still alone, and Juan still wasn't home.

I hated that I was bitter about it, but I understood.

"Looks like you bought the whole store." He lightly laughed, trailing me into my room. I had no idea if he noticed that there was a slow buildup of items in my room or not, but again, he hadn't been home.

"Just getting a few things for the baby."

He leaned against the door frame, his black dress pants pressed and paired nicely with his white dress shirt.

"Well...here's one more thing you can add to the list." He slid a white box into one of my bags, wearing a sheepish smile.

I watched as he took a step back, like it was no big deal that he had just purchased something for my baby. My heart skipped a thousand beats, like it was about to burst.

I blinked.

"Thank you...here, I want to open it." I shuffled a few steps so I could set the bags down.

"I have to head out, it's no big deal..." he hedged, but there was no way he was getting out of me opening it in front of him. The fact that he was leaving again scratched at my lungs, like I wanted to sob for him to please stay with me. I was sick of being alone, but I wouldn't.

I had no idea where he was going, but with his dark skin and that raven hair...it was an effort not to jump him. My hormones were going crazy, and the attraction I had to him was becoming impossible to handle. It was probably a good thing that he had put space between us, because that night things had gone way too far...it hadn't been until he mentioned the baby the other night that I realized he had pictured having sex with me, with current pregnant me and not future non-pregnant me. For whatever reason, this banter we had, this flirtation...I thought it was just a game, a buildup for when I wasn't pregnant anymore. No guy would just fuck a pregnant girl unless they cared about them, right?

So, I freaked out.

It was a lot to take in at once, and of course images of him fisting my hair and fucking me from behind were on repeat in my head for days.

I began digging through the bag he'd slid the gift into.

"So, find out the gender yet?" he asked, walking closer.

My heart froze, that feeling of panic surging to the surface. I wanted to, especially after my talk with Fatima in the store—I'd learned her name and ran into her three times since our first meeting. She told me she'd been asking for the baby section more often in hopes she'd see me. I felt like I'd made a friend, and with Mal gone, it was nice, even if I did have to splurge on spending money just to see her. I supposed I could maybe ask for her number...maybe.

"Um...not yet." My fingers wrapped around the box he'd given me. It was solid white without any packaging indicating what it was. Scrunching my brows, I began tearing at the sides to get inside.

Juan picked up a pack of newborn diapers, tilting it in his hands. "Holden won't go?"

I hadn't asked him. After I hadn't shown up that night at his dorm, he'd ghosted me again, and when I saw him on campus, he pulled whatever girl was near him under his arm and walked away.

"No." The box opened, and out slid a small machine about the size of my palm. With it was a headset wrapped in plastic and a few cords.

"Fetal doppler..." My eyes jumped to his.

He rubbed the back of his neck. "So you can hear her...or his heartbeat whenever you want to. There's a speaker, but I think you can plug in those headphones. You can record it on your phone too, so you don't have to apply that stuff to your stomach each time if you don't want to."

I had tried so hard not to cry in front of Juan. So many times I had wanted to...but I held back. I was terrified on a regular basis, and the longer I was pregnant, the more I felt like I was just on a runaway train, headed for a cliff. But he made me feel safe, like not everything was about to go up in flames.

"Thank you," I whispered, resisting the burning behind my eyes and the urge to jump into his arms.

"It's not a big deal." He turned away about to leave, but suddenly I wanted him to stay. I couldn't ask for that, though.

He had been creating space between us, setting up a new habit so that we knew where the other stood regarding this thing that had been flickering between us. It was like a fire that just wouldn't take. We'd burn to ash, and that would be the end. I turned and started putting things away in the closet. There was nothing set up in there, just empty space, so I'd been setting everything on the floor.

"Set up the appointment. I'll go with you."

My head snapped up, now in the closet, and he was still by my bed. I ambled out, tripping over a bag but not falling. "No...you've done enough for me...us. You don't need to—"

"I offered. You didn't ask," he said curtly, then he was clenching his molars together, acting as if he wanted to say something else, but he exited my room instead, leaving me with a kernel of hope in my chest that I didn't want to take root. I couldn't bear to face that appointment alone, and here he was offering to help me again. It made me feel warm and grateful. That feeling paired with the attraction I had to him, and it was an impossibility that I wouldn't allow myself to imagine.

♥

I TUGGED the sweater around my belly, thankful I'd grabbed a ton of cozy maternity things for the upcoming winter. We didn't always get winter in North Carolina in the same way other places did, but it was still unpredictable, and the temps still dipped, or it rained. Today it was raining, a miserable freezing sort of drizzle.

I'd been attending classes for over a month; October had crept in and suddenly there were pumpkins and harvest decorations all over the town. Fall was my favorite season, so I was giddy with excitement as I tugged on tall boots and wrapped myself in cozy sweaters. I was especially excited today because I'd received a call that the imaging center was able to schedule my ultrasound appointment.

I had done what Juan had suggested and set it up, ignoring all the flutters in my stomach about what could happen if I saw my bean up on the screen and fell in love with it...only to have it taken from me. I couldn't dwell on it.

Walking around campus was starting to get difficult with my book bag and purse, so I decided at the last second to cut through the building instead of skirting around it. Overheated and a little annoyed, I tracked through the entire building and exited the opposite side, and then I halted. There across the quad, leaning against a lamp post, stood one of my father's men. I knew it was him with his dark wool coat, the collar popped, and with the way his cold eyes moved, measuring each student that passed as a possible target.

I also knew if he was standing there, he already had me boxed in, and if I tried to run, they'd give chase. It was how my father's wolves operated, and how they never lost an asset or a target. Swallowing the lump in my throat, I walked toward him, never more grateful for buying an oversized maternity sweater than I was in that moment. Seeing me straight on, especially covered in a charcoal sweater, it was hard to tell I was pregnant; it was the side profile I had to be wary of.

"Hercegnő," the man muttered in Hungarian, chewing on a toothpick. Icy blue eyes assessed me while he relaxed against the post. He had at least a week's worth of scruff along his neck and jaw.

"I'm no princess," I bit back in a tone as cold as his gaze. "What does he want?"

"Your father wants to make sure you're local," he drawled, blue eyes flicking down my frame, "close by, and ready for Markos." He adjusted the toothpick in his mouth. I wondered how many more pairs of eyes were watching us.

"I have until December."

"You have until he says you do. Don't forget who your father is, little bird." The man chucked under my chin then turned and walked away.

I was fuming, my face heating and my chest burning. I knew he'd come; I'd known it for years and even more so as the time dripped slowly by, moving closer to my birthday. I knew and yet this man's presence was like being shoved under water.

"Taylor." Someone called my name, and I realized too late it was Juan, his hand wrapping around my elbow and tugging. "Who was that?" His dark brows caved in, those whiskey eyes flicking over my shoulder to where the man had disappeared.

"No one...just an old hookup." I shrugged out of his hold and walked toward my car. I could feel my fortress of ice start to freeze in place once more, to protect more than just me. Juan could get hurt if I wasn't careful.

"He's a little old...why is he here?" Juan trailed after me.

He never used to ask me questions. I hated how far he'd unraveled within the span of just a few months.

"A professor." It was a lie, but I couldn't bring myself to care.

Juan's scoff skittered down my chest, darting into my heart like a bullet from a gun.

"Well did he upset you? You seem..." He assessed me, and he should have just saved himself the time.

"I'm fine. I need to go." I slammed the car door and pulled away from the lot, refusing to see if Juan stood there watching. My heart galloped with panic, and my baby kicked as if aware that something was wrong.

What if another one of his men was sent and saw that I was pregnant? What if he decided to call me back sooner than my twenty-first birthday?

I sniffed, forcing the tears to stay at bay as I drove toward the opposite end of the city and headed back home to my mother and stepdad's house. At least there, I wouldn't have to face Juan, and if his men followed me, it wouldn't endanger him.

CHAPTER FOURTEEN

Juan

Greying clouds overcrowded the sky, erasing any natural light that would normally pour in through the kitchen windows. It put me in a shitty mood. I might as well have been a fucking house plant for how much I loved the sun; it always made me feel better and more alive.

I continued chopping bell peppers, hating that I was curious if Taylor had taken her coat or not. I wondered about her more often than I should, and it was happening more frequently than I would ever admit.

I was so involved with chopping and worrying I didn't even notice when the front door opened.

"Primo!" my cousin Hector yelled from the living room.

"In here." I moved the peppers to a plate and started on the onions.

"Look at you, Martha fucking Stewart." His laugh was muffled by his meaty palm coming up to smother it. I couldn't help laughing with him. He could be goofy as fuck when he wanted to be, and I was sure I looked ridiculous wearing the apron over my suit. "Why you dressed so nice?"

I cut the vegetables, keeping my eyes on the knife in my hand and my curled fingers. "I had an interview with one of the head coaches for the Bears." I looked up in time to see the blank look on my cousin's face. "It's another hockey team, up the coast a bit."

"Oh...you know you're set for life, even without lifting a finger. We're here for you...Pops was talking the other night about how you're supposed to be taking over." Even though my cousin's tone softened and his posture went lax, I snapped.

"I'm not fucking coming back." Not to the outfit, not the family... none of it. I checked on my parents out of duty, and I checked on my little sister because if I didn't, she'd end up as used as a communal toothbrush. She loved the attention of El Peligro and the lifestyle. Riding in low riders, packing, fighting, fucking, and stealing—she lived for it.

Hector stayed quiet for a second, his dark brows wrinkling while his hands came out in front of him.

"Why you here, anyway?" I dumped the onions into the sauté pan and began stirring.

"My dad told me to come over and make sure you knew about the panic button."

I paused mid-stir and stared at him. "You fucking with me?"

His chest moved as laughter rolled through him; contagious, it filled my lungs as well.

"Serious, man...let me show you." He stood and waited for me to follow.

Once I turned off the burner, I untied the cloth around my waist and followed him.

"Pops set it up for himself, because he was going to live here, until his new wife said she wanted to live closer to the shops." Hector shifted left into the study and walked toward the massive desk in the middle of the room. Flicking his hand underneath, he suddenly froze.

His black tee didn't seem to move an inch.

"Dude, you gotta come over here and see what I'm actually pressing."

"How many buttons are under there?" I joked, moving closer and ducking down. Sure enough, there was a silver switch built into the sturdy wooden writing desk, along with a 9mm strapped underneath. "Well, I'll be damned."

"El Peligro is your family whether you want it or not...we're here for you."

I stood, watching my cousin with confusion.

"Is there something you know that I don't? Some danger you happen to think I'm in?"

Our entire lives, Hector had never been a good liar, so long ago, he'd stopped trying. If he had to hide something, he'd kill first just to avoid having to spill it. But with family? He didn't waste his time. He didn't play poker, didn't do anything at all that could lead to him having to lie... so now, staring at him as he waited to tell me what he knew, I wasn't sure why, or really how he was still hesitating.

His black lashes fluttered, his smile cracking as a small laugh erupted in his chest. His hand came up, slapping my shoulder as he headed back toward the front door.

"Not for you...but for who hangs around you."

I turned, following him with my eyes. "Like Mallory?"

He reached the door and turned. "If you need us, hit that button, primo. That's all I'm saying." Then he was gone.

♥

THE INTERACTION with Hector was still in my head as I headed to school. I stretched my fingers at my side so I wouldn't be tempted to get my phone out of my pocket and double-check my messages. Taylor was supposed to notify me when she had the date for her ultrasound. I'd offered to go with her, mostly because it would just be a shitty thing to go to alone, but there was something deeper there I was ignoring, some desperate need to be included, involved, to experience that moment with her.

It was Thursday afternoon, a few days since that moment by the admin building where I saw her talking to some stranger. Her words had flung back at me like little rocks. There was something she wasn't telling me, that much I knew...but I wasn't sure what. It left me wondering who that man was. I noticed the smallest bit of a tattoo on his wrist when he moved his arm; it looked like something I'd seen in one of my history classes, something similar to the Turul bird from the creation myths from somewhere in Europe. The hardness of the man, the way his eyes looked at Taylor...it reminded me of the way the captains in El Peligro looked at one of their targets.

"Fuck it," I muttered, hanging right toward a large pillar. It was past two in the afternoon, which meant Taylor was out of her classes and should have been leaving campus or already home. She'd been staying at her mom and Charlie's off and on, and I didn't fucking know why. I had decided to back off after she recoiled from me that night in her bed. I'd done my part in setting up distance for us, but now it seemed Taylor had decided to do her own thing, and I didn't fucking like it. I wanted it to stop, and maybe when we went to the ultrasound together, it would.

My fingers moved as the sun bounced off the science building to my right and the breeze blew gently passed, mussing my hair and reminding me that winter was on its way. Thinking of winter made me think of Taylor's baby and whether or not she'd stay with me once she had it. Again, there was some deeper part of me that, if I were being honest, I'd admit wanted her to, even more so after I'd gotten to know her better...but my basic survival instincts wouldn't let me acknowledge or ever admit that out loud.

Focusing on the cell in front of me, I punched out a text to her.

Me: You never told me the date for the ultrasound.

I waited, seeing the little bouncing dots jump and die down. I looked up, realizing I was too attached to this situation, too attached to my mind wandering, thinking about who Taylor was with, who she was seeing, and if it was Holden fucking Winters. Finally, after several minutes and once I started walking again, her reply came in.

Taylor: About that...Holden said he'd go. No need to come, you're off the hook.

I froze mid-step in the middle of the walkway with students moving and bustling around me. Someone jostled me from the side and another from the back, but all I could do was stare at the screen. My heart was doing something funny, something strange, like it had beat so hard it had escaped and somehow fallen, swooping into my stomach, forcing it to churn anxiously. I could usually sense when she was pushing me away, but in this...with him, there was no clear way to tell, and I didn't have enough heart to risk to find out.

Spinning on my heel, I marched toward my car and decided I needed to ruin this, whatever the fuck it was. It had to end, because the tearing sensation happening in my chest couldn't surface again.

CHAPTER FIFTEEN

Taylor

"This chair is pure magic," I said wistfully to Fatima. I rocked while she used a scanning gun on specific items.

"You need to be doing this yourself," she said, and I peeked an eye open to see her shaking her head. It was difficult to tell if she was truly annoyed with me or not. With Mallory it was always easy to tell because she was annoyed with me frequently. I had that way about me, I supposed. Unintentional as it was, sometimes I didn't pick up on social cues that came easily to others. I'd been raised with monsters most of my life and spoiled for the other half. I was incorrigible, regardless of how frequently I desired to change this about myself.

"You don't have to do it, Fatima." I sat up, bracing my hands on the sides of the chair to stand. She made a sound I could only identify as a sassy scoff.

"Girl, I never said I didn't want to do it, only that you should be, so you know what you're registering for." Her dark brow rose as she pivoted toward the stack of diapers next to her. Using the scanning gun in her hand, she began to scan each box.

I scooted out of the chair and knelt down next to the stack.

"Why are there different sizes here? Shouldn't I be registering for the small ones for when it comes home from the hospital?"

Fatima turned her honey-colored eyes toward me, her mauve lips slung in a disappointed frown. "It? Didn't you find out the gender, and don't you have a name picked out?"

Right, that whole thing. I shrugged with indifference, feeling my internal, solidified fortress reinforce with more resolute emotional steel than ever.

"The doctor penciled me in, but not for another week or so." What I didn't tell her was I'd canceled twice now because I was too chicken to go by myself. Regardless of what Juan had offered, there was no way I'd endanger him by letting him go with me, especially if my father's men were watching us. I shouldn't even have been going to his house, but I was having a hard time not being local throughout the week.

"Look." My new...or *almost* friend turned toward me. "The ultrasound is just to make sure the baby is healthy, and you can even request they don't tell you the gender. There are lots of people who go that route, but you should still go to make sure the baby is okay and there aren't any concerns that could have been caught early."

A new kind of panic blossomed in my chest. It was as if someone had just lit a flare gun and shot it in the darkness, which also happened to be my mind. How could I be so naïve? So stupid? I had only been thinking about myself, not the little bean, and because of that there could be something wrong, something I could have prevented.

"Hey..." Fatima put her hand on my knee, and I realized there were tears streaming down my face when she gently swiped one away. "It's normal to be scared, and it's normal to avoid specific things...trust me. You're a good mom—look at all this stuff you're registering for."

I sniffed, peeking at the spread in front of us. I'd registered for nearly the entire baby department. My mother had said she'd help with anything, Charlie too. Even Mallory wanted to start spoiling the little bean, but no one knew what to get, so I said I would come in and register for a bunch of things. In the end it had just been Fatima telling me what I would need.

"I've been so selfish," I croaked, swiping at new tears.

"You haven't," my new friend reassured me, "and these numbers on the box"—she pointed her finger at the numbers going from the letter N to one and so on until she hit the number four—"the different sizes I mentioned...you want to be prepared because these babies grow so fast and it's good to have some on hand."

I nodded, moving past my meltdown and rising off the floor.

"I'll call the office and see if they can get me in as soon as tomorrow."

"Good, that will change everything for you. And pick out a boy name and a girl name...or a gender-neutral one."

I nodded, picking up the things we'd brought out to scan. I wanted to see everything so I knew what to get if I came on my own. Fatima had been sweet enough to accede to my demands.

"Here, text me a picture of your little one when you go, okay?" She handed me a small piece of paper, which forced a knot to form in my throat and a burning to singe the backs of my eyes.

"Okay, I will," I whispered, not finding my voice. She smiled and sauntered away, likely not aware of how monumental it was that she'd given me her number or helped me today. I wanted to thank her, do something that would pay her back for all her help...but I knew if I flashed money at her, she'd back away and think I was trying to buy her friendship. I wasn't; I just didn't know how to be in a normal friendship without those things. Maybe Mal would know.

As I started out of the store, my mind still on Mal and a little bit on food, I nearly missed the two jackets darkening the space near my car. They lounged against the hood of the minivan opposite mine, their collars popped, sunglasses perched on their noses, covering their eyes, all while smoke billowed from their lit cigarettes.

This time I didn't feel right about approaching or going to my car, and since they hadn't looked up yet or noticed me, I slunk back inside and headed back toward the baby section where I knew I could sit and be out of anyone's eyesight.

Once I was there, I tugged my cell free and swallowed my pride. Punching in Juan's number, I waited for the call to connect, except it never did. I redialed him five times with no success and got no response to any of my text messages, so I waited.

I waited and waited. My fingers shook, and my heart throbbed as the hours passed. I was terrified to leave the store, and I had no idea if Fatima was still working. I had shot her a text asking if she was but got no response, so there was a chance she had other things to attend to, and I didn't want to get her in trouble. I contemplated calling my stepdad, but I knew he was up in New York with Mallory and Decker at the moment.

I had no one, and the realization of that truly began to sink in for the first time ever. I wanted to melt, break, and shatter, but I had nowhere to do it. I had a feeling I'd be escorted out of the building in the custody of the police, which would be horrible because my father would see that as a sign of weakness, or an attempt to escape him, both of which would be addressed with reminders or lessons.

Suddenly I heard the sound of thunder rumble softly outside the store and perked up at the chance that rain might accompany it.

Grabbing my bag and water bottle, I started back toward the front doors, only to see the two men making their way inside. Thankfully, I had eyes on them and was able to skirt around their entrance right as a larger family was exiting. I blended until I got to my car, where I crouched and gingerly crawled inside. Rain indeed was coming down in a massive downpour, thankfully covering my exodus from the parking lot.

"After this, we're getting a massive SUV, little bean," I muttered out loud, shutting the door. I waited for a blast of thunder to boom to start the car, and then I was pulling out of the lot as fast as lightning. If they saw me leave, I didn't know. I just knew I had to go, get out, and get away. Instead of driving all the way to my stepdad's and because I knew he wasn't there to protect me, I ended up driving past the city.

The rain pelted my windshield as I drove down the road at dangerous speeds. My father had finally come for me, and it was sooner than my twenty-first birthday. I'd known it would happen, but still it felt like a jolt of lightning to my system.

How could I have been so stupid? Why hadn't I run? Why had I just waited like a rabbit stuck in a trap for the hunter to come and gather me up? What had I done? Even now, I could run...I could drive and drive and never look back. The image of my sister's face, devastated that she'd never see my daughter, and the gentle way Charlie's eyes flickered with amusement when he looked at my mother, and...*Juan*...they all stopped me from keeping my foot on the pedal and my car going straight.

Instead I took a sharp turn at sixty miles per hour. The sign suggested thirty-five, but I had driven this road so many times I knew it like the back of my hand, even drenched in inches of rain.

Houses and buildings began to spread out, more and more sparse the further I got out of the city. I pushed down the gas pedal as anger surged forward, boiling my blood. This hate had simmered under the surface for years as I was forced to do things against my will, forced into this life I never asked for. Now I had this one light, this little gleaming hope, and he would steal it from me.

I couldn't allow it. I wouldn't.

Seeing the half-broken sign indicating that trespassers would get shot, I cranked the wheel to the right and pulled into the narrow drive, hidden by dense brush. The tail end of my Beamer jumped and swung but straightened after a few seconds. There was thick mud, but the road itself was mostly gravel, so I stayed straight.

Plowing down about a mile, I finally pulled under a large tree and put my car in park. The sky was dark, but there was enough light for me to do what I needed to. I tugged my collar up, zipped my coat, and pulled up my hood. Grabbing my phone and headphones, I popped the trunk and moved toward the back of the car.

I tugged out the pair of tall rain boots first, slipping off my shoes, then pulled the tall rubber up to my calves and set my shoes in the trunk. Shoving a dark blanket out of the way, I grasped a small black case. Unclipping the latches on either side, I pushed the top open, removed the foam from the top, and took a deep breath.

Black matte metal met me as my fingers wrapped around the handgun. Cradling it in my hand, I adjusted the adapter, twisting the suppressor in place. With me being in my third trimester, I had to be careful with extra noise that might hurt my baby's hearing, so I had purchased a way to silence the gunfire a while ago, knowing if I wanted to shoot during this time, I'd need it.

The rain finally dissipated, leaving behind a wispy fog. I hadn't been out to this spot in months, and now, with a much larger stomach, the hike was trying.

Finally making it to the clearing, I checked on my targets.

They seemed to be intact, a little warped and faded, but the circles and coloring were still there. Walking toward the middle of the clearing, I faced a large hill. At the base were my marks, each nailed to a piece of plywood, tilted to stay in place.

I stood in the middle, digging a scratch in the mud. Pulling my earbuds out, I set up my playlist and increased my phone volume then swiped until it was on airplane mode. My fingers flexed, twisting the gun to prep it. First, I pulled the clip out and made sure it was full, then I slammed it back into place and pulled the hammer back until it was ready to go.

Lining up the sight on my gun, keeping both eyes open, I aimed for the center first. Just as the haunting sounds of "Save My Love" rocked through me, I readied my stance and began to shoot.

Wood splintered as the bullets slammed into the colored circles, a few going wide at first, as expected. The small sounds coming from the extra barrel on the gun were still mostly blocked by the music, but the ripple going up my arm always seemed to make a sound. It was always as though I was back in that room as a little girl, my tiny fingers wrapped around the trigger.

I continued on, moving over to the furthest target until I hit the center. I did the same with the far-right board, squeezing the trigger in quick succession until I was nailing the center over and over. Moving to the left, I began to aim at the third target stand, then a flash of something dark darted in front of the stapled paper.

My breath caught as the bullet released from the gun and the dark object that had swooped down at the wrong second fluttered to the ground. I lowered my gun and tugged out my earbuds, my breaths suddenly echoing loud in the silence. My feet were frozen as my eyes roamed the ground, falling on the brown lump near the three stands.

"Oh my god," I murmured to myself, wishing so badly someone else was with me so I didn't have to see the animal alone. Not again. I never wanted to do this again.

Tucking the headphones into my jacket pocket, I slowly began to walk toward the fallen animal. My heart thrashed in my chest like a rogue flame consuming a forest.

What had I done?

My knees bent as my free hand came out to cradle the bleeding creature. Bloody feathers caked my hand as I inspected the bird. He had a razor-sharp beak, a long neck, and large, golden eyes. He looked like one of the falcons I had seen at the zoo once, his talons massive and powerful.

"Why did you fly in front of me?" I blubbered, tears streaming down my face.

Once again, I'd gone back there to that room, staring at what my father had done.

"Papa, please don't make me do this," I begged.

"Shhh, enough now, Aurelia...this is a lesson. We need those in life sometimes. My hand will cover yours, so you know what to do," he whispered in my ear as his large arm came around me.

"I don't want to do this." I eyed the dark wolf pup stranded in the center of the room. Around his neck was a rope, keeping him locked in place.

"You will do this. You are my daughter, and you won't argue with me," my father snapped, forcing my hand up, my tiny finger to the trigger. *"Now, Aurelia. Pull back,"* he ordered.

"I can't," I cried, tears lining my eyes, making it impossible to see.

"You will, and for defying me, you will stay in here with the creature once you've killed it." His finger ghosted over mine, adding pressure, until a loud boom filled my ears. Seconds passed while the overhead lights flickered in and out. The room we were in was used for things I didn't want to know about. The floor was stuined red, and most of the walls too.

Our hands lowered, and all that was left was the puppy, bleeding out in the center of the room.

"You have excellent aim, értékes."

My father walked out of the room and locked me in, but not before turning off the lights.

I sniffed as rain began to pour in buckets across my back and neck and through my hair. Ensuring the safety on the gun was flicked on, I put it in my jacket pocket and tried to pick up the bird. Maybe I could save him; I knew there were rehabilitation centers for birds who had broken wings and had been hit by cars. Hope fluttered in my chest, but just as fast, it left when the bird's chest stopped moving.

"No. Please," I begged with a small cry.

I was still that girl who murdered innocent animals.

I carried the bird to where the trees met the hill and buried him under three large rocks. Sobs racked my chest as I did it. At least with this animal, I was able to bury it. With all the others, I was never given the chance.

I partially hated myself for needing this stupid outlet of mine. Long ago, I had wanted to learn how to use a gun to protect myself and not be afraid of them. For so many years, I was afraid because of what my father had forced me to do, but now I just wanted the choice, the freedom to make my own decisions. I had come out here because of my fear, but also because of how I had handled the ultrasound situation, how I had lied to Juan about Holden. Somehow, I knew it must have felt like a slap to his face to tell him I had Holden. Even if Juan didn't have feelings for me, he was very protective of me.

Swiping the tears from my face with the back of my jacket sleeve, I turned and headed back toward my car.

♥

I WAS WRAPPED in a fluffy robe, standing in a dimly lit kitchen when the front door finally opened, and Juan walked in. He was soaked to the bone, his shirt stuck to his chest, and his hair was slicked back, revealing his dim eyes. He drew closer, which revealed dark circles under his eyes, making me pause. Had he not been sleeping?

After I was done walking around the clearing, I had trekked back to the car and driven home in the dark. Once I'd pulled into the driveway, I realized Juan wasn't home, but once I had taken my phone off airplane mode, there were about thirty-five missed calls from him.

I hadn't responded to a single one.

"You're soaked," I said as a form of greeting.

"Where the fuck have you been?" His chest heaved up and down, his eyes wide and full of panic.

The realization that he may have been worried about me made me feel foolish. I tucked a stray piece of wet hair behind my ear.

"What do you mean?"

He stalked forward until he was in my space, tipping my face back.

"I mean, you called me several times, then when I came home, you were gone. It's been hours. Mal hasn't heard from you, and your GPS wasn't working."

I narrowed my eyes on him, a smart remark on the tip of my tongue... but there was something about the look in his eye that stopped me. He was truly worried for me, so much so that I had no idea what dark images had haunted him those hours I was gone. If the tables were turned, I'd be so angry with him.

Cradling his wrist, I peered up into his eyes and gave him the only truth I could that wouldn't endanger him.

"I lied to you."

Warm whiskey eyes settled on me, releasing a flutter of hope in my caved-in chest where nothing seemed to live or grow anymore.

Blinking away a tear, I softly explained it to him. "Holden isn't in the picture. I didn't want you to be in..." I paused, realizing I couldn't tell him the real reason I had lied...so I could only give him a partial truth. "I didn't want your pity, so I lied and said he was going with me."

His thumb swept away my tear and then rubbed the wetness along my bottom lip.

Seeing his emotions reflect in his eyes always gave him away. Juan cared about me, more than he should...more than I could afford.

He would only get hurt by caring for me.

"When do you go?" he asked, a gentle touch landing on my hip. I could still feel it through the thick material of the robe.

"Tomorrow." I hesitated...he couldn't go. If I was being followed, they'd kill him.

"But Juan, I can't—"

"I need to check my schedule," Juan said coolly before turning on his heel and putting distance between us. I had hit a glass wall made purely of assumptions, but it bruised and left a mark. I had stupidly thought he was about to offer to go with me again...but he was only offering to check his schedule. Good then. We needed the space, I'd go alone, and he'd be safe.

His brow knitted when he faced me again, this time closer to the stairs.

"You calling earlier...what was the issue?"

I swallowed, forcing burning tears away. "Umm...I can't remember."

He stared at me as though he knew I was lying, but would he call me out on it?

"Where were you?" His hands linked across his chest while a dull look crossed his features. He was still angry with me. I was probably just an inconvenience. He'd likely had plans tonight and now he was missing them because I wouldn't answer my phone.

"I was at Target...but then..."

He sneered, bringing his hand to his hair. "Of course you were just shopping. Shallow as fuck, and you don't even think about the people around you. Why would you call me several times in a row and then just go radio silent? Do you have any idea how fucked up that was?"

A burning sensation filled my chest, bubbling over, filling every pore, every fiber of my soul. I had opened up to him, told him the truth, confronted the fact that I had lied to him, and I had assumed he'd forgive me, like Mallory always did.

"I'm sorry," I whispered, already wishing I could just go back to my forest and disappear there.

"I don't think this is working, you living here," he stated, bringing his fingers to the bridge of his nose.

Silence stretched between us as he stood with his confession in the air.

I swallowed every other word I wanted to utter. What could I say? I refused to let my heart sink or let the feeling of being insignificant wash over me. I steeled myself and nodded, walking past Juan. He deserved so much better than me, and the sooner I moved and exited his life, the sooner he'd find it.

"Okay."

"That's all you have to say?" he asked, his voice cracking.

I stared up at him, getting closer to where he stood. "What do you want me to say?"

His eyes flared with need, but it wasn't the same kind of need he'd had when he watched me walk toward him in the pool. This need was something deeper, something that had a beat and a thrum, like it was tied to him, inside his chest, under his skin. "I want you to ask me why."

I wouldn't. That would be dangerous, and I'd never do anything to endanger him.

"You've made it obvious. I'll be gone tomorrow," I replied evenly then walked past him, up the stairs, and shut myself in my room.

I heard something land against the wall downstairs before I turned off the light and climbed into bed.

CHAPTER SIXTEEN

Juan

The rain just kept pouring, and with it my mood soured into an emptiness I had never experienced. I'd never worried about another person like I had tonight...I'd never sat feeling helpless and afraid that someone I cared about was hurt...or dead. Even through everything I'd endured growing up, I had never been afraid in this way.

She had no idea what she had fucking put me through.

Her first few calls that afternoon had gone to voicemail because I was in another interview with a hockey team from New York. That meeting went similarly to the others: no team on the east coast would touch me. So, it was all a colossal waste of time. I was in a shit mood after that and went for a drink. I hadn't wanted any company or anyone to talk to while I stewed over the defeat.

Moving out of the area was becoming the only viable option, and yet...the thought of leaving just...fuck. It was only her that kept popping up in my head every single time I'd go through the reasons I didn't want to leave. Not my family or my friends...just her, and that pissed me off even further because of the shit she had pulled with Holden and the ultrasound appointment.

She didn't want me.

Yet somehow, I wanted her.

No matter how hard I had tried to keep her at bay, to keep this from happening...she was still there, and then she wasn't. I had tried to call her back and repeated that goddamn cycle for hours. I drove to her parents' house and forced Charlie to look up her location, knowing he had tracking on her. That didn't work, and I wasn't sure why Charlie kept glancing over at his wife with a look that should have told me more than it did.

It was as if they'd expected this. Taylor's mom sipped her coffee like she hadn't a fucking worry in the entire world. All she said was, "She'll turn up."

And fuck her, but of course, in the end she was right. There Taylor was, in a robe, looking comfortable and at home in my house, and then she told me Holden wasn't in the picture and all I wanted to do was fuck her, sink my dick so far inside her she'd never forget where it was she belonged. I wanted to ruin her the way she'd ruined me, because, like a thistle in the palm of a lion, she'd dug into my heart, into my flesh and bone, wreaking havoc on my entire existence. Anger like I hadn't known surfaced, forcing the words out of my mouth, the decision that had to be made.

When I asked if she wanted to know why, I was fully prepared to explain that it was for her attempts at stealing my heart. I wouldn't tolerate it. I wouldn't. Not from her. Especially her.

But she hadn't asked, so this feeling just festered in my chest. I needed to talk to her, tell her I cared for her, but fuck, she was so duplicitous...I didn't like that I cared for her. I hated myself for it. It was the greatest weakness I could have, and I had it, but she wouldn't offer to help relieve me of it. She was probably already packing.

I sat up, still shirtless and in my boxers, suddenly needing to know that she was still in her room, still home. We had to talk about this shit before she left. She needed to know why this had ended, and she needed to realize it was all her fucking fault. She'd ruined this. She'd made me fall for her, and I refused to. I couldn't afford to. I was leaving, and that was important to remind her about too.

I left my room, noticing right away there was light coming from downstairs...which meant Taylor must be up or had gotten up and left the light on. She never usually left it on...but then, I had essentially kicked her out. Had she already left? Two fast steps down the hall and I heard a sound, a thudding of some kind from below, followed by a slap and a woman's cry.

I ran.

My feet moved too slow along the carpeted floor, and I cursed the fucking house for being too big. Trailing past Taylor's room, my gut twisted as I realized her door was open and her bedroom empty.

Fuck. Fuck. Fuck.

What was going on?

I heard muffled screaming coming from the living room, and from over the railing I saw the backs of at least three men, wearing the same jackets I'd seen on that man talking to Taylor outside the school.

"If you knew, értékes, why am I here?" a man yelled in a thick European accent.

Silently, I ran toward the office, skimming the backside of the staircase and, more importantly, avoiding the men in the living room. I ducked in, kept low, and crawled under the desk, flicking the silver switch my cousin had pointed out. I had no idea if he had been telling the truth, but it was worth a shot. About six inches from the switch was the 9mm gun kept in place by a Velcro strip. Pulling it free and ensuring it was loaded, I carefully shifted back to the hall. I moved to the right, away from the living room, so I could ensure there weren't any more men I didn't know about, then I carefully minced back toward the living room.

Another slap resonated from the room, forcing my feet to move faster. My heart kept even pacing as adrenaline and fear burst through me at sickening speeds.

The back of the room was littered with men standing shoulder to shoulder, holding silencers. There in the center of the room was a tall man with blond hair that was slicked over, little pieces falling into his face. He wore a white dress shirt and a gunmetal grey suit with a long overcoat, and there on the floor, gripped by her hair, was Taylor.

Wearing a thin nightgown that barely covered her ass, she grimaced in pain at the hold on the back of her head. She didn't seem surprised... which meant she had been expecting this.

"Nincs mondanivalód?" the man in the middle asked, leaning his face into hers.

"Baleset volt," Taylor replied through clenched teeth.

My stomach dropped out. Whatever language she was speaking, it was with perfect fluidity and dialect that matched his.

Creeping along the opposite wall, I moved into the kitchen and grabbed a large butcher knife then veered back toward the sentinels crowding the back of the couch.

Twisting the blade in my grasp a few times to get the motion down, I crouched down and, before I could talk myself out of it, cut into the tendon behind the man's knee who stood closest to me. Then I slid on the floor and cut into the man standing next to him. By the time he was down, the third was moving, and I'd already stood, lunged, and stabbed into his neck.

Pulling it free, I spun, pointed my gun toward the man near the side, and pulled the trigger. It landed in his shoulder, forcing him down. The gun was aimed at the man in the center a second later.

"Let her the fuck go." I breathed out heavily.

I wasn't out of shape, but I hadn't used a blade in that way in over three years.

The man looked over my shoulder, so I dodged around and pointed my knife at him.

"Do you know who I am?" I didn't know why I asked it, but there was something familiar about the man holding Taylor, about the men with him. He was a part of *it*, the disgusting mess that was my entire family, what I grew up with. It was darkness I recognized, so I wanted to know if he recognized me too.

The man let Taylor go, but only so he could laugh and remove his jacket while looking around the room.

"If this blade flies, I promise you it will land exactly where I want it to," I swore, glancing at the men bleeding out behind me.

"Do you know who the fuck you're messing with, boy?" he asked, straightening and fixing the cuffs of his shirt until they were rolled up his arms. "Have you not heard of Ördög up and down this forsaken coast?" His white teeth clicked as his thick accent flowed out of him.

A sliver of fear splintered, but I wouldn't let it show. I had heard of the devil. Everyone had. He was the Hungarian warlord who'd moved his operations to New York and now ruled more territory than my own family did. He was our biggest competition. This was about to be a bloodbath in about thirty seconds if Hector pulled through. I just needed Taylor out of it.

"I have heard of you, old man." I flicked my gaze to the back of the house where I saw a few headlights bleeding through the parted curtains. Relief swelled in my chest as I realized my cousin had been telling the truth about the panic button. I had to keep the devil and his men occupied while they made their entrance. "But tell me, you sick fuck"—I spit on the blood pooling near my feet—"how stupid are you to sneak into *my* house while I sleep and touch *my* things?"

I walked closer to him, the men around the couch flanking me with their guns pointed at me, but my weapons were still pointed at their boss. One of them looked oddly familiar and younger than me. I eyed him curiously. Those eyes...*I know those eyes. I sat next to them for an entire semester. Decker's eyes...is that his brother?*

The man laughed. "We touched nothing of yours. I came for her." He gestured with his head toward Taylor. She was on her ass, leaning back on her palms while looking up at the man. Why hadn't she run? Why was she still there?

I gestured toward her with the gun. "She's mine."

"And who the fuck are you, boy?" He tilted his head in a menacing way.

Right on cue, glass shattered toward the back of the house.

"Fucking El Peligro, you son of a bitch," I seethed while the echo of chaos erupted around us.

The man's eyes went wide as my family crowded the room, Hector leading them, two guns in his hands pointed at the men aiming theirs at me, my uncle next to him, a desert eagle in his hand, pointed at the man in the center. At least a dozen others walked in behind them, some with bats, most with guns or knives.

My family outnumbered his men ten to one, so each of the men surrendered their weapons to my family, but the fucking devil himself saw the moment his window closed and grabbed Taylor, using her as a shield.

"Manuel died by my own hand. El Peligro died...unless..." His eyes swung around the room before landing on me.

My stomach flipped over like I'd just been dropped off the top of a rollercoaster.

"I will talk with you once you've let her go." I tried to distract him from the pieces of my father's life and mine that he was putting together.

He laughed, smoothing her hair back. I wanted to cut that fucking hand from his body.

"If I let my daughter walk to you, I'm dead."

Daughter?

"Then talk fast." I lowered my gun but gripped the blade in my hand tightly.

"You said she's yours, but she's promised to another...and it looks like she's gotten herself knocked up. Are you telling me you're the father? Because my only plan is to take her and kill him."

"I am the father. Do you plan on killing me?" I raised my arms, letting him see the tattoo that ran down the back of my arm. My cousins and family began laughing around the room at the notion of this man killing me.

He spit on the floor once he registered the connection he'd been pulling together. "You're the son, aren't you?"

I stared at Taylor, her eyes going wide in shock.

"You're the new leader...the little boy who used the blade?" Her father shook his head, rubbing his chin. "I always wondered what happened to the little boy who knew how to handle a blade so well it struck fear into the hearts of men up and down the coast. They used to call you kis szellem—*little ghost.*"

"I'm not here to talk about my past, or yours. Let her go. Now."

I wasn't in the mood to get into the tangled rumors that had gotten out of hand after I merely defended myself when I needed to. My father used to hand me a knife and tell me to sit outside the door of whatever deal he was brokering.

"So, you're also the father?" His blond brows raised, and now that I looked at him, he resembled her. She had the shape of his eyes and his nose.

"I am. She's *mine*. You're touching something that doesn't belong to you." I eyed him again, trying to catch Taylor's gaze. She was staring, breathing through her nose, her hair wild, mussed, and I could see a tiny trail of blood dribble down her neck; her lip was bleeding too. "You'll pay for that." I pointed toward her face.

"She's *not* yours. She has been on borrowed time until her twenty-first birthday. She knew she was coming home, knew Markos would be waiting for her. It was all arranged long ago. Her entire future has already been sold."

Fuck...I hoped to everything holy he wasn't talking about Markos Mariano. I couldn't show how much the idea of her going to him messed with me, or how shaken I was by this entire thing. These were big players, and I was drastically out of my league.

"She *is* mine. The baby *is* mine. *They* are both fucking *mine!*" I yelled and took two steps closer. She was worth something to him; he wouldn't hurt her. "Now let her the fuck go and speak to me like a man."

"Give me something that guarantees you won't kill me," begged the pathetic piece of trash.

"You're my child's grandfather. No harm will come to you as long as you don't do any harm."

"A new deal can be made," he offered, releasing his hold on Taylor.

"You're not in a position to barter," I reminded him, drawing closer.

He laughed. "I am here as a courtesy. The man she's promised to will come for her, and if I go missing, he will bring his entire operation to wipe your fucking pathetic family off the face of this earth. No one will remember you. The Mariano family will come for you. But, if we work together, form a new deal, then I will let her go."

Fuck. It *was* the fucking Mariano family. El Peligro had started as a cartel but over the years transitioned into a gang, the largest on the east coast. It would be lucrative for him to ally with us with something as strong as a marriage, but I wasn't even involved in any of this shit. If I said yes right now, it would mean I was in, back in with my father's legacy...in with the one stain on my soul that I'd always wanted removed.

Taylor's flushed face and growing injuries had me dropping the gun and blade.

"Deal. Let her go, let me clean her up, and we will talk about a new deal."

"You swear it?"

I nodded. "On my family."

His hands dropped, taking a step back from Taylor, and thank fuck she went along with the ruse and ran to me. I opened my arms, and she plastered herself to my chest, her arm going up around my neck.

Hector came over with a blanket and placed it over her shoulders, tucking it around her.

I wrapped my arm around her protectively.

"We talk tomorrow. Get the fuck out of my house. You'll be welcomed back for brunch at eleven. Come with three men only. You will be safe. If I go back on my word, you can go to war with my family."

The man gave Taylor one last look before he nodded at me. They grabbed their dead and injured men and began to leave.

"See that they're gone, and get some men to clean this place up," I said to Hector before I turned and cleared the walkway, keeping my arm around Taylor, who was shaking.

Once we were clear, I picked her up and carried her up the stairs, past her room.

"Where are you going?" she whispered, her voice shuddering.

"You sleep with me now."

I opened my door and walked to the bed. It was larger than hers, with a much nicer headboard and much larger window.

Setting her down, I crouched in front of her.

Her hands immediately went to her face, blocking my view of whether she was crying or upset.

"Hey." I tugged on her hand.

She sniffed, and I realized her body was shaking still.

"Take a sip of water, here..." I handed her my water glass, unsure if that would bug her or not. She let go of her face and accepted it, draining it completely. The darkness in the room kept her face shadowed, but the lights from outside allowed me to see the way she seemed to curl in on herself.

"What the hell happened down there?" I asked quietly. The image of her being held by the hair was going to haunt me for the rest of my life.

She sniffed again and leveled her chin.

"Don't you have to go and check on things or something?"

I shook my head. "Not until you talk to me."

"I don't want to talk."

"You owe me something." I carefully ran my hands up her thighs, just so I had an excuse to touch her. I was shaking too, although I hid it better than her. What if I'd been too late? I couldn't even protect her in my own fucking house. How pathetic.

"I owe you nothing, Juan. You said this wouldn't work out and now you're claiming me? What the hell?" Her voice cracked on the tail end of her tirade, and it nearly made me wince.

"I needed to keep you safe," I whispered, bringing her knuckles to my mouth.

"Why did you have to keep me safe—why do you care?"

I paused, unsure if I should say it, but ultimately, I wanted to know. "Earlier tonight, I asked you to ask me why this arrangement wouldn't work, but you wouldn't. Why?"

Her pink tongue darted out, wetting her cracked lips. There was reluctance in her eyes, and I wanted to know why she didn't want to just come out and tell me.

"I'm exhausted. I really don't want to talk. I'm freaking out about my baby...I just want to get this blood off of me and go to sleep." A few tears slipped down her face along with her admission, and it cracked something inside of me open.

Standing, I pulled her by the hand and walked her toward my bathroom.

"Can you sleep in one of my shirts?" Our feet hit the marble floor and I went over toward the bath, but Taylor stopped me.

"A shower is fine, and yes, a clean shirt will work…but are you…?" She paused, her eyes darting back and forth over my face. "Are you sleeping somewhere else, or…?"

"I don't know yet." I ducked my head into the shower and turned the chrome knob to the left. I grabbed a clean towel for her then left her alone in the bathroom.

Now that she was in the shower, my heart wouldn't stop pounding, reminding me how close I had come to losing her. Even if he didn't kill her, he would have taken her. The image of how she looked that first second…the way he gripped her by the hair…fuck.

I stormed back into the bathroom and found her crying while crouched on the shower floor, the water pounding into her back. Opening the glass door, I walked in, shutting us in the steam box, still in just my boxers, and pulled her into my chest. Swiping her wet hair out of her face, I cradled her in my arms while we sat on the bath tiles, the heat pouring over us while my girl let out her demons. There was something unhinged about her tears, like she'd pulled out a hidden box that hadn't been revealed in years and now she was shuffling through all the pain that had been locked away.

It was with slow clarity that I realized there was more to Taylor's life than I knew…in fact, I hardly knew her at all. The events of the night had begun to frame her in an entirely different light. All of our interactions, the way she seemed so selfish…if she had grown up with Ivan Varga as a father, then by all rights she should have been way more deranged and screwed up than she was. She was good…her soul was beautiful, but now I was finally seeing that she wasn't just a flower; she was one who'd constantly been covered in dirt, with limited light. She should have been withered, dead; instead, she was vibrant, and I…

Something in my chest expanded as I continued to wipe her hair out of her face. I couldn't speak to her about my emotions or my feelings because it would ruin everything...like it had that night she pulled away from me. Instead, I spoke to her in Spanish and hoped it would heal the brokenness cracking her apart.

"Cuando pienso en ti, no puedo respirar." *When I think of you, I can't breathe.*

"Te has llevado la oscuridad que habitaba en mi." *You've stolen the darkness out of me.*

"Perdóname si trato de aferrarme a lo poco que queda de ella por un tiempo más. Es lo que necesito para protegerlos a ustedes dos." *Forgive me if I try to cling to it a little longer, my soul. I need it to protect you both.*

I held her until the water ran cold then kissed her forehead and helped her up. Steam filled the room and clouded the glass, which helped to distract me from how naked Taylor was, and how much her belly had grown in the last few months. She had no stretch marks, which didn't surprise me; somehow this girl didn't have to endure much when it came to this pregnancy. She still painted her toenails with ease and didn't have swollen ankles or cravings that I had noticed.

"Here." I opened a large white towel and wrapped it around her back. Right as I tried to walk past her, she gripped my wrist, stopping me.

"Why?" Her voice was rough now that she'd sobbed for nearly half an hour.

I knew she meant the question I'd asked earlier tonight, but now I didn't want to tell her. I had been feeling brave earlier, before all this happened, back when I thought she might walk away and leave me to my one-sided feelings. Now, looking at her, after holding her in such a tender way, she'd fucking crush me.

I opened my mouth to say something...I wasn't sure what, maybe the truth, but a knock on the bathroom door stopped me.

Taylor's head whipped toward the closed door, her body already responding to the threat with adrenaline. I gently pushed her behind me while I walked toward it.

"Yeah?"

"Primo, we need to talk about what you want set up out here," my cousin Hector said through the door. Taylor wrapped her dainty fingers around my hand as if she'd stop me from going. This was good; I wasn't ready to tell her my confession anyway, and this would give us some distance.

"I'll be right out," I yelled then turned toward Taylor. "I have a shirt for you. Get in bed and try to get some sleep. I'll have someone posted outside the room all night." I opened the door, a waft of steam following me out. The bedroom lights were still off, just the outside security lights beaming in through the open shades in the window.

"Where will you be?" Taylor panicked, walking right behind me.

"I'll be here, making sure things are okay. Get some sleep," I repeated one last time before opening the bedroom door and slipping out.

CHAPTER SEVENTEEN

Taylor

A GENTLE KICK TO MY STOMACH WOKE ME. THE BABY HAD BEEN doing that a lot lately, making it nearly impossible to sleep past five in the morning. Thankfully I wasn't really getting up at all hours of the night yet, although I heard the last month would do that to me. Stretching, I turned from my side onto my back and absently felt the side of the bed for Juan.

I had no idea what made me think he'd be there. It wasn't like he'd made a real vow of any kind the night before, had just saved my life and my baby's...we owed him ours now, forever. I'd do anything to repay that debt, including leaving if that was what he really wanted. Light poured in through the split curtains as a tiny shard of pain sliced through my chest, hollowing it out as I sat up and registered that Juan had slept in the chair by the window.

His knuckle was pressed against his temple, a blanket wrapped around his shoulders, and a pillow was stuffed under his arm. He looked uncomfortable, and I had been miserable all night, worried about where he was...worried he wasn't with me. I tried not to relive the evening prior, but that significant moment when Juan had claimed us and my father let me go...it was unlike anything I'd ever felt in my life.

Freedom, safety—it was fake, I knew as much, but something in my soul latched onto it as though it was real, and now I wanted to be near Juan as frequently as possible. He'd protected me. Even angry with me, upset...hurt by my actions, he protected me.

The memory of him expertly holding that gun and the blade...I touched my temple as I remembered seeing my father's men fall, and then the bloodbath near his feet when I'd run into his arms. Juan had done that. He'd killed those men within seconds, as if it was nothing.

He'd mentioned a name...that name was so familiar, but even now, I couldn't recall what it was.

"Are you overthinking over there?" Juan's scratchy voice asked from his spot by the window.

I smiled, tucking a few stray strands behind my ear. *God, my hair must be a mess.* I hadn't combed it after the shower, had just slipped into one of Juan's shirts and crawled into bed. His shirt wasn't as loose as I'd hoped; with the belly it was practically glued to my body. Juan had never seen me this undone before, and I didn't know if I was ready for him to, so I pulled the blanket around my shoulders.

"Why'd you sleep over there?" I crinkled my eyebrows at how he cracked his neck to the left.

"To give you space." He smiled lazily, and I wanted to grab my phone to snap a picture of him. I found myself wanting to do that more and more frequently with him.

I shrugged, trying not to make a big deal out of his sentiment. "This is a big bed—it won't bother me if you sleep here...especially if you're serious about me sleeping in it from now on."

He stood, stretching his arms above his head. The sunlight caught on the glossy black strands of hair that fell over his eyebrow. His whiskey eyes landed on me, and without a shirt, those black boxers hugging his muscular thighs...holy shit.

His semi-hard erection.

My tongue was nearly rolling out of my mouth at how good he looked, and my hormones were screaming at me to jump him, straddle him, and force him to love me forever.

His strong legs carried him to where I was perched on the edge of the bed. My head tipped back to track his progress, and before I could process that my breath had hitched, he reached for my head and tilted it to the side.

"Just checking for any bruising, or if we need to have anything checked today," he said, pushing hair out of the way so he could see where the blood had pebbled last night.

"It's sore...but I think it will be fine." I swallowed thickly.

His soft touch caressed my ear and jaw, his fingers trailing down my heated skin in a much more sensual way than was probably necessary. It made me squirm uncomfortably.

I had no idea if he knew the effect he had on me, but part of me thought he did, especially when he got that specific look in his eye and the side of his lip twitched upward. With his dick in near proximity, I could see now that the bulge had grown and looked painful. His fingers wrapped around my neck and began to rub circles into my shoulders while his other hand gently tugged on rogue pieces of my hair.

I moved my hips, the ache between my thighs getting to be unbearable.

"Hormones hitting you pretty hard?" he lightly joked, smoothing his fingers down the length of my hair until it stopped at my breast. The backs of his knuckles grazed my hardened nipples, and I let out a small whimper.

"Yeah." When had my voice become so breathy?

"Check out my tub—there's a pretty nice jet system in place that might help out." He winked, letting my hair go.

My face burned with embarrassment. Of course he wasn't interested in helping me himself. After that night on my bed, we hadn't had any more moments where we almost crossed another line. He made sure of that.

"Yeah, okay. Thank you." I ducked my head, shoving my frizzy hair behind my ears. He still hadn't moved away from my space, and now, after his comment, it was awkward.

"I'm going to check on things downstairs. Don't come down wearing that shirt...my guys are down there." Juan's jaw clenched as his whiskey gaze moved over my peaked nipples, down to the fabric of the shirt, barely covering my thighs.

"Why does it matter if they see me in this?" I laughed lightly, still feeling the heat of his eyes on me, wishing he'd touch me, hoping he wouldn't. It would be easier if he kept this distance between us.

"Because I don't want them to look at you, Taylor. Not fully clothed, not partially clothed, sure as fuck not like this when you look like you were recently fucked. You probably have no idea how you look right now, but over my fucking dead body is anyone else seeing you like this."

He began to walk out of my space, away from me, and my veins were made of acid now. I stood, watching his muscled back as he bent to grab a pair of sweats.

"Why would you say that to me but refuse to touch me?" I stammered, wishing my voice had come out a little stronger.

He stood, his fingers still wrapped around the band of his lounge pants. "Why would you think I don't want to touch you?" His eyes stayed on the phone he'd grabbed off the dresser like this conversation was the last thing on his mind.

I crossed my arms over my chest, hating how now that I was standing, I had to pee.

"You just..." What could I say to explain this to him without feeling stupid?

"I'm giving you space. You seemed to want it...or did you forget that night where you pulled away from me without explanation?"

My mouth opened, but before I could respond, someone knocked on the door, just like the night before. I was already over these guys being in the house. Juan gave me a soft smile before ducking his head.

"Gotta go. See you down there."

Then he was gone, and I was left wondering what in the hell I had done to ruin the chance I had with him.

♥

THE FEELING in the house was tense.

When I opened Juan's bedroom door, there was a man standing guard. I gave him a small smile, but he didn't return it; he only lowered his face and moved to the side. It served as a reminder that I'd somehow been thrust back into a world similar to the one I came from.

I kept my eyes up and roaming as I descended the stairs. My feet briskly made their way past the living room, where several dead bodies had lain the previous night, until I was treading into the kitchen.

My eyebrows crinkled in confusion as I tried to piece together what was in front of me. A female, short and round with greying curls and deep brown eyes, was dicing green chilies on a cutting board. A taller woman, somewhat close in age but with eyes that matched Juan's, stood next to her, tossing chopped tortillas into a skillet.

"No me ha dicho nada de ella," the taller woman said in the same lilted accent that Juan had when he spoke to me in Spanish. The memory of the night before surfaced, the way his lips moved against my ear and the cadence of those haunting words. It felt as though he was confessing something, but I had no idea if that were true. He could have been calling me a massive cow for all I knew, but it felt tender and real.

The women looked up right as I placed my hands on the back of the barstool.

"Hello." I smiled, trying to be kind. Something told me these women were Juan's family, or somehow part of all the family that had shown up.

Both women stared at one another, the taller one whispering something to the other under her breath in Spanish.

"Hello, I'm Marie." The shorter woman wiped her hands on her apron, moving around the island. "Juan's aunt."

I shook her hand and tried to relax as her eyes dropped to my belly.

"You're so big, my goodness...but all belly. The rest of you is so thin." She held her hands out, a wide smile erupting on her face.

No one had really acted in a positive way about my belly bump except for Juan, so it was different seeing her smile, as if me being all belly was a good thing.

"Do you eat?" the taller woman asked, glaring at me from her perch at the counter, dicing and chopping items and tossing them aggressively in the skillet.

"Uh...yes," I replied, a little confused by her question. Of course I ate.

"So skinny—doesn't look like you eat anything."

My mouth opened as Maria made a clicking sound with her tongue. I eyed her disapproving look for her family relation then swung my head toward said woman at the counter.

"I eat...not as well when Juan isn't cooking for me, but I do eat." I nervously moved toward the corner of the kitchen, grabbing three coffee mugs. "Would either of you like coffee?" My face burned, but I wasn't sure why. I supposed it was because I'd never played hostess before or met anyone's aunts or family...not that Juan was a someone to me, but he was the closest I'd ever had.

The women began whispering to each other, Maria sounding more angry with the taller woman with each passing second.

"Yes, I'd love some," Maria finally replied sweetly.

"You move around my son's house like you own it," the other woman chided, letting out a scoffing sound.

I looked down at the mugs in my hand, feeling a strange sensation open inside my chest. It was cold but also searing hot, as if rage was burning me from the inside out. This was Juan's mother, and she sounded as if she hated me. She had just met me; how did she already hate me?

"You're Juan's mother?" I whispered, turning away from the counter.

She didn't turn, just kept chopping with her lips drawn into a thin line.

"I am, and you're not good for him," she snapped right as Juan walked in.

"Mama, no sabes nada." He said it coldly enough to force his mother's head to snap up, her hands freezing in place.

"Ella es una perra," his mother yelled, throwing her hands out passionately.

The skylight accented her tan face, her whiskey eyes, and her dark hair. She was as beautiful as Juan. All it did was make me think of what

I'd heard the night prior about Juan's father. Juan was called the little ghost because he used to kill people...

Juan's loud slap against the counter had my thoughts scrambling and forcing me to jump.

"You will not call her a whore while in my house. You haven't even met her, haven't even given her a chance." He seethed.

My spine snapped straight, unfamiliar with the sensation of being defended. It had never happened before.

Juan walked over, shoving his hands into his pockets. He was already dressed in a nice suit, sans the jacket, the sleeves of his white button-down rolled up to his elbows. It was only nine in the morning and he already looked like sin.

He wrapped a hand around my waist, drawing me closer to him until his lips pressed against my hairline.

"If you can't understand this or respect it...then leave," Juan explained, softening his voice only a small amount. I watched his face, his lips drawing down while his eyes stayed firmly on hers.

"You're already changing. You don't want this. You have never wanted this, and now she's forcing you into it," his mother yelled again, slamming her hands on the counter, shoving the cutting board forward.

I nearly jumped again, but not because of her. It was her choice of words. They might as well have been as sharp as the knife she'd used.

"Get out of my house."

"It's his house, their house...El Peligro's house. She's the daughter of the man who killed your *father*, and she's living in your home like nothing is wrong. She should be traded back to that monster." His mother spat the words, her face twisting with rage.

A few men filtered into the room, immediately looking to Juan, watching for him to tell them what to do. I recognized the look in their eyes; it was how my father's men used to look at him when they were prepared to dispose of a problem. Lethally.

I wanted to say something, but Juan squeezed my hand, encouraging me to tuck my chin and wait it out.

My chest heaved as I waited for him to respond, as I waited for him to seal any fate we might have. I couldn't be with a man as cruel as my father. I wouldn't be, not even to keep up pretenses. If Juan was physical with his mother or killed her, I'd leave and never come back.

"Mama, I know you're worried about me. I know you love me, but taking your fear out on Taylor is the wrong move. She hasn't done anything. She's innocent in this."

My eyes snapped up, desperate to see the tenderness in Juan's face that might match his velvet voice. His mother crumbled; Juan left me to hug her. She cried into his shoulder, speaking in Spanish as she sobbed. After a few minutes, he ushered her out of the kitchen.

I spun back toward the coffee machine, trying to hide my watering eyes. Busying myself with the buttons, I didn't notice Maria sneak up behind me.

"You'll have to develop thick skin if you're going to be in this family."

I looked over my shoulder, hoping my tone wasn't as rude as I currently felt. "My skin is made of Kevlar. I'm not fragile. I am, however, petty as hell."

Maria laughed, swiping a few crumbs from the counter.

I brought my coffee to my lips, sipping it while I waited to hear Maria's piece. If she noticed I hadn't made her coffee, I had no idea...but my kindness evaporated while being called a whore.

"You have to understand...Anna and Manuel, Juan's parents...they were in love for so many years. El Peligro has never had a queen, but if it did, she would have been it. Her husband was the leader, and her son the young prince of the outfit. Back then, product was being moved between Mexico and the southern border...and it was Manuel's father who decided to move it up the coast, into New York. He built this business with his bare hands."

I continued nursing my cup of decaf, listening, and gathering up all the information she was giving freely.

"Anna loved her husband and son, but she hated this life. She was depressed and anxious all the time. Manuel cheated on her, often...he was so handsome and powerful, it was hard not to be drawn to him." She tucked a few pieces of hair behind her ear, a rosy coloring filling her cheeks, and I wondered if she had been an admirer of Juan's father. "Anna once caught him with someone in their bed, and that was the last straw. She left with Juan, going down to Mexico for five years. She met Leo, a simple cook who worked for the outfit, but only on the fringes. She fell in love, or at least something similar to what she had with Manuel, although most of us knew she'd never love another the way she loved that man. Regardless, she allowed her son to be raised by another man, a good man. It didn't change the fact that Manny had Juan with him while he worked and tried to harden his heart with the evil he exposed him to, but he had a good man at the helm who led him onto a different path."

My mind tugged at the pieces; how eerily similar Juan's life was to my own. Both sired by monsters, both saved by brave mothers who found better men to raise us, now forced to return to the mess our fathers created.

"His mother never wanted this life for him. She's scared, but give her another chance to show you who she is." Maria pressed her gentle hand to my shoulder while moving out of the kitchen.

I nodded, watching her retreating form. Of course I'd give his mother another shot...her words had been mean, but as I pressed my hand to my growing belly, feeling my baby kick—I could understand where she was coming from. I'd want my child to have the best life possible, and being born into my family, I'd murder someone if anyone ever tried to drag them back.

Taking my mug, I sipped it while walking toward the back patio doors. Shattered glass had been everywhere the night before, at least that was what it had sounded like. Now, there was nothing to show for Juan's family breaking in, save for a piece of plywood along the back wall.

Every morning, if I had the time, I liked going out there. I liked the way the sun rose over the orchard and the orange and purple streaked along the sky, like a toddler using crayons. I usually took a history book, my coffee, and a blanket to curl under. Juan had tried to accompany me a few times with his own book, but after the bed incident when I jumped out of his lap, he'd stopped.

There were men walking around the perimeter of the house, carrying guns...and once again, it was like someone had opened a portal and I was transported back to my childhood. This wasn't what I wanted, yet I knew I'd never outrun the life my father had planned for me. Just turned out I'd tricked him by shuffling the deck. I had no idea what I would have done if it weren't for Juan pretending to be mine.

"Hey." He broke into my thoughts, taking the chair across from me.

I smiled at him. "Hey, your mom okay?"

His grimace told me he wasn't happy with her, and the way his lips turned down made me want to crawl into his lap and hug him. *This is all my fault.*

"She's just worried about all this. Word spread pretty rapidly about this whole situation...my mom and aunt were here before I even woke up."

"They love you." I tried to lean forward to set my cup on the glass table, but my belly was making it difficult, so Juan reached over and grabbed it from my hand.

"They do...in their own way."

"I guess I can understand that...it's why my mom tears Mallory down. She sees her as a threat to me, or my position in my stepdad's eyes. For a long time, she tried to get me free of this by marrying me off to a wealthy, connected man." I ducked my head, feeling shame wash over me. What must Juan think of my mother and me? He had called her a gold digger last spring...he wasn't wrong, but it clearly showed his opinion of her.

"Speaking of...your father will be here in a while, and before then, I need to talk to you." Whiskey eyes settled on mine, reflecting the same fear and confusion I had about how all this would work out.

I nodded my agreement and allowed him to grab my hand and help me up.

"Where are we going?"

"Somewhere private."

CHAPTER EIGHTEEN

Taylor

Settling into the plush chair near Juan's window, I suddenly wasn't feeling so bad that he had chosen to sleep in it the night prior. The buttery fabric was soft and instantly relaxed me. I noticed someone had brought up its twin, positioning it right next to the one already stationed there so there were two by his large window. My heart jumped a little at the notion that he'd thought of this, of sharing his space with me, for however long this ruse lasted.

"We don't have long. Tell me the basics first," Juan said, propping his elbow on the arm of the chair and resting his knuckles under his chin.

I let out a tiny sigh, leaning back into the plush cushion. "My father is Ivan Varga, or as you referred to him last night, Ördög." I watched as Juan's eyes stayed steady on me, encouraging me to keep going. "I found out I was promised to Markos Mariano when I was thirteen years old. The custody arrangement at the time was that my father had me every summer...my mother used to joke that the custody was just a string my father liked to pull on when he grew bored or wanted to punish her. It didn't really mean anything to him, seeing as he could easily take me whenever he wanted, but it worked for his schedule to only have me a few months at a time. Anyway, when I learned about the arrangement, I went back to my mother and begged her to find a way to get me out of visits."

"Your father went along with it?" Juan asked, leaning down to grab my ankle. He pulled my bare foot into his lap and began rubbing the soles of my feet, and while it was still early in the morning, they were already aching.

"Uh..." I wet my lips, pushing past the urge to moan. "With one condition: I return when I turn twenty-one and agree to marry Markos. My mother agreed, so did I...but then she immediately married Charlie, thinking the wealth and power would help create a buffer of protection for us both, mainly me."

Juan's eyes went wide and his lips parted as though he was finally connecting the dots. Yes, my mother was a gold digger, but she would have done anything to protect me. No one would ever know that she had fought it, that she hadn't even meant to meet Charlie, or that he had fallen for her, offering his riches before she ever had a chance to steal them.

"Being married to Charlie did shield us. He was there that night I came back after hearing about Markos. I was sobbing on the floor of our one-bedroom apartment...Mom and I had shared a bed...we were so poor, but still I preferred it to visiting my father. That weekend, he'd stayed local instead of going back to New York. He had planned to deliver a reminder to a family that had forgotten where their loyalty lay. Markos had shown up to assist my father...he..." I couldn't even bring myself to say out loud the horrors I had witnessed that night, why I hadn't been able to stop crying or screaming, why I couldn't risk being married off any sooner. "Anyway, Charlie made sure we had extra security around us at all times...not just because we were the heirs to a massive fortune, but because of Ivan and his wolves."

"Which is why the townhouse was always occupied by his security team," Juan mused.

I nodded. "I tried everything to get myself out of this, which is why I tried to take over the New York office for Charlie last spring...I was terrified to go back to the city, but I thought if I had a position of power, my father would leave me alone. In the end, I was just a fool playing a game, like a little girl wearing her mother's shoes and pearls."

I tucked hair behind my ears, hating how my face heated. The shame from all my antics, how much I had left Mallory out of...how much I was willing to take from her father, just to keep myself safe.

"So, what's your real name then? Taylor isn't Hungarian...neither is Beck." Juan smirked, moving his hands up my calf. I wore shorts or a dress most days due to the humidity, and I was never more grateful for that than right in this moment.

"My name is Aurelia Varga. I changed it after my mother left with me and put me in public school. Kids made fun of me, and I didn't want my father's enemies to come for me. So, I picked names from celebrities I followed at the time."

The man rubbing my foot narrowed his eyes, his dark brows wrinkling. "Taylor...and Beck?"

My face warmed as he attempted to figure out my childhood obsessions.

"Taylor Swift?" His eyebrow rose.

I covered my face. "Yes. Oh my god, don't make fun of me."

"And...what's Beck from?"

"I was obsessed with David Beckham," I confessed through parted fingers, barely revealing my tomato red face.

"My, my, my..." Juan chided, shaking his head.

I tried to kick him in the chest with my foot, but he grabbed my ankle with one hand and slid his other up my leg.

The heat from his fingers burned my skin, leaving me fevered. My hormones were so intense that even the lightest, playful touch was getting me worked up.

"So..." I tugged my foot free. "Your turn."

Tan hands tunneled through raven hair, forcing the wayward pieces back. It was a really fucking hot move, and I wanted him to do it again and again, preferably while I touched myself.

"Maria, your aunt, told me a little bit about your mom, and your dad…or dads…" I tugged on the hem of my shorts. "Seems we have a similar past."

Juan nodded, watching my fingers play with loose strings.

"When we came back to the States, my mother was still tied to El Peligro, whether she wanted to be or not. She had little choice, same with Leo, the man she married. Manuel wasn't easy on us and was constantly taking me without their permission. He'd force me to watch everything he did, make shipments, meet with clients, get drinks with associates. He'd even fuck while I stayed outside the room in the hall, listening to every disgusting sound happening on the other side. He was a rough man, and I'll never forget him opening the door once and seeing the woman inside, crying while dabbing at her bleeding lip."

"I'm sorry you went through that." I ducked my head, wishing I could have somehow protected him from seeing or hearing what he did.

"Something tells me you went through a few things similar. Otherwise you'd be outraged, not just sorry."

My eyes bounced up, meeting his, truly seeing him for who he was, what they'd made him into. It was like looking in the mirror, seeing someone who finally found the tucked-away pieces of yourself, the ones you hoped no one would ever find…only to find they had the same exact ones.

"My father used to teach me lessons," I mumbled, unsure if I wanted to confess this.

Juan captured my other foot and began rubbing slow circles into the soles.

"What kind of lessons?"

"The kind where I shot innocent animals and stayed in the room while they bled out."

"Fuck," Juan whispered, shaking his head.

I lifted my shoulder. "We're a fucked-up duo, aren't we?"

His eyes bounced back up, seizing me. "We are."

"So, what's next?" I eyed the desk clock and saw that we were running out of time.

"Now, we run with this lie until everyone believes it. Your dad needs to trust there's an actual shot at a deal being brokered here, otherwise he'll find a way around it and kidnap you."

"But this is going to mess up your whole life, Juan. The only way he'll believe it is if you step into the role your father had, right?"

Juan's head dipped, hiding his eyes from me.

I pulled my foot free and moved until I was sitting on my knees in front of him, my hand cupping his jaw.

"I can't ask you to do this. I knew this was coming. I'm strong—his darkness doesn't scare me anymore."

He lifted his face, bringing his palm to cover mine, pinning us in place. "You're a fucking liar. I can see it in your eyes, in the way your limbs shake and your lips thin. You're terrified, if not for you then for your baby."

"It's my issue, not yours. I can't ask you to do this." My voice cracked, betraying how much this hurt. I hated that he was being put in this position, that he was choosing this.

His forehead pressed into mine, our hands still connected on his face, our lips dangerously close. "You didn't ask me to do it. Stop saying that, preciosa. You didn't ask, and I wish you would have. I wish you could see how badly I need you to ask."

His lips parted to say something else, but someone knocked on the door, and his head turned toward the sound.

"Time to go. You need to remember that in front of my men, and in front of your father's especially, you are mine. Got that?" Both his hands cupped my face this time, ensuring I understood how serious he was.

I nodded. "I understand."

His lips briefly pressed against mine in the slightest touch before letting me go.

♥

JUAN'S HAND wrapped around mine as we walked downstairs. Three men trailed us, and three more were at the bottom of the stairs waiting for us. I wanted to make a point to meet them, especially if they were going to be around for a while. I tried to give one of the men a smile, but he only met it with a serious glare, his eyes watching the room around us.

I'd forgotten these men were trained killers.

Juan pulled me closer as we made our way outside, toward the patio. Once we cleared the glass doors, there was an entirely new barrage of men standing guard. This time they were my father's men; I knew from the clothes they wore, the heavy knitted coats despite the heat, and the specific tattoos they had. Each one of my father's men had his moniker tattooed on their knuckles. *Ördög*.

Ignoring the butterflies in my stomach and my desperate desire to have my own gun in the palm of my hand, I focused on Juan. He was my protector and would ensure my safety, as well as my baby's. We bypassed the patio furniture and headed toward the pool house, which had a slight covering off to the side. Underneath a myriad of hanging flowers and twisted vines sat a long slab of glossy wood fashioned into a table. Eight wooden chairs, each with white cushions, sat around the space. On the opposite side, three were occupied by my father and two of his men. Jakob was on his left, giving me a small smile, and there on his right was a familiar face. My breath hitched as I tried to place him, but as Juan pulled out my chair and helped me into it, my eyes flicked to the man in question and my lungs stalled. His eyes landed on mine, softening just a fraction before he looked down.

What the fuck is Decker's little brother doing here?

"She doesn't need to be a part of this," my father declared, forcing my eyes away from Kyle and toward the monster I knew as Father.

Another man sat next to Juan on the other side of him while at least ten men flanked us. Juan's hand tightened on my own before bringing it to his lips, then he put it in his lap. I gripped his thigh, leaning into him.

"First of all, I told you three men. You brought over ten. The fact that you weren't killed on sight was a kindness. As far as Taylor's presence, I won't speak to you without her," Juan said evenly.

"She's a female and has no say in the deal we broker," my father said, his icy eyes landing on me for a fleeting moment. This wasn't new to me. He used to treat my mother like a sack of moldy potatoes, so I didn't expect much from him.

"I'm not sure how you treat your women, Ivan, but in my outfit, we treat them equally. Taylor is mine, my other half, my queen, my entire fucking soul. You'll treat her with respect while in my house."

My breath hitched while heat infused my neck and face. Did he mean that, or was it just for show? Jesus, he couldn't just say shit like that and not expect me to get confused and blur our already murky lines. Not being able to stop myself, I leaned over and kissed his neck, moving my fingers that were in his lap to graze his dick. His responding smirk only made my blush deepen.

"Fucking tizenéves." My father shook his head.

Juan raised a brow, looking over at me in question.

"He called us teenagers," I explained.

"Ah. Well, we certainly are as horny as them. Let's set the terms then and be done with this. We have an ultrasound appointment to get to." Juan snapped his fingers, signaling one of his men to walk forward. He placed a rectangular tablet in front of them. "These are our terms." Juan's eyes narrowed on the way my father grappled for the device, narrowing his eyes. I knew from when I was a young preteen that my father would have to put his reading glasses on, but how did Juan know that? It was a way of flushing out my father's weakness.

"It says to fuck off and leave you alone." My father's face snapped up.

Juan sat back, showing his white teeth in a brilliant smile. "That's where I'd like to start."

My father spat, lunging over the table to grab for Juan's throat. Two silencers pressed into his forehead a second later, Juan's men already surrounding my father's.

My eyes went to Kyle and the man sitting in front of him; I now remembered he'd attended my sister's wedding. They must have both been related to Decker in some capacity then. The man watched me with zero emotion on his face, while behind him, Kyle kept shifting, as if he was uncomfortable. I knew he looked up to his older brother, and it made me curious if Decker knew about this. My father was a dangerous man; anyone working for him would be expected to do illegal, unspeakable things...the fact that Kyle was even attending this meeting meant he'd moved up in the ranks faster than most.

My father fixed his sleeves, settling in his chair once more. "Try again, dog."

"What were the terms with Markos?" Juan asked, moving his hand to my thigh. His fingers dipped dangerously close to my center, making me aware of how short my cutoffs were.

"The deal? She'd marry him, he'd get access to our transportation services and political contacts, and of course we'd be allies."

"What would you get in return?" I watched the mood shift around the table, and something told me there was more to the deal with Markos than they were letting on.

"One point two million, for starters, and one third of their product to use as we want," my father answered, his eyes flicking up to my face then over to Juan's. There was something he was leaving out.

I squeezed Juan's hand. When he glanced over, I leaned forward and spoke.

"Before anything is official, I'd like to review the initial contract you had with Markos." My mind kept circling to why he wanted to wait for my twenty-first birthday, and not my twentieth or eighteenth. There was ample opportunity for him to grab me, even if he was busy in Hungary...there was something he wasn't telling me about the deal with Markos.

"You don't get to ask me for that. You're nothing but a—"

Juan's loud voice cut through my father's, forcing him to shut his mouth. "If you speak about my woman one more time in an unfavorable fashion, you will force my hand. We'll go to war with you and that will be fucking that. Do you understand me?"

My father sneered, slamming his fist against the table. "You'd risk a war over a piece of pussy?"

Juan leaned forward but didn't remove his hand from my leg, his fingers still dangerously close to rubbing the center seam of my shorts. "She carries my child—this is more than a piece of pussy, old man."

"Fine. Fuck. I'll get the contract for you to review."

Juan's pointer finger pressed into my core, along that middle seam. I nearly grabbed his wrist to hold him in place. Instead, I went lax and spread my legs wider. There were men behind us, but not close enough to see what we were doing, and no one sat next to me.

"Excellent."

"I want Taylor with me until the deal is finalized. I don't want her running," my father demanded, his gaze shifting between Juan and myself.

Juan pressed his digit in, adding more pressure than I could stand. We hadn't had any type of physical connection since that night on the bed, and I'd been dying to rectify the fact that I had freaked out and walked off.

"She stays with me," Juan replied easily, adding more fingers over my center. "Until then, we will be in touch." Juan began to stand, removing his hand from me and leaving me cold.

My father tipped his head back, watching as Juan stood. "That's as far as you're willing to go today? We came all this way—I expected a deal."

Juan barely paid him any notice while snapping, "You came all this way to kidnap my fiancée. You came here to steal her from me—don't test my patience."

My father stood, pointing his chubby finger at me. "I should just take her and give her to Markos. He will abort your child and keep her as his whore."

Something slid from Juan's wrist, fast as lightning. Within an instant, a small dagger plunged into my father's left shoulder, another poised to ready to fly.

"I warned you. Now you've not only threatened Taylor, but my child. Now get the fuck off my property. I will entertain a conversation with you once I get the contract delivered to me, by someone other than you. You aren't welcome here again until we're ready to discuss terms."

Juan grabbed my hand and walked briskly away, ignoring all the yells from my father behind us. There was no gunfire, so that was at least good news, especially as more men filled the patio space, emptying the house.

Three guards followed us to Juan's bedroom, walking in ahead of us to sweep the space. Juan delivered me to the bed, and once the men were through, he locked us inside.

CHAPTER NINETEEN

Ivan

I LEANED AGAINST MY FOREARM THAT WAS PINNED TO THE DOOR. My body faced away from Taylor while my frame vibrated with the need to stop Ivan from breathing. I was still having a hard time understanding that he was so cold and cruel toward his own flesh and blood. Then again, I had no doubts that my own father would have sold me if he was offered a high enough price.

I wasn't sure how my new fake fiancée would respond to my need, but I was at the edge of reason and didn't frankly care.

"I need to touch you. Even if it's just to hold you, I need to feel you..." I swallowed, unsure how to explain it to her. She was consuming me, in my veins, my lungs, my head. She was everywhere and nowhere because of whatever her fucking reasons, but she wasn't mine in any real way. I just needed to feel her warm skin against mine as a reminder that she was here with me, safe.

Taylor waited a few seconds before responding. "I feel too restricted in these clothes. I'm going to get more comfortable." I nodded silently.

After a few seconds of breathing, willing my pulse to calm, I turned around.

She reclined on the bed, her shirt gone. Instead she had on a see-through, lacy bra that held her tits in place over the swell of her creamy stomach. Her shorts were gone now, and in their place was what seemed like a strip of lacy fabric, probably a thong or something, but with her stomach, they just seemed nearly invisible.

I swallowed.

"Come feel the baby kick." She held out her hand toward me, and I couldn't tear my eyes from her. Stripping out of my clothes, down to my boxers, I joined her on the bed.

I gently placed my ear to her belly, being careful not to add too much pressure.

The little jolt against my face had me sitting back.

"Did he just kick me?" I smiled.

Taylor laughed, her nose crinkling. "I guess I will find out today if it's a boy or girl...but yeah, she kicks a lot."

"You want a girl?" I rubbed my hand down the expanse of her belly, over her protruding outie.

"I want a healthy baby."

My hand moved along the lower part of her abdomen, right over the top of her underwear.

"I figured we'd need to get used to being in bed together, like this. With, um..." She hesitated, her face flushing. "Less clothing. I don't usually sleep in a ton of clothes...I hope that won't bother you," she confessed quietly.

I nodded, knowing she was right but a little surprised that she was the one to suggest it. "We need to leave soon, for the ultrasound," I stated, trying to divert my thoughts, dragging my fingers up her stomach, away from the band of her panties.

Taylor's eyes jumped to mine, her mouth gaping. "You're coming with me?"

"Of course I am."

"I figured after last night..." She trailed off.

I didn't move my eyes from seeing how my dark hand looked against her creamy skin.

"Last night I was feeling a lot of really big things."

Taylor wet her lips, cupping my jaw. "You wanted me to ask you why."

I nodded, still nervous about confessing this, but as I stared at her stomach and the way she looked in my bed, I realized I needed to say it.

"Why?" she asked, voice just barely above a whisper.

I looked away from her stomach and swallowed the thickness that had strangled my throat, realizing she deserved the truth...but at the last second, I changed my mind.

"I haven't stopped thinking about that night on your bed...I got really jealous when you said Holden was going with you to the appointment."

Taylors fingers slowly pushed through my hair while she watched my lips. "You don't like that you felt jealous?"

I shook my head in answer. I was too cowardly to tell her I might be falling for her, especially after learning more about her that morning...all my emotions were gathering in my chest like a tidal wave, drowning all my resolve to stay away from her.

"I haven't stopped thinking about that night either...I was just scared. I left because I realized you cared about the baby, and I wasn't used to that," she explained, stroking my jaw. Then she whispered, "I think we should finish what we started that night."

My eyes snapped to hers.

"Are you sure?" I'd already decided I was going to touch her, but I had been certain it would still be something PG considering how the last time went.

Her small intake of breath told me she was struggling. "I'm positive."

Moving until I was down by her feet, I started kissing her left foot, kissing the top then moving up her ankle and calf. I shifted to the other foot, repeating the process.

I smiled at her, dragging my lips along her inner knee. My fingers trailed forward, up her thighs, my body closing in until I was on my stomach directly in front of her parted thighs. Before she had a chance to fight it, I pressed my tongue into her panty-covered center.

"Oh shit." She breathed out, bucking her hips.

I smiled again, and this time, I gently tore the fabric at her hips, and then I devoured her. Swiping my tongue up her folds and then circling her clit, I added a finger into her cunt while I worked her with my tongue.

"Yes." Taylor rocked her hips into my face while I sucked her outer lips into my mouth, adding another finger into her wetness.

I palmed her ass, bringing it closer to my mouth, and continued to suck on her clit while fucking her with my fingers.

"Add another finger," she begged, panting while her hips rocked.

I did as she requested, realizing she needed to be filled with something and knowing our little game was coming to an end. I was going to fuck her while she was pregnant, and there was nothing she could do about it.

I just wasn't sure when, but it was going to happen.

My tongue swirled while I added pressure to her clit, and after a few more strokes, she was coming undone with a sharp cry.

I fisted my erection, pulling it free of my boxers. Getting to my knees, I pushed her leg outward while I rubbed my weeping cock through her soaking wet folds. She was still gasping for breath, her eyes on the ceiling while I stroked up and down, rubbing the tip through her arousal.

I only planned to see how it would feel, and it felt like fucking heaven...but I knew we weren't ready for more. When I took her completely, I wanted her to be mine, without this fake shit between us, or this ruse. I wanted her entirely.

So, I began to stroke myself, using her arousal as a way to lubricate my shaft. I stroked up and down while wiping up her juices with my fingers and bringing them to my mouth.

"You taste so fucking good." My voice was raspy as I felt my balls begin to strain with pain. I wanted to be inside her.

Taylor wet her lips, bringing her hands to cup her breasts through the lacy material holding them in place. "Can I taste you?"

I paused mid-stroke, positive I hadn't heard her correctly. "Fuck yeah."

She tried to move, but I leaned forward, placing my hand on her chest then inching closer to her while gripping my cock.

"Open your mouth."

Her blue eyes drifted toward mine, then those pink lips opened in compliance.

I gently and carefully slid my length onto her wet tongue, allowing her to taste herself. The humming sound she made vibrated down my shaft, tearing a groan from my chest.

She wrapped her lips around me, using her hand to twist around the base, then she sucked and fucking sucked until I was about to explode down her throat. Ready to pull out of her mouth, I began to withdraw my hips. She let go with a pop of her lips and her brows caving in.

"I said I wanted to taste you. That means all of you." She narrowed her eyes then grabbed for my erection once more, opening her mouth and swallowing my hardened cock. I couldn't hold back. I pressed forward, hitting the back of her throat while groaning my release.

Her eyes bore into mine while she swallowed every last drop of my seed, moaning every fucking second. Once she had completely taken everything, she let me go and used her tongue to lick the top of her lip.

"You taste fucking delicious too."

I met her smile with a broad one of my own and then shook my head in disbelief. Taylor fucking Beck was in my bed. She had just had her mouth on my cock, and she'd enjoyed it. I'd had wet dreams about this a year ago, and now it was happening. It was too surreal to comprehend.

"Let's get cleaned up." I bent down and pressed a kiss to her hairline, nervous about kissing her lips. I'd stolen plenty of kisses from her, but I was ready for her to give them up freely, and part of me still worried she'd pull away.

♥

"TAYLOR BECK, here to see Dr. Kline," the pregnant woman at my side said shyly to the woman behind the glass.

The woman at the reception desk clicked a few screens before smiling at Taylor.

"Go ahead and leave your sample, then come back and he'll be right out for you."

Taylor turned toward me and gave me an awkward smile. "I have to go to the bathroom. I'll be right back."

If this had all been done prior to her father showing up, I'd have let her walk away from me, but instead I grabbed her hand and smiled at the receptionist.

"We'll be right back."

Taylor led the way down the hall to a small alcove, whisper-yelling at me the whole time.

"Do you really need to come with me?"

She opened the door to a single-person restroom, and I followed her in.

"Are you really that worried about peeing in front of me?"

She scoffed. "Yeah...I'm still in that stage of wanting you to think I wake up looking like a princess and don't fart or burp."

I cracked a smile. "Why do you care if I think those things about you?"

I wanted to know. I needed to. I had to have something to hold on to, proving that she was in this, falling into it as much as I was.

"Because I'm a girl. Now wait outside." She pushed my shoulder blades until I was moving.

I waited for the outside her door, pulling my cell free to answer a few texts and check my bank account. My parents had me on payroll at their restaurant, and if I was there for a few hours a week, they generally paid me under the table. With my payout from the Hornets, I had enough to float on for a while, enough to see Taylor through this. We had class in a couple of days, and I hoped that was enough time to sort shit out because there was no way I was leaving her alone on campus.

I heard the toilet flush on the other side of the door but punched in my banking password for a quick glance. Right as the door opened, I saw my balance was over nine hundred thousand dollars.

"What's wrong?" Taylor asked while drying her hands with a paper towel.

I looked up, giving her a smile. "Nothing...just some banking stuff I need to clear up."

I knew it was my uncle, but fuck, I wasn't ready to accept it. I wasn't ready to accept El Peligro, or any extension of them.

"Taylor, there you are." One of the doctors came up, smiling at Taylor. Dude was older than us by at least ten years, but he wasn't half bad-looking. He looked like he worked out, and I knew from the way Taylor blushed that she found him at least semi-attractive. Fuck, the more I looked at him, the more I realized he resembled that soccer player she'd chosen her namesake from.

His eyes narrowed briefly, taking me in before putting his hand at the small of Taylor's back.

I followed after them, thinking through how much trouble I'd get in if I broke his wrist.

"How are you feeling?" the doctor asked, helping her sit down on the elevated table.

"Okay…just a little achy and tired. Same as usual." She pulled up her shirt, leaving her in a small tank top, and slipped off her sandals.

"How are the hormones?" he asked, his eyes bouncing to me nervously then back to Taylor.

"Not as bad since the last time…" Taylor brushed her hair behind her ear while a new patch of red invaded her neck.

What the fuck was going on here? I watched as Taylor stood, grabbing hold of the waistband of her shorts, ready to drag them down her thighs. The doctor's eyes moved from the computer screen to her in a sleazy-as-fuck way, then went back to his screen like he was trying not to notice that she was about to get undressed.

The doctor flicked his gaze once more toward Taylor before typing on his computer. "I was surprised when I saw that you had moved your appointment to a Saturday. Usually I see you much later in the afternoon, and usually you're alone. It's nice that your friend could come with you."

"I have my ultrasound appointment today," Taylor said, moving right past the comment about me being a friend. She was about to unclasp her bra when my eyes swung back to the doctor.

"What the fuck are you doing?" I eyed the doctor even though my question was directed at Taylor.

She let out a little gasp of shock. "Juan, chill, this is how visits go."

I spun to look at Taylor, and a bone-weary anger began surfacing in my stomach.

"So, you undress in here, in front of him, before every visit?" *Please tell me she doesn't. Please fucking tell me she doesn't.*

Taylor's face turned red. "These exams are all pretty up close and personal. I know how it must seem from the outside, but—"

"Dr. Kline," I said, cutting her off. My voice was a warning, and he seemed to realize that as his face began to flush red. *Motherfucker.* "Go find a female doctor. If you can't find one then return with a female nurse."

He stood, letting out a little scoff. "This isn't what you think."

"I think you need to go do as I said before I smash your face in with that laptop."

Shaking his head, he eyed Taylor once more before moving toward the door.

Her eyes darted toward the closed door. "What the hell, Juan?!"

"Tell me the truth—have you ever let him get you off?"

Her eyebrows hit her hairline. "What…that's crazy…"

"Answer me." I was barely containing the rage rolling through me. I wanted to kill him, fucking murder him.

Her lips thinned while the rest of her neck and face turned an angry pink color. "Not on purpose."

My eyes narrowed, my fists clenching at my sides. "What. The. Fuck. Does. That. Mean?"

She pulled her tank top back on slowly, linking her arms over her belly. "He was asking me how my hormones were doing, and at the time I was going insane. Nothing was helping, and I felt like a deranged sex addict even for struggling. So, he offered to show me a stimulation tactic that would help."

I was going to go to jail. That was just the end of it.

"So, he touched you?"

Taylor lifted her shoulders just slightly.

"Did he touch you?" I upturned the metal tray of tools that were out for the appointment. I needed an outlet for this rage. *He fucking touched her...he...*

Taylor winced, clenching her arms tighter over her chest. "He showed me the movement, yes...and he did it until I came, so I knew it could be done."

My voice cracked as I worked to swallow the lump in my throat. "Did he keep his gloves on?"

Her shuddering features told me enough.

"He took his fucking gloves off, stuck his fingers in your pussy, and made you come, and you think that's fucking normal?"

Her cheeks flushed a deep pink while tears lined her eyes. "I've never been pregnant, I don't know what the hell normal is...they stuck a big-ass wand covered in a huge condom up my vagina the first time I came in here."

It was when her voice cracked that I realized I was being too harsh on her. I wasn't even angry with *her*; I was just pissed as hell at the man who'd taken advantage of her.

Walking forward, I cradled her head in my hands and pressed a kiss to her forehead. "Hey, hey, I'm sorry."

She hiccupped as tears began to stream down her face. "I didn't know that wasn't normal...I thought my reaction to it was embarrassing, and I was so ashamed, but he promised me it was completely normal. I mean his hands are always in my vagina every time I come in for a checkup, so I thought it was normal. He told me he had to remove the gloves in order to show me...so I could feel it."

Rubbing circles into her back, I kept kissing her hairline.

"It's okay, baby. You didn't do anything wrong."

The door opened, and a female nurse walked in, her eyes already softening at the sight of Taylor's tears. I grabbed a Kleenex and handed it to Taylor while I slowly slipped toward the exit.

"I'll let you set her up, and please explain to her exactly what should be done every single time she comes in for a visit. I'm pretty sure it isn't normal for her to strip down with the doctor still in the room each time she comes in for a checkup."

The nurse's mouth gaped.

Taylor grabbed my wrist, a silent question about where I was going and what I was about to do.

I gave her a small smirk, hoping to lessen the worry in her eyes.

"I need to talk to Dr. Kline."

Her blonde eyebrows narrowed. "Juan…"

"I'll be right back" was all I could get out. If the nurse knew what I was about to do, she'd call the police. I waited, unsure if Taylor would put up a fight or not.

She slowly released my wrist, giving me a tiny nod, and I knew she understood. She'd grown up with the devil…of course she understood. I leaned forward once again, pressing my lips to her forehead before exiting.

I walked down two doors until I saw the shitbag in question typing away on his computer. His face was still slightly red, and if he'd had any sense in his goddamn brain, he would have left the building.

I walked into his office and shut the door behind me.

Dr. Kline stopped typing and rolled back in his office chair. "I don't think you should be in here."

I tilted my head. "Really? How strange. I think it's you who shouldn't be here."

"She's a fucking tease, did you know that? She came in with these tiny shorts and her shirt showing half her breasts. She'd openly talk about how horny she was…she was asking for it," the shitbag explained through clenched teeth.

"So, because she's a beautiful girl and unsure of how these appointments are supposed to go, not to mention completely alone…you preyed on her?"

I stalked forward, forcing him to cower into his bookcase.

"No. She wanted it. She wanted to get off, and I just helped her."

"Would you have fucked her? Is that what you had planned for today? Thinking you could take advantage of the fact that she's in her third trimester and so hot and bothered she would need a mediocre fuck to help her?"

The good doctor clenched his teeth while he shook his head.

"No. No, it was a one-time thing."

I drew closer until I was directly in front of him, hardening my tone as I asked again, "Were you going to fuck her today?"

"No...I..."

I slammed my hand into the bookshelf next to his face.

"Okay, fine...fuck. Yes, I was going to. If she wanted it, I was going to offer it."

I grabbed him by the collar and slammed his face into his desk. His hand rested next to his keyboard, and I didn't waste any time pulling a blade from the holster hidden under my shirt. I sank it into the back of his hand and covered his mouth to smother his scream.

"The only reason I'm not cutting off your hand is because I have an appointment to get to, but trust me...if I want it gone, it will be." I pulled the blade free and wiped the blood on his face. Hovering close to his ear, I asked, "Do you understand?"

Finally, he nodded, and I let him go.

"Clean yourself up. Try to call this in, and you might be signing your death certificate." I placed a single playing card down on top of his bleeding hand. It was the calling card for El Peligro, the king of hearts with a bleeding black heart inked into the middle.

The way the doctor's eyes bulged meant he knew who it belonged to.

I left him there to figure out what he wanted to do with it. I walked out of his office and down two doors, until I found Taylor's exam room.

"Okay, she's all set. The ultrasound takes place at this location. It's out this building and down the street." The nurse held up a card with an address on it. "They will be expecting her in about twenty minutes."

I held my hand out and helped Taylor up. The nurse gave us both an apologetic look while Taylor grabbed her purse.

Once we were out the door, we walked right past Dr. Kline's office. The door was still closed, and not a single siren or security guard moved while we passed by.

Once we were clear of the building, Taylor looked up at me.

"Did you hurt him?"

I shrugged, shoving my free hand in my pocket.

"Did you kill him?" she clarified quietly, like shame coated each word.

"I should have." I blinked at the bright sun. It was getting later in the afternoon; the shine should have dulled by now, especially for how late in October it was.

"So you did hurt him?" We turned the corner and headed into a glass elevator.

"Taylor, I'm going to hurt anyone who touches you. Period."

She stared up at me in shock as the doors opened. This entire ruse was getting away from me. I'd never been this protective of a single person in my life, but the idea of anyone touching her—it made my blood boil. I wondered, not for the first time, if I should just come clean and offer her my black, bleeding heart.

What would she do with it though? She had no use for it, and none for me…I was merely a lucky break; any other guy could have fit the role. With that idea in mind, I bit my tongue and held back any other wandering thoughts.

CHAPTER TWENTY

Taylor

My stomach seemed to pinch with panic as every minute passed and we waited for the ultrasound technician to call my name. Juan took a seat in the waiting room, tugging my hand until I was sitting next to him. I couldn't explain to him how embarrassed I felt. Juan used to make snide remarks about how much of an easy lay I was, how I was essentially a slut with an open ticket to anyone who wanted a ride.

I had never explained to anyone why I had sex as frequently as I did, and I guess it honestly didn't matter. Once someone made up their mind about you, you would be hard-pressed to change it. I didn't care what others thought of me, except for Juan. His opinion mattered very much to me. I could feel myself begin to shut down, just like I had back in the spring after Juan came in and told me he had wished I would just disappear.

My chest tightened as assumptions and that inner voice began to speak and tell me I was worthless and didn't deserve to be a mother. My fight-or-flight instincts kicked in, mocking me and telling me to just give up already and run. I nearly choked on the sob working its way up my throat, then suddenly my phone vibrated on my knee.

Fatima: Hey girl, didn't hear from you…how did the ultrasound go? You know I'll be waiting on a picture of that baby.

It was like an air mask had been placed over my face, filling my lungs with air. I inhaled a silent breath and decided to face Juan and whatever it was he thought of me.

Looking over at him, I tried to gather the tiny specks of bravery I had gathered, knowing it would be like trying to hold on to sand.

"I never encouraged him…I know you must think the worst of me, but I never once asked for anything from him. From the beginning he set up our appointments in that way, explaining that it was normal and telling me to relax."

I looked down at my stomach. I wanted to throw up. He'd taken advantage of me, and the realization hadn't really hit until now.

Rubbing my forehead, I felt tears burn behind my eyes. God, I was so stupid. Of course it would be me who would get taken advantage of, simply because I was naïve. Self-hate smothered me. I didn't deserve to be a mother. I didn't deserve to be in Juan's life, or to have his protection.

"Taylor Beck." A man wearing green scrubs stepped out, holding a clipboard.

Juan grumbled under his breath. "Great, another Beckham lookalike."

Threading our fingers together, he walked in behind me. The room was dark and quiet with two large screens set up along the wall to our right. In the middle was a plush leather medical chair, already reclined.

"Go ahead and sit down, and your husband can sit over there, next to you," the tech advised, typing away on his computer.

I didn't correct him regarding Juan. Instead, I settled into the plush chair while Juan took my purse and set it next to the chair next to mine.

"Okay." He turned toward me holding a hand towel. "I'm going to tuck this into the band of your shorts, but I'll have you unbutton them first, please." My eyes immediately went to Juan, now unsure who was being honest and who was just taking advantage.

Juan's gaze was already on the tech, who seemed to grow red under his inspection.

"Give us a second, please," Juan asked, moving to take the white cloth from the man's hand.

"Sure, just pop your head out when you're ready." He rolled his stool to the desk and then left us alone.

Juan sat next to me on the edge of the chair. "You're shaking."

"I don't know what's normal." My voice shook as I tried to calm down, blinking away tears.

Juan slowly unbuttoned my shorts and splayed the denim open, revealing the top band of my underwear.

"You know, most women probably want to kill you for not having to wear maternity shorts. These cutoffs look like sin on you...it's not fair that you're about to give birth and can still fit in them."

I laughed, trying to relax into the chair. "I haven't indulged in a single craving, so I think it's plenty fair."

His eyes met mine while he slowly tucked the rag into the band of my underwear, flipping it so it protected the opening of my shorts. The tech wouldn't be able to see anything except the cloth.

Juan's lips pursed, his brows caving as he spoke softly. "I know I've said some pretty shitty things to you in the past...I know I can be an asshole occasionally, but there's no one on this earth that sees you the way I do."

I sniffed, letting the tears I had been holding back fall free.

"I see you fight and get bruises in places no one can see. You stand when everyone else around you falls. You love when everyone has given you a reason to hate. You have a beautiful heart, preciosa, and I'm doing my best to help you see it. But this whole thing with the doctor...it's heavy as fuck, and I would really like it if you left it in this room so we can enjoy what comes up on that screen."

I nodded, swiping at my face.

He wiped my hair out of my eyes and then raised my shirt up, tucking it under my bra line so my chest was covered, only showing my stomach.

After giving me one last look, he went and called the technician in.

The ultrasound tech reclaimed his position on the rolling stool and then began to set things up.

The sonographer made a sound of approval. "Let's get this show on the road."

Warm gel squirted in an undignified way along my abdomen, followed by the pressure from the transducer being pressed into my skin.

Immediately the screens hanging on the far wall came alive with flashes of white against a black screen.

"Okay, let's see where baby is hanging out." The transducer wand moved over my stomach and then pressed pointedly into one specific area, revealing the baby's head and face on the screen. The tech paused, drawing boxes around the head and typing away on his computer. "Here, you can see the lips and nose."

Tears fell freely as I saw my child blink and bring their thumb up to their mouth.

"That's the most beautiful thing I've ever seen," Juan said in awe.

I turned to see his expression, and seeing tears line his eyes shifted the glacier in my chest, melting it entirely.

The sonographer moved on to the feet and hands, shoulders, and rib cage taking care to zoom in on the heart. The little fluttering valve was the most insane thing to witness.

When the wand moved and we had a view in between the legs, I held my breath.

The tech made a humming sound before letting out a sigh. "Looks like a healthy baby girl."

I half laughed, half sobbed, so excited and happy I was sure I'd burst. I looked over in time to see Juan was already smirking, shaking his head.

"Of course it's a girl," he joked.

The sonographer smiled. "You sound like that might be a little bit of a handful."

Juan leaned over, kissing my nose. "If she looks anything like her mom, I'm going to have my hands full."

My heart cracked. It had been chipping in little pieces from the moment Juan first kissed me in the spring. Unlike every other guy in my life, my walls didn't keep him out, and now he'd claimed me in a way that would never make sense...it was fake, but the way my heart had just split in half for this man felt as real as ever.

Pictures printed from the machine, and suddenly the appointment was over. The technician began to pull out the rag that had been tucked into my jeans, but Juan stopped him.

"I got it from here. Thanks."

The tech raised his hands like he was surrendering and walked out.

Juan wiped my stomach and held out his hand to help me sit up. "How do you feel?"

Moving to stand and button my shorts, I felt my lip wobble. "I feel like my heart just split in half. It's such a strange sensation...but she's so beautiful."

Juan handed me the few photos that had printed. One had a little note written on the top that said, 'Hi Mom and Dad.' I kept my head down so Juan wouldn't see my breakdown. If I had one wish, it would be to have this be real, to have Juan be the dad and me the mom, to have this little girl loved by us both and raised by us.

I knew my feelings were dangerous. For once I wanted to keep something for myself, and it terrified me that I wouldn't be allowed to. Even if I was able to convince my father that this entire thing was real, how long would Juan play pretend for? He had a life to live, and there was no way I could expect him to keep up pretenses, nor would I want him to. I had a baby coming soon, and that would require long nights and lack of sleep. I couldn't ask this of him. We were both so young; his entire life was just beginning.

As difficult as it was for me, I began to tuck away every rogue emotion that had rolled out, every feeling, every hope. It wasn't a perfect remedy for what I was feeling, but it would help. I had to protect Juan as much as I had to protect my daughter, and in order to do that, I'd fight not to fall in love with him.

♥

AS SOON AS we'd parked the car, Juan's cousin was there updating him on everything, including the contract my father had drawn up for Markos. We settled into Juan's room while rain danced along the windows, casting the room in a gloomy glow. Wrapping myself in a soft blanket, I began to pore through page after page of information, passing each one over to Juan as soon as I finished.

"So, your dad didn't lie, but he also left out the part where Markos would be the successor to the outfit if something should happen to your father," Juan summarized, shuffling the papers back in order.

I spun my chair to look outside, staring at the varying shades of leaves along the top of the orchards. "He also left out that our first child would be given to Ivan to secure another deal were Ivan to be in good health when the baby was conceived."

"Interesting that he didn't immediately suggest that the baby be dealt with," Juan mused while rubbing his eyes.

I didn't want to talk about it anymore. My stomach churned with disgust that my own father would stoop so low…that he would treat my offspring like a piece of livestock.

"Then there's the part about your trust going to Markos, the one you can't access until you turn twenty-one."

That explained why he was so adamant about this specific birthday; it must have been a request from the Mariano family then. I had no idea what the trust included, but they must have known.

"Come on." Juan grabbed my hand, helping me up. "It's colder out now, so you might want a sweater, or something warmer." Juan walked into his closet, and when I headed toward his bedroom door, he stopped me. "It's all in here now."

Letting go of the doorknob, I slowly followed him into his massive walk-in. Shelves lined each wall, along with various shoe racks. Juan had an impressive shoe collection, but it still didn't take up all the space. He had a built-in dresser with gliding drawers on one wall, and as I turned around, I noticed the opposite wall had one set up too.

Curious, I pulled it open. All the folded items from my dresser in the guest room were now in the drawers. I tipped my head to the side, and there, hanging to the right, were all my skirts, dresses, and shirts. I still hadn't brought my whole wardrobe over, so there wasn't much, but it was still nice to see it all neatly hung and put away.

"Juan, you didn't have to do this." I gently touched the fabric of one of my sweaters.

With his back turned to me, he murmured, "It was no big deal."

I smiled, turning once more, only to notice more hanging items on the far wall. This time, it was all the baby clothes I'd purchased so far. Tiny pink hangers held rompers, dresses, and little outfits, while the gliding drawers kept blankets, diapers, and folded onesies.

All the ice I'd infused into my heart since the ultrasound melted again.

"No one has ever done anything like this for me," I whispered, slowly dragging my hand along the fabric of a soft blanket. "Did you have your men do this while we were gone today?"

I turned to look at Juan. He was still turned away from me, but I wasn't letting this go until he faced me. His face was stern, like my heart had been before this moment.

"I did most of it while you were sleeping." He tugged on a simple Henley that gaped at his throat, revealing his strong muscles.

I walked closer to him, slowly moving step by step to avoid spooking him.

He watched me with apprehension, a wariness to his eyes as I brought my hand up to his chest. Right when I thought he'd pull back or tell me we should get going, I made my move.

Leaning in, I gently pressed my lips to his. Once I knew he wasn't going to push me away, I settled more into his space, tipping my head to the side and pushing in for access. He met the smooth glide of my lips with his tongue, dragging his left hand up my back while his right hand held my hip in place.

He broke away, pressing his forehead against mine. "We keep peeking over our walls, as if we want to climb over, only to realize how far the drop is..."

I blinked as reality hit me, rushing in as cold as a tidal wave. He was fighting this as much as I was...except he was doing a better job. He didn't want this. He didn't want me.

I stepped back; his grim expression only served to confirm that he was right. I wanted to keep him safe, but I was also falling in love with him. I had to stop this. Taking another step back, I tucked hair behind my ear and turned away from him. I couldn't watch his expression as I put up another layer between us. It was what he wanted too, so there was little comfort in each step I took.

His warm fingers threaded through mine, tugging me out of the closet.

"Let's eat."

CHAPTER TWENTY-ONE

Ivan

It was close to ten at night, and my cousins and other men employed by El Peligro sat around the table. Forties and glasses full of Patrón sat in front of each person, and a few blunts were being rolled at the end of the table while a few men wandered the property. My mind kept wandering thinking of how Taylor was settling in my bed.

I had stared at her the night prior, standing over her while she slept, just watching as her chest rose and fell. I stared until the image of her being held by her hair finally left my mind, then I reluctantly tucked myself in the damn chair. I wanted to respect her, not overwhelm her... but now that she'd told me I could sleep in the bed with her, it was all I could think about. Even if it wasn't smart, even if I shouldn't.

"So, this deal...what are you planning to ask for?" my cousin Luis asked between sips.

"In order for it to work, you'd have to marry her before he can really discover that we're fucking him over," Hector added, taking a drag from his joint.

We'd lightly discussed the terms, how he'd snuck in terms without Taylor knowing, and how we could have the same courtesy when getting our deal together. Honestly, Ivan could fuck himself with the deal. All I wanted was for Taylor and the baby to be safe. I didn't want anything he offered, but El Peligro was already foaming at the mouth as opportunity came knocking.

"This whole thing is still crazy. I didn't even know you had a girl… just last week, I was talking about that Angela chick coming by, and here you have this side piece. She's so fucking hot, but—"

Rage sputtered in my chest, running down my arms. I wanted to slam my fist into his ugly mouth. "Shut the fuck up, Kane."

The man, who was barely older than me, held up his hands in surrender. "Jesus, sorry bro. Just saying, she's not marked, and neither are you. If I had known she wasn't, I would have moved in so much faster."

He laughed, slapping hands with the guy next to him. I knew them well enough from parties and other shit throughout the years, but I was ready to throw them both out on their asses.

"Taylor doesn't need a mark."

Hector looked over at me, his eyes hooded while his high kicked in. "And you…do you need one?"

These fucking marks. It was tradition for El Peligro men to mark if they were taken, so if they were to ever die in a fight, by their bodies we'd know that there was someone left behind. The women wore the mark of their man so there weren't any issues with other men trying to step in and make a move, especially if the man was out on a job. In some cases, there were members that traveled to the border and back, forcing them to be gone for weeks at a time, if not longer.

"She's pregnant, dumb fucks."

My cousin kept his eyes on me while a cloud of smoke billowed in front of his face. "Then put a ring on it, primo."

I shuffled the papers in front of me and sipped on the whiskey I'd poured. "Let's move on, finish this up. I want to go to bed." I also didn't want to talk about this shit anymore, not with how suspicious my cousin was already. He knew why I was hesitating, and it had nothing to do with Taylor.

"We have to give him the final answer soon, which will require another meeting. Where is it going to be held?" Kane asked, finishing off his blunt.

"I'll let you know. I need to talk to Taylor about it first."

Everyone around the table chuckled, shaking their heads. I stilled, halfway to standing, and looked back and forth between their expressions.

"What?"

"Nothing, primo. It's just...Manny never ran things like that, and neither did my pops," Hector joked, putting his hands behind his head.

"I'm neither of them."

Kane and Luis started talking to each other in Spanish toward the end of the table while Hector ran a hand over his bald head.

"It's just...the women aren't involved. I know you said she was your equal, but I thought that was just to piss off the old man. She can't have that place here. You can't make your decisions based on what she says... you're the king, and we've never once had a queen."

I stared at each of them through the thin cloud of smoke hanging over the table. The tone in the room had grown somber, and I knew, depending on how I answered, things could go poorly. I didn't want to fight with my family, but all of this just felt like one big-ass lie, and I was merely playing a part.

Something I was eager to put an end to.

"You're right." I dipped my head, scooping up the cards I'd been shuffling. "You don't have a queen, probably never will...but *I* do. It's her life, her future. She's mine, which means you will show her respect, you will answer to her, you will lay down your life for her. Do you understand?" I met each stare, each gaze...and once each of them nodded their agreement, I stood. "We'll meet up tomorrow."

♥

I CLOSED the door and locked it, keeping to the shadows. Taylor's sunshine hair was muted by the dark, all of it fanning out on the pillow behind her. She only wore a sheet across her body, barely covering the swell of her breasts, her swollen stomach outlined. My heart did this strange fluttery, panicky thing. I could feel tears burn the backs of my eyes as I tried to wrangle the rogue emotion invading my chest.

She was beautiful, so innocent lying there in my bed, completely at peace. Not a single worry in the world, and soon she'd have a baby. I already thought of what she'd look like, omitting any thoughts that the baby might have Holden's looks. In my mind, that little girl would only look like her mom.

Dragging a hand down my face, I began to strip out of my clothes, carefully placing them on the foot bench so I wouldn't wake her. Once I stripped down to my boxers, I grabbed a blanket from the end of the bed, gently padded toward my spot, and reached for my pillow. I'd sleep in the chair again, to give her the space we both needed. I'd seen it in the way she'd backed away when we were in the closet earlier, when I mentioned our walls...though part of me had hoped she'd press in and deny it. I wanted her to fight for me, like I had fought for her. I wanted her to want me, plain and fucking simple. She knew what she was doing, just as much as I did, and still she wanted distance.

"Hey," she whispered, moving a fraction to pull the sheet up over her shoulder.

I shifted, pulling the pillow free. "Hey, sorry I woke you."

Suddenly she sat up, the sheet falling to her breasts. "What are you doing?"

"Just grabbing my bedding for the chair."

It was too dark to see if hurt flashed in her eyes, but her tone revealed as much. "What are you talking about? I told you this bed is big enough."

I couldn't sleep next to her. It would start to feel too real.

"I'm okay on the chair."

She moved, losing the sheet, revealing she wasn't wearing anything except maybe some underwear. I swallowed, thankful the shadows were mostly concealing her.

"I'll throw on some pajamas so you're not uncomfortable." She turned, tossing the sheet aside.

"No. It's not that—get back in bed." I moved until I was next to her.

My hands were on her shoulders, her face tipped back, looking up at me.

She whispered, "I want you to sleep here...I feel safer when you're next to me."

I pushed a few stray strands out of her eyes and tucked them behind her ear before leaning down and kissing her on top of her head.

"Okay."

Her smile was enough to get me moving until I was crawling across the mattress and settling in next to her. She pulled the sheet over us and snuggled into the crook of my arm.

"Please don't try to sleep apart from me again."

I smirked at how tired she must have been, her little slur evident. I rubbed her shoulder, staring up at the ceiling. My chest was doing that strange ache where all I wanted was for this to be real. Eventually I closed my eyes and said the only thing I could.

"Always."

CHAPTER TWENTY-TWO

Taylor

Getting back to normal was an effort.

Juan had promised he was handling the deal with my father even after I offered to be the point of contact so he didn't have to speak with my father or go any further into this thing than he needed to. Juan had laughed, kissed my hairline, and told me not to worry about it, but I did, and I couldn't stop. I was planning a way out of this; I just needed to know what my father was planning and where he was staying while in North Carolina.

Resuming school was key to feeling back to normal. Juan had told me his men would be watching from afar, but I never saw any of them. He, however, was ever present.

My feet ached, and my back too, so I sat in the uncomfortable wooden chair with my eyes closed in front of a plate full of food I was slightly too exhausted to even eat.

"I think you might be ready for maternity leave, babe." A smooth voice skittered down my spine as warm fingers brushed along the nape of my neck. My eyes popped open right as Juan spun the chair next to me and straddled it.

"I am taking it in November. I can hold off until then."

"You just yawned twice." He smiled, brushing his knuckles down my face.

I still wasn't sure how to react around him. He'd held me and touched me the other day, at my request. Since then, he'd been careful to treat me as if I was made of glass and a single press of his finger to my skin would shatter me. At night, he'd slide into bed late, and I always woke up each morning, somehow cocooned in his arms, but he'd merely let out a heavy sigh and quickly get out of bed so nothing would happen between us. It was getting annoying.

I wouldn't pressure him to actually treat me like we were in a real relationship. He was already doing enough, but he'd gone so far that day of the ultrasound, and part of me thought he wouldn't mind doing that again...or more than that. But that had been because I'd asked him to. I wasn't eager to do that again; it made me feel like I was using him somehow. So, when I would wake up in the middle of the night and see that he was asleep, I'd head to the bathroom to relieve the pressure my hormones kept building between my thighs. It was partly why exhaustion had taken over my life so completely.

"What if you don't make it...do you have a backup plan in place?" Juan leaned forward, snagging an apple slice off my tray. His jaw worked in a delicious manner while he chewed. The light cutting through the tall windows in the cafeteria worked to his benefit, casting him in a glow too brilliant to handle.

I shrugged, grabbing for my water. "I'm prepping to finish classes online, so I guess that's my backup plan."

Juan's eyes settled on me in a gentle way, silent and careful, almost like he was worried I'd catch the concern lining his sharp features. His whiskey eyes darted down to the tray, and his jaw clenched tight. People walked around our table, a few people casting glances in our direction. A small group of girls gathered in a cluster two tables over, and at least four of them kept glancing over with wide eyes and gasping shock.

"I think your friend is curious about this development," I said, my eyes staying on the group of girls. I knew Angela, the girl who'd been in the locker room with him, was in the center of the cluster, but I wasn't sure if Juan knew, or worse…if he cared.

He didn't even turn around, and shit, it did something to my chest.

"Not worried about anyone in here but you."

Then why wouldn't he touch me? He was hard for me all the damn time; he just never did anything about it. It was so difficult to decipher his true feelings for me, but maybe there weren't any left. Maybe he just felt duty-bound to protect a pregnant mother, and sometimes he got hard because I had a pair of boobs and a vagina.

Maybe there was nothing left but his concern for me as Mallory's little sister.

I noticed his gaze hadn't left mine, even while he ate my lunch.

"I think…" He dipped his head, which forced his hair to shift, and I found myself desperate to run my fingers through the glossy strands. "I think I should be seen with you here…Ivan is keeping tabs on you, so we need to make sure it seems like we're together."

My chest pinched tight. Sometimes it was easy to forget that Juan saw me as a duty, a job to complete. I knew it was ridiculous to ask that he see me as anything more, which was why he was still putting distance between us, but hurt found a way between my ribs anyway.

"What did you have in mind?" I ducked my head to hide my emotions.

Looking up just in time, I caught a smile displacing his furrowed brow and contemplative features. How could I not fall in love with him? It was impossible.

"Stand up," he ordered, moving his own chair and grabbing his backpack.

I slowly stood, already knowing he'd grab my bag for me. Then before I had a chance to even catch my breath, his hands were around me, cradling my hip and bracing my jaw. His lips caught mine in a possessive move and he moved his head to the side, sliding his mouth against mine, leaving no room for anyone in the cafeteria to question our relationship or what it was we were doing. I returned the kiss with fervor, because I'd already been so desperate to feel his hands and lips on me again.

Tears nearly pricked my eyes as I leaned into his touch and met every sweep of his tongue with a fevered push of my own. He stood over me, his hand dragging up my spine until both cradled my head. It was the sort of kiss that would leave a mark forever. When I closed my eyes, I'd see the way his eyes shuttered with need before those lips landed on mine. When I slept at night, I'd dream of how good it felt to be held by him, to be owned and claimed in such a way.

Even if it wasn't real for him, it would always be real when I remembered.

He broke the kiss with a heaving chest and wild eyes that burned for more. He wasn't finished with me, and I hadn't even begun with him.

Turning away, he threaded our fingers together and pulled me toward the exit so I'd make my next class. As we neared the door, I found a pair of angry blue eyes pointed at me. Holden stood watching with his jaw set and a furious expression clouding his face. I saw him but turned my head as if he was no one of consequence...because ultimately, he wasn't. He'd made his decision, and now I was making one so that his daughter would survive.

♥

"YOU SEEM OFF," Juan said, coming up behind me.

His fingers ghosted over my hips before they were buried in his pockets. I was off because as much as I wanted to do the right thing and keep distance between us, it was absolutely killing me. The sexual tension was getting so insufferable that I had straight up almost humped the arm of the couch the other night. I felt like an animal in heat.

Juan would rub my shoulders, my feet, and my calves, would braid my hair...he was always touching me but never doing anything more. We hadn't shared any more kisses since the school cafeteria, and while we shared a bed each night, he kept it platonic. He held me, wrapped his arms around me, but nothing more.

I missed going out and doing my own thing too. I missed freedom and being able to just pick up and go to the store when I wanted without worrying about who was with me and which guard was assigned to me. I missed Fatima, but complaining that I was being guarded and kept safe would only prove how much of a spoiled brat I was. Juan had risked everything for me, and here I was ready to just whine at the first hint of boredom.

In an attempt to stay busy, I'd cook with Juan, watch television, read, prep the baby stuff…or I'd sulk. Today, it seemed I was destined to sulk.

"I want to go to the store to grab a few things." I let out a sigh.

Juan stood like a statue behind me, breathing warmly on my neck. I wondered what he thought of this entire thing. I knew he was still taking interviews for hockey; he just didn't seem to want to tell me. I also knew Angela kept calling and texting him. His phone was always going off with notifications, and even if he didn't read them or spend time looking at them, it bothered me that he wasn't just blocking her.

Why should he though? His relationship with me wasn't real…he kept putting up walls, and so did I, for the sake of this stupid charade, or for the sake of our own hearts. I just wanted it to end, but I hadn't quite connected the dots yet for how that would happen without involving Juan.

"Can I come with you?"

I turned, facing this man my heart had latched onto with such a ferocious grip. "Of course."

We drove to the store, and I walked hand in hand with Juan to the baby section, where my friend was working.

Fatima was using a scanner gun on a few items when we found her, and as soon as her brown eyes landed on mine, a smile crept up her beautiful face.

"Hey." I smiled awkwardly at her, feeling a little insecure about my fragile new friendship.

"Oh my gosh, hey…I feel like I haven't seen you in forever." Fatima walked forward and hugged me with one arm.

Once we broke away, she looked down at my belly and pressed her hand against my side. My daughter kicked right away, causing another smile to light up my friend's features.

"You're getting so big, oh my goodness. You have to be almost ready to pop, right?"

I rubbed a hand down my belly. "A couple more weeks."

Right around my birthday, when I was supposed to be sold off to Markos. That fate still felt like it could happen, as if it were lingering in the back of my life like a storm cloud.

"Well tell me everything—how did the appointment go?" Fatima's eyes went big as she took in the man who stood behind me.

"It went fine. Hey, this is Juan. He's the..." I started, unsure how to word the lie just right so she didn't think I had been dishonest with her.

"I'm the dad." Juan held out his hand, and she shook it, all while her eyes went wide, her arched brows dancing near her hairline.

"Well, it's nice to meet you. Sorry we didn't wait for you when we registered...Taylor didn't tell me."

He waved her off. "No, it's fine."

Fatima eyed me again, silently begging me to explain, but I'd have to wait until I had her alone.

"Well, here..." She walked over to a pillar that seemed to have a small register built into it. "You can look up everything she registered for here, so you're at least in the loop."

A slow and steady smile worked its way across Juan's mouth, and I nearly gripped his face and kissed him. "Thank you, this is great."

"I have to head to the back for a bit, but Taylor, call me and we will catch up." Fatima hugged me once more and gave me another silent look that told me I owed her a conversation.

"She's nice," Juan said, waiting for the sheets to print off.

"She's the best...hey, you know we can just look it up online, right?" I pointed at the pages printing. *God, how much stuff did I register for?*

He smiled again, gathering the stack in his hands. "Yeah, but this is fun too."

My stupid heart perked up at his excitement and decided to flipflop around in my chest as Juan walked with me, looking for each item like we were in some life-sized version of an *I Spy* book. He'd pick up each item, turn it over in his hands, and ask what it did. Currently, we were on a somewhat outdated nose aspirator with a bulbous end and long, narrowed nose.

"Stop laughing at me," he whispered, setting the package back on the shelf.

I wheezed, halfway bent over, tears welling in my eyes. "You thought it went..." I couldn't even say it.

"Why is it shaped like that then?" Juan argued, moving down the aisle to the nursing pillows.

"Because it goes up their nose!" I choked.

His eyes darted around, making sure no one heard. "Why would anyone need this much nipple shit—isn't it pretty straightforward with all that?" He eyed my chest, and I couldn't fight the smile erupting. I pushed his shoulder like we were flirting, and when the side of his mouth screwed up, I couldn't help but relax into the sensation.

He'd been climbing my walls day by day, metaphorically of course, but it was getting so hard to keep him out, to keep it clear that he was supposed to stay safe on the other side and I was supposed to find a small crack to somehow crawl back to a different fate, one where my father couldn't reach my daughter and I kept him safe.

"So, do you feel ready to have her?" We walked, still eyeing the different baby items, half of which I had no idea what they did, and even the nursing question I wasn't sure about. I figured it would be straightforward, but what did I know?

My finger brushed across a bottle set. "I think so..."

"You are." His eyes sparked with something I couldn't name. "I can tell."

My face heated under his praise, and I loved the warm sensation moving through my chest. However, a shrug was my only response because I wasn't sure how to respond to the sweetest thing anyone had ever said to me.

"What are your plans after she comes, after graduation?"

We walked to where the highchairs and little bouncer seats were on display. I fidgeted with buttons so he wouldn't see how blank my expression must have turned.

I cleared my throat, trying to stay positive. "Not sure. Just getting through the delivery first...you know, and everything." The deal, the getting free...the not leaving behind the people I loved just to be safe thing. That was on my dream board at the moment. "How about you?" I moved around until I could see his face in case he tried my tactic.

The shrug gave him away. "Just enjoying the moment for now."

His smile settled on me soft and slow, light as a caressing feather. I returned it, letting our eyes feast, climb, and devour...we seemed to thrive in the in-between, where no words were needed. I knew what he wanted to say, and I knew why he wouldn't say them. It was the same reason I turned away and gave a pained sigh.

Longing. We were both longing for what we wished could be but knew would never happen.

CHAPTER TWENTY-THREE

Juan

The weather had turned unusually warm, and while I was perfectly content with using the air conditioning in the house, the poor guys walking the perimeter asked for a break in the pool. Taylor thought it was a great idea and suggested we do a big pool day where there were nachos and margaritas for everyone. She went on and on about services we could call to cater both things and how we could even get a DJ for the party.

It was easy to see the old Taylor, the one who partied all four years of college and who had numerous flings and boyfriends at her beck and call. While that girl used to drive me insane, it was nice to see little glimpses of her every now and then, especially when she'd smile in my direction or run her hands over my shoulders while walking past me. It seemed like an absentminded movement, like she wasn't even thinking about it.

Our previous evenings where we watched television together had resumed, which made me happier than I could afford to be. She'd bring down one of her books and settle in between my legs, even if I was watching hockey or sports. She wouldn't even ask, and I realized I had started just opening my arms on instinct, expecting her to crawl into my lap. Occasionally she'd seem like she wanted to say something, or even do something...but she'd just settle for sitting in my lap and then snuggle into me. Other times, she'd come downstairs with wet hair, and I'd immediately start pulling her strands into a braid.

At night, by the time I got to my room, Taylor was fast asleep. She was usually snoring, and most of the time, I'd just stand there and watch her like a freak, but it was hard to believe she was with me...in my home, in my bed, curling under my arm at night and resting her face against my chest. I was already infatuated with her, but it had always been mixed with a little bit of resentment for what she'd done to me that day in her apartment when she said she thought I was Holden. I still hadn't gotten over that shit. It still burned in ways I was too ashamed to talk about.

I considered that it was the reason I kept my hands to myself at night. It wasn't easy, especially when Taylor would wake up in the middle of the night, horny and uncomfortable. She'd excuse herself to the bathroom, and I'd hear the shower turn on, or occasionally the bath. I knew she wanted me to touch her, like I did the day of her ultrasound, but I couldn't help but realize the walls she'd begun to put up the minute we started driving home. She was always letting me in, only to push me out a second later...and I was doing the same back, just to feel safe.

I tried to push those thoughts down as I walked out toward the patio. I could already hear the guys splashing and joking around with each other. Taylor must have been out there too since she wasn't in the room when I came out of the closet after changing into my swim shorts. The sun nearly blinded me as I joined the twelve or so different guys jumping in and out of the pool. A small group of them were huddled toward the ledge, grouped around something...or someone. Most of them had drinks in their hands. One of them tipped his back, creating an opening in the circle, and that was where I found Taylor.

Seated on the ledge, kicking her legs in the water, she had a pair of large sunglasses on her nose and that same fucking bikini I'd told her didn't fit her anymore. No wonder the guys were all huddled around her with that belly, that protruding belly button, and those full tits barely concealed by the scrap of fabric. Shit, the guys were likely salivating...but they knew she was mine. Why the fuck were they around her?

I picked up my pace, grabbing a few towels on my way to where she was sitting. There was a basketball resting on the concrete, near the pool house, so I bent to grab it then tossed it toward the group. It splashed behind them, getting their backs wet and making them all turn to see who'd thrown it.

"Move."

Their eyes went wide as they must have realized their fuck-up, especially when I walked behind Taylor and tossed a towel over her chest and lap.

"Hey, what are you..." Taylor started, but I wasn't listening.

"The fuck are you guys doing?" I crouched down to get eye level with my men. Three of them had already gotten the hint and swam away. Two of them remained, one of them standing way too fucking close to Taylor for my liking.

"You said you didn't need to claim her...which means she's free game. I see no ink on your chest, boss."

I stood, pushing my foot into his torso until he was flopping back in the water.

"Hey," Taylor whined, protecting her face from the splash.

I bent low again to look her in the eye. "And you, what did we talk about? I'm pretty sure you said you wouldn't wear this"—I put my finger under the thin black strap at her neck—"again."

She tipped her glasses up, resting them on her head. Her blonde locks were wrapped in a messy-looking bun, allowing little tendrils to tickle her neck. Her freckles were on display from her not wearing any makeup. She looked like home, like the rest of my life, and my chest did a pathetic thump at the image: her in the pool while our kids splashed around us, me holding a baby gently and carefully to shield them from the water. I wanted an entire herd of kids with Taylor, starting with the one currently in her belly.

"You said a bunch of bullshit then I stripped in front of you...should I do that again?" Those pink lips twisting into a smirk created a problem for my board shorts. Over my dead fucking body would she be doing that little routine out here.

"Get out of the water, Taylor."

She leaned back onto her palms, giving me a better view of those tits straining against the flimsy bathing suit. "Why?"

Even her asking was too much pushback for me as the leash on my control began to fray.

Bending down, I scooped her up in my arms then headed toward the pool house. Hector saw me coming, so he opened the slider for us, and Taylor waved at him, giggling under her breath.

My cousin left, shutting the patio doors behind him. Once I set Taylor down, I walked over and shut the curtains, which transitioned the bright room into gloomy darkness. With Taylor standing in the center of the floor, waiting for me...it was brighter than ever.

"What's your plan, Mr. Hernandez? You going to punish me?" Hips made for sin rotated as she stepped closer, dragging a finger down through the center of her cleavage.

I inhaled a silent breath, watching her draw near.

My resolve snapped.

I stepped forward, keeping my eyes on her. "I can't punish you the way I'd need to in order to properly teach you a lesson."

I smirked, but suddenly Taylor faltered...as if she'd just run into a glass wall.

"What...what did I say?" This was just like the last time, when I had said something wrong and she shut me out. I stepped forward until my hand cradled her elbow and drew her closer. She ducked her head, shaking it back and forth...and I fumbled, trying to figure out what it could be. Then suddenly I remembered what she'd said after her father had shown up.

"My father used to teach me lessons."

"Shit, I'm so sorry...that was the wrong thing to say." I rubbed my hands up and down her arms.

"No, it's okay...it's just sometimes that word hits me like a sledgehammer in the chest. I'm never fully prepared for how it will feel."

I kissed her hairline, gathering her in my arms. "Don't shut me out... I'm sorry I said it."

Suddenly she tipped her head back, giving me those ocean eyes.

"I won't. I want to do what you brought me in here for."

I chuckled, running a finger up her back, trailing close to the edge of her bikini bottoms.

"I brought you in here to watch you strip, then to see how much you'd let me get away with while I touched you."

"Why don't you do it then?" she whispered, carefully placing a kiss to my chest. My heart was beating intensely behind my skin.

Bringing the finger that was trailing down her spine up to her neck, I tugged on the black string until it fell away, leaving her tits bare and those rosy, pink nipples peaked and primed for my touch.

"Beautiful," I whispered, tipping her head back to capture her lips.

She wrapped her hands around my neck, clinging to me while she melded her mouth to mine, allowing our tongues to dance to an angry beat of conquest and obsession.

I moved my hands down to her hips to bring her against my erection. Of course, her belly made that trickier than normal, but I still tried it, which ended up making Taylor laugh as she kept her lips against mine.

In response, I shoved her bottoms down, holding her hand to help her step out of them. She in turn lowered to her knees and tucked her fingers into the waistband of my shorts. My erection strained against the material, popping free the second she tugged them down.

"Glorious." She let out a heavy sigh. "You have the most perfect cock, Juan. I haven't ever told you this, but it's a work of art. The perfect length, all dark veins, and that head—my god."

I inhaled a sharp breath, looking down at the top of her head, watching as she stroked me up and down and then leaned forward until she was taking me in her mouth. The groan I heard wasn't mine; even though I wanted to let a sound loose, it was the girl on her knees deep-throating me who was groaning like it was the most pleasure she'd had in her entire life. It was so fucking hot that I had to concentrate on something else so I didn't blow my entire load down her throat.

She let up until she was sucking on just the tip, swirling her tongue around the head a few times until she was lifting my cock and pulling on my balls, opening her mouth to fit one in fully.

"Fuck!" My hips jerked forward with the sensation. No one had ever done that to me, and damn...it felt really good.

She continued to suck then moved to the next one, repeating the process while precum leaked down my shaft.

"You weeping for me, baby?" she murmured with hooded eyes. Sitting up, she released my dick, licking up the precum that coated it.

I rocked my hips to match the rhythm she'd picked back up, until I pulled completely out and gripped my shaft, pumping it until ribbons of white shot out, landing all over Taylor's chest.

Her lips twisted into a seductive smile while she rubbed the mess into her skin, over her nipples, and then took my seed and rubbed it in between her legs. I was already ready to fuck her, but that image had me hard as stone, nearly in pain from how badly I needed to be inside her. Taylor reached her hand out for help up, and as soon as I lifted her, she let out a pleased sigh and walked past me to the bathroom.

I turned to watch as she cleaned up, curious what on earth she was doing.

"It's really weird...getting you off felt just as good as if it were me getting off, and now I'm sleepy. Come lie down with me."

I smothered a laugh, because how could I say no to that?

An eighty-inch television displayed some TV show while we crawled into the massive bed, and Taylor pressed her cheek into my chest, closing her eyes.

My hand went to her back, my fingers trailing down her smooth skin while a cool breeze came in from the oscillating fan.

"What do these mean?" She ran her fingers down the black numbers along my forearms.

"Seven-one-seven means perseverance...a long time ago, someone decided those numbers would outline the parameters of our family, along with the black heart. So, when people see those digits with the black heart, they know who we are...where we come from."

She sighed, running her finger along my throat. Sometimes I

wondered how she viewed me, how she viewed my family. There was a small speck of pride over what my family had built, but it was minuscule. My overwhelming hatred for it smothered the feeling. I didn't need her approval or her understanding, or for her to know that the tattoos had been forced on me at the age of thirteen by my father.

"What did that guy mean, about being claimed? I saw a few guys with black hearts inked on their chests…does that have something to do with it?" Taylor asked with a yawn.

I smiled, wrapping a few of the loose strands of her hair around my finger.

"In El Peligro, our calling card is the king of hearts, and on each one is a black heart."

"The leaking ink heart, right?" She yawned again.

I smirked, trying not to be affected by the way her naked skin felt against mine.

"Yeah, it means someone is waiting for them at home. In a way it's like a wedding ring. If one of the guys comes up dead or missing a few fingers, at least we know there's someone waiting back home. When you ink that heart onto your chest, it's for life. It's as close to claiming a mate that we get."

She smiled against my chest. "Like animals?"

I laughed. "Guess so. It's also a way that men know to back off…if someone has a black heart inked onto their skin and is seen with a woman, socially or physically, everyone knows she's completely off limits."

"So, I'm technically still fair game, because there's no ink stain on your chest?" She was smiling again, like this was a joke.

"Yeah, pretty much." I hated that we were talking about this. I hadn't told her that getting that inked meant your loyalty to El Peligro, that once you committed to the black heart, you'd essentially agreed to give away the rest of your body and soul to the gang, and I wasn't ready to do that. I was still planning a way out of this shit.

"Poor you, you'll just have to deal with guys hitting on your fake fiancée."

I reached down and pinched her ass. She gave a little yelp while giggling.

"Or I can make you moan my name so loud no one out there would question it."

She laughed, and the sound was like sunbeams breaking through storm clouds.

"You finally ready to fuck me, Juan? You seemed so reluctant..." Her blue eyes held a challenge. She knew I had been holding back and for good reason. I wasn't ready to hand it all over to her yet. When I fucked her, I wanted her to be mine.

Giving her a wicked smile, I said, "No, just ready to make you come so hard you see stars."

"Baby, you make me see stars regardless of what we're doing." Her confession was soft, but the words landed like boulders in my stomach. That felt a lot like it was real, real enough that it made my breath hitch.

"How would you have me take you, hmm?" I moved until I was hovering over her.

That blonde hair splayed out on the pillow beneath her, and her pink lips twisted into a smile she kept trying to fight.

"Any way you want to. I mean, pretty much any position is safe... that's what one of the on-call doctors said."

"Is that so?"

Pink invaded her neck and face as she ran her fingers along my chest. "I've actually kind of been dying to know what it feels like to...um..."

"Don't be shy. We're way past that."

She squirmed as I casually pulled her hands together until her wrists were pinned in place above her.

"Uh...I want to know what it feels like to ride you...like, if it's too big, or just...I don't know...how it would feel, I guess."

"Hmmm." I held her wrists captive at the base of the headboard and trailed down her body with my lips and tongue, sucking on her hardened nipples, then over her belly button. "Let's see how wet you are." I moved my free hand down until I was gently pressing into her slick entrance.

Letting out a hiss, I shook my head. "You're wet, but not quite wet enough. I'm going to need to fix that."

I released her with a lingering press into her skin, hoping she knew it was a veiled promise for future fun. Then I moved down her body, carefully lifting her knees until I pushed on the backs of her thighs and her left leg was thrown over my shoulder. My tongue darted out, sweeping through her core.

"Oh god." She cried out as I repeated the process, swiping up and down her cunt.

I pressed my tongue flat against her. "So perfect, so fucking delicious." I sucked her clit into my mouth before pressing my thumb against her asshole.

"Juan." She moaned, tugging on my hair.

That was probably enough foreplay for her. She was likely going to be too sensitive if I made her come then tried to fuck her.

Giving in, I turned until I was lying flat on my back. "You win. Take what you want."

A fire lit in her eyes as she scrambled to her knees.

"You sure?"

My dick jumped at her eagerness. "Fucking positive, baby."

"Um...are you, uh...have you been with anyone?" She hesitated while rubbing her hand up and down my shaft.

I chuckled. If she only knew. "No, I haven't had sex in over a year, and it's entirely your fault...but I'm clean."

"Yay, me too. Okay, here we go." She bypassed my comment about it being her fault, which was fine; that would lead to a conversation we likely weren't ready to have.

Narrowing her eyes on my dick, she sat on her knees, seeming a little lost.

"What's the problem, babe?"

"I'm trying to figure out how to get it to fit."

That made me laugh again, a full one that made my chest ache. Before I could respond, she was doing some kind of low squat, hovering over my dick while trying to guide it into her pussy. She went slow, pushing the head up and down her entrance, coating it with her arousal. She hummed and moaned while she slowly lowered herself onto me, inch by inch, stopping every few seconds.

"Is that too much?" I tilted my head, watching...nervous that I might hurt her.

She shook her head, a pink flush working its way up her neck. "No, you're just big, and that's perfect, but it's a lot of sensations...I want to make sure the baby is okay."

That freaked me out. "You said the doctor approved." My tone sounded strained as I lifted my head to watch her mount me.

"She did. She said this is good for me, as long as it's comfortable. I'm just making sure it is."

I watched in horror as she kept lowering herself, sliding down my dick, each spare inch of skin disappearing inside of her. Finally, there was nothing left. She was completely full, and I was holding my breath.

The sensation, being bare...I'd never gone bareback with anyone. I hissed, my hands going to her hips as her eyes went wide, and before I even had a chance to adjust, she was rotating her hips forward.

"Oh my god, Juan. This is..." She gasped, putting her hands on my lower abdomen while she fucked me. "This is more than I thought it would be. Oh god." She threw her head back, rocking forward.

I was careful, jutting my hips up, but just a little bit. I was terrified of hurting her, so I just let her grind against me as needed while moving as much as I could without fucking her into oblivion. This must have been some cosmic joke, to finally have this girl and have to show restraint.

"You have to go harder than that, Juan. I need it harder."

"The baby..." I gasped as she moved. "I don't want to hurt the baby."

"You're not going to, I promise you. It's okay, please just move. I'm begging you."

Fine. *Fuck.* I let go jutting my hips up to meet hers, letting out a groan as ecstasy pummeled through me like liquid heat. My movements increased in speed while her hips rocked faster and faster, her hands moving to her tits, pinching her nipples while her eyes watched the ceiling and her mouth gaped.

"I'm coming. Oh my god. Oh my god. This is...fuck, Juan." She screamed while I continued pumping my cock. I wanted to flip us, get her up on all fours, get her against the wall, in the pool...but all of that would need to wait.

I came with a groan and a myriad of muttered curse words. One year without fucking. Well, more than a year. I couldn't even remember the last girl, but she was blonde, and I had imagined Taylor while I did her.

Now, here, with my eyes open, watching as Taylor came down from her orgasm, it was making things in my head and heart muddled. I'd been falling for her far longer than I was comfortable admitting, but these last few weeks felt like she'd fallen too, and now at the bottom, there was nothing left but this...us...our bodies finally catching fire after breaking against each other, over and over, like two stones. I couldn't withstand being away from her, and now that we'd crossed this line, I worried she'd chalk it up to something physical when it was far deeper for me.

She carefully crawled off, lying next to me while my seed made a mess between her thighs. She held her belly while she worked to catch her breath.

"You okay? Is she okay?" I gently rubbed my hand down her stomach.

Taylor smiled at me, brushing her fingers through my hair. "We're great. I just haven't had an orgasm like that in...um...I think forever, and it feels amazing. I feel like I'm about to go into a coma."

I got up, walking toward the linen closet Taylor had found before, and pulled out a rag. Rinsing it with warm water, I brought it back and carefully wiped between her thighs, cleaning her up. Then I pulled the sheet back over her.

"Sleep, baby," I whispered before tossing the rag in the hamper and crawling in beside her.

CHAPTER TWENTY-FOUR

Taylor

November had snuck up on us, giving me mere weeks before the baby came. My routine with Juan felt real, comfortable. The only thing that reminded me that it wasn't was when I'd see my father's men lingering around at school, always in places Juan wasn't or couldn't see, which was something because Juan made it a point to escort me to every class and wait for me as each one ended. There were messages and reminders sent, and Ivan had even shown up at the house a few times to discuss new terms. Apparently he wasn't happy with the addendums Juan had suggested after reviewing the contract.

It was difficult for me to push myself to care. I had to because in the back of my mind, it was the right thing to do—figure a way out of this and free Juan from it. Still, my father was getting antsy, and Juan was stalling. While my fake fiancé continued to push away more talks and discussions with my father, he'd keep me up late at night with his head between my legs or his dick carefully running through my folds.

He was careful not to penetrate unless I was the one who initiated the sex. I think he was scared of hurting me, but I didn't want to seem like I was a tease, or only interested in using him. I wanted him to want it, to want me.

Even though I wanted him as often and frequently as he'd let me have him...occasionally reality would hit, and I'd remember what Juan was giving up by pretending to be with me. I realized how much time had passed and continued to slip away while he acted as the leader of a gang he didn't want to be in. Sorrow and selfishness would battle it out for dominance in my soul. Usually selfishness would win, and that was when I'd indulge in Juan's smiles and touch. This morning, however, I realized sorrow would be a strong enough contender to force my hand.

I sat at the kitchen island, seeing Juan's mother and aunt there once again, cooking.

"Good morning." Maria smiled at me; her hands were full of cornmeal-like dough.

I returned her smile. "Good morning."

Juan's mother looked up briefly, her lips twitching before she relinquished a half-hearted greeting. We'd slowly been working on our relationship, if that was what you called it. She saw Juan and me kiss frequently enough that she knew we were into each other, even if it did hurt that she sometimes pointed at his chest and muttered, "Idiot."

It hurt. Unfortunately, I had noticed several people asking Juan something in Spanish and pointing toward his chest then shaking their heads. It made me feel strange, like I was a fool, being unclaimed by someone who was obviously taking me to bed. It was like we'd suddenly been transported back to a time where I was obviously the lover, but not the queen.

"What are you making?" I asked, even though I had heard a few people say tamales. I didn't want to seem stupid if I was wrong. My stomach grumbled with my question, which I quickly tried to cover with my hand, as if that would work.

"She's starving." Anna stilled her hands, raising her gaze until her brown eyes clashed with mine.

"No, I'm okay."

She started yelling in Spanish toward the living room, until Juan entered. For some reason my face heated upon seeing him, especially as his eyes settled on me, gentle as always. Juan looked at me like he was stealing a glance he wasn't allowed to have, a look he would be punished for taking. It made me burn in a way I had never experienced before.

"Why is she hungry?" Anna held her hand out toward me in accusation.

Juan gave me a little smirk as he moved forward. "She's always hungry, Mama."

He wasn't wrong.

Anna clicked her tongue. "Get in here and cook her a proper meal."

I stood, scooting the stool behind me. It let out a horrible squeaking sound. "No, I can grab my own food. He's busy—it's completely fine."

"Nonsense. Juan, come make her eggs."

Juan's hand landed on my lower back while his lips landed on my hairline. I melted into him instantly, threading my hands into the material of his shirt and finding harbor under his chin. He was like a fortress, always shielding me when he didn't need to.

"Let me help you at least," I whispered, already knowing there was no way I was going to sway him.

"Okay, grab the eggs."

We stood side by side with his mom and aunt while he made eggs, bacon, and toast. I grabbed one of my yogurts to pair with my meal then sat and ate my food while listening to Juan and his mother and a few other women milling about, laughing with one another about Juan's stepdad, Leo. They seemed to joke about his surly demeanor and how he didn't know how to season things properly. I was smiling, enjoying myself, this new version of Anna, and this little glimpse of the old Juan I used to know through Mallory, the goofy one always laughing and joking with her.

It was sometimes difficult to remember that the man I was falling in love with was the same one I'd known the last four years as my sister's silly, joking best friend. I was mulling over Juan's character with a smile on my face until Anna asked Juan about hockey.

"That man, Mr. Delgado, called me the other day. Told me to talk some sense into you."

I kept my head down so as not to let on that my ears had perked up.

Juan didn't reply, just silently chewed his breakfast while taking sips of his drink.

"Says there's a team from Chicago that wants you."

Was that true? I thought Juan had been interviewing for other teams—why would he suddenly turn them down? He hadn't said anything about it…but then again, our entire focus had been on my situation with my father, and the baby…and orgasms. There wasn't room for anything else.

"So?" Juan remarked slowly, still acting as though this wasn't news. His jaw tensed as he chewed, and I had the urge to shake him. Of course he should go after it. Hell, why wouldn't he go after it?

Because of me.

"So, you should take it. From the sound of it, the team is from the NHL," Anna explained, sounding increasingly agitated.

Juan continued chewing his food in silence, only reaching for my thigh under the island to squeeze it. Then his stool made that sound as he stood and gripped my hand.

"We need to get going."

I followed after him but gave one last look to his mother, who was giving me a lethal glare as we exited. Her whiskey eyes narrowed as she tossed a dish towel on the counter and began muttering in Spanish. By the way Maria winced, I had a feeling I wouldn't like what she had to say. I didn't like that Juan was doing this. I didn't want to keep him from it either, but what was I supposed to do?

A desperate burn began in my lungs, warning me to get some clarity around this entire situation. It hurt that Juan hadn't told me about the offer, but I understood on some level…he was still keeping me at arm's length.

I needed a second to think and process all the feelings that were swirling in my chest, making it ache.

Holding his hand, I walked with him toward the study. "He was supposed to give me until my birthday," I said as Juan secured the door by locking it. I paced, bringing my hand to my forehead. "That's still a month away. I want to leverage that, get a little bit of time so we can figure something out."

Juan's head snapped up as he turned toward me.

"Time for what?"

His eyes narrowed in a way that had me questioning whether or not this was a good idea. I didn't want to hurt him, but I also couldn't allow him to give up his life for mine.

"Time to think of a way out of this fake deal...so you can go back to living your life, and I can move on with mine."

Hurt flashed across his features briskly. He lowered his gaze once more before I could fully process how he would feel about my comment... but even if he was attracted to me, there was no way he felt the same way for me that I did for him. Memories of his pointed words about how he wished I would just disappear came rolling back into my mind. It wasn't like he hadn't meant those words; he'd merely felt it his duty to step in and help me, regardless of how he felt about me.

"So, you want to figure out how to get out of this?" He raised his eyebrow, walking around the room until he drew closer to me.

I scoffed. "This?" I moved to the desk, sitting on the ledge. "Juan, you were forced into this, and I couldn't be more grateful, but I can't ask you—"

"You didn't fucking ask me." Juan pushed his left hand angrily through his hair.

The muscle in his firm jaw jumped, making his face look deadly. The light from outside poured in, invading his study, casting a glow along the wooden desk and soft oak-colored floors.

I cleared my throat, barely speaking above a whisper. "I want to go home, see my mom...talk to Mal about everything. I just need some time."

"You can't talk about my family with Mallory."

That muscle in his jaw jumped again while his eyes stayed on the carpet.

My breathing slowed, unsure why that would matter to him. I told Mal everything...we were overdue for a conversation, so me not explaining this to her wasn't going to work.

"She won't tell anyone...you know that."

He shook his head. "This is part of my life I share with no one."

"Juan, she—"

His gaze burned through me as he turned his head to the side. "Don't test me on this, Taylor. I won't put my family at risk just because she's curious and has a noble sense of justice."

"She's my sister," I explained.

"And you're my home, yet you're leaving to go find something from that family I can't provide you here. So, I'm asking you to just leave my family out of it." He stepped closer to me, gently holding my chin in his massive hand. "But Taylor..." he whispered, tipping my head back until I was staring into whiskey and sunshine. *Home.* "This isn't fake...we're not fake."

I opened my mouth to argue merely for the sake of his own future, but his lips crashed against mine in a way that promised destructive and toxic methods of punishment, methods that involved red handprints across my ass and rope burns on my wrists.

His tongue delved into my mouth; his hand went to my hip, holding me in place. Warm fingers brushed across my neck and through the open collar of my shirt until he was palming my breast through my bra.

I let out a moan as he deepened the kiss, moving the hand at my hip up under the hem of my shirt and around my back. The cadence of him marking me was a song I wanted to dance to in the dark. It was beauty and pain, everything we both wanted but could never have. I wrapped my arms around his neck to keep him closer. The thought of losing him was too much to bear, regardless of how impractical and useless it was. Juan would be ripped from me regardless, this much I knew.

Juan broke the kiss, moving his lips to the shell of my ear, muttering, "I want to fuck you. Do you have any idea how many times I have pictured you bent over this desk?" He added pressure in the form of a tight squeeze to my breast, but the space between my legs was where I needed the weight. "I know I can't yet, but hear me, Taylor: I will fuck you on it at some point."

God, I was on fire. Clawing at his shirt, I lifted my hips as much as my stomach would allow and removed the space between us. Finally, one of his hands fell away from my chest and moved lower until he was flicking the button on my denim.

"Again with these fucking shorts." He lowered himself until his face was even with the molten space between my thighs. I stayed perched against the desk while he worked the button and slid the fabric down.

His face tipped back, locking eyes with me while I stepped out of the material and kicked it across the room.

The man kneeling before me didn't waste time. My leg was gently lifted, going over his shoulder as my palms landed behind me for balance. His hot tongue pushed through my folds and he emitted a low groan.

He acted like I was the sweetest-tasting thing on earth, especially as he sucked my clit into his mouth and brought his other hand up to work two fingers into me.

"God, yes." I tossed my head back, moaning while grinding against his face.

It was when he slowed down, removing his face but keeping his fingers there that I nearly burst apart.

"Look how wet you are for me," he mumbled, watching my sex while his fingers pushed apart my pussy lips. One finger went in, and then out, then two went to my clit and began rubbing in slow circles. "I'm going to ruin your cunt, baby. When I can, I'm going to fucking ruin you."

He continued to play with me, watching while his fingers moved up and down my slit, separating my folds, rubbing my clit. Every now and then he'd bring his fingers to his mouth and suck before returning them.

My hips bucked, begging for pressure and friction, all while I moaned and begged him to fill me. Subconsciously I knew the men could hear us, knew his mother was somewhere outside those doors, but I didn't care.

"Juan, I need you to stop playing and fuck me."

He leaned forward and pulled my clit with his teeth, pinching it with just the smallest amount of pressure before sliding his wet tongue through my arousal once more.

I begged him, tears lining my eyes with how badly I needed him. "Please, Juan."

Suddenly, he stood, laying a kiss on my mouth, moving that same tongue that was in my most private place through my mouth, devouring me, owning me.

"Come here." He pulled my hand until I was stumbling away from the desk. He moved the chair positioned behind us until it was spun and placed with the back against the desk. "Put one leg on the floor and your knee on the cushion here while your hands hold on to the back."

I did as he said on trembling legs, leaning forward, using the cushion of the chair to support my weight. I couldn't see Juan, so I had no idea what he was doing, but suddenly he was there behind me, touching my ass, running his hands over the bared skin.

"So fucking perfect for me," he whispered.

I didn't have time to respond. He was moving the leg I had on the floor back, and I felt the tip of his cock pushing at my entrance. I wanted to see him fill me, see the throbbing veins on his impressive length disappear inside me. I closed my eyes as he slid further, moving so slowly I almost screamed.

Once he was seated inside me fully, he groaned while applying a punishing grip on my hips. I rocked backward, desperate for friction, even though I knew he was pausing to help me adjust and to be sure I was comfortable.

Finally, he pulled out entirely only to push back in with more force. I bit my lip while I watched the sun pour in the windows through little gaps in the curtains and fall along the floor. I wished for a second that we had the house to ourselves, without anyone demanding anything from us. I half expected Hector to knock and interrupt us like he had every other time.

Juan pumped in and out of me, moving his hand to my arm so he had more leverage to thrust. I was desperate to have a rough fuck from him. I needed him to push my face against the desk, slap my ass, and ride me so hard I couldn't see straight. I wanted my legs to be so wobbly I couldn't stand any more, but I knew we had to be careful. I knew it, yet still I was desperate for more.

I pushed backward, which only made him pull my leg further, granting him deeper access. A grunt left him as his pace quickened.

"I need more, Juan..." I forced the words out through gritted teeth, imagining how he must look with his balls slapping my ass with every push of his hips.

"You need this, baby girl? You need me to fuck you harder?"

His cock slammed in firmer than before, still careful enough that I wasn't worried, but it made me cry out. His hand came around my hips until his fingers were buried in my pussy, fucking me while he pushed in from behind.

Just when I thought he'd increase his speed, he slowed down, making more measured movements with additional powerful thrusts. That paired with how slowly he rubbed my clit had me nearly coming. I finally combusted when he added pressure to my clit and thrust inside me, bringing his fingers with my arousal on them to my lips.

"Come for me baby."

It was filthy and so erotic that I came with a moan while his digits slid across my tongue and he emptied himself inside me.

He groaned his own obscenities into my neck while he finished pumping into me. He'd spent himself, but he hadn't softened, so he kept going at a dizzying pace, pushing harder and harder, fucking me ruthlessly while my hair was wrapped around his fist. A pinching sensation pricked at the back of my head as he tightened his hold and thrust.

"God, what the fuck is this...I can't get enough of you." He rotated his hips, going deeper and harder than before.

I had no words as another orgasm ripped through me with a throaty scream.

"Fuck, fuck...shit, baby," he snapped, breathing heavily behind me, finally slowing and going slack against my back.

We stayed pinned together like two pieces of Velcro for long minutes until he was finally pulling away.

Juan turned from me, buttoning his slacks. Once he returned, he had my shorts in his hand. My chest heaved, and there was the slightest cramping sensation in my lower abdomen, not enough to panic...but it was slightly freaking me out.

"Do you want anyone to go with you to your mom's?"

I watched as he moved around the room as if we were just getting back to business, so unlike it was in the pool house when he cared for me then lay next to me. The pinching sensation moved to my heart. Even though I understood why he was doing it, it still hurt to experience his own walls coming in to protect him.

"No, I'll be fine...thank you." I turned to leave, but his voice stopped me.

"Just be sure to come home tonight."

I watched the door, feeling like a hole had been opened in my chest.

He sounded like he was in pain when he added, "Please."

He cared if I came home... he'd called me *his home*.

"I will," I muttered in response before exiting.

CHAPTER TWENTY-FIVE

Taylor

I'd called Mallory and found out she was staying in Pinehurst with Decker, but I wasn't lying about wanting to go back home. I drove to Mom's, but neither she nor Charlie were home. So, after a shower and changing my clothes, I headed toward Pinehurst, ignoring the low ache radiating in my lower belly every now and then.

It was probably just in my head anyway, but to be safe I called my doctor and told her what I was feeling. She dismissed it, saying they were Braxton-Hicks contractions.

Veering into the gravel driveway of my brother-in-law's house, I pulled in behind Decker's dark truck and put the car in park.

Grabbing my purse and water cup, I managed to half walk, half waddle to the door with a bit of a wince. The Braxton-Hicks were kicking my ass, and if they were any indication of what the labor was going to be like, I was going to pass out.

"Oh my gosh, you're huge!" Mallory exclaimed, opening the front door.

I flushed red, loving that her rounded eyes went to my belly but also feeling a strange sense of panic that I was bigger than normal or something.

"Not that big."

My sister's arms wrapped around me in a tight hug, and I nearly broke. She was my rock, my person when the world sucked, and it had been sucking so much lately, but I hadn't told her about any of it.

Disconnecting, I tried to take solace in her calm green eyes and wild russet hair. She had on red lipstick and wore a pair of ripped jeans with a loose tank top.

Crinkling my brows together, I moved into the entryway with her. "Why are you dressed so informal?"

"I don't know, because I want to..." She laughed, walking toward the back yard.

"Not once over the summer did I find you wearing anything remotely informal...so what is going on?"

"I'm spending less and less time at the office, and we're training someone new—which means I'm writing more for Kline Global!"

I pulled her into a hug. "Oh my god, that's incredible!"

"I know...Dad promised it wouldn't be that permanent, so I'm excited."

She walked toward a new area that looked recently renovated. There was a small cooler and fridge space, and she pulled out two cold bottles of water. My gaze flicked toward the middle of the massive yard, where my sister's husband walked in a straight line, pushing a red mower. Bare skin glistened under the sun and bounced off the dark bill of his hat. He certainly wasn't hard on the eyes, but he wasn't Juan.

I looked down, feeling my chest pinch tight and an ache that went so deep tears began lining my eyes.

"Hey, you okay?"

I grabbed the water bottle she extended and shook my head. "Just hormones...and some other stuff. I actually need to catch you up on several things."

"Okay, yeah...I don't like how pale you just got. Not at all." She leaned forward, putting her hand to my forehead.

Was I pale? I felt a little nauseous and weak, but I probably just needed a snack.

"I'm fine…"

Mal gave me a reserved look but sat back and settled into her chair. "Okay, tell me what's going on."

I rubbed down the length of my belly, unsure of where to even begin.

"Did I ever tell you about my birth father?"

Mal tilted her head, leaning forward to grab her water. "My dad actually told me a bit about him. He sounds scary as hell…"

That was putting it mildly.

"When I was growing up, he used to talk about the people who betrayed him paying penance. I had to watch him execute those people… and when it was time for my own lessons, they were taught in a dark warehouse, where blood splattered the walls and animals were brought in and tied up for me to shoot."

Mal gasped, putting her hand to her chest. "What the fuck?"

I blinked, moving forward. "I was a piece of property to my father, a game piece to be moved around as needed…and he determined that he wanted me on my twenty-first birthday. It was how we got away from him for so long…my mom made a deal."

My sister's eyes went wide with surprise, her dark brows hitting her hairline. There was silence while she seemed to slowly connect the dots. "Which is why she married my dad so quick…"

I nodded, looking out over the lush grass, the fresh scent of it being cut hitting me hard.

Another gasp from Mal brought my gaze back to her. "Tay…you turn twenty-one in a month."

So I told her everything. I explained my father breaking into Juan's house, how her best friend saved my life, leaving out why he felt so empowered to do so. I told her nothing about Juan's family, just like he'd asked. I could tell by the way her eyes questioned there were pieces not matching up for her.

My sister was pacing the patio at this point, her hand at her chest. Decker had looked over at us a few times from where he worked on something with a motor near the garage. Worry lined his face, but he didn't make a move to come closer, which I appreciated.

"Holy shit, Tay…just, what the fuck," she sputtered, jutting her hand toward me.

I hadn't disclosed anything that had happened between Juan and me physically. For some reason, I felt like if I said it out loud and to the one person who probably knew him better than even me, our bubble would burst, and he'd be taken away from me.

"I can't even…I don't have words for what I want to say."

"You don't have to say anything. I have an idea of how to get out of this, and how to get Juan free of all of it."

Mal stopped pacing and moved until she was crouched in front of me.

"Look, I don't know what is going on between you two, but I know him. I know he would never do anything he didn't think through first. If he did that, Tay, it's because he wanted to."

I wished I could stand and storm off. I mean, I could have, but I'd need her help to get up, and that would sort of defeat the purpose. She didn't get it. She saw Juan as the nice, sweet guy who had become her best friend. He was a great guy, but she hadn't seen him as the head of a dangerous gang with a birthright he wanted nothing to do with. She didn't realize that Juan had had no time to decide if he wanted to claim me; he'd seen it as the only possible way to save my life.

Which reminded me…

"There's something else you should know, and I'll let you decide if you tell your husband or not, but—"

"Hey party people! I'm here—you have my permission to have fun now." A loud voice boomed from inside the house, through the open French doors.

Decker's younger brother Kyle walked through, holding a bag of chips in his hand and looking entirely different from the last time I saw him. Instead of the tailored, tight black suit he had donned while standing next to my father, he now wore a loose tank top and board shorts, his hair askew. He looked like a real teenager, and it made my heart ache for what he must have been involved in. At the sight of me, he froze in place, and his face went deathly white as if he'd seen a ghost.

"Hey." Mal smiled, but it only took her a few seconds to take in his response to seeing me, and somehow, I knew that she knew. She must have, because her lips thinned while her green eyes bounced between his tall form and mine.

"What are..." Kyle started, but he stopped once his brother came into view.

"There you are. You were supposed to fucking help with the lawn over two hours ago. Where have you been?" Decker snapped, and I wondered if Kyle's hands were soiled like Jakob's hands used to be. Whenever the older man would hand me a piece of gum, his skin would have red stains inside every crevice and crack.

"Sorry, got tied up." Kyle's gaze flicked to mine once more, and this time everyone caught it.

Decker's face was a stone mask as his eyes drifted down to me, back up to his brother, and then over to his wife. Mal did the same thing, and Kyle's jaw tensed, his eyes on the floor.

Decker snapped his fingers and curtly demanded, "Sit." Kyle made some muttered objection, but Decker only doubled down. "I said to fucking sit."

"Hey Kyle, where's Rylie?" Mal asked, bracing her elbows on her knees.

"Haven't seen her in a while."

Decker scoffed. "You haven't seen your best friend in a while? That's not exactly normal for you, is it?"

Kyle shrugged one shoulder. I continued rubbing a hand down my belly as a new cramping sensation started up, similar to what I'd felt earlier.

Decker lowered to his haunches in front of his brother. "What have you gotten yourself into?"

"What do you mean?" Kyle tilted his head as if he and Decker were playing or joking around.

"I mean, what has Scotty gotten you mixed up with?"

"Nothing...I told you..." His light green eyes moved to me again as his blond brows caved in. "Why? What did she tell you?"

I chuckled, because now it was all over for him, and I hadn't even said a thing.

"Nope. Fucking. No." Mallory stood and walked over to Kyle. It happened in a blink. Faster than a single breath, she slapped Kyle across the face. "Did you or did you not have something to do with the break-in and attempted kidnapping of my sister?"

My heart swelled at the rage in Mallory's voice, at the way her fists shook. To have someone love me, care about me in that way still completely undid me.

Decker's jaw clenched tight while his fists curled. "Answer the fucking question."

Kyle held his face still while glaring at each of us, until finally he let out a measured breath. "I can't tell you. I—"

Mal's hand flew again, this time on the other side of his face.

"Jesus Christ! Will you stop?" Kyle's palm came up to cradle his other cheek.

She pointed at me. "Tell me you had nothing to do with that psycho breaking into Juan's house and pulling her up by her hair while his men watched. She's pregnant, Kyle. Fucking PREGNANT!"

I flinched at how loudly she screamed. Kyle's red face only worsened as Decker stepped up to stand behind his wife. She was crying; somehow I'd missed it, but tears streamed down her face.

"Scotty told me we had to go…it was a way to secure our place. I didn't know it was Juan's house, or that Taylor would be there."

Decker let out a few muttered curse words while running a hand through his hair. "Why were you with Scotty at all? Do you have any idea how dangerous it is to get involved with that shit?"

Mallory's arms were a band of tight steel in front of her chest. Her lips thinned, and her gaze bounced between her husband and Kyle.

"Sorry if I'm not exactly worried about your safety at the moment, Kyle. You put my sister and her child at risk. If Juan hadn't been there, what would have happened to her?"

Kyle winced, ducking his head. "We had no idea she was pregnant, or that the kid was his...we wouldn't have broken in if we knew who he was. He would have come for us..."

"What is that supposed to mean..." Mallory's dark brows wrinkled while she glanced at Decker then looked back at Kyle. "What do you mean about not knowing who Juan was?"

Shit. I absently rubbed my forehead, wishing I was positioned right to kick Kyle so he didn't say anything.

Kyle glanced at Mallory then me.

"Juan is the son of Manny Vasquez."

Decker's face twisted in confusion, and Mal looked anxiously between them.

"Who is that? What does that mean?"

My heart rate tripled, my panic flaring out of control. He wanted to protect them, and I'd fucked it up.

"Manny was the leader of the largest gang this side of the country. It started as a cartel down in Mexico, and it's called El Peligro. They're more dangerous than any outfit this side of the Atlantic Ocean, save for ours."

"Why the fuck do you keep saying that? It isn't yours," Decker snapped, smacking his brother in the back of the head.

"Because whether you like it or not, I *am* part of it. I'm a part of *him*," Kyle yelled back, his throat straining to contain the rage he had rolling through him.

I yelled back before anyone else could. "No, *I'm* a part of him. You have no idea what you're doing, or how far into this you really are, or what is going to happen the first time you choose not to kill a child, or kill a mother... have you ever killed before, Kyle? I promise if you haven't, you will, and that sort of damage to your brain, to your heart...it won't ever go away."

I stared at Kyle, my fists clenched tight in my lap, my baby kicking furiously at my lower abdomen. One of the kicks was so hard I nearly lost my breath, but I gritted my teeth and kept a straight face. Decker shook his head, stalking off toward a different part of the patio. Mallory glared at Kyle before following after her husband, leaving the two of us alone.

The sun was out, shining down in a way that made the awkward silence stretching between the boy next to me and myself not as horrible. Still, it didn't change the fact that there were some unspoken things between us that needed to be cleared up.

"So, are you going to tell him I'm here?"

Kyle leaned forward on his elbows, resting them on the tips of his knees, then he tilted his head until he was peering over his wide, round shoulder.

"You're my family, Taylor. I wouldn't hurt you...I know you can't ever know if I'm telling the truth, but if Juan hadn't shown up, I would have stepped in. There's no way I would have let Ivan hurt you."

That made me feel better. A marginal amount, but at least it was something. I turned in my seat, ignoring the cramping in my stomach.

"Then help me...I need to set up a meeting, and I need to do it without my fiancé knowing."

Kyle smiled, laughing as if I had told a joke.

My brows caved at what might be so funny. Maybe it was the mention of fiancé in light of the swap with Markos and Juan.

I was too curious not to know.

"Why are you laughing?"

Kyle leaned closer, seeing that Mal and Decker were threading their fingers together and turning back toward us.

"Because your boy just had a meeting with *your* dad, claiming you two have already tied the knot."

CHAPTER TWENTY-SIX

Juan

Taylor was off today; I could sense it. Maybe that was why I had demanded her touch, her lips...that fucking space between her legs. She had no fucking clue it was the organ in her chest I craved the most. It was something I knew she'd never part with, and still I wanted it.

The fact that she wanted to go home without me, without protection meant she was planning something. I could feel it in my bones, so I may have taken the opportunity to cut her off at the head and make a deal without her. She'd be pissed, but if she had any plans whatsoever about doing this herself or doing something heroic, she was wrong.

The front door slamming was the only warning I had that my beautiful, fake bride had returned and somehow learned of our artificial nuptials. My guess was that she'd somehow run into Decker's little brother, a loose end I needed to tie up.

Her flip-flops slapped against the marble as she charged toward the kitchen. I had asked the men to start doing rotations outside the house, giving us more privacy, especially after how hard we'd fucked that morning. There was zero percent chance we weren't doing that again.

I leaned against the kitchen island, crossing my arms, just waiting for her wrath. If I was lucky, she'd end up wanting to take it out on my dick with her mouth.

"Juan," she snapped, coming into view. Her golden hair was down in loose waves, and tiny freckles were splattered like paint across the bridge of her nose. She wore a loose-fitting dress, which meant she had to have changed from our little romp that morning. She was all boobs and perfect, round belly, and my chest ached at her overwhelming beauty.

"Babe," I replied casually. I wondered if I should cook her something. She always seemed to be hungry these days.

"Was there something you forgot to tell me?"

I smiled, deciding if we were going to eat, it would just be better if we feasted on each other.

"What do you mean?"

She stepped closer, her blue eyes narrowing. "Are you kidding me? Why did Kyle say you told my father we are already married?"

Knew that fucker had told her. The fact that he had been close to her today didn't sit right with me, and I likely would be requiring a private conversation with the little idiot soon.

The sky was darkening. She'd left early in the morning, and now it was nearly dusk. I hated that my chest ached, questions dancing on the tip of my tongue about her day. I wanted to know how she was feeling, what she'd had for lunch. I wanted to show her the new baby swing I'd bought for her with the help of her friend from the store.

"Because I did tell your dad we are already married. Are you hungry—have you eaten?" I turned away, heading for the fridge. I could order us dinner; I could even eat some of it off her body. I was about as horny as a fucking middle schooler right now, and I needed to calm down.

"But why would you tell him that?" Taylor followed me around the kitchen, holding one hand out.

"Because it changed the game board." I ducked, looking in the fridge. My mom had made enchiladas.

Taylor crowded the stool closest to the fridge and gingerly slid onto it.

"I'm so confused. So, now you're...what?" She pressed her palms into her eye sockets. "My fake husband?"

I stood up straight, grabbing a water bottle. "There's nothing fake about it. You're mine until I say you're not."

A pink flush overcame her face while she shook her head. "This is crazy."

"What would be crazy is if you tried to cut me out of this...I'm half tempted to marry you for real, just so you can't."

She looked up from under her lashes. "Marry me for real?"

Was that shock in her voice?

I stalked closer. "Yeah, you know, you and me, baby girl...why not?" I shrugged, feeling a fluttering sense of hope begin to spread through my chest. I tried to stop it before it crushed me, but I wasn't fast enough.

Her scoff was like a knife against my chest, cutting with a serrated edge.

"Because we hated each other not very long ago, we're not good together, you have an entire life ahead of you with a beautiful wife and kids, and I have unfulfilling single mom sex with the single dads from school in my future. My highest hope right now is that I end up like my mom and find some Charlie out there who will take pity on me, Juan. Pity. My only future relationship will be one birthed from pity, and that sure as hell won't be with you."

A thick ball of pain swelled in my throat. It felt like I was going to cry or some shit. I cleared the sensation with a quick cough. Of course, it was just a joke to her; I'd known that even when I had stood in front of Ivan and told him I had already taken his daughter, told him he'd need to figure out his shit if he wanted anything from me.

"Well regardless, your dad thinks it's real, so just fucking roll with it, if that won't be too much trouble for you."

I stalked out of the kitchen before she could reply.

♥

A SOUND from outside in the hall woke me in the middle of the night. I threw the covers off, hating the feel of the shitty thread count, and maybe just hating the fact that it wasn't mine. After my argument with Taylor, I had ended up taking a bottle of whiskey with me up to the guest room and then proceeded to pass the fuck out.

I had washed down my presumptions with the burn of the alcohol and let my self-hate surface in hopes that it would drown. That was hours ago, though, and I hadn't even had dinner with her. I'd just left her standing there with that fucking comment she'd made. I had locked the door too, so there was no chance of her coming in and using me to get off.

I was bitter knowing that the only pleasure she had in me at all was that I was a convenient fuck, an easy way to get off without any drama or strings attached.

The sound rumbled from the hall once more as I moved, pushing one palm into my eye socket and grappling with the locked door with the other. I swung it open, grateful that most of the lights were out, except for the one at the end of the hall.

"That's my bedroom light," I muttered out loud…or probably, more accurately, I mumbled it. I wasn't drunk anymore, which meant it was likely in the wee hours of the morning, but I sure as fuck didn't feel well.

I stumbled down the hall until my room came into view, and the sight before me sobered me immediately.

"Taylor? What's wrong—what happened?" I ran to her crumpled form on the floor. She had her phone in one hand and gripped the sheet with the other. There, tangled around her thighs, were the rest of my white sheets, like she'd fallen out of bed…but… "Fuck. Why is there blood? What's going on?"

I pulled her face back so I could see if she was coherent, but all I could see were her eyes tightly closed and her jaw clenched shut.

She was making some kind of low whining sound, so I at least knew she was conscious.

"Taylor, baby? What's going on?" I moved my hand to her belly, and it was hard as a rock.

"I think…" She gasped, breathing in through her nose and audibly out through her mouth. "I think I might be in labor."

I grabbed the phone from her hand to check her outgoing calls; the screen was open on the dial pad, with just the number nine dialed. I finished it off, calling for an ambulance. The operator began asking a myriad of questions, and I put the phone on speaker so Taylor could answer them. She kept her eyes closed while gripping my hand.

"Am I going to lose her?" Taylor whispered while a few tears fell down her face.

"Shhh, no, baby, no." I rubbed her back, praying I was right.

I stayed there, soothing her back for ten minutes until a man and a woman wearing dark blue uniforms came running up the stairs with equipment. I moved so they had full access to Taylor. They seemed to take forever to check her vitals and asked her ten thousand fucking questions when all I wanted was for them to get her to the ambulance.

Then everything changed in an instant when the female EMT looked up at me with a calm expression and said, "Sir, your wife is in active labor. She's too far along for us to move her, so we're going to deliver the baby here. If you aren't comfortable being in the room, please leave."

I tried to catch a breath, realizing I was about to hyperventilate right there in my boxers. Taylor's baby girl was about to be born, and I wasn't even dressed. I blinked, walked toward the closet, and pulled out a pair of sweats and a t-shirt. Then I grabbed a baby blanket and one of the diapers Taylor had set up in the small travel caddy thing. I wasn't sure what she'd need, so I nearly grabbed every damn thing in the closet.

I could hear both of them talking in soothing tones to Taylor while they moved her to the bed. I heard one of them mention that they'd called Taylor's doctor, but she hadn't found a permanent one and like fuck would Dr. Kline be delivering this baby.

I pulled up my phone and dialed my mom.

"Mom, Taylor's in labor...I need you."

My mom gasped then muttered a few things sleepily to my dad in the background. "I'm coming, mijo."

I hung up and moved back toward Taylor. Hector and a few men had migrated in, hovering outside the door, unsure how they could help.

"We need clean towels and extra sheets. I need you to come and get behind her, help keep her propped up," the paramedic directed while she set up a few medical tools from her large bag.

My men ran off, hunting for extra towels and sheets while I did as they said. Taylor was in the middle of the bed, wearing some kind of soft robe that was tied at her breasts but opened over her belly; otherwise she was bare from the waist down. She had her knees up and was breathing in the pattern she'd learned in one of her Lamaze videos.

I crawled up behind her, and she immediately gripped my hand in support.

"That's right, keep breathing, baby." I kissed her forehead, feeling panic begin to swell as the EMTs began to direct Taylor on what to do. They said someone was coming to help deliver, but I had a feeling this baby was coming before anyone could get there, including my mom.

"Daya, I've never done one of these," the male paramedic said nervously.

"Patrick, seriously? Just get up there and help keep her leg up," the female snapped, keeping her eyes in between Taylor's legs. "She's crowning. You need to push, Taylor, okay?"

Taylor nodded vigorously while biting her lip.

"You have to keep breathing, honey. I know it hurts. Keep breathing. Here, you, hold her leg in place, like he is." She looked up at me, and I jolted into action, grabbing her knee cap. "That was a great push. Take a break, rest for a second, then we're going to do it again, okay?"

Taylor rested her head against my chest. Her forehead and neck were sweaty, and all I wanted to do was grab a wet rag and wipe her down. Right as I thought it, I heard loud shouts and a few slamming drawers and doors from downstairs. I tensed for a second before my mother's dark head of hair came into view.

Dressed in flannel pajamas, she walked in holding a bundle of dark towels and wash rags.

"Idiots, they know nothing of sheets and towels."

She wasted no time in setting them down and moving toward the bathroom.

"Is that..." Taylor tried to catch her breath while trailing my mom with her eyes. "Is that your mom?"

"Here, wipe her brow with this. Keep her comfortable, Juan." My mom walked over, chiding me. She worked at setting up what looked like a small Bluetooth speaker, and before I knew what was happening, peaceful music began to spill into the room, like something you'd hear in a spa. "This will help her relax. These lights are too much too. They have head lamps they can work with. Lessen the lights on her."

I didn't move, because I knew she was going to do it. I realized Taylor began laughing while tears streamed down her face. I felt a few tears begin to line my eyes too.

"Here we go, another big push, Taylor."

My girl made some sound I could only describe as a war cry. It was loud and terrifying, but it was followed up by the sweetest sound in the entire goddamn universe.

"She's beautiful, Taylor," said the woman in between her legs in a happy sort of awe. The baby continued to cry while the EMT handed the baby to my mom.

My mom looked down on the baby with a reverence that had tears welling up.

"Preciosa." She carefully set the baby on Taylor's chest and then waited to be sure Taylor was looking her in the eye. "It means beautiful."

"Hi, sweet girl." Taylor smiled, dropping her gaze to her daughter.

My heart felt like it might explode. I stared at the tiny bundle in my girl's arms, and with my head I knew she was hers, knew she wasn't mine, but as I looked down at her and saw how perfect and small she was... something clicked in my heart, telling me this little girl was mine. She'd be mine her entire life. No one would ever take her from me. I loved her as much as I loved her mom, just in a vastly different way.

I bent down, pressing my lips to the baby's head, letting my own tears fall. I was tired of fighting them. I was feeling so much and couldn't hold them back anymore.

"Hi, *preciosa*." I eyed Taylor to see if she realized it was the name I'd called her all those weeks ago when she thought I'd said cow. "Welcome to the world."

"Alexandra...Alex for short," Taylor whispered.

I smiled, rubbing a hand down Taylor's back. "It's perfect. It suits her."

"Do you want me to clean her?" my mom offered, stepping close to us but still giving us space.

Taylor didn't take her eyes off of Alex. "I want to hold her a little longer if that's okay."

"She's yours—of course it's okay."

"I've never had anyone that was just mine..." Taylor whispered, keeping her eyes glued on her daughter's.

My heart swelled again, thumping wildly to combat her statement. She had me. I was hers and no one else's. I moved away from her to hold back the sensation. I needed to stop...she'd shut me down just hours earlier, showing me that she didn't want this. Yet, two seconds into birth and I was ready to lay down my cards, showing her everything.

Alex stayed curled up against Taylor's chest, and an on-call midwife stopped in. She went over about a million different things while the paramedics cleared out and my mom headed downstairs. I stayed next to Taylor, listening and trying to keep up with all the terminology, the fact that Taylor was going to need to be careful when she got out of the bed, and that she'd need to wear a big-ass ice pack in her underwear to help with the swelling and tearing.

She ended up having to help Taylor to the bathroom so she could check a few other things before she left, so I got to watch Alex. The midwife instructed me on how to hold her, the proper way to care for her head, and how to cradle her so she felt protected.

I sat in the chair over by the window and stared down at her while I rocked at a slow and careful pace.

That sensation burned again, daring me to hope even when there seemed to be no reason to. I bent down and kissed the top of Alex's forehead as I whispered, "Hi, beautiful. You're mine...your mama doesn't realize it yet, but both of you are."

Taylor was fucked. There was no way she was getting away from this now. I'd fight like hell to keep them both; now I just needed to convince her I was worth keeping.

CHAPTER TWENTY-SEVEN

Taylor

THE FOLLOWING TWO WEEKS WERE A TOTAL BLUR. MALLORY DROVE over the morning after I delivered to see me and Alex, bringing Decker with her. Both of them seemed to fall in love with Alex within the first few minutes of holding her. Juan was never in the room while they visited. I saw him and Mallory have a tense stare-down for about five seconds, but Mal's focus returned to me and stayed there for the next week. She stayed in Juan's bedroom with me, effectively kicking him out, and Decker went back to New York to oversee things. I had no idea what was going on with my father, but Juan must have had it well in hand since he never seemed worried or anxious.

Juan came in while I was nursing a few times. He'd smile at me, ask if I needed anything, then leave once Mal came in. It was obvious they were in a fight and she wasn't speaking to him. I had a feeling it had to do with what Kyle had revealed about Juan's background. I couldn't get involved; it was their friendship and their issues to work out. I focused on enjoying my sister's help and having her close as I nursed and navigated how to take care of an infant each night. We'd stay up watching *Friends* and eating snacks we shouldn't have eaten, but it was the only way either of us could stay awake. Then when Alex would sleep, we'd curl into each other and pass out.

This process was on repeat for days, and while I loved seeing Mal, I was getting irritated by Juan's ghostlike appearance in my life. Finally, after the ten-day mark, Mal decided she'd go back to Decker and check on me the following weekend. It was a bit of relief mixed in with sadness. I loved having her be a part of this process, but I needed to get on with my life too, and more importantly, I needed to know if Juan was still part of it.

With her gone, it finally allowed the gaping hole between Juan and me to fester. Our conversation from that night hadn't gone anywhere; it had taken up residence in my mind and heart, and like that night before I went to bed...I wanted to talk to Juan about it.

That said, part of me felt I had pushed him away, and maybe that was exactly where he should stay—safe, and alive, *away from me*.

Once Mal left, Juan slowly started wandering back into the bedroom, especially when he knew I needed a nap or a break. He'd take Alex and tell me to sleep, and while I wanted to fight it, I never could. I'd pass out, and then when I was awake, he'd hand her back to me and leave. At night, he was in and out, sleeping while I was awake then swapping with me so we never really had time to talk...and there was no touching whatsoever. I felt like he'd become a stranger, and I wasn't sure how to rectify that, or if I was doing him a favor by leaving it. We repeated this process for two weeks, and each day a little more of my heart seemed to wither.

Finally, close to Thanksgiving, I couldn't take it anymore. I put Alex down for a nap, and now going on four weeks after I'd given birth to her, I was up and walking around just fine...still sleep-deprived, but not nearly as sore.

I knew Juan had a lot of family in and out, and I supposed they had decided to have Thanksgiving here at Juan's house...although from what I understood, it wasn't like typical American feasts. There were tamales and other dishes being prepared that I wasn't familiar with, but they all smelled so amazing that I didn't mind. With my lack of connection with Juan, part of me wondered if I was even invited. Maybe he just expected me to drive to my parents' and have it there with them. The other part of me thought this entire thing was crazy. I knew Ivan was coming…it was merely a matter of time.

With it being close to dusk, I wanted to see if Juan would sit with me by the fire while Alex napped in her bassinet in the living room and talk to me about Ivan, the plan…us. Everyone had cleared out for the day, save for a few men walking the property, so it would be more private than usual, which would be a nice chance of pace.

After looking for a bit, I couldn't seem to find him anywhere, until I walked past the front door and voices carried in through the open window to the left.

Juan was on the front steps…with Angela.

I stood where they couldn't see me, but I had a perfect view of them.

Her big brown eyes seemed frantic, her caramel hair blowing in the breeze. Juan wore loose jeans and the same white t-shirt I'd seen him sleep in the night before. His feet were bare, and for some reason, her seeing him in bare feet set me on edge. It was too personal.

"Just listen to me," Angela begged; her left hand reached out to grip his shirt.

My heart hitched into a tight knot at the familiarity of it.

"Your mom just wants you to be okay…she just asked that I come and talk to you. You have like three offers on the table, Juan. You'd be crazy to turn them down," Angela explained.

"I know. I just…" Juan ran a hand through his hair, shaking his head in frustration. "It's not that simple. I have obligations here."

The air in my lungs seemed to slowly leave, like a rock had suddenly been placed there. Was that how he saw me…us? An obligation?

"She can take care of herself. You don't want to tie yourself down with someone who doesn't even care about you…why would you do that? She'll literally just walk away the second Holden comes around. There's already talk around the frat house parties that Holden's gearing up for some big display of love so he can win Taylor over. She'd trade you for him in a heartbeat. You know I'm right."

What a little bitch. Even if that were true, how the fuck would she know? Better yet, how did she know about me being here and being able to take care of myself? Juan's mom had told her that much? This shit wasn't supposed to be talked about; lives were at stake...did she not understand this? Ivan had ties to the Russian, Italian, and Irish mobs; he was the Hungarian transplant who'd nearly usurped them all by making backdoor deals, undercutting, and killing off the competition. He did this because he was patient. He'd wait for the opportune moment and attack, which was how he'd built his empire along the east coast.

El Peligro likely wasn't even on his radar after he'd killed Manny, but now he'd systematically work to cut them down, especially if Juan didn't broker a lucrative enough deal for him.

These fucking morons were out here spilling all our business and would get themselves killed. With having previous ties to the cartel, I figured they knew this, especially Anna.

I watched as Juan looked down, and my heart ached, wishing I could see his face, even though I knew already it was likely pain etched into his features. Angela took advantage of the moment and stepped up, twisting her fingers further into his shirt and pressing her lips to his.

I waited for him to push her away.

I waited...and yet, he didn't look like he was kissing her back, but he wasn't pushing her away.

It was when his hands went to her hips that I knew this was it—my moment to set him free. He was torn up about losing the offers that were somehow on the table, another thing she knew that I didn't. He hadn't told me about them. She was here, and he wasn't pushing her away. My chest constricted as my heart rapped urgently against my ribs.

I didn't belong here.

I never had. This was just a game, and my time was up.

CHAPTER TWENTY-EIGHT

Ivan

I TAPPED OUT A BEAT ON THE TABLE, MIMICKING LEO'S FAVORITE song. My mom was droning on and on about something that didn't fucking matter, and I was trying to show some modicum of respect, but she was testing my good will. She'd sent Angela to my house, to my fucking home to try to stir shit up. It was absolutely unacceptable, and she needed to understand that it wouldn't be tolerated.

"Are you listening to me?"

I laughed. "No, Mama. I'm not." I stood, pulling out my cell phone. "You crossed a line tonight, and for what?"

My mother stared at me with watery brown eyes, the dim light from the living room barely casting enough light for me to see the concern in her eyes. "For your future, son. How can you not see that?"

"A future I don't want!" I yelled, slamming my hand on the table.

I hated myself when her shoulders moved with a wince. My father had been violent with her, always angry and brutal...I never wanted to be like him. I never wanted his blood flowing through my veins, and yet as this entire shitstorm with Ivan pressed against me, I found myself turning more into a monster than a man. I wanted to protect what belonged to me. I had to; it was a constant burn in my chest, a hollow sensation in my veins, an urge that wouldn't go away. I'd kill for it. I'd lose everything for it. As long as they were safe.

"How can you say such a thing? You worked so hard for it, only to have it ripped away from you by this cursed gang."

I rubbed the stress out of my forehead. "A gang my father and you ran, side by side. Don't pretend you didn't have a hand in it. It's in my blood, and yet you act as though you have any right at all to make these calls for me."

My mother crumpled into a chair. We were in her small apartment; they lived modestly and would take nothing extra from me or the family business. It was my stepfather's only method of standing on his own against El Peligro. She rested her hands under her chin while tears welled in her eyes.

"Why won't you do this?"

I crouched down in front of her chair and took her hand in mine. "Because I love her. I love them both. I don't want a life that doesn't have them in it."

My mother cried in response. In her mind Taylor only led down one path, and the baby would only guilt me into staying. She didn't understand that I had fallen in love with the idea of being with them, of starting a life with them. When Angela had come to try to stir shit up, something in me had snapped. I'd gone numb for a moment at the idea of Holden winning Taylor back, and everything went quiet in my mind for too long, long enough to miss that she'd started kissing me, long enough to realize the future I wanted was already within my grasp and I just had to wrap my hand around it and take it.

I just needed to clear my fucking head and figure out how to convince her. December was days away, and Ivan had stopped calling... which made my gut churn. When I'd told him that Taylor had the baby and we needed time to recover, he had made a comment about how that had no bearing on this and I needed to man the fuck up.

He was right, but only in terms of how I consistently chickened out around Taylor. I was worried she still felt the way she had that night she went into labor...like this was fake, and she just wanted a way out. If she was looking for a way out, that meant she didn't want me in, and that nearly ripped my black heart out.

Still...fuck.

What did I have to lose just explaining this shit to her? I supposed more rejection, but maybe if I hadn't dicked around about a sloppy marriage proposal, she would have taken me seriously. Now, Holden was going to come over and start playing daddy? Fuck him.

I stared at the different flower options for nearly an hour, not knowing her favorite kind. All this time with her, and I didn't fucking know what kind of flower she liked. It was then that I got the phone call that nearly made my blood go cold.

"Yeah?" I snapped. It was nearly midnight—why was my cousin calling me?

He let out a sigh, and fuck that made me panic. "Why did you text us to leave? I've been trying to call you."

I turned on my heel, grabbing a bouquet before I left. I dropped cash on the counter right as the clerk's eyes went round and I pushed into the glass door to exit.

"What the fuck do you mean?" I was almost to my car.

"I got a text from you telling me to pull the men back...that you got word Ivan was hitting the restaurant."

Fuck.

I started the car, tossing the flowers in the passenger seat. "Where is Taylor?"

The silence on the other end was deafening.

"Where the FUCK is she?" I gassed it, the tires squealing as I peeled away from the asphalt.

"Primo...you said she was with you."

I slammed my hand into the steering wheel as rage and panic began to seep into me. "Get back to the house NOW!" I tossed the phone and pressed on the gas, praying I wasn't too late.

♥

THE HOUSE WAS EMPTY. My men slowly began to filter back in, helping me search...but both the baby and Taylor were gone.

My stomach was tilting so much I was on the verge of losing everything inside of it, but I wouldn't let anyone see that. I just kept pushing forward, knowing we needed to check footage in the house to see what had happened. The study held several computer monitors that were connected to the security feed around the house. Currently there were feeds in the halls, near all the exits, and along the perimeter of the house. Pulling up the footage from earlier in the day, I began scrolling through times and sections of the house, then I suddenly stopped.

There, by the front door, stood Taylor, looking through the window while I was out there talking to Angela.

Dammit.

She saw Angela kiss me, and what was worse, she saw that I didn't push her away right away. Shit, she thought I wanted Angela? What a joke. I nearly laughed as a frustration so low in my gut nearly made me cry. She had left; I knew she had. I confirmed it as I scrolled through the feed. She hadn't left right away; she had waited for me for over two hours before finally giving up and leaving with Alex.

I couldn't hold back the anger ripping through me at a forceful rate. It had taken so much work to get the progress we had made with one another, and this was...shit, this was going to set us back, maybe even drive her into Holden's arms.

I had to fix this immediately.

Running upstairs, I made sure there was nothing I had missed, like her phone being left behind...and fuck, there it was on the dresser next to a note.

Gently I picked it up and inspected it, reading it without really processing it.

Juan,

You should know that I have loved you far longer than you probably know. I kissed you back in March because I wanted to know what it was like, at least once before we graduated. Then you kissed me back and acted like I was the air you needed in order to breathe, and it scared me because I could never endanger your life...so I lied to you.

I was never expecting Holden. It was always you.

It's been you forever. It destroyed me when I saw you with Angela at the wedding. I thought...see, it doesn't even matter what I thought, because there was never a future with us.

This was always going to end like this, because I already made a deal for my future, and the only thing that could possibly bring me peace is knowing that you go live yours.

Sign on with Chicago. Give Angela a real shot. Live your life free of this place, of the dark thing your father left you...I know you hate it. So, cut ties, baby, and be free.

I love you.

I'll always love you, Juan.

Think of me from time to time, because I'll always be thinking of you. I'll always be yours, in that place neither of us can touch but will always feel. We'll always be together there, in that place where the sun breaks through dark places and shines when it shouldn't. I'll be there loving you still.

Taylor

Fuck. That. Shit.

I crumpled the note in my fist, shaking my head, refusing to get emotional. Rage shuddered and quaked inside me like the way the earth shuddered before an impending war.

I knew of one person who could tell me where she'd gone, and if I was fast enough, I'd grab her before she did something stupid, like agree to go back to her father's.

CHAPTER TWENTY-NINE

Taylor

Rain whipped against my windshield as I pulled into the gravel driveway. No one was expecting me, so there was a small chance I had missed my opportunity to see Kyle entirely, but even if no one was here, I'd just sneak into Mal's old fifth wheel that she and Decker had stayed in when they lived here.

The side garage looked like it was open with the lights on, a sleek black car was parked inside with the hood open, and Decker's kid brother hovered over the engine.

Bingo.

I flicked my lights off, and right as I was about to pull up in front of the garage, right as my foot was about to transition to the gas, I saw a girl appear on the other side of the hood. She smiled at Kyle, tossing a dirty rag at his face, which he caught...gosh the smile he gave her was so sweet. I wondered if she was his girlfriend.

I smiled, only for a second, before I realized that girl looked around the same age as Kyle, which meant she was likely seventeen or so...which meant Kyle was endangering her by working for my father. I wondered if she knew about that...or wondered where that expensive car came from. She seemed more like Mallory with her flannel shirt and ripped jeans.

Her long dark hair was like a glossy sheet of perfection that surely belonged in a Pantene Pro-V commercial.

The girl's smile faltered when her eyes flicked in my direction and saw my car just awkwardly sitting in the driveway. Kyle's head peeked out a second later, his brows caving in confusion.

Shit.

I put the car in drive and pulled up closer so it didn't seem like I was spying on them...at least not any more than I already was.

"Taylor?" Kyle opened my car door for me, holding it while I got out.

The girl in the garage folded her arms in front of her, not defensively...more like she was afraid of me and those arms were supposed to protect her. Did she know who I was? It only worsened when her eyes went big and round when I grabbed my baby from the back.

"What are you doing here?"

Grabbing Alex's bag and my own, I shut the back door and walked toward the garage so I was out of the rain.

"I need to talk to you." I let the carrier hang in front of me while my gaze bounced between Kyle's furrowed brows and the girl's fearful composure.

With a heavy sigh, Kyle ran an oil-stained hand through his hair. "Yeah, okay...head inside, I'll be there in a second."

I nodded, giving the girl a small smile before walking away. Before I got to the door, I heard the girl mutter.

"That's his daughter...my dad showed me a photo once. She's dangerous, Kyle...why is she here? What's going on?"

So, she did know who I was.

Kyle let out another sigh.

"Rylie, just...chill, please. I'll call you later."

Oof. Wrong thing to say to a girl who he looked at like he might love. Not my problem though.

I walked into the small, attached entry and slipped off my shoes before settling into a chair in the living room, where I waited for the only boy who had a one-way ticket through the back door into the underworld.

♥

KYLE SAT across from me on a couch that had a flower pattern similar to something found in the seventies. He kept glancing at me then looking up, like he was uncomfortable. I could tell by the way his knee bounced in place and how he kept checking his phone.

"It's just breastfeeding...it's normal, Kyle," I said, looking down toward my daughter, who was feeding like a champ. She'd had a difficult time latching the first two weeks, so the fact that she was going to town made me ecstatic.

"I know, it's just..." Kyle let out a sigh, keeping his eyes on the ceiling.

"She's almost done, anyway." I rolled my eyes at his dramatics. Closing my nursing bra, I lowered my shirt and set Alex up on my shoulder to burp her. "Okay, it's safe."

Kyle let out a dramatic sigh and lowered his eyes. "Finally. No offense, but that was awkward as hell."

I laughed. "Maybe for you. I created a fucking human—you're going to try to tell me it's weird when I feed her?" I raised an eyebrow. "Besides, most of my breast was covered by her blanket. You're being really dramatic. Have you ever even seen a boob before?"

Kyle's face flushed a violent red. *Oh my god.* Was he a *virgin?*

"Just tell me why you're here."

I bit my lip so as not to laugh at how his voice cracked. He was still just a kid. I hated that he was working for my father and mixed up in grown-up shit he had no business being near. Yet, to get what I needed, I was willing to drag him into it.

"I need a meeting with Markos."

Kyle tossed his head back, laughing.

I frowned in response. "You don't have to be an ass."

"Sorry, it's just...the shit you've put me through—do you have any idea what sort of shitstorm has gone on behind the scenes? Ivan is pissed. He wants nothing to do with Markos, Juan, or any other fucking guy. He's got a price on your head."

My heart stalled in my chest.

"What?"

"Yeah, he wants to fucking list you on the black market, the sick fuck. Your only hope is to hide behind El Peligro."

I shook my head. "That's not an option."

The boy across from me leaned forward, resting his elbows on his knees.

"Taylor, you're fucked. If El Peligro isn't a choice, then…" He shook his head back and forth.

A few tears threatened to fall as I held Alex tighter against my chest. Maybe I could just leave. Maybe if I started over, he'd never find me…but what would he do with Juan?

"Markos will want the meeting, trust me…please just try," I pleaded.

I had no idea what sort of man Markos was now, but I was banking on the fact that his pride had been bruised by me exiting the marriage contract. He'd want me back if just to brag. That would place me under Mariano family protection, which was about as good as being behind El Peligro.

"I'll see what I can do." Kyle stood, grabbing his cell from his pocket, already pulling it to his ear.

♥

I WONDERED what the day would bring while I watched the darkness wrap around the house. I was still in the living room, pacing with Alex cradled in my arms while I waited for Kyle to come back down. He'd mentioned in passing that his mom was on a shift at the hospital so I could make myself at home, but that was impossible. I felt like I was waiting for the Grim Reaper to come and claim me.

Kyle finally came down the stairs, looking exhausted even though it had only been about thirty minutes since I had arrived. He didn't look defeated though, so that was something.

"Good news and bad news."

I walked closer, lowering Alex into her carrier so I was more prepared for what he was about to say.

"Markos agreed. He has an address for you to drive to."

"Okay, that's good..." It wasn't. It was about the same as being sold, but at least I knew who I was going to with Markos...and at least it would still piss my father off. "Bad news?" I asked, buckling the straps in the carrier.

"Decker called me, and Rylie called him..." His hand came up to his hair again, tunneling through it. "He's on his way here. I don't know if Mal will be with him or not, but he's not happy."

Well shit, I had better get going then, and fast.

"Send me the address for where I'm supposed to go. Here's my new number." I handed him the note I'd already prepared. I had a burner phone I'd bought on one of my trips to see Fatima.

Padding back toward my bag, I shoved it up on my shoulder. If I didn't beat Decker, he'd never let me leave, and depending on when Juan found the letter...I had no idea if he'd come after me, but part of me hoped he wouldn't. I meant what I'd written in that letter. I wanted him to have a happy life. I wanted him to have everything.

"Kyle...thank you. By the way..." I turned with my hand on the doorknob. "The second you get a chance to kill my father, you should take it. It's the only kill you'll ever make that won't make you feel like a monster."

With that, I opened the door and headed toward my ending. Whether I lived or died...a life without Juan was no life at all.

CHAPTER THIRTY

Juan

Gravel sprayed behind my car as I pulled on the e-brake, blocking in Kyle's borrowed shit from Ivan. Decker's truck was here, which was good…maybe he'd help me hide his little brother's body. Maybe not—didn't matter. The way I was feeling, I was half tempted to murder them both, just for the sake of simplicity.

I flexed my fingers as I slipped on a pair of brass knuckles and walked toward the front door, knocking politely. I had no idea if their mom was home, but fuck, at this point she wouldn't stop me…no one would.

Kyle opened the door casually, saw me, and tried to slam it shut, but my hand was faster. I grabbed the door and pushed it open, causing Kyle to fall. He quickly got on all fours, trying to get back to his feet while crawling to put distance between us.

"Fuck. Juan, calm the fuck down—you don't understand!" he screeched, still pawing at the carpet to get purchase. I walked up behind him and kicked him behind the foot, forcing him down again. A few lamps were on, but he nearly knocked one of them over when he tripped. Maybe I could use one and beat him over the head with it.

I bent down, grabbing him by the shirt and halting his progress. He twisted his face toward me, which was the wrong thing to do.

I didn't even hesitate. I drew my arm back, and my fist flew into his jaw.

I let him go a second later as he groaned, holding his face. I hadn't broken anything, but it was pretty fucking close. Hopefully I had his attention.

"Brass fucking knuckles...shit." Kyle spat blood out on the carpet.

"Stop it—why are you doing this?" a female screamed, running into the room, her long dark hair swinging around Kyle like a shield. She had pale blue eyes that shone with tears as she looked up at me and held her palm against Kyle's chest.

Decker casually wandered into the living room, his hands shoved into his pockets while he watched his little brother. His face was expressionless, like this situation didn't faze him in the least. His eyes flicked once to the girl, and their gazes seemed to lock for long enough for something to pass between them. The girl suddenly looked down at the person lying under her, and it was as though pain had suddenly been etched into every surface of her skin.

"You going to do anything?" Kyle yelled, aiming the question at his older brother.

Decker finally broke his stare with the girl and looked his brother in the eye. "The way I see it, little brother, you're headed toward an early grave. Not sure how to get your attention, so maybe Juan here can knock a little sense into you."

The girl hung her head in defeat, removing her hand from his shirt. "You didn't stop, did you?" Her whisper might as well have been a trumpet for how loud it felt between us. She was disappointed in Kyle, and the way his face twisted in remorse told me he cared what she thought of him.

"Rylie, it's not what you think," he muttered while trying to get to his feet.

I moved forward and pressed my boot into his chest to stop him.

"Are you working again? It's a yes-or-no question, Kyle," she yelled, tears glimmering in her wounded expression. There was obviously some story here, but I didn't currently give enough fucks to figure it out.

The girl scrambled away from Kyle, getting to her feet and running from the room, and that was when I took advantage and punched him in the stomach.

Kyle rolled over, groaning.

I spoke carefully, trying to control my tone. "Where. The. Fuck. Are. They?"

"Fuck this...it isn't worth it. She..." He swallowed thickly, trying to catch his breath. I moved to hit him again and he put his hands up. "Okay, okay. Just...Jesus."

"Start talking," I commanded with my fist ready to slam into his nose.

"She came here, asking for a meeting with Markos."

I didn't want to believe that. She wouldn't...but...fuck. She would.

"Did he accept it?" I stood over him, removing the brass knuckles, feeling my anger dissipate for a brief second. Now that I knew where they were, it felt a little easier to breathe. Not that I liked where she was, but not knowing was half the fear.

"He did...gave her an address for where to meet. I have it."

"Get it." I turned away to give him room, walking toward Decker, who was still just watching things play out.

"You done with him?" my best friend's husband asked me, raising a dark brow.

I nodded, pacing around the room while Kyle got to his feet so he could pull out his cell.

"Here..." He handed it to me with the screen illuminated, and I put the address into my phone while Kyle held his stomach. "You should know...Ivan...he put her up for sale."

My fingers stopped moving as my heart seemed to flop the fuck out of my chest. Impossible...but it seemed her own father doing something so evil was too, yet here we were.

"What does that mean?" I whispered.

Kyle shook his head, wiping at the corner of his mouth. "It means I told Taylor El Peligro was the only safe place for her, but she said she couldn't go back and needed Markos...said it was the safest place for her."

We'll fucking see about that.

Kyle grabbed a bag of peas from the freezer and plopped it against his jaw. "Ivan is after her. He wants to sell her as a form of punishment for going against his wishes. He isn't honoring any deals or anything set up with you or Markos."

"Then he's declared war against me."

I turned to leave, but Kyle's question stopped me.

"You didn't get that memo when he broke into your security feed, had your lead man called off, and completely emptied your place?" The shit scoffed, which renewed my anger.

I clicked my teeth shut. "Why, if he wasn't planning on taking her?"

Kyle shrugged. "To flex...show you what he's capable of. You don't think he knows she went to Markos?"

I turned to leave without replying because it was just fucking noise at this point, but Kyle stopped me.

"Wait, hold up—I'm lost. I know the baby isn't yours...hell, Taylor isn't even yours, so why are you doing this?"

I turned around, flexing my fingers, getting used to the pain still vibrating along my knuckles from hitting Kyle. I hated explaining myself. My decisions were always my own and I didn't owe anyone anything, but Decker was basically my family since he'd married my best friend, so I decided to explain for his benefit, but only his.

"If you ever find someone you'd be willing to kill for...I mean really kill for, someone you'd die for because living without them won't mean a goddamn thing, you'll do whatever it takes to keep them."

I didn't wait to hear him respond. I turned to leave, but the screen door snapped shut again as I scaled the porch steps.

Decker's voice stopped me as I reached my car. "Juan, I can't not tell Mallory about this. It's about two of the most important people in her life. She's still pissed at you about leaving her out of the stuff about your past."

The rain fell lightly against my car as I stared over the roof at my best friend's husband.

"Tell her I'm fixing it."

"That won't be good enough and you know it." Decker stepped closer, panic urgent on his face. I wasn't sure what he wanted from me, but whatever it was, I wouldn't be giving it up.

"She's your problem now. Do what you have to, but this is out of your league…out of hers. Her dad can't fix this. In fact, both of you need to stay away from this shit and let us sort it out." I opened my car door. "Taylor and I…we were born into the same pack of monsters. We're cut from the same piece of glass, and because of that, she's tough enough to withstand whatever is about to happen…you wouldn't be."

Decker's jaw tensed, but he nodded, letting me get in the car without saying anything else.

♥

THIS SORT of shit took a minute to work through. As badly as I wanted to walk in there and just start demanding Markos hand over my girls, I knew it wouldn't be that easy. I needed to rely on my family, on the power the name gave me. This was the entire reason I had agreed to claim Taylor in the first place that night in my living room, to extend protection to her. Fuck if I cared if she wanted it or not.

She'd have it.

She'd have me.

"Hector," I said over the phone, trying to explain the entire situation to him, bringing him up to speed. I'd driven to New York, walking into the house my father once owned that now served as the center point of operations for our family in the city. Each larger city along the eastern border had a main office or central location where members of El Peligro would meet, get orders, stand guard, and watch and move product.

Punching in the access code I had set up, I greeted a few men who roamed the property armed to the teeth.

"There's been news," my cousin said in my ear, and I held the phone there while moving through the large courtyard.

I eyed one of the men guarding the front door; he seemed hesitant to move until someone next to him leaned in and whispered something. He immediately straightened and opened the door for me.

"There was a leak in our communications. Javier says he's narrowed it down to the location Ivan was staying at while he was visiting. We think he's planning something."

I moved through an opulent room where multiple computer monitors were set up, and there were crates of guns and more crates of unopened shipments. I was going to shake shit up with this family, and I didn't really care who stuck around for it.

"Ivan has decided to go to war with us," I stated plainly.

"Seriously?"

I ignored my cousin's rhetorical question, jogging up the steps. Three women were lounging on chairs with their cell phones in front of their faces, their small dresses riding up with their legs draped over the sides of each chair.

I didn't have time for this. "Get out."

They each dropped their phones and stared up at me. Dark lips, long lashes, caramel skin...all beautiful, and all completely wrong for me.

"Now!"

They scrambled up and ran downstairs in a rush.

"What do you need?" Hector asked, likely understanding that I wasn't exactly in the mood to stay on the phone any longer than I needed to.

"Men. Guns. Taylor is currently in the company of Markos Mariano, and we're going to relieve her of said company tomorrow morning. Be ready."

"It'll be done, primo, but I just want to be sure..." Hector began but stopped like he wasn't sure he wanted to say it.

I walked down the hall and gently knocked on the black door that had a holographic spider sticker set in the center. The man I was here to see greeted me with a nod and led me to a reclined chair in the middle of the room.

"Just say it," I bit out.

Hector let out a sigh on his end, likely running his hand over his head. "You do this, and it means you're in...no backing out after this."

I pulled my shirt over my head and tossed it in the corner of the room.

"I know." I hung up and set the phone aside while I prepared for war.

CHAPTER THIRTY-ONE

Taylor

Heartache wasn't a new sensation.

My heart had been slowly breaking since I was young, since that first time my father shot someone in front of me, my ponytail caught in his meaty fist when I tried to run away. He wanted me to watch, to see what betrayal looked like. He wanted me to be a tool for him, a broken doll he could pick up and place where he needed me as he saw fit.

So this new feeling flaring to life shouldn't have been new...but somehow it felt different. The loss of a life I had convinced myself I might be able to keep...all it did was drive the hammer into what was left of my heart at a much more damaging pace.

I blinked, watching the rain smear the glass near my face. I'd been leaning against the balcony door for what felt like an hour, tucked away in the Mariano mansion. There was a courtyard three stories below my window, and inside the fortress stood a myriad of foot soldiers pacing the property carrying semi-automatic weapons. Surely, they weren't always this obsessive or alert...there had to be something that had them on edge, and the hope that flared to life like a tiny match was unwelcome.

I didn't want to think that Juan would come for me. If he came, they'd kill him, and I'd have nothing left but a broken heart and a baby girl who would likely grow up in the exact same fashion I had.

A small knock on the guest room door had me swinging my head around.

Markos strode in, giving me a small smile. His dark hair was slicked back in a menacing way, the black strands matching his all-black suit and gleaming ebony watch. He'd grown to be a handsome man, but he had a darkness inside him that matched my father's, so I found myself dreadfully repulsed by him.

"Just checking on you...and..." He looked down at the swaddled babe lying on the bed.

He seemed unsure of how to process her existence, but he was crazy if he thought I wasn't on to his ruse. He had picked me up at the meeting location the previous night with a comforting arm around my shoulder and a gentle welcome to his mansion. He'd even prepared this beautiful room for me, not pressuring me into his or trying anything reprehensible.

I knew he'd only accepted this as a way to assuage his pricked pride, that or he had another use for me because, for all his faults, I believed Kyle when he said my father wasn't making a deal with Juan or Markos. That meant Markos was now making his own plans, and he had just picked up two new pawns to use on his gameboard.

"Her name is Alex." My arms banded across my chest as I looked down at her sleeping form. Markos looked too, but nothing changed in his features; they didn't soften or transition to anything fatherly. Once, when my mother was feeling maternal and opened up about how she knew Charlie was someone she could trust, she had said she knew based on how he looked at me, someone who wasn't his child. She had told me he was the only man she had ever met who didn't look at me like I was a ticket or a price tag. She said his features would transform entirely when he watched me, and said it was the same way he looked at his own daughter.

I had doubts back then about that statement because he loved his daughter and treated her like she had hung the moon and sun. Now, comparing how Juan had looked at Alex to how Markos looked at her, I understood what my mother meant. Juan looked at Alex like she was his, his to protect, to love, to raise. Markos looked at her like she could prove to be useful, but he wasn't sure how yet. I wouldn't give him the chance to find out.

"How are you settling in?" Markos moved his greedy gaze to my cleavage, slowly perusing my form in a sensual way. I was still healing and hadn't hit my six-week mark, so there was certainly no way I could have sex...but I wasn't sure if Markos was the kind of man to care about details like that.

"I'm okay." I shrugged.

I had only told Markos that I needed to get away from my father and would find a way to secure all the original terms of his contract regardless of what my father said. Markos had said we'd discuss it, but for now he was happy to resume the planned marriage.

"Well, I wanted to let you know that we received something today. I'm hesitant to give it to you, but..." He pulled out an envelope, looking down at it with his dark brows caved in question. "I think it might help you put whatever happened behind you and get closure so we can move forward. I'm planning to have our ceremony take place this weekend."

My brows arched, hitting my hairline. "So soon?"

"I think it's best we do not tempt your father any more than we have."

I looked down, ignoring his smarmy smirk. Something about him made my skin crawl. I hated not knowing what plans he had for me, what assurances he'd made for himself where I was concerned.

"What if that's from my father?" I gestured toward the letter.

Markos gave me a little scoff with a lift of his shoulder then he handed it over to me. A leaking black heart was stamped into the middle of the white surface.

"Something tells me it's not." Markos ran the back of his knuckles down the side of my face, tucking a few strands behind my ear. "You grew up to be more than I imagined, Ari. We will have to get to know one another once again. I've always cared for you, even when I learned that you had gotten involved with..." He looked down at the letter in my hand. "No matter. We will right everything and put it behind us." He gave my face one last stroke before turning away. "I'll give you some privacy to read it."

I watched as he walked away, and once the door clicked shut, I turned back to the falling rain and broke the seal on the envelope. My heart hammered behind my breast, telling me not to hope, begging me not to give in to this feeling that began to swell inside me. The letter was probably just a response to mine, wishing me well and telling me to have a nice life. Knowing Juan and how he'd reacted to all the times I had brushed him off or acted as though I preferred someone else over him...he usually just went along with it.

He allowed me to indulge in my lies, even if it meant I'd drown.

My journal entry paper was used, the same jagged edge from where I'd pulled it out crinkling the sides. It made my stomach flutter for some reason.

Then, readying my heart, I began to read.

Lie little pup.
Lie with those ocean eyes.
Lie through those pretty red lips.
Lie with your legs wrapped around my hips.
I don't care for any of your truths.
Just stay with me.
For as long as you are able.
Give me your stars, your moons, and all your light.
We're monsters, you and I.
The darkness is where we'll hide.

I reread the entire thing ten times before I folded the paper into a neat square, then I tucked it along the same inner lining of my bag where I had my gun hidden. I ignored the tears that fell in drops against the leather of my purse and swiped at my face.

It didn't matter. His poem was beautiful, but it was pointless. I'd already gone out of his reach, and there was nothing left for us to do except mourn the future we were both now forced to live without one another.

CHAPTER THIRTY-TWO

Juan

I hadn't slept. It seemed impossible with the knowledge that she was there and I wasn't. The image of that letter she'd left me was in my mind every time I closed my eyes. She had tried to end this...she'd tried to walk away. Deep down, I'd always known she would. It was obvious with how we seemed to entertain the idea of a relationship but required each aspect of it to be guarded with a chain linked fence, like she didn't know how to love people without fences, walls, or rooms, enough space to keep her demons hidden away. My brave girl...she should have known me better than that. By now, she knew my demons looked just like hers, knew I had been raised by a monster too and the roaring in her blood was the same that echoed in mine. She was meant for me, and I was going to have her.

"What are we waiting on?" Hector asked, standing close so the others wouldn't hear.

My cousin had brought up all of our numbers from Rake Forge, Greensboro, and the other surrounding cities to convene in New York. There were armored cars, trucks, weapons, and enough members of El Peligro in one place that if the FBI caught wind of this little meetup, we'd be fucked.

"Just for my letter to be delivered." I rubbed my thumb across my lip, thinking about her reading it. I'd sent it that morning, and while I didn't know Markos Mariano, I had a feeling he was the sort of man who wouldn't shy away from letting his newfound bride have one last letter from the man who had claimed her without permission.

It had been roughly an hour since I had delivered it, so by now she'd know I was coming.

"Let's head out. Have all the men been instructed on what to expect?" I asked Hector as I pulled on a bulletproof vest.

He already wore one, along with his bandanna folded and wrapped around his head with the colors of El Peligro. All the men wore the colors...all of them but me. I would start instating changes in the family as soon as this business was done, one of them being the colors. I had a feeling I'd get some pushback, but with time, they'd start to see things my way. We could be a family...one of honor, one that lived and worked by a creed, one that helped and benefited the cities we existed in. I didn't want El Peligro to be a stain on the population anymore. I wanted it to be a symbol of honor, of safety and peace.

I knew I was stretching my hope and you can't ask a monster to suddenly shed its teeth, so I'd determined to be patient as we worked toward that goal, something none of them knew anything about. Once Taylor and Alex were safe with me, we'd begin to build that dream.

"The men know we're there to protect Taylor and the baby...but what we don't know is if Ivan's men will be there. We're all a little nervous about our numbers compared to theirs."

I nodded, understanding that concern. We'd tried to get a pulse on Ivan and his wolves but had been unsuccessful. "Just assume the worst. Prepare for Ivan's numbers, along with the Marianos."

"You say that, but we don't have the numbers on both..." Hector laughed like he finally realized how unhinged I was.

"We'll manage."

I knew it was senseless. Hell, I even knew the odds were stacked against us. I also knew I was risking men who would follow me in. For that, I knew I had to say something, so I climbed up into one of the truck beds and yelled into the mass of men who had gathered.

"We're likely outnumbered. They have the advantage, being at home, and this could very well be a suicide mission. If your heart isn't in this, leave. No harm will come to you, no expectations of blood and bond. I am doing this for my own gain, my own reasons. I can't ask you to sacrifice your life for my own goals." I looked down, seeing several eyes stare back at me, unchanging in their demeanor. "But...as your leader...I'm asking that you help me bring home my queen. She walked in through those doors as a way of protecting me, and I won't rest until I've pried her out of there and brought her back home. I may die trying. If I go down, I ask that you get her out. Get the baby out. Neither of them can stay there. If you're with me, come with us...if you're not, drive home."

I leapt down, ending my speech and trying to push past the nerves rattling inside me. My entire life I had avoided this, avoided my father's footsteps and the life he'd led...but for her, I'd gladly walk it out.

I didn't watch to see if anyone followed as I entered the armored car I'd be driving in. Hector climbed in next to me.

"You inspire them, primo...we haven't had that in a long time," he declared, sounding somber.

The driver of our car started north, merging onto the freeway toward the Mariano compound.

Hector looked over at me, his gun resting in his lap. "Did you ever know our gramps?"

I peered over at him, crushing my brows in question. "My dad's dad?"

My cousin nodded. "He was the leader back then. I obviously was too young to be in the regiment, but I remember him. I remember my pops talking about how Gramps was a good man. He cared about the things other men in the business didn't...cared about the weak and helpless. He inspired the men to be great, to do good with their love and devotion to El Peligro. He used this family to keep the streets of his city safe, used his money to feed the widows and orphans. He cared for people, and because of it we had more pledges and people asking to sign on to this life than we ever had before."

I was silent as the car carried us closer to my girls. My heart thundered rapidly as I heard about this man who shared blood with me...who didn't sound like a monster. He sounded good, like the kind of man I would hope to be.

"All I'm saying is...it wouldn't be the worst thing to have that kind of leadership again."

I glanced away from him, looking back out the window as a knot formed in my throat. I had assumed the men would leave me and I would ruin this thing they had created, but stepping into a legacy my grandfather had originally created didn't seem to feel like I would be losing a dream. I did love hockey...but I loved it like I loved football or any other sport. I liked playing it, but it wasn't my dream.

Creating change felt like a dream worth chasing. Being someone who created safe streets and helped in ways other organizations couldn't sounded like a dream. Knowing what was going on with the black market and human trafficking rings, being able to help...that felt like a noble dream. A small fire lit inside me as I considered what it would be like to help people with the power of El Peligro at my back. It would be worth it, all of it, regardless of the fact that I had already made my decision about staying. Hearing this only helped soothe my worry that I might end up like my dad someday.

I'd do anything for Taylor and Alex, but now I had a new goal in mind...something that felt fresh and new, a legacy of my own that would start an entirely new chapter for this gang.

"Once we get there, I want to take the lead," I muttered, still looking out the window.

Hector didn't respond, but I had a feeling I knew what he'd say if he did. He'd be right there with me regardless.

We sat in silence as the rain poured and we traveled toward the outskirts of the city.

CHAPTER THIRTY-THREE

Taylor

THE MEN AROUND THE COMPOUND DIDN'T PAY ME MUCH NOTICE. In fact, no one besides Markos paid me any notice. I wasn't complaining, but it felt odd...there was something I was missing.

It had been about an hour since I cried in my room, tucking Juan's letter away and firming my resolve to put my love for him behind me. This life with Markos was my future now, and I needed to get it through my head. Never my heart...it would never follow, but my mind needed to get on board.

I sat in a velvet chair tucked into a long dining room table, with Alex resting in her carrier on the seat next to me. I was unwilling to leave her with any of Markos' staff or maids, even if they were lovely women who seemed friendly enough. I wouldn't leave Alex with anyone.

"So, there are a few details I'd like to cover before this weekend, and I thought to start out, we needed to clear the air." Markos took a large bite of the egg whites in front of him.

I pushed my breakfast around my plate with a fork. A yawn overtook me as I looked longingly at my cup of tea. I hadn't asked for tea, I had asked for coffee, but one of the maids told me tea would be better for my milk supply. She was probably right, but I hadn't slept the night prior and was running on fumes.

"What do we need to clear?"

Markos shifted in his seat, facing me with one long arm braced along the table, the other on the back of my chair. I didn't like how close it brought us.

"We need to clear up this issue with your father...so, I've invited him over to discuss terms."

I scooted my chair back immediately. "No. He can't come here—he won't agree to any deal with you."

Markos trailed my movement with a confused expression. His thick brows crowded his brown eyes, and his lips seemed to thin.

"I think you're being a little dramatic...sit back down, Ari. We'll speak to him together."

Just as I was about to say something, the sound of muffled voices and movement sounded near the foyer, out through the dining room doors.

"Is he already here?" I seethed, lowering back to my seat, but only to dig into the inner lining of my bag.

"He is...he'll be having breakfast with us."

Shit. This was going to be bad. I had to find a way to protect Alex and get the hell out of there before my father sabotaged this entire situation.

"You don't underst—" I was cut off by a loud boom from outside. It shook the house, the chandelier above the table vibrated, and dust rained down from the ceiling.

Everyone was frozen around the room, including the two large men on their way into the dining room.

I slowly pulled my gun free and pulled the strap of my bag around my chest then gripped Alex's carrier with all the strength I possessed.

"Who was that?" Markos asked with an eerily calm voice, the kind of tone that pranced along the edge of a knife.

Gunfire sounded from outside and glass was shattering, but it wasn't in the dining room...it was everywhere else. The foyer, the living room... the cars outside. Everything seemed to be exploding as the purr of automatic guns rang through the air. I ducked under the table, dragging the car seat with me. I hovered over my daughter, protecting any open space that might expose her.

Shouting commenced, along with the sound of more shots and yells. I remained where I was under the table, but within seconds, there were large hands grabbing at me.

"No!" I screamed, desperate to fend off the person.

I reached for the gun I had set down next to the carrier, pointed the extended barrel at my attacker, and pulled the trigger.

Three shots quieted by the barrel pummeled into the soft stomach of the man grabbing me. Another man took his place, and I kept shooting.

Panic seized my lungs as I realized these were my father's men. Markos had been hauled out of the room by his own men, and they hadn't given me a second look.

It was telling enough of my future with the man, but I didn't care. At this point, I was just going to run away with my daughter and be free of these men for as long as I could.

"Come now, Aurelia, don't make this difficult," someone cooed from above.

My father's face came into view as he sank to his haunches, and I gasped sharply. His blond hair was slicked out of his eyes, but not well enough as strands fell into disarray. He eyed Alex next to me, and his lip curled in disgust.

I didn't wait for him to threaten me again; I pulled the trigger with as much force as I could.

But nothing happened. A click sounded. I did it again and again, but it was just empty clicks that emanated from my gun. I was out.

Oh my god. I was out. He would have me, and I couldn't defend myself.

"Climb out, little értékes." He laughed, his large shoulders shaking with delight.

I shook my head, climbing backward on my palms.

"Now, now...I'll spare your little child if you come with me. How about that?"

I looked around the table, seeing the chairs all askew around the room. Long legs stood in their place, proving that he had me cornered. There was nowhere to run. So, on shaky limbs, I crawled out and met my doom.

♥

MY FATHER STRANGLED my shoulder with his meaty fist and led me toward the exit. A man behind us carried my daughter in her carrier, and I forced my gaze backward, which annoyed my father.

A tight pinch shot through my arm as his grip intensified.

"You will learn your pla—" His voice cut off as we came to a sudden stop.

My eyes flew forward to see what had halted our walk, and that was when I realized the courtyard had become a war zone. Cars blown up, glass everywhere, a hole in the brick wall that surrounded the Mariano compound. In front of the exit were at least a hundred men, all with guns and folded bandanas across their foreheads, all save for one.

My breath hitched.

"What the fuck are you doing here?" my father yelled toward the man standing in his way. He was wearing a black bulletproof vest over a white t-shirt and dark denim tucked into thick combat boots. My heart swelled so much I thought it might burst.

He'd come for me. *For us.*

I let out a strangled sound as I tried to walk forward but was jolted back by my father's grip.

"Ivan...funny seeing you here. I came here to pick a fight with Markos, but it looks like you're trying to run away with his fiancée."

The words burned from the top of my head to the soles of my feet. I wanted to scream that I didn't belong to anyone but him, that Markos was no one and nothing.

"She belongs to *me*. Not you, not Markos...no one but me...so fuck off and get the hell out of here." My father started forward, his men falling in like a V in front of him.

"See, you're wrong again," Juan yelled above the sound of the men moving along the debris.

"Not this again with the baby being yours." My father rolled his eyes.

Juan laughed, giving us a beaming white smile. "No...not with that. You're right—by blood, she isn't mine."

Juan stepped down from a large piece of rubble, drawing closer, his men fanned out behind him. My father staggered back a step as he saw what I saw. Juan had them outnumbered, vastly so. If Markos allied with Ivan, he might have had a shot, but it was clear that Markos wanted nothing to do with this; he and his men were nowhere to be found. My father had made a massive mistake by not bringing in his full force.

"Do you know what laws we live by in El Peligro?" Juan asked, casually skirting a car that was on fire.

My father spat on the ground near my feet. "I care not for your fucked up family."

"Well, you will care for this, because it's law," Juan yelled in response; the echoing silence seemed to spread around the courtyard.

The feeling around the space was uneasy. I held my breath as I waited for him to speak, knowing there would be gunfire shortly after.

"You see, these laws are absolute, and they matter, so when I say those two are mine, that means they've been claimed by me. No one else can have them, and they fall under my protection. There's nothing you can do to fight it, other than going to war with me over it, of course."

"I'm not at war with you," my father shot back, sliding away nonchalantly while keeping his gaze on the men who were suddenly everywhere, surrounding us.

Juan began taking off his vest, unstrapping one Velcro piece at a time until he was slipping it over his head. "You see...you're wrong again. You declared war when you tampered with my communications, and again when you attempted to leave here with them."

"They're mine!" my father yelled, moving his grip until it was a solid piece of steel around my arm.

Juan bared his teeth and suddenly ripped his shirt, exposing his chest.

"Wrong!" he snapped with so much venom I winced. "They're *mine!*" he yelled so every single soul in the courtyard would hear him.

The look on his face was devastating, like a warrior toeing the line in battle, a man ready to fight his way until death claimed him.

There on his chest, right over his heart, were two black hearts inked into his skin. I hiccupped as I realized what he'd done. He'd claimed not only me, but my daughter as well.

"Mine, and it is law in my family. Their hearts are now on my chest, so you will let them free of your grasp, without issue, or you will go to war with me, right now, right here."

My father seemed to struggle with his decision as he staggered backward. I could feel the tension in the air as the men around him began to look back and forth between El Peligro circling them and my father at the center of their circle. I tried to look behind me at Alex to ensure she was okay. She was starting to stir, her little blue eyes opening, no doubt searching for something familiar. She couldn't make me out this far away; the man handling her held her carrier down near the ground, just barely hovering above it, which made me instantly nervous.

These men killed for a living. They'd killed entire families, women, children…probably babies. They'd have no qualms about dropping my kid or tossing her entire car seat toward the enemy. I realized as I glanced back, seeing our surroundings, Ivan had surrounded himself with his men but backed us into a wall so that Juan's men wouldn't be able to circle from behind, which only meant he'd have more leverage to use me or Alex as hostages.

"I'll go to war then," my father finally said through clenched teeth, grabbing a hold of me tighter than before. "The first casualties in this battle will be the two hearts on your chest, you fucking idiot."

I screamed.

I screamed so terrifyingly loud that I thought my voice would leave me entirely. I thrust what I could of my body backward to try to protect my daughter, but whatever I thought was going to happen didn't. My body went slack as my father's grip released me and he staggered forward. I watched in confusion as blood began to bubble from his lips, and his men seemed to be at a loss as well. Then Kyle sidestepped the man he'd just killed, the bloody knife dangling at his side.

Decker was behind the man holding my daughter, holding a gun to his head. The man who had been with them at the wedding, their Uncle Scotty or something, was behind another man, holding a gun to his temple. My father's men lifted their arms in surrender and stepped away from the circle they'd formed with Alex and me inside.

I unbuckled my daughter as she began to wail, and I clutched her to my chest as I tried to soothe her. Kyle handed the bloodied weapon back to his uncle, who tossed the knife under one of the burning cars. Decker lowered his gun, handing it over to his uncle as well.

"You..." I started but couldn't speak over the bubble in my throat.

"He wanted to go to war...problem was, he chose to battle against my family." Kyle crouched down, getting eye level with me. He shrugged, giving me a small grin before he stood up and walked off.

Decker crouched next, placing a solid hand on my back. Tears nearly blinded me as I gave him a watery smile. "You?"

He met my smile with a sad one of his own. "Mallory is my life, and she was two seconds from driving here herself to get you." He shook his head back and forth. "My morals grew grey after that shit with Elias, and my hand...I guess this side of the law doesn't really feel too foreign to me. My Uncle Scotty has been in this business for a long time too, so there's that."

Yes, his uncle had worked for my father. I ducked my head, trying to ignore that I had to share family with a man who was tied to my own personal monster. The man in question walked past me, giving me a completely stoic face, no emotion whatsoever. He was in his mid-thirties with dark hair that matched Kyle's and Decker's. I had to remember that my monster was dead now, and their family member had been on the right side of this war, defending me and my daughter.

The rain fell in angry spurts as the fires around the compound began to hiss and flicker. I went to stand up with Alex cradled to my chest, and warm hands landed on my arms, helping me.

Whiskey eyes, muted by the greying sky but no less warm, stared back at me. His black hair was getting soaked, forcing stray strands into his eyes. He smiled at me, pushing the pieces back.

I didn't wait another second; I just walked into his arms and allowed his strong hands to pull me against his chest. He'd found a zip-up hoodie somewhere, and the fabric was wet under my face as I pressed into him. A second later, he was standing back and guiding me toward the hole in the massive wall.

"Come on, babe," he murmured, kissing my hairline.

Tears flowed freely as I nodded and followed him to his car.

CHAPTER THIRTY-FOUR

Juan

I HAD OUR DRIVER TAKE US TO MALLORY AND DECKER'S PLACE IN the city. I knew she'd feel safer there than anywhere else right now, even with me. I knew she needed to see Mal and get a second to collect herself.

I had dialed my best friend letting her know we were on our way and then pocketed my phone so I didn't have to answer a million questions from her.

Taylor had wanted to buckle Alex in the middle because it was the safest place in a car, so currently there was a baby between us. As I kept looking over at Taylor, it was getting more and more difficult not to touch her.

"Unbuckle, Taylor," I said, voice low and commanding.

I didn't dare take my eyes off her as she brought those ocean eyes up to meet my brown ones.

She must have understood what I needed because she didn't question me or say anything. The sound of her restraint unclipping hit my ears, then she was moving. We were in a rather large SUV, so it was easy enough to move around in. She hunched her back and moved until she was close enough, then I pulled her into my lap.

She buried her face into my neck as her hand went up to grab my shoulder.

I rubbed her side, hating how close I'd come to losing her.

"I'm not sorry that I left," she whispered in my ear, stroking my neck and dragging her finger along my collarbone.

"You left assuming I'd be better off without you. How would you feel if I had done that to you? Agreed to marry a different person, giving you no choice in the manner, because I thought it was best for you?"

She let out a small sob that seemed to get caught in her chest. "I couldn't think that way, Juan. You were never mine to begin with...I was never going to be able to keep you."

"I've always been yours. Yours and no one else's," I explained coldly. My anger began to rise, making me hold her tighter against me. "I love you...I can't..." I snapped my mouth shut, trying to get my emotions under control. "I won't live without you, Taylor. It's not a life I want."

Her finger moved down to my chest where the zipper to my hoodie latched. She slowly dragged it down until she could see my chest and the two hearts tattooed there.

"You claimed us. For real this time." Her eyes found mine, watery and red and yet still the most beautiful thing I'd ever seen.

My hand came up to cover hers. "For real and forever."

She nodded and pressed a small kiss to my chest, which only made me want those lips on mine. I tipped her chin up until her mouth was accessible for me, and then I claimed it just like I did her life, her heart... her entire existence.

♥

Taylor

MY SISTER LIVED at the top of a thirty-story building, in the penthouse suite. She and Decker hated it and couldn't wait to hand off the reins to the person they were currently in the process of training for the job.

I was at the window again in her guest bedroom, sipping decaf coffee, while I watched the city turn white under the December snow.

Alex had been bathed, fed, and burped, so now she was sleeping soundly in the crib my sister had ordered and set up for when I came to visit. I had turned to goo when I saw how many things she'd already bought for my baby girl.

The door opened with a click then shut, and I knew it wasn't the man who was sharing this room with me tonight who had entered.

"I've been patient, but I need to know what the hell happened, and I know this is super shitty, but I'm not going to lie—at the top of my nosey list is why the hell you walked in looking at Juan like he was your knight in shining armor, and why you're sharing a room with him...and why you never mentioned anything while I practically lived with you for ten days?"

I smiled at her, snuggling into the plush chair she had by the window. She settled on the bed, cradling her own mug of coffee. *Probably isn't decaf. Bitch.*

"Did I ever tell you I had a massive crush on Juan?"

My sister's green eyes grew into huge saucers. "What? No, you never told me that. How am I just hearing about this?"

I blushed and brought my sleeve up to my face, trying to hide my smile.

"I saw him play hockey my freshman year at RFU, and at first it was just the way he moved on the ice that I was drawn to, the way he seemed to glide so beautifully...it was like he was made for it. I couldn't keep my eyes off him, and when he took his helmet off on the players bench..." I blushed again, shaking my head. "Mal, it was like everything faded away. Nothing had ever felt like that before. The way he shook his hair, the way he swept it out of his face...god, I was completely obsessed with him. I tried to talk to him after the game, but he ignored me. He walked right past me like I didn't exist, and that was the first time anything like that had happened to me...with guys at least."

"So, you saw him as a challenge?" Mal smiled at me over the brim of her cup.

I shook my head. "No...I just wasn't expecting it. I was actually super embarrassed, but then I saw him again at a local hangout spot, that place off First Street, and that feeling came back...like everything else had just become a blur, except for him. I watched him like a stalker that entire night, and no joke...I tried talking to him again."

My sister laughed, tossing her head back, and it made me laugh too.

"So, what happened that time?"

I covered my face in shame. "He ignored me again...totally talked to a different girl and ignored me."

"Did you happen to grab a different date that night?" my sister asked, knowing me too well.

"Of course I did...I thought I could make him jealous, even though he didn't know I even existed."

"Poor freshman Taylor."

I wiped my eyes, loving how good it felt to laugh with her again.

"I was seriously so obsessed with him. I knew his favorite places to eat and hang out...then I made all these ambitious plans over the summer before sophomore year, and what was the first thing that happened?"

My sister covered her face, cradling her mug between her legs. "I became friends with him."

"Not just friends—*best friends*, and suddenly all he saw me as was Mallory's little sister."

"Still, you should have told him...or me, for that matter."

I shook my head again, biting back another smile. "I ended up making a move on him senior year, right before I found out I was pregnant. I stole his number from your phone and texted him to come over..."

"Was this around the time Juan gave me crap for not being there for you?" Mal's voice rose a little as she narrowed her eyes and pointed her finger at me.

I shrugged. "Close to it...it was a little before. Anyway, I kissed him. Then when he kissed me back, I told him I thought he was Holden."

"No!" Mallory threw a pillow at me.

"Yep." I nodded furiously.

Mal's voice lowered. "Is that why you two didn't get along?"

"Sort of...I hurt him pretty badly when I said I was waiting for Holden, and he came by one morning like he always seemed to back then and said something awful to me. Then he took that girl to your wedding, and it was just..." I blinked, looking out the window to clear the emotions away. "Anyway, as you know, I ended up staying with him, and then everything with my dad happened, but we had preexisting feelings...so things sort of moved along."

"Wait a second," Mal said conspiratorially. "Have you two had sex?"

I blushed.

"Oh my god! You have and you didn't tell me!"

I covered my face. "I'm sorry...I was so worried about Juan being tied to his family stuff that I didn't have time to be myself with you."

My sister softened. "It's okay, oh my gosh. My best friend and my little sister—I'm so excited." She squealed and jumped off the bed.

"Does this mean you talked to him about everything and you're not mad anymore?"

She ducked her head, watching her coffee. "He talked to me while you were bathing Alex, and I kind of get it now...I think. I mean, I don't want any of you to feel like you can't talk to me just because of what I do for a living."

"You write about this stuff specifically, Mal...of course we're going to be hesitant."

She moved her head, sipping the last of her coffee. "But I get it. I mean, with Decker and Kyle...I would never do anything to endanger them, and the same goes for Juan. He's my family. Even more so now." She stood up, kissed my forehead, and then leaned away. "I'm going to go hug him and tell him how excited I am that he's going to marry into my family."

"Hey, who said we were getting married?" I sat up quickly. Where was this coming from?

Her hand paused on the door handle while she looked back at me. "Are you for real?"

She did know everything we had gone through, but Mal was the number one person who'd argue for me not to get married this young, regardless if she had done so herself.

"Taylor, you don't get it. He doesn't just love you—that boy craves you. There's no way he's not putting a ring on it the second he gets a chance."

I sank back into the chair as my sister left. I wasn't sure how I felt about getting married right away. All I knew was that I wanted to be with Juan...but I didn't think that required marriage. Did he think differently? I half wondered if the ideas about Holden coming back around lingered in his mind the way that image of Angela pressed against him lingered in mine.

CHAPTER THIRTY-FIVE

Juan

It was late when I opened the door to the guest room and closed myself inside. Taylor was awake with the side lamp on, holding Alex in her lap. I stood by the door for a second, just watching how Taylor's hair was swept up into a loose bun on her head with little strands falling to her neck. Her face was bare so her freckles were showing, and all she wore to bed was a white tank top with some kind of built-in nursing thing, underwear, and a pair of tall socks.

My dick twitched at just watching how her nose scrunched as she laughed and cooed with her baby girl and dove in to kiss Alex's cheek and feet.

Watching them together felt like my entire life was playing out before my eyes, like I was dreaming. They were it for me, and I didn't even know if either of them would ever know how monumental that was.

"You just going to stand there, or are you going to come get in on these snuggles while she's awake?"

I smiled, jolting out of my stupor, and walked toward the bed.

"Watching you two is like a dream...like something I don't ever want to end."

I moved, crawling onto the bed until I was lying in front of Taylor's crossed knees and Alex was between us. Holding my head up with my palm, I peered down at the little bundle of perfection, taking in her dark hair and blue eyes. Her gaze drifted up until she was looking at me, then she smiled, warm and bright, and it was everything. My heart felt like it grew a thousand sizes in a single instant, and all I knew was that this girl was mine. Regardless of who her biological dad was, she was mine, and would be forever.

"She knew about your hockey offers," Taylor suddenly said, still looking down at Alex.

My eyes jumped to hers. She...*shit*.

"I didn't tell her."

She eyed me, grinning at the sweet face below her. "You didn't tell me either."

"I'm sorry about that entire thing, babe. I was exhausted, and she said she had something from my mom, which is why I went out there to begin with."

"You didn't push her away when she kissed you."

I stared at her while she stared back, the silence stretching.

"I was tripping pretty hard over her Holden comment. I'm worried you'll leave me if he comes around. I don't want her...just you. Only you."

"Holden hasn't contacted me," she said quietly, stroking her daughter's hand, grabbing her tiny fingers.

I mimicked her along Alex's other hand but didn't respond. Even if he hadn't reached out, that didn't mean he wouldn't.

Taylor suddenly touched my face, forcing my eyes up until I was meeting hers. "You make us whole, so even if he one day decides he wants to be in her life, you were here first. You loved her first. She's yours, Juan. Just like I am. If you want us...then you have us."

Fuck, she broke me. I had never felt this broken, but this was it. I was done for.

I moved so I was lying next to Taylor, then I pulled her until she was lying in my arms, and the baby too.

"I love you both. I *want* you both. So, if you'll have me...then..."

"Yes," Taylor rushed out.

"No more games...no more walls. You're mine, and I'm yours," I said, meeting her eyeline.

She sat up gently and set the baby in the lounger across from where we were entwined.

"No more games." She pressed a kiss to my bottom lip. "No more walls." She moved until she was pressing her lips into the corner of my eye. "You're mine." Her tongue darted out, tracing the shell of my ear until she was whispering, "And I'm yours."

I grabbed her, gripping the side of her face until our lips landed in chaos against each other. My tongue swept into her mouth while my lips pressed a solemn promise into hers. Our mouths moved in cadence while Taylor's hand delved into my hair, pulling on the ends, deepening the kiss.

"I love you. I have loved you for so long." She broke away, gasping, then slammed her lips back to mine.

"No, I've loved you...you've driven me crazy for the past two years." I returned the messy rhythm of kisses along her jaw and neck.

"I have you beat. I've loved you for four, not counting this year...so I've loved you longer."

I moved until she was cradled under me, my arms caging her in. I dipped my head until I was licking the swell of her breast.

"You may have loved me longer, but I'll probably outlive you, so in the end it will be me who loves you longer."

A scoff left her lips, which rumbled in her lungs and forced a smile from my lips. "You think I'll die first?"

"You eat like crap, babe. Sorry."

I smiled, shoving her shirt up, marking my way down her stomach. It wasn't entirely flat yet, so I wasn't surprised when she tried to shove me away, but I stayed where I was.

"No. I get to love you and touch you, fuck you at whatever physical size you happen to be. Don't ever push me away from loving this body." I pressed a kiss to her belly button. "This skin."

She let out a sigh.

"You're too sore still?" I asked, raising an eyebrow.

"Not sore, but the doc said six weeks, and we're only at four…"

I kissed down her underwear, nuzzling her pussy from behind the cotton barrier. "Then we'll wait, but you can still orgasm without penetration, right?"

She gave me that lazy smile that answered without using words. I smiled and returned my lips to her body.

I ended up kissing her until she fell asleep, and I gladly took a shift with Alex, walking around the room with her tiny body cradled in my arms. I watched the skyline of the city as I sang in Spanish. Her big round eyes just watched me in fascination. Taylor said they can't really smile at this stage, that it was probably just gas…but every time Alex looked up at me, she smiled. It was like she knew who I was, even when I didn't know who I was.

I loved her more than I could anything on this earth besides Taylor, but this love was so different. It was a roar in my chest, a war drum in my veins, demanding I protect her, keep her safe, and buy her anything she'd ever want in her entire life. I didn't care what Taylor said…we'd get her whatever she wanted.

I ended the night watching both my girls sleep, and while they slumbered, something inside of me came alive.

CHAPTER THIRTY-SIX

Taylor

Juan's mother sat across from me with weary eyes and a frown that made her look decades older than she was. She'd been apologizing for the past half hour and had even brought me flowers and a baby gift for Alex.

"You think I'm bad for him?" I asked at about the fifteen-minute point, and that was when Anna switched gears from kissing my ass to being real with me. I always preferred that people be real; it saved time.

"I think you tied him to this life, and he didn't want it," Anna explained, her voice soft.

My heart broke a little bit. She wasn't defensive or being mean. She finally understood that I wasn't going anywhere and we needed to figure this out for the sake of her son.

"I tried to leave so he wouldn't be."

The sun broke through the clouds, offering a little bit of warmth. The fire roaring near our legs was still warmer. Juan was inside with Alex while his mother and I had stepped out to the patio to chat. It was mid-December and my twenty-first birthday. A date that had held such fear for me all those years had turned out to be nothing but perfect peace. Juan woke me with a searing kiss, which led to us dry humping. I still hadn't been cleared by the doctor for sex, but we'd been touching, kissing, and sucking like crazy. Dry humping in our underwear had become one of our favorite pastimes.

I always finished Juan off with my mouth, and while he always wanted to reciprocate, I wasn't ready to have him near me in that way yet, so he'd take out his cock and let it fill the space between my legs while I wore my underwear. Then I'd rotate my hips and grind against him until I was screaming. After our orgasms, Juan took us to breakfast; he'd even bathed and dressed Alex for me. Fatima, Mallory, and Decker, along with my mother and Charlie, were on their way for my birthday dinner, but before then, Anna wanted to make peace.

"I know you did, and that's how I knew you were the one for him. He never would have risked so much for someone who didn't mean this much. I will never interfere in your relationship again, and I hope in time, you can grow to trust me...and allow me to love Alex like she's my own grandchild."

I reached over and grabbed her hand in mine. "Of course. I want nothing more than to have that. Juan and I will marry one day and have more kids. I want to have a good relationship with you before that happens."

We hugged and talked about Juan's plans for the family. Hector had talked to me about Juan's dream for El Peligro, which prompted me to ask Juan about it. I ended up crying from how proud I was of him and how badly I wanted to partner with him on making it better. Anna cried too, and I watched as the worry for her son began to lessen and eventually drift away.

"You ready for your big night?" Juan walked up behind me, his hands going to my hips, his lips to my bare shoulder. I moved my hair to the side as he took up residency in his favorite place. We danced like this, him behind me, holding me. We watched Alex sleep like this. It was often how he let me know he wanted me. I loved this position.

"Did you know Kyle is coming and bringing that girl with him?" Juan teased, biting my earlobe.

I spun in his arms. "She forgave him?"

Juan shrugged. "They might be coming as friends, but they are coming. I told them to bring their mom too and decided we'd just turn this into a big Christmas party. Also, you have a visitor," Juan whispered, brushing his lips against mine.

I stiffened in his arms. The only people I wanted in my life were in this house or on their way.

"He's downstairs, on the back patio."

Panic surged forward. "Alex?"

"She's safe, and I'll be there if you want, or not. It's your call."

"I want you there."

Juan kissed me. "Okay."

♥

HOLDEN WORE a suit that was too big for his body. Not by much, but I had grown used to seeing Juan in his tailored suits. He paced the patio, near the fireplace, his long stride seemingly nervous with every step. He also had flowers with him.

Oh boy.

"Holden," I said by way of greeting.

Juan had walked me out but hung back toward the bar, where string lights hung overhead, illuminating the glass bottles and different tumblers. He was close enough to hear, but not too close that Holden would feel threatened.

"Hey...wow, you look beautiful. You don't even look like you just had a baby."

I wasn't sure what that meant. I had stretch marks under my clothes, along my inner thighs, and on my sides. Juan kissed them every chance he got, but I very much felt as if I'd just had a baby. My body had changed significantly.

"What brought you out tonight?" I asked, trying to be polite.

He jolted forward, handing me the flowers. It brought him a few steps closer to me.

"Thank you." I accepted them as gracefully as I could. I wanted to ask where the gift for his daughter was, maybe a pack of wipes or a little wad of cash to help out?

"Look...I wanted to..." He suddenly looked over at Juan, who was staring at Holden while he stirred his drink. "Does he have to be here?"

I laughed. "Yeah."

He narrowed his eyes on Juan but finally moved on. "I wanted to come and tell you that I'm ready to step up. I want us to be a family."

Aw, poor thing. Did he consider the flowers and showing up on my birthday a declaration of love?

I clicked my tongue, noticing that Juan had stepped closer, sipping his drink. In all black, he looked like the devil there to seduce and sway the feeble minds of man to the dark side. I was already hot and ready for him; I wanted to try to test how far we could go. My six weeks was over in a few days, but it was my birthday, so there had to be a chance it would be fine. Maybe if we only did half his cock, or the tip...maybe if we went really slow and careful it would be okay.

"You're welcome to see Alex during scheduled visitations. I'll expect you to begin paying child support, and we can set up a parenting schedule for her. However, the family aspect is already covered." Right as I finished, Juan walked up behind me and resumed my favorite position with his hand at my waist. "I have a family. Alex has one. If you want to make your own with Alex, you can...but I won't go easy on you. You have to prove you'll be there for her. You can't flipflop—you have to decide you'll be there for her forever. You can't quit parenthood. It's forever, Holden, so you need to decide on that."

A red coloring overcame his face. Maybe six months ago I would have felt bad for him, but he hadn't even texted back when I had called letting him know that Alex had been born. He hadn't done anything, so I owed him nothing.

"I thought we discussed that your dad would cover stuff. I want to be involved, but I'm still in school...how am I supposed to manage helping and going to school?" he pathetically asked, his eyes flicking around the house as if my dad had bought it. I wanted to roll my eyes.

"Holden, Charlie will happily help with anything and everything I need, but as I said...I have a family." I covered Juan's hands that were at my waist with my own. "We're covered...but that doesn't mean you get a free pass on responsibility. It takes work to be involved in your kid's life. If you decide you'd like shared custody, the financial obligation changes, but for right now, while she's this young...you have to show me you're serious about it. Anything you give will only be used for her or set aside in a savings account for her."

"This is bullshit!" Holden yelled, shaking his head back and forth.

"You're welcome to leave. It is, after all, Taylor's birthday party you're crashing," Juan advised smoothly from behind me. He still held me tight against his chest.

Holden took the opportunity to dig himself a grave. "You know what...fuck you man." Holden stepped closer to me, trying to get into Juan's face. We stayed steady for a second before Juan must have felt the mood shift. Within seconds he was pushing me behind him, and Holden punched him in the jaw. Juan's face barely moved; in fact, it looked as though the hit hadn't even registered. Stupid Holden—he had no idea who he was dealing with.

"That was one. I'll let you have it, let you walk out of here thinking you've got the upper hand. You don't want this, man." Juan's tone was hard as stone, allowing no room for argument.

Holden crowded Juan's space as if he was ready for another hit. There was even a bit of chest puffing if I wasn't mistaken.

"You can't keep my daughter from me." Holden shook his head.

"No one said anything about that. Taylor laid out the terms clearly—take it or leave it, but you've now outstayed your welcome."

The man who shared DNA with my child sucked in his lip and nodded his head heavily. His eyes darted to me and then Juan.

"Fine...I'll go, but you can keep your fucked family. I don't want anything to do with it, and I won't be paying you a dime, so if you want the baby, you can fucking have her."

Holden stormed off around the corner of the house. Juan stayed facing the way he'd been talking with Holden. I tugged on his sleeve to get him to turn around.

"You okay?"

His whiskey eyes burned through me. "Me? Are *you* okay? That wasn't what I had planned for your birthday."

I laughed, stepping under his chin. "I feel relieved, I guess. I mean, I didn't mind if he wanted to be in her life, as long as he was serious...but if he's not going to be, I don't want him here. I feel like we know now."

Strong fingers ran down my spine as a rumble reverberated under my cheek.

"What, you don't agree?"

"I think he was caught up in expectations and emotions tonight. I think it wouldn't hurt to give him another shot, if he wants to humble himself and apologize," Juan replied smoothly.

Floored—Juan always left me floored with his goodness. I simply nodded into his chest, overwhelmed with gratitude that I got to call him mine.

He walked forward, reaching down to thread our fingers together.

"Happy birthday, baby. Let's go celebrate your life, because you are worth celebrating."

I followed after him, entering the house where all of our loved ones had gathered to support me. I smiled as the snow began to fall, and I realized I deserved to smile. I deserved to be happy, and most of all...I deserved to be loved.

EPILOGUE

Juan

Six months later

"You should just record yourself singing to her."

I turned and looked over my shoulder to see Taylor sipping from a mug of coffee while leaning in the doorway to the study. I had Alex against my chest, my hand softly patting against her tiny back while she dozed off to the sound of my voice.

"So you can have it easy on your shifts?" I smirked, moving around the desk and a few boxes on the floor.

Taylor laughed but quickly covered her mouth so she didn't wake her daughter. "Easy...are you kidding me? This teething shit is for the birds. Even with your voice, it's work, but during my shifts...I don't know." She shrugged her slender shoulder. "I miss you."

I walked around Taylor to the mobile crib we kept in the study. We weren't quite trusting enough yet to just leave Alex in her crib and rely on video feeds to watch her. We wanted her close at all times. It made for an interesting dynamic in the house. The men who came in already knew to take off their shoes now that Alex was big enough to sit up, and soon she'd be crawling. They also knew to whisper, unless they saw her awake.

I carefully set my daughter in her crib then turned back toward the woman I planned to marry. I'd started calling her mine in my head, out loud...other people would call me her dad. I had no idea if Holden would ever come around, but I wasn't waiting for him to. Alex would grow up knowing me as Dad; there was no changing that.

"You know, I never did get to have you on that desk, and now we're moving...the desk is staying here, so I think we owe it to each other to fulfill that promise."

Taylor's pink lips pursed in thought as she tilted her head to the side.

"We aren't taking it?"

I grabbed her waist and began pushing her toward the desk. "Nope. I want to get one of those built-in unit things, where you have half the space and I have the other half." We had slowly started working together, utilizing our position within El Peligro to begin digging at the roots of the organization. It would take time, but for the time being, Charlie had asked if Taylor would be interested in heading up a new nonprofit for young girls who grew up in abusive or violent homes. He thought she'd thrive in a company built on helping young teenage girls overcome their anger and direct them toward a hobby or trade.

She hadn't entirely committed yet since Alex was still young, but I loved seeing the look in her eye when she began reading up on the vision behind the nonprofit. I knew it was something she was excited about. She'd finished school online between nursing, pumping, and sleepless nights. I couldn't have been prouder of her efforts and determination to finish her degree, and I had decided I wanted to invest in changing the city for my little girl. I wanted her to have a safe space to play when she went to the parks or walked home with her friends.

So, to start things out, Taylor and I were moving. We wanted to be closer to Decker and Mallory, so we planned to live between Rake Forge and Pinehurst, still close to my family and her parents. It would be a smaller house, which we both preferred, but it still had the opulence of the place my uncle had purchased. Part of the change we wanted to create in El Peligro was how leaders lived fat and lazy while the rest of the family worked tirelessly for scraps. As a leader, I wanted to live within my means. If we ended up needing more space, we'd adjust, but for now it was perfect and private.

Taylor ran her finger along the wood finish on the desk then turned and hopped on top of it, swinging her legs in front of her.

I stepped between her open thighs and brought my fingers to her jaw, brushing aside a few stray strands that had fallen out of place. Her hair was tied up in a ponytail, but she'd slept in it, so it was loose and falling out. She still had on her tank top and tiny sleep shorts, similar to the ones she used to wear in front of me when I'd come and check on her in the townhouse. She used to drive me insane with how she'd walk around with half her ass showing.

"So, we should say goodbye to the desk?" she whispered, gripping my t-shirt, pulling me closer until her lips sealed against mine. I moved slowly while she seemed to be in a hurry. I wouldn't be rushing through this. There were times I had taken this girl fast and hard, but while our little girl slept, I wanted her mother slowly and passionately.

"Yes, preciosa..." I said against her lips, moving my hands down her body.

Our lips moved firmly but slowly against each other, her wet mouth melting into mine, her tongue sweeping out in a vicious claim. I moved my head to the side, and she followed, wrapping her hands around my neck. The urgency in her touch had me letting loose a growl into her mouth. With my hands on her hips, I moved them down to her thighs and pushed them apart, spreading her legs as wide as they'd go. My palm pressed against her chest, forcing her to lie down on the desk. She pulled up her tank on her way down and tossed it into the corner of the room.

I stared down at her body, her creamy skin, still so perfect that sometimes I thought I was dreaming. Her pink nipples hardened under my stare, and her fingers quickly moved to gently caress them; since she was still nursing, she couldn't apply much pressure. She must have seen the predatory look on my face, because her hips bucked without so much as a touch from me.

"Are you already aching for me, baby?"

I pushed my thumb into her center and began rubbing over the fabric of her shorts. She moaned, palming her breasts while she tried to move her hips to gain purchase somehow.

"Juan..."

"If I move these shorts, how wet are you going to be for me?" I skimmed up and down her slit, and I could already feel her desire through the material. "Should I do this until you soak your shorts?"

Her tongue darted out to lick her full bottom lip while those ocean eyes stayed on me.

My dick thickened in my sweats to a painful degree, making me impatient and eager to taste her. Dragging her shorts down her legs, I tossed them over my shoulder then, with my eyes on her, got to my knees.

I pulled on her ass until she was on the edge of the desk, and then I ran my nose along her soaked slit.

"I was right. Look at this...fuck, baby," I rumbled into her heat then spread her folds with my finger and licked.

"Oh my god, Juan!" Her voice was still muted enough not to wake up the sleeping baby, but I wasn't sure how long that would last. "It feels too good." She moaned, bucking her hips.

"I want to ruin this desk, baby. Put your feet on my shoulders." She did as I said, which spread her legs wider, and I leaned in to take advantage of the new position. I knew the stretch was a bit much for her, but she liked that. She also liked it when I stretched her in other ways, like when my fingers pressed into that tight bundle of nerves along the crack of her ass.

Today, I wanted to fuck her and ensure she was properly lubricated for the occasion.

I gently lowered her legs, and they dangled there while her chest heaved, her fingers still caressing those perfectly pink nipples.

"I was so close, Juan," she whined, and I smirked.

"You get too sensitive to enjoy my cock when I give you an orgasm with my mouth."

She rolled her eyes. "Then are you going to let me ride you?"

"You want to ride me on this desk?" I raised an eyebrow at her.

She began sitting up, a small smile cresting her lips.

"Yeah, I do. Hop up here, buddy."

I laughed, shaking my head, but she moved a second later so I had room to get on top of the desk.

First, I dropped my sweats. Neither of us bothered to wear underwear at night. We were always grabbing each other for a quick fuck, or, in Taylor's case, so she could pull the crown of my cock into her mouth whenever she craved it...which, fortunately for me, was frequently.

I turned, sitting on the desk, and then transitioned so I was lying flat on my back, a smile cracking my lips.

"You overestimate how big this desk is...you're going to fall off my dick and break your face."

She stifled a laugh and began getting on the desk, then she took my hardened length in her palm and began to rub up and down.

"Looks like I wasn't the only one weeping under my PJs, was I?" She leaned forward and licked the precum that had been leaking from my dick for some time.

She wet my length with her tongue a few times before she was fulfilling her plan to ride me. Using my chest as leverage, she slid down and adjusted to the fullness of it, then she moved, bracing me with her knees, kicking her feet behind her in true cowgirl fashion.

My hands went to her hips, unwilling to admit to her that this position actually felt fucking phenomenal.

"Well ride me, baby." I smiled up at her, loving the red flush in her cheeks.

She took a second, but as if a silent beat had begun, she started rotating her hips while her hands went to her heaving tits, palming them while she moved.

There was no reprieve from how hard she rode me, bouncing up and down and rotating until my length hit that spot inside her that forced her head back and a loud enough moan from her lips that I knew she may be in danger of waking Alex.

"Juan, god...more." She wheezed, circling her hips, pushing down against me.

I jutted up as hard as I could, pulling her waist down against me, which forced Taylor forward, her mouth gaping while sounds of pleasure and pain left her in a song of pure seduction. If anyone were to accidentally walk into our house right now, they'd likely turn right around with a heated face. The sounds she made were purely pornographic.

"Oh my god, Juan..." She moaned, and this time it was as if she were trying to get my attention, but I couldn't stop, jutting up and pulling her wet heat onto my shaft, up and down. "Juan, noooooo, fuck—" She gasped, her hips still moving in a rhythm of desperation. "I'm not...I'm not on birth control yet, and you didn't..."

She didn't get to finish, because I did.

With a roar, I pumped my hips up while she rocked against my cock. I spilled my release into her until I was entirely spent, and then she screamed her own release, digging her nails into my skin at the same time. With a heaving chest, Taylor finished her sentence.

"You didn't wear a condom."

My eyes widened as realization barreled into me.

"Can that happen this soon after?" I looked over as if Alex would be standing there watching us.

Taylor bit her lip. "I think so..."

We'd been careful every other time...it must have just been the packing and the exhaustion from our late-night shifts.

Even still, the idea of another baby with her wasn't an unpleasant thought. In fact...the more I thought of it, the more I liked it.

She crawled off of me, walking toward the bookshelf, grabbing a few Kleenexes to clean up, but I snuck up behind her, wrapped my arms around her, and carried her back to the desk until she was leaning over it. She let out an excited gasp as I gripped my firm length and ran the tip of my cock along the smoothness of her ass.

"Would it be so terrible to be pregnant with my baby?" I whispered, pulling her hair back and kissing along her neck.

She rocked back into me. "Of course not. You know I want more."

I gripped my erection and moved it to her still wet opening. "Do you want me to stop?"

I slowly pushed into her, one small inch at a time. She moaned in response.

"I need an answer."

"I dare you to try, big guy...fill me up and see what you can do." She gave me a sly smile, which only encouraged me.

So, I held her by the stomach, flush against my chest while I thrust into her. Her hand went to the edge of the desk as I pummeled into her slick heat, but there was no finding purchase there. I moved too recklessly and fucked her so hard that her entire body quaked against mine. She screamed my name as I thrust hard enough to move the desk forward.

We ended up going another round before we finally ended up on the floor, sweaty and spent. I looked over at the hair falling into her face and smiled.

"You're my perfect ending."

It sort of just tumbled out of my mouth, like it had been locked away somewhere in my chest.

Her lips curved, her face pressing against my skin while her finger ran along each groove of muscle in my stomach.

"Funny, I was just thinking about how you're my perfect beginning."

This girl.

Wrapping my arm around her shoulder, I brought her closer until our lips met. "Here's to forever then...the beginning and the end." I kissed her nose as she ran her hand up my torso. "And to all the happy moments in between."

Scotty

"You've been in my employment for over ten years, Scott. I don't want to do this."

I exhaled, bouncing my leg over my knee, as if this shit wasn't a big deal. The head of a family had died, garnering attention from every other head mafia member, in addition to Ivan's two brothers back home. Shit was fucked ten ways to Sunday.

"Then don't do it, Gino."

My old friend's eyes narrowed on me, as if I was fucked in the head. He wasn't far off, but I ignored the look and focused on the gloomy room. I hated these shitty meetings. So dark, and depressing. The curtains in the room were practically shut, only a slice of daylight bled into the murky room, but I was using it as an anchor. I knew what it was like to go underground, to not see the light of day for weeks on end. I knew, and I'd never take light for granted again, no matter how marginal.

"Then bring me your nephew, so I can deal with him."

I shook my head. "Can't do that."

His bulky shoulders moved under a pained exhale. The boss of the Melonette family did not take no for an answer, and I knew I was pressing my luck, but Kyle wouldn't survive the retribution. The fact that he was involved in the first place was my fault, there wasn't a chance I'd let him burn for this.

"It's been six months, I have allowed him the time to get the fuck out of here...but instead, he takes money out of my men's pockets at the street races. He's making a fool of us, so he will either heel by becoming an employee, or he will die."

Gino leaned against an armchair closest to his desk and lit a cigar, once the zippo clicked shut, he narrowed his eyes again. He had crows' feet, aging his blue eyes, his salt and pepper hair showed it too. My friend was getting old, and soon enough that pacemaker wouldn't keep up anymore, and there'd be a gap. I didn't like gaps. They were messy, and a fucking headache to deal with.

"You will bring him in, or I will take out everyone. Your sister, her sons, their women. *Anyone* who would miss them. Do you understand?"

Wrong fucking move. It was one thing to threaten my family, but if Juan even had a hint that his woman had just been threatened, he'd go to war...problem was, he wouldn't survive this one. Not when Melonette would pull in every other family this side of the coast.

"I'll get him."

I gave Gino a firm nod and headed for the door, biting but the massive 'fuck you' that sat heavy in my chest. No one threatened my family. Fucking no one. I'd repay the favor to Gino, but in time.

I'd get my nephew, but I wouldn't be bringing him back.

♥

Click Here to read Kyle's story, it's Free with Kindle Unlimited

ALSO BY ASHLEY MUNOZ

Small Town Standalone's

Glimmer

Fade

The Rest of Me

Tennessee Truths

Only Once

Vicious Vet

What are the Chances

The Wrong Boy

New Adult Romance Series

Wild Card

King of Hearts

The Joker

ABOUT THE AUTHOR

Ashley resides in the Pacific Northwest, where she lives with her four children and her husband. She loves coffee, reading fantasy, and writing about people who kiss and cuss.

Join her Newsletter so you never miss an update
www.ashleymunozbooks.com

She's most active in her Reader Group on Facebook, so be sure to join there too!
Book Beauties

ACKNOWLEDGMENTS

Thank you so much to the team of people that has helped me through this journey, and I'll try and make it short and sweet.

My husband who shares the load of raising four kids, working full time, and keeping our house ridiculously clean, and always doing our laundry when all I wore were sweats days on end while finishing this deadline. To my kids, my two teenagers, thank you for stepping up and helping with meals you have no idea how much that helps me and dad. To my two younger ones, thank you for snuggles, ISPY books, and always bringing me treats.

Tiffany Hernandez, you make my world go round. Thank you for always being on top of my schedule and encouraging me. You do so much more than I could ever ask.

To my publicist, Jennifer and the entire Wildfire Marketing team, thank you for everything you do, and making sure my books become everything they can be, and all the connections you help me build with bloggers.

Savannah, from Two Daisy Media, I was so insanely thankful when I found you. I can't wait to see what we do together, and what becomes of this series.

To my beta readers, Amy, Kelly, Brittany, and Gladys. You guys ALWAYS come through for me, and I couldn't be more grateful. I am so honored to have you as members of my team.

Amanda, the design of these covers and all the marketing material was spot on, I couldn't be happier.

To my editor, C. Marie, once again, you've perfected my books and I couldn't be more grateful to have you polish and shine this beast.

And as always, thanks to God, my creator, who has provided the gifting to create stories, and has filled my life with more blessings than I'll ever be able to count.

Made in the USA
Las Vegas, NV
07 March 2025